MRS. NASH'S ASHES

Praise for *Mrs. Nash's Ashes*

'An unequivocal delight. Fans of Emily Henry and Sarah Hogle,
you've found your newest obsession'
Ava Wilder

'This is a treasure of a story that lived and breathed inside my heart'
Anita Kelly

'Full of zippy banter, gorgeous prose, and tender-hearted characters,
it's a complete delight'
Carley Fortune

'This unforgettable road trip runs on deeply felt romance
[and] a profound sense of the unexpected – we loved every mile'
Emily Wibberley & Austin Siegemund-Broka

'Adler crafts a tale full of humor and heart, proving that
love sometimes finds us when we least expect it'
Ashley Herring Blake

'Instantly addictive! Pure rom-com gold'
India Holton

'Adler has it all – fresh characters, fabulous
writing, and enormous heart'
Sarah Grunder Ruiz

'Witty, beautifully written, and laced with
sexual tension and suspense'
Sarah Hogle

MRS. NASH'S ASHES

SARAH ADLER

QUERCUS

Published by arrangement with Berkley, an imprint of
Penguin Publishing Group, a division of Penguin Random House LLC

First published in the United States in 2023
First published in Great Britain in 2023 by

QUERCUS

Quercus Editions Ltd
Carmelite House
50 Victoria Embankment
London EC4Y 0DZ

An Hachette UK company

A CIP catalogue record for this book is available
from the British Library

PB ISBN 978 1 52942 915 2
EBOOK ISBN 978 1 52942 917 6

10 9 8 7 6 5 4 3 2 1

Printed and bound in Great Britain by Clays Ltd, Elcograf S.p.A.

Papers used by Quercus are from well-managed forests and other responsible sources.

To Houston—

You were right; this was the one.

Content Note

While this is a book with a happy ending and hopefully lots of laughs along the way, it also includes instances of, discussions about, and references to ableist language; death, including parental death (in the past, off-page); grief; historical homophobia; the objectification of girls and women; and toxic relationships. If any of these are potentially sensitive for you, please read with care.

MRS. NASH'S ASHES

1

• • • • •

ROSE McINTYRE NASH DIED PEACEFULLY IN HER SLEEP AT AGE
ninety-eight, and now I carry part of her with me wherever I go.
I do not mean that figuratively. She's inside a small wooden box
tucked away in my backpack as we speak. Not *all* of her, of course.
Geoffrey Nash wasn't about to hand over his entire grandmother
to the weird girl who lived in her spare bedroom. But Geoffrey
was kind enough to give me three tablespoons of her ashes (again,
not figurative; he portioned her out with a measuring spoon from
the kitchen). Probably not the request he was expecting when he
asked if I'd like something to remember her by, but he didn't seem
to mind too much. I think he was mostly relieved I didn't want her
highly collectible radioactive Fiestaware.

Geez, this is making me sound like a total wackadoo. I'm not,
though, I promise. I know that's exactly what a wackadoo would
say, but I'm really just a relatively normal person who happens to
be traveling to Key West with a small amount of human remains.

I'm going about this all wrong; let me start at the beginning.

Mrs. Nash had been living in Apartment 1B for almost seventy years when my boyfriend and I moved into Apartment 1A. Thanks to rent control, she was paying like five dollars a month for her two-bedroom between Dupont and Logan Circles. And we became fast friends, because I am a damn delight and so was she. So when Geoffrey and the rest of the extended family began fretting over her living alone around the same time things with Josh imploded, I moved in with Mrs. Nash. It was the perfect situation: Geoffrey let me live there for practically nothing in exchange for cleaning, cooking, running errands, accompanying Mrs. Nash to her medical appointments, and generally attending to his grandmother's needs. But mostly what Mrs. Nash needed was friendship, which I was more than happy to provide since that's mostly what I needed too.

Well, one day about three months ago, we were in the living room, me sprawled on the Persian rug with some book on the War of 1812 I was reading for work and Mrs. Nash sitting with her eyes closed in her favorite threadbare chair, the sunlight covering her plump little body like a blanket. She appeared to be napping, but suddenly her cornflower-blue eyes fluttered open and she sat up straighter.

Millie, she said with a sense of urgency in her voice that sent a jolt of panic up my spine. I was relieved—albeit momentarily confused—when she continued, *I would like to tell you about the love of my life. We met during the war. Her name was Elsie.*

Anyway, that's the ultra-abbreviated version of how I wound up here, sitting cross-legged on the floor at National Airport, waiting to board a plane to Miami with a bit of Mrs. Nash in my backpack. There's a lot more to the story, of course, but right now I'm a bit too distracted to tell it properly—a man across the gate's

waiting area keeps glancing my way when he thinks I'm not looking. Like he thinks he might know me from somewhere and is
trying to figure it out. That's nothing new; people still recognize
me sometimes, even though I haven't been on TV since I was
fourteen. It's not a big deal when they do since I'm about as extro-
verted as they come.

Usually the way this situation plays out is they approach me,
saying something like, "Hey, aren't you that girl from that show?"
Then I respond, "If you mean the actually kinda problematic kids'
show from the early aughts about the time-traveling redhead and
her poorly rendered CGI lizard companion, then yes. That's me.
Millicent Watts-Cohen, also known as Penelope Stuart on *Penelope
to the Past*." Then they say, a little sheepishly, "Right. Yeah, that
show was awesome, and you were great in it." Except I know they
are lying because the show was *terrible*. The history it taught was
inaccurate at best and flat-out offensive at worst, the special effects
sucked, and I was never talented at acting so much as at having a
cute face and a good memory. Sometimes they'll mention a *Penelope* episode they claim was their favorite, but it's usually a confla-
tion of two or more, or even a different show altogether. I never
bother correcting them, just smile and nod. And I'll usually agree
to a selfie when they say, "Oh my god, my friend/sibling/partner/
parakeet will never believe this!" because it keeps them from taking an unflattering stealthy pic of me eating a corn dog a few minutes later, and also staves off the biannual tabloid rumors that I've
died from huffing glue.

It's possible this guy is a fan; he looks about my age, give or
take, and thirtyish is the right demographic. Except something
about the way he's looking at me feels familiar. Like maybe he
recognizes me from real life.

I think I might recognize him too. But I can't seem to place him. Did we go to school together? Not grad—my master's program was small and absurdly insular—but maybe undergrad. I'm running through a mental catalog of various classrooms I've been in over the years, hoping he'll snap into the memory of one of them, when a man's voice interrupts my mental riffling.

"Hey, are you . . . ?"

I turn to find an almost perversely muscular dude in a tank top, which feels like a real choice on a cloudy day that didn't even break sixty-five degrees in the DC area. His shaggy, sun-bleached hair sticks out from the edges of a flat-brimmed Nationals cap with its iridescent sticker still in place. His biceps are the size and color of whole honey-baked hams. He's wearing sunglasses—indoors. This person is what I imagine would result if a beach bum and a lax bro had a thirtysomething baby.

My meeting-a-fan smile automatically plasters itself to my face as I stand. "Penelope Stuart on *Penelope to the Past*," I say. "That's me. Millicent Watts-Cohen."

"Whoa, yeah, I thought it was you. That's so rad. I can't wait to tell my boy, Todd. He won't believe it." He pulls out his phone and holds it up. "Can I get a selfie?"

"Yeah, sure," I say.

We lean in toward each other, and he angles the phone downward to get us both in the frame. His proximity assaults my nose with the scent of beer and an excessive amount of musky body spray. Even after he snaps a few shots and tucks his phone back into his shorts pocket, his grin remains. "Todd and I watched every episode of *Penelope to the Past* like a million times back in the day."

"That's great. Always nice to hear that people enjoyed the show," I say.

"Ha, no, the show itself was kind of garbage—no offense."

My smile droops in response to this surprising development. Not that I'm offended (I mean, I wholeheartedly agree with him), but these lines aren't part of the usual script for this interaction.

"You were like the hottest girl our age we'd ever seen. Especially that episode when your family was on vacation in Mexico. You know, the one where you went back to Aztec times? You were in this little yellow bikini, and your, you know . . ." *Don't do it*, I think. *Don't do it.* But he raises his hands to his chest and palms invisible breasts, then mimes them bouncing while he slo-mo runs in place. ". . . when you had to escape from the human sacrifice." He laughs and nudges me with an elbow. "Ha, yeah. You know what I mean. You know."

Oh god.

It's not that I was unaware until this moment that my awkward fourteen-year-old body starred in a lot of my fellow teenagers' early sexual fantasies. It's that most people keep this shit on the internet, where they can say gross things anonymously and without inflicting it directly upon my person. That's one of the main reasons I don't do social media. I learned a long time ago that I can't stop the world from objectifying me, but I can choose to shield my brain from absorbing the worst of it. Luckily (and perhaps surprisingly) this is the first time in years someone has been so candid when meeting me. But as much as I want to call out this dickhead for what he's said, my mouth is paralyzed in this sort of horrified gape, which he's unfortunately taking as encouragement to continue voicing his disgusting train of thought.

"Wow. I had so many dreams about you in that yellow bikini back then, you can't even imagine." He lets out another laugh. My whole face grows hot with this terrible combination of embarrassment and fury. "You look good, still, by the way." He lifts his sunglasses, and his eyes travel over the front of my body like a dog show judge might check out the standard poodle before taking a closer look at its teeth. "Really good."

A warm hand cups my shoulder, and I flinch before I realize the touch is coming from somewhere behind me. From someone who has yet to comment on either the past or present state of my tits and is therefore very welcome to enter this conversation.

"There you are," a voice says as the hand leaves my shoulder and slides down my arm, spreading a strangely reassuring heat over my skin. "I know you said you put the hotel info in my bag, but I can't find it and I need the phone number. Can you come look?"

I glance over at my rescuer as he hands me my little leather backpack and grabs the handle of my rolling suitcase. He's the guy from before, the one I remembered but couldn't place. Except now that he's closer, I can see his features clearly: dark chocolate–colored hair, mussed in a fashionable way where you can't tell if it's deliberate or if he really did just roll out of bed; light olive skin; full lips surrounded by the kind of stubble that manages to be ever-present yet has zero aspirations of becoming an actual beard. And I'd never forget those eyes in a million years—one blue-gray, one cognac brown, staring from behind round, tortoiseshell glasses. I've definitely had those mismatched eyes focused on me before.

"Yeah, sure." I hug my backpack—and Mrs. Nash—to my chest and mutter a quick, "Nice to meet you," to the fan, even though it wasn't nice to meet him at all.

"Sorry to interrupt, man," my new companion calls out as he guides me away. Then he adds in a hurry as if he just can't help himself, "But also, hey, learn some fucking appropriate boundaries maybe."

The memory comes together like a time-lapse video of a jigsaw puzzle. The crisp, late-September air on my face, chilling my tears as they tumbled down my cheeks. The whooshing sound of city traffic that replaced the restaurant's hubbub as I stepped outside into the night. A man's voice—*this* man's voice—reaching out of the dark, asking, *Hey, you okay?*

Hollis Hollenbeck. From my ex's MFA cohort. One of those fancy literary friends Josh talked about and constantly compared himself to but rarely let me interact with beyond hasty introductions and quick hellos at parties. Hollis was there that horrible night eight months ago, leaning against the brick wall beside the restaurant's entrance, the light from the old-timey lantern suspended above him highlighting the different colors of his eyes.

Now, Hollis leads me to the row of chairs in front of the floor-to-ceiling windows as a plane zooms down the runway in the distance. His blue duffel bag waits in front of the seat he vacated to save me. I consider joking about how he must have missed the last twenty years of PSAs about not leaving your bags unattended in an airport, but instead I say, "Thank you. That was getting . . . gross." I am grateful, of course, for his intervention. But I also can't ignore the tiny twinge of shame deep in my stomach, as if part of me feels like what that guy said is somehow my fault, that I should have shut it down or prevented it or been able to walk away without Hollis's assistance.

"Getting? Dude rocketed past gross and was well on his way to abhorrent." The look on his face is almost comical, the way his mouth droops into a perfectly symmetrical arch. Like a postcard of St. Louis.

"Hey. I know you, don't I?" I say.

His thick eyebrows raise in question. "Do you?"

"You know Josh Yaeger, right?" Somehow my smile stays perky and unaffected by the name coming out of my mouth.

"Yeah. And you . . . also know Josh."

He doesn't say it like "Wow this is so awkward because you dated my friend for three years and probably would be engaged to him right now if he hadn't betrayed your trust." It's more of an "I can only guess that's why you know me, but I really have no clue who you are." So maybe he wasn't looking at me because he remembered me after all.

"Um. He and I were together for a while," I say.

"Right."

"Back in September . . . at Josh's book release party at that restaurant in Georgetown. You drove me home," I explain, hoping to jog his memory. "So I probably owe you a thanks for that too."

"Oh. Did we . . . ?" He waves a finger back and forth between us.

"What? No. You didn't even come upstairs, just waited to make sure I got inside okay then left."

"Then you must be mistaken. That doesn't sound like me."

I don't understand the game he's playing here, why he's fighting against my good impression of him. "Well, from the little I know, helping a woman out of an unpleasant situation sounds very much like you."

"No way." He shakes his head. "I never do anything out of the goodness of my heart."

"Then what was that a minute ago?"

"Purely selfish. If I had to listen to another word about that guy's wet dreams, a tidal wave of vomit would've escaped my mouth and swallowed up this terminal."

The mental image of that makes me chuckle, but his expression remains serious. "Whatever," I say. "Regardless, I'd like to thank you somehow, both for today and for that night."

I immediately regret the open-endedness of my offer as his eyebrows raise again, but he eventually shakes his head. "Not necessary. Like I said, I was just being selfish. Now, not to be rude, but I went over there to stop a conversation, not get roped into a new one. So if you'll excuse me . . ."

Hollis navigates around his bag and sinks into the chair. He pulls a clicky black pen and a small red spiral-bound notebook from the front pocket of his duffel. By the way he focuses on the pages as he scribbles something down, it's clear he does not intend to pay me any further attention. Which is fine, because he's kind of being a dick.

I stand there, searching the terminal for somewhere I can go to leave Hollis alone without the creeper taking it as an invitation to resume our conversation. There are about a dozen airline staff huddled around the little desk (which, frankly, seems excessive, but what do I know?). Perhaps if I sit close to them, I'll blend in with the hustle and bustle . . .

Hollis lets out a heavy sigh and looks up at me. I stare back. He moves his eyes from me to the chair beside him repeatedly, wordlessly directing me to take a seat and stop annoying him.

I have to admit, remaining in Hollis's little bubble of protection and apparent exasperation isn't a hardship. Especially now that I'm sitting beside him and I can tell that he smells really good. Comforting. Like the scent version of reading your favorite book in a worn leather chair with a cup of Earl Grey tea while rain patters against the windowpane.

"Although, cinnamon rolls," he says abruptly.

"What?"

I'm about to tell him that, while delicious, those don't really fit with the vibe of the scene I'm imagining when he says, "I accept payment in the form of cinnamon rolls." Hollis nods toward the Cinnabon stand near our gate.

"You want me to buy you a cinnamon roll?"

"Yes. No—actually, two of them." In response to my raised eyebrow, he says, "Hey, according to you, I've helped you out twice. So two cinnamon rolls and we'll call it even."

I roll my eyes, but there's a smile on my face again. I'm not sure one dessert per good deed is the correct exchange rate, but if that's what will make Hollis feel appreciated, that's what he shall receive. Besides, I'm really not buying this "Oh, I'm just selfish" act of his. I bet he's a secret cinnamon roll himself; he's just hiding it underneath a thick layer of . . . burnt toast for some reason.

After making my purchase and getting the name of the artist who did the cashier's extremely cool mermaid tattoo in case I ever get over my fear of needles, I return to Hollis with a massive stack of napkins and a Cinnabon box in each hand. He's still sitting in front of the windows, his expression that of someone who would never say *harumph* but is constantly thinking it. "Here you go," I say, holding out the containers. "Thanks again."

But he only takes the fork and one cinnamon roll, leaving the other still in my possession.

"What about the—"

"I don't like eating alone," he says, lazily waving the fork toward the seat to his left. "Sit."

"Um. Thank you." I lower into the chair beside him, then spring back up. "Oh, but I only grabbed one—"

Hollis hands me the black plastic fork, stands, and places his container on his chair. A minute later he returns with another fork and settles back in beside me.

Again, I'm struck by the strange juxtaposition of his personality. He's not very nice, and yet he's so *kind*.

"I'm Millicent," I say, realizing he probably doesn't remember my name. "Most people call me Millie."

"Millicent. Right." He digs his fork into his cinnamon roll. "I'm Hollis. Hollis Hollenbeck."

"I know."

He raises his fork, topped with a giant bite that's mostly icing. "Cheers," he says, barely making eye contact before he shoves it into his mouth. For someone so grumpy, he's awfully cute.

We're quiet for a while as we eat. Well, quiet except for the occasional satisfied hum from Hollis. Then he asks me to hand him a napkin, and I figure it's as good an opening as any to start a conversation.

"So you're headed to Miami?" I ask.

"Yep," he says around a mouthful of cinnamon roll.

"For business or pleasure?"

"Both." I think that's all I'm going to get, but after he finishes chewing, he continues, "I promised my agent a finished draft of my new project by the end of next month, but, uh, I can't seem to get words on the page lately. So I'm hoping a week . . . relaxing with my, uh, friend will get me unstuck. She's been . . . helpful in the past. With relaxation."

I add up his "uh"s and pauses until they make sense. "You're going to Miami for a sex appointment?"

"That's not the expression I would use." His eyes shift over to me for a moment before returning to the Cinnabon container. "But yes."

"And you think that'll cure your writer's block?"

He puts down his fork and directs his full attention toward me for the first time since I sat down. I get a long and direct enough look at his eyes to notice that the cognac brown one isn't actually all brown, just about 80 percent; there's a bit of blue in the top right, like the sea meeting sand.

"It's not a block," Hollis says. "It's a . . . minor clog. Nothing a week with a gorgeous woman in an oceanfront condo can't knock loose."

"Well, I hope it's . . . satisfactory?"

"Thank you," he says as he takes another bite. He pauses, eyes closed, savoring, finding way more enjoyment in it than anyone should be able to find in airport food. Then his eyes flit open behind his glasses, the moment of ecstasy apparently over. "What about you? What are you going to be doing in Miami?"

"Not much. I'm only staying one night, then driving to Key West first thing in the morning."

"Vacation?"

"Not exactly. I'm going with a friend," I say.

Hollis glances around the terminal as if trying to scope out the location of my traveling companion. "Meeting them there?"

"No, no, Mrs. Nash is dead and in my backpack." The part of me that should have registered that this is a weird thing to say seems to be on a late lunch break. Well, it's already out of my mouth, what can you do?

He almost chokes on his next bite. Maybe I should've bought him a bottle of water. "Um. I'm . . . sorry for your loss?"

"Thanks. I'm taking three tablespoons of her ashes to Key West to reunite her with the love of her life. Give her the happily ever after she deserves."

"Sure. I know I never leave my house without my wallet, keys, phone, and a dime bag of cremains." I glance over at him and see that his expression matches his deadpan tone.

"This isn't doing me any favors, is it? I'm sure Josh has told everyone all sorts of stories about how weird I am."

"Oh, absolutely. And he said that's why he ended things."

So Josh is claiming that he broke up with me. I knew from the moment I left him at the book release party that this was how he would spin it. That he was the wounded one, totally innocent, and that I drove him away by being too difficult in my weirdness. But knowing someone is probably talking about you behind your back and hearing that someone *definitely is* are different things. Josh blaming the breakup on my personality instead of owning what he did shouldn't hurt, but it does.

"Not that I put much stock into anything Josh Yaeger says," Hollis continues. "Never met a bigger asshole. If he ran over a little girl's cat, he'd tell the story as if he were the real victim."

"That's a strange way to talk about your friend," I say, even as his words fill me with hope that he's seeing me through his own glasses instead of Josh-tinted ones.

"I wouldn't exactly call us friends. We're more . . ."

I remember the things Josh used to say about Hollis and his writing. *Nothing but a glorified gonzo journalist. Wouldn't have even been accepted into an MFA program if his dad wasn't a big-shot lit scholar.* "Frenemies?"

"Competitive acquaintances," he counters.

"Hmm. Hate mates."

Hollis gives me another perfectly arched frown. Like a drunken *C* that fell onto its face. "Whatever the opposite of a way with words is, Millicent, I think you have it."

He probably meant that as an insult, but for some reason it feels like a compliment. Something tells me that Hollis Hollenbeck is reluctantly finding me amusing, and that's my favorite sort of power to have over a person. What would it be like to make him smile? What would that even look like on his handsome but stony face? I would love to figure out what it takes to flip that *C* onto its back before we board the flight and go our separate ways.

Maybe I'll try a knock-knock joke.

A sudden commotion distracts me from my efforts to remember the punch line to the one someone told me on the bus last week. It's not localized, though; exclamations and profanity have overtaken the entire terminal.

"What's going on?" I ask Hollis.

"I'm not sure . . ." he says, stretching his neck to see farther. "Oh shit. Flight's canceled."

Why are people waiting for other flights upset about ours being canceled? Or wait, did he say "flight's," as in "flight is," or "flights," as in plural? I glance over my shoulder to look out the windows in case the weather has taken a sudden turn, but other than a few puddles left over from last night's thunderstorm, it's a dry, late-May day. "Why?" I ask, as if Hollis knows any more than I do about what's happening.

"I don't know," he responds with some irritation, still looking in the direction of the arrivals and departures board across from our gate. "But it looks like it's . . . most of them."

The airline staff who were amassed around our gate's desk have dispersed and stand like guards around the terminal, preparing to do battle with a bunch of irate customers—not a great sign. "Good afternoon," a woman's voice says over the PA system, just barely audible over the din. "The passenger service system used by multiple airlines is currently experiencing a nationwide outage. For your safety and security, affected flights have been grounded until systems are restored. Passengers should speak with their carrier's customer service representatives concerning refunds and rebookings."

Another outbreak of disgruntled noises fills the terminal as the announcement is repeated. Hollis tosses his empty Cinnabon container into the trash can near his seat without looking up from his phone.

My heart flutters with anxiety as I go over my options. One: Hang around here and hope they either fix the problem soon or that I can find a seat with an unaffected airline. Unlikely, considering it's Memorial Day weekend; it was hard enough to get this flight on short notice. Okay, so two: A train? Could this problem somehow affect train bookings too? And how long is a train ride from here to Florida anyway? Three: I could try to catch a bus. I don't know if there's a DC-to-Miami direct route, but there must be one that goes at least a little south, and that's progress. Four—

"Welp," Hollis says, clapping his hands to his thighs before he stands. "I'm going to head out and get on the road before there's a mass exodus." He checks the black watch on his wrist. "Maybe I can get through Virginia by dinnertime. Good seeing you again, Millicent. Best of luck with the whole dead-lady delivery thing." He and his duffel bag are strolling away before my brain can finish processing his words.

"Wait!" I grab my backpack and the handle of my carry-on. My shorter strides and a wonky suitcase wheel slow me down, but I somehow catch up with him a few gates away. "You have a car?" I manage through my embarrassingly heavy breathing.

"I do."

"And you're driving to Miami?" I struggle to match his pace. He's probably around six foot even, but I am only five-foot-one on a good day. My short little legs need to take two steps for every one of his, and my body resents being forced into cardio.

"I don't see what other choice I have," he says. "I'm not going to waste my limited vacation time waiting around for the airlines to get their shit fixed. According to airline industry people on Twitter, it could be hours, maybe days. And then dealing with the red tape of getting rebooked on a new flight? On a holiday weekend, when everyone else is also fighting for limited spots? Nah, driving will almost definitely be less of a headache. And it'll give me time to think."

"Let me come with you."

"What?"

"Let me come with you," I beg. "Please. We can even split the driving."

Hollis shakes his head. "No one drives my car but me."

From what I remember, Hollis is an English teacher. Or maybe a lecturer at one of the local community colleges? Something that Josh criticized as low-level but that he was secretly super envious of. Regardless, I doubt he's rolling in money. "I'll pay you for your trouble. Name your price. Really. I'm desperate to get to Florida as soon as possible."

"Sorry. There aren't enough cinnamon rolls in the world."

"Wow. *Wow.*" I stop walking and put my hands on my hips.

I half expect Hollis to keep moving forward, leaving me behind without a second thought, but he stops. He turns toward me with an audible sigh. "Look, don't take it personally, Millicent. You're pleasant enough company, I'm sure. But this trip is about two things for me: dirty, dirty sex and inspiration. And unless you can supply one or both of those, the benefits of your presence seem unlikely to outweigh the nuisance." He reaches out and pats me on the head. "Sorry, kid. Safe travels."

The gesture is so goddamn patronizing that I want to hurl myself onto his back as he walks away. Stick to Hollis Hollenbeck like a barnacle and refuse to remove myself until he agrees to take me with him. But the logistics of doing so while holding onto my backpack and my suitcase are too complicated, so I glance up at the sign above my head and follow the arrow pointing to the rental cars.

2

. . . . .

MIKE SEEMS NICE. I MEAN, I KNOW THAT A LOT OF PEOPLE *SEEM*
nice but aren't. There are probably some really nice-seeming serial
killers out there. But what are the chances that I just happened to
approach a nice-seeming serial killer out of all of the people waiting for a rental car at DCA? I'm not a statistician or anything, but
the numbers are undeniably on my side here. Besides, we've known
each other a full ten minutes now, and Mike's already shown me
about a hundred pictures of his wife of twenty years and their three
elderly pugs, Rockem, Sockem, and Robot. He's large and looks
cuddly. Total teddy-bear vibes, assuming the teddy bear's wearing
a greige pinstriped suit from Men's Wearhouse. He's probably in his
late fifties, and he definitely has no clue I used to be on TV. My
instincts tell me that Mike here is about as harmless as they come.
And most importantly, he's procured one of the last rental cars in
the metropolitan area and is willing to accept $400 in exchange for
allowing me to ride with him to Charlotte, North Carolina.

As we wait for the overworked rental car staff to track down the keys to our Hyundai Sonata, my new friend gives me a genuinely concerned look. "And you're sure you're not on the run from the law or anything, right? Nothing that'll get me in trouble?"

"No, no. I'm just on a very important mission."

"'A mission from God,' eh? I do love *The Blues Brothers*." He chuckles to himself. "'It's 106 miles to Chicago, we got a full tank of gas, half a pack of cigarettes, it's dark . . . and we're wearing sunglasses.' Kidding, we're goin' to Charlotte, don't worry. Though Chicago does have some great hot dogs. Hey, did I show you the video of Rockem and Robot fighting over a hot dog yet?"

See? Harmless.

But just in case, I should probably let someone know I'm doing this. I'm not about to terrify my parents. They don't even know I'm taking this trip in the first place; they turn into nervous wrecks whenever I travel alone and then inevitably guilt me into calling every thirty minutes to reassure them I'm alive and well—*Call, Millie, not this texting nonsense. We need to hear your voice.* Not to mention my father would alert every extended family member and old friend we have in the state of Florida that I'll be "in the area," making me look bad when I don't drive five hours out of my way to visit them. My younger brother is currently studying abroad in Denmark, and I'm fairly certain if I'm out of sight I'm out of mind when it comes to him. Not someone I would trust to notice with any expediency if I go missing. And while I have a wide swath of people who appreciate my company in small doses (or maybe hang out with me because they like being able to say they know someone who used to be famous), I don't really have any actual friends. Just Mrs. Nash, and she's gone.

So I pull out my phone and text my favorite and least judgmental cousin, Dani: Was flying to FL but flight canceled so getting a ride to NC.

If you don't hear from me by midnight tonight, tell the police I was last seen with Mike Burton from Charlotte. Late 50s, Black, bald, pretty tall, and very huggable.

Within seconds, Dani sends a thumbs-up emoji.

Mike is going through his phone, still searching for that video of Rockem and Robot with the hot dog when the rental car lady returns with the keys. But as I turn toward the exit we need to reach the Parking 1 garage, Hollis appears behind me, his arms folded tight across his chest.

"Hello again," I say.

"Hi." Hollis gestures to Mike with his chin. "Who's this?"

"Hollis, meet Mike. Mike's a hospital exec headed home to North Carolina from a conference. Mike, this is Hollis, a grumpy, blocked writer on his way to a sex appointment in Miami."

Mike gives Hollis a questioning look but says, "Nice to meet you."

"Likewise," Hollis replies.

"Mike has graciously offered to let me travel with him to Charlotte."

"But you're going to Key West. Charlotte's not even halfway."

"Thank you, Captain Obvious," I say. "I know how distance works. But beggars can't be choosers. I'm sure I'll figure it out. Maybe the planes will be up and running again by the time we get there, or I can find my own rental car, or a bus, or another friendly stranger . . ."

Hollis rubs his hands through his hair and makes a noise somewhere between a sigh and a groan. "Fine. Grab your bags, Millicent."

"What?"

"Grab your bags. You can ride with me to Miami."

My hands find their way to my hips. I should probably be glad he's changed his mind, but right now I'm mostly annoyed. If Hollis was going to give in and let me go with him, why couldn't he have done so earlier? We've already wasted so much time—time I don't exactly have. "I thought you said that unless I could offer sex or inspiration, you didn't want me around."

Mike's eyes bounce between us. It's like the video he showed me of Sockem observing a tennis match at their local park. Apparently, the pugs are very popular on TikTok.

"Sorry, if you could just give us a minute," Hollis says to Mike while guiding me off to the side so we can continue our discussion in relative privacy. "If it's either your luggage in my trunk or your dismembered body parts in someone else's, I'd prefer the former."

"Excuse you. Mike is lovely and very not-murdery."

Hollis looks back at Mike, who is smiling down at his phone and humming "Soul Man." "I'm not worried about Mike. Mike's probably fine. But it's a long trip from Charlotte to Miami, and you apparently have very few qualms about requesting rides from strangers. So excuse me if I'd rather know for sure that you arrive in Florida safe, sound, and with all of your limbs intact."

"Ooh, stranger danger," I say, wiggling my fingers in the air. "Did you forget that you're a stranger too, Hollis?"

"I'm not a stranger. We've met before."

"You don't even remember it."

His frown deepens. "Well, *I* know you're safe with me. And since I'm doing this for my own peace of mind, that's what matters here."

"Oh, right. Right. Because you only do kind things out of self-ishness."

"Why are you saying it like that?" he asks.

"Like what? How am I saying it?" I smile up at him, watching the way his pulse jumps in his neck. Him finding me amusing is great and all, but I have to admit there's an appeal to him finding me frustrating too.

"Ahem. Sorry to interrupt," Mike says, appearing beside us. A blush sweeps over my face as I realize Hollis and I have been having a stare-off for the last minute and a half. "I need to get rockin' and rollin' if I'm going to get home tonight. Millie, are you still riding with me, or . . . ?"

"Ah, sorry, Mike. As much as I was looking forward to being the Joliet Jake to your Elwood, it probably makes more sense for me to go with Hollis since he's traveling farther south. I'm really sorry for keeping you from getting on the road. So uh, here." I dig my wallet from my backpack and pull out two fifties. "Here's a quarter of what I promised you, to make up for the inconvenience."

"Oh, you don't have to do that." But after I insist, Mike tucks the bills into a money clip and it disappears into his pants pocket. "Thanks, Millie. But for the record, I'd've been Jake. Belushi had the better voice." He barks out a laugh, ending in a wide smile. "You take care now. Be safe."

"You too," I say. "Give my best to Carla and the puppies."

"The puppies, huh?" Hollis says as we walk toward the exit.

"Mike and his wife are proud pug parents."

Hollis sighs and rolls his eyes but doesn't say anything as he walks ahead. After a short and silent journey, we arrive at his car in the Parking 2 garage. Considering the circumstances—that I was weeping and suddenly single—I didn't really notice his car the night he drove me home, but I assume this navy Volvo sedan is the same one he had a few months ago. He tosses my suitcase into the trunk beside his duffel bag. I settle into the passenger seat, my backpack on the floorboard between my feet. When Hollis starts the engine, he lets out a little annoyed huff that might be directed toward me or maybe just toward the world at large.

"Thanks for changing your mind," I say.

"I didn't have much of a choice."

"Don't even. I would've been perfectly fine with Mike."

He grips the steering wheel so tightly his fingers lose their color. There's a beat of silence, and it lets a realization float into my brain.

"Hmm," I say.

"What?"

I wait until he's safely backed us out of the parking space. As he predicted, there's a lot of extra traffic in the garage due to the mass cancelation. "Well, I was just thinking . . . there's something I don't understand."

"Oh, it seems like there are a lot of things you don't understand. Like basic self-preservation."

"Why were you there, Hollis? By the car rental kiosks, I mean. That's the Parking One garage, and your car was parked here, in Two." I watch his profile, waiting for him to respond. When he doesn't, I continue. "And you had a head start. About twenty minutes between when you left me and then when you showed up again. If you'd come straight to your car, you would've already been making your way down 95 by the time I met Mike. Yet there you were, skulking around the rental car kiosks—"

"I wasn't skulking."

"Then what were you doing?"

He doesn't respond.

"What I think," I say, "is that you were about halfway to the garage when you realized there'd be a mad dash for rental cars. And your conscience refused to let you leave me potentially stranded, so you hung around to check on me."

"You should be glad I did," Hollis says. "Who knows what kind of mischief you would've gotten yourself into, getting into cars with strange men."

On a more charming person, that would be said with a little smirk. But Hollis's expression reads as completely serious, as if he doesn't see the irony.

"Admit it," I say. "You really are a cinnamon roll underneath that ridiculous burnt-toast disguise."

"Huh? If you're trying to imply that I'm secretly nice, I'm not. Still just selfish. You think I want to deal with the cops showing up at my door, all 'Mr. Hollenbeck, we'd like to ask you some questions. It seems you were the last person to see Millicent Watts-Cohen alive'?"

"Of course. Nothing to do with you being a good person. Forgive me for suggesting it."

"I'm not a good person, Millicent, and you best believe it. I'm a real jerk. A bad apple, through and through."

I laugh. "You sound like Pee-wee Herman."

"Excuse me?"

"Not your voice but like, you know. 'You don't wanna get mixed up with a guy like me. I'm a loner, Dottie. A rebel.'"

"I have no idea what you're talking about."

I let out an intentionally wistful sigh that I know will annoy him. "I bet Mike would've understood my references."

"Enough about Mike. Jesus." Hollis taps his fingers against the steering wheel and bites his cheek. "You were really going to pay that man four hundred dollars to drive you six hours south?"

So much for enough about Mike. "I would've paid a lot more. I told you, I'm desperate."

For a split second, he takes his eyes off the road and looks over at me. "This trip really means that much to you?"

I squeeze my backpack between my sneakers, giving Mrs. Nash a little makeshift hug as I remember promising her I would find Elsie. It was right after she told me their story.

I just wish I could have said a proper goodbye, told her how much I still loved her, she whispered, blowing her nose into the tissue she kept tucked into her stretchy silver watchband. *Even after she died, she never felt gone to me. She still doesn't.*

What if I can find out where she's buried? I asked. *Then we can go visit.*

Oh, Millie, but what would be the point?

So I can meet her. I smiled up at Mrs. Nash from my spot on the floor.

You're such a silly thing, Mrs. Nash said, returning my smile. She called me a "silly thing" with such regularity and with such affection that it was better than any standard term of endearment. *Well, I suppose, if you find the time to search that internet of yours—*

I'll make the time, I announced. *I want to reunite you with Elsie, however symbolically.*

Of course, I didn't make the time until it was already too late. Mrs. Nash passed away in March, and I never got to tell her that the love of her life hadn't died in Korea after all.

But now Elsie actually is living out her last days in hospice care at a Key West nursing facility, and I can't afford any delays. That's why I dug into my *Penelope to the Past* money—"That's supposed to be for your retirement!" I could almost hear my father shouting as I moved the funds over to my checking account—to spring for an outrageously expensive plane ticket and hotel rooms during one of the busiest travel holidays of the year instead of waiting until next week.

"It means more than anything," I tell Hollis.

"I suppose a thousand dollars is fair, then."

"What?"

"As payment. For me to take you to Miami."

"No way," I say. "I offered to pay you and you said no. 'Not enough cinnamon rolls in the world,' remember?"

"I just saved you from getting stranded in Charlotte. Or worse. I think I deserve some sort of compensation for helping you, yet again."

"I never asked for your help. And Mike was a very nice man. I would've been perfectly safe with him."

"Again, less concerned about Mike than whomever you might've stumbled upon after him." Hollis flails his right hand in the air. "That wide-eyed, trusting thing you have going on practically screams 'Hey, come murder me and wear my skin!'"

I snort. "Do you always assume the worst of people?"

"Yes. Do you always assume the best?"

"Usually."

"*Faaantastic*," he says through clenched teeth. The word acts like punctuation, announcing that the conversation has come to an end as far as he's concerned.

However, I don't do well with silence. "So," I say. "What kind of stuff do you write?"

Authors are practically bound by law to answer this question. "Nonfiction novels, mostly. My first book's being published in November. It's about a pyramid scheme that caused all sorts of scandal in a small town in Minnesota."

"Nonfiction novels? So, like, *In Cold Blood*?"

He contemplates the comparison, then concedes, "This one has less murder and more casseroles, but basically yes."

"Wow. Sounds great. I'll have to preorder it."

To my surprise, Hollis smiles. It's the smallest smile I've seen on anyone ever, really only visible at the corners of his mouth, but it's something. If he knows this is my go-to line for meeting authors that I perfected while dating Josh, he doesn't seem willing to call me out on it.

"And you?" he asks. "What does Millicent Watts-Cohen do when she's not fending off creeps or jumping into cars with randos?"

"I've been freelancing as a historical accuracy consultant for TV and film for the last few months. I did some research to help out a director friend while I was finishing up my master's. She recommended me to others in the industry. There's a lot more demand than I expected. Apparently, Hollywood people still think of me as one of them, and they like keeping everything in the family, so to speak."

"Your master's is in history then?"

"Yeah. I've always been interested in it. Plus, it felt necessary to somehow atone for *Penelope*'s sins. And there were a lot of them. I mean, there's an Appomattox episode that *extremely* does not hold up." He doesn't comment. "Did you watch the show?"

"My sister did."

"But you didn't?"

He raises one shoulder in a lazy shrug. "I caught bits and pieces of episodes here and there, but it wasn't really my thing."

It's a relief that Hollis is probably not doing all of this for me because I'm ever so slightly famous or because he's hoping to role-play some weird teenage sexual fantasy. I'm basically an E-list celebrity, or maybe even F-list if it goes that low, but you'd be surprised how many people are only interested in knowing me because of that. Like Josh, it turns out.

Thinking about my ex makes me remember what Hollis said about him, about how Josh has been telling his friends—and frenemies, apparently—that we split because I'm too impossible, strange, needy. And that makes me get that sinking feeling that accompanies knowing there's someone out there who doesn't like me. It's never fun, but it's so much worse when it's someone I assumed I would marry one day.

I reach for the stereo, hoping for a distraction. When I press the button to turn it on, a velvety voice fills the car, talking with sharp enunciation about the flight cancelation hullabaloo.

"What is this?"

"WAMU."

I wrinkle my nose.

"What do you have against NPR?" he asks.

"Nothing," I say. "It's great. I have the utmost respect for public radio. But it's a horrible soundtrack for a road trip."

"I'm sorry I don't have a perfectly curated playlist with which to caress your discerning ears."

"That's okay." I pull my phone out of my backpack's front pocket. "I've got us covered." I dig around until I find my aux cord, and soon The Alan Parsons Project's "Eye in the Sky" fills the car. My mouth opens to belt out the lyrics, but I'm not a talented singer—like, I'm actually objectively bad—and it's probably too early to subject Hollis to that. Making someone's ears bleed isn't a great way to show your appreciation. So I restrain myself, settling for swaying in my seat. Of course, by the time we get to the chorus, there's some shimmying and eyes-closed head bobbing going on too.

"What's going on over there?" Hollis asks. "Do you need to pee already?"

"I'm dancing."

"Of course you are."

The playlist I made this morning for driving from Miami to Key West is on shuffle, but as the next song starts, I decide I'm quite pleased with the music app's choices.

"God, I love Steely Dan," I say, adjusting my swaying to the more subdued tempo of "Dirty Work." "I actually just found this album on vinyl at a record store in Silver Spring last week." I bought it even though I don't currently own a record player; Geoffrey's daughter wound up with Mrs. Nash's.

Hollis groans. "When I agreed to let you come with me, I didn't realize you were secretly my uncle Jim in a tiny woman costume."

"I bet your uncle Jim doesn't have my moves." I gyrate in my seat in time to the saxophone solo.

Hollis watches me out of the corner of his eye—the blue-gray one. "That he does not."

Fleetwood Mac's "Dreams" comes on next, but before the end of the first line, Hollis says, "Ugh. Can we please listen to something else?"

"Excuse me, do you have something against Stevie Nicks?"

"Her voice sort of gets on my nerves."

I sit in stunned silence, attempting to find a suitable reaction to this blasphemy. I finally land on a simple, "How dare you. How *dare* you."

Hollis reaches over and turns off the stereo.

"Hey!" I go up an octave in my outrage.

I think I see the slightest tilt of his mouth into a smile again, which only annoys me further. How dare he disrespect Stevie Nicks and sort of almost smirk about it! The *impudence*.

"Tell me more about this mission of yours," he says.

I fold my arms over my chest, pouting. "What about it?"

"Like . . . why? Clearly, it wasn't a priority for your friend to get back to this old lover."

"It was, though," I say. "She wanted to find her, more than anything. But I'd only just started looking when Mrs. Nash died."

"Her?" The eyebrow over the blue-gray eye raises.

"Yes. Elsie. They met during the war."

"The war?" he asks. "Vietnam?"

"World War Two."

Hollis lets out a whistle through his teeth. "Man. That's a long time ago."

"Yeah. Well," I say. "So are a lot of things."

"I guess I wonder why any business left unfinished after so many years shouldn't remain unfinished."

"Because she didn't mean to leave it unfinished in the first place. Mrs. Nash and Elsie kept in touch at first, after the war ended. They wrote tons of letters. But then . . . it's complicated."

"Millicent. We're going to be stuck in this car together for hours. I'd much rather hear a long and complicated story than listen to middle-aged-man music the entire time. Go ahead."

"All of it?" I know this story by heart. In fact, I have thought about it every day since Mrs. Nash told me how she and Elsie met. But I've never had to tell it to someone else before. It's intimidating. What if I can't do it justice? And something tells me Hollis

Hollenbeck isn't exactly a romantic. I swear, if he disrespects Mrs. Nash and Elsie like he disrespected Stevie Nicks—

"Well, why don't we start with the beginning and see where we wind up."

"Okay, fine," I say. "So . . ."

Key West, Florida
November 1944

BEING STATIONED IN KEY WEST FELT LIKE SOME SORT OF COSMIC reward. Rose McIntyre had suffered through eighteen cold, dark Wisconsin winters, but in late November 1944, the US Navy gifted her more sun and warmth than she knew what to do with. Even the fact that she spent a majority of her time scrubbing nest boxes and dumping bird droppings into a trench kept behind the loft solely for that purpose—"living the glamorous life of the new girl," as she later described her early days at US Naval Air Station, Key West—couldn't diminish the freedom promised by a place blessed with eternal summer. The first day she found herself off-duty, Rose turned down her bunkmate's invitation to go bicycling along the sea wall with some of the other Women Accepted for Volunteer Emergency Service, and instead made her way to the rocky shores of Boca Chica Beach. She found that the rhythmic sounds of the sea made it easier to push her frustrations and disappointments with her duties out of her mind. Focusing on the endless turquoise water stretching out into forever eased her homesickness, even though this place was so different from her frigid Midwestern home.

That's what she was doing when she first saw the mermaid. Rose wasn't a fanciful girl; she knew that mermaids were not real. Yet she could find no other explanation for the way the creature glided through the water with the ease of someone born among the frothy waves. Rose watched, trying to catch a glimpse of shining scales or the tip of a tail fin, but from a distance she could make out only light hair and tanned skin that appeared to glisten when covered in water droplets. "Come closer," she whispered. "Come closer so I can see you better." Perhaps the breeze delivered her message, because she only had to wait a moment before the mermaid swam toward the shore.

Of course, it was a human woman who emerged, not a mermaid. If Rose still had any doubt, it was erased when she saw two long, bronzed legs stroll out of the surf.

"Hello there," the woman said with a smile as she walked past where Rose sat cross-legged in the sand. Rose turned her head to glance over her shoulder, where a towel lay draped over an arched piece of driftwood. Rose felt somewhat foolish that she'd assumed the otherworldly woman had swam to her directly, as if they were magnets compelled together, because surely the towel was what brought her here.

"Hello," Rose said, attempting unsuccessfully to avert her eyes as the stranger dabbed at the saltwater beaded along her taut midriff. From the closer distance, she saw that the hair that clung to bare shoulders was honey blonde while wet—it would be almost platinum, certainly, when dry. As her gaze drifted to the unmistakable points of nipples showing through the saturated thin material of her bathing suit top, a thought drifted through Rose's head that she had only entertained once or twice before—thoughts she'd only ever thought about her best friend, Joan, in the safety of her dark bedroom back in Oshkosh.

Rose was startled from her reverie when the woman lowered to the ground beside her. "Oh, I just love this place, don't you?" she asked, her voice melodic and lightly accented; perhaps she was from Missouri, or some other place not quite the South or West.

"It's gorgeous," Rose said. She wondered if the woman had caught her staring at her body, and she considered leaving to avoid having to concoct some innocuous compliment about the stranger's bathing suit to explain her odd behavior.

"Funny we haven't come across each other here before."

"I only arrived a few days ago," Rose said. "This is my first week on base."

"Nurse or WAVE?" the woman asked.

"WAVE. A pigeoneer. You?"

"Nurse." The woman's shell pink lips parted, and her tongue poked out to wet them before she spoke again. "What's a . . ." She laughed, and it sounded like someone strumming a harp. "What's a pigeoneer? Someone who keeps pigeons?"

"Yes, exactly. We breed, care for, and train them to deliver messages. There are eight of us total here."

"That must be fascinating work."

"It's better than taking dictation at least." In actuality, Rose wasn't convinced that sweeping away the mixture of corn, rice, and excrement that fell to the loft's floor after the pigeons' twice-daily ten-minute feeding frenzy was in any way superior to sitting in front of a typewriter while an admiral paced the room, but her pride refused to admit that she had yet to be trusted with any of the more interesting aspects of pigeoneering.

"The birds probably aren't as handsy as naval officers." The woman winked, and something inside Rose's chest tightened in an uncomfortable way that made her consider again taking her leave. "I'm Elsie Brown. From Elgin, Oklahoma."

"Rose McIntyre. Oshkosh, Wisconsin."

Their handshake was brief, and Rose couldn't ignore the sense of loss she felt when the other woman pulled away.

"It's a pleasure to meet you," Elsie said. They sat in silence for a moment, and Rose's heart began thumping in a way that would probably concern the nurse beside her if she could hear. She moved to rise and escape Elsie Brown's strange pull, but a hand cupped her shoulder before she made it to her feet.

"Say, Rose McIntyre, pigeoneer. What are you up to for the rest of the afternoon? I have a box of chocolates under my bed, and I've been dying to share them with someone before they melt."

3

· · · · ·

"THAT'S A GREAT LINE," HOLLIS SAYS.

"What?"

"About the chocolates. It's a great line. I'll have to use it sometime."

"It wasn't a line. Elsie wasn't . . . Why am I even bothering trying to explain it to you? You probably don't believe in love and romance. Only lust and suffering and . . . and . . ."

"No, you're right. Lust and suffering, that's about it."

"I just don't understand how you can listen to what I told you and all you come away with is, 'That's a great line.'"

"I never said that's all I came away with. I also learned that pigeoneers were a thing in World War Two, and that Elsie Brown was a total fox circa 1944." The corner of his mouth creeps up. "Look, I'm not sure what else you want me to say. No matter how pretty the story, love doesn't exist. At least not the romantic, enduring kind you're talking about. Not the kind that lasts for seventy-some years. People fall out, get bored, move on. They forget. I mean, how do you even know Elsie *remembers* Mrs. Nash? Or, if she does, that she'd want a sandwich bag of her ashes? What exactly do you expect her to say when you give it to her? 'Thanks for bringing me some dust that used to be a former fling?' You have to see how this whole reunion scheme is extremely presumptuous, Millicent."

I flash him my angriest look while my stomach sinks like it's full of concrete. "You don't know what you're talking about. You don't know *anything*. You're just bitter because . . . because you lack emotional fortitude."

Even as I say it, I wonder if Hollis is right. What if I'm the one who's too afraid to process the world around me and come to a new conclusion? Maybe this *is* a ridiculous and presumptuous thing to do. "I promised Mrs. Nash I'd find Elsie," I say, refusing to confess to even an inkling of uncertainty. "That they'd be together again, in some way. If she lived, if I found her before—" Tears well up behind my eyes. I groan, the effort to keep them corralled making my nose burn. When the feeling subsides, I continue. "The point is, true, lasting, romantic love exists, whether *you* believe in it or not. I know it does because that's what Mrs. Nash had with Elsie. And that's that."

Except I know, deep down, that that's *not* that.

Of course I'm doing this for Mrs. Nash, both because I promised before she died and because I loved her. She was my best friend in the whole world. But now that I've had a moment to process, to slow down and analyze . . . I have to admit that I might be doing this for me too. Because if I could be so wrong about Josh, what else could I be wrong about?

What if I've been a naive fool my whole life, putting my faith in things like happily ever afters and humanity's overall inherent goodness? I need reassurance that it isn't stupid to believe that two people can love each other and keep on loving each other as long as they live, no matter what obstacles get thrown into their path. That hoping I might find someone who will never give up on me isn't as pointless as it's sometimes felt lately. As pointless as Hollis seems to think it is.

"You look like you want to punch me," Hollis says, glancing over.

The thought honestly hadn't crossed my mind. But now that he mentions it, I do. I really do. "Well, you'd probably deserve it."

"Probably. But keep your weapons holstered while I'm driving. We'll have to stop for gas at the next exit. You can take a swing at me then if you want."

The uncharacteristically violent urge is eclipsed by others by the time we pull off the highway and up to the pump at a Wawa somewhere west of Fredericksburg. I was actually dancing before, but now I do have to pee something fierce. When I come out of the convenience store, Hollis is leaning against the car. He hooks his fingers together and reaches his arms toward the sky. The stretch makes the striped T-shirt under his open black hoodie ride up, exposing a few inches of skin and a trail of dark hair that presumably continues both northward and southward. No matter how grumpy and rude he is, I cannot deny that Hollis is an attractive guy.

He's exactly my type, physically. In fact, now that I think about it, he looks a little like Josh. Only a better version. Like Josh was an artist's first attempt at figure drawing and Hollis his hundredth. Which is probably one of the reasons they're frenemies and not friends; I learned too late that Josh can't truly like another person unless he's certain he's superior to them in every way. And considering Josh could be the poster boy for white male mediocrity, that leaves very few people for him to like.

Hollis pulls his phone out of his pocket and types something quick. Probably letting his friend with benefits in Miami know he won't be there as scheduled. Part of me wonders what Hollis's muse is like. But most of me wants to know absolutely nothing about her. Because if I know things about this woman, I'm going to start forming an opinion about her. I'm going to start comparing us, because that's how being a human being works. And if I wind up having negative feelings about her that have nothing at all to do with her, that's not exactly fair. Not to her, and not to me.

Anyway, Miami Woman is no doubt disappointed that Hollis won't be in her bed tonight. Well, sister, honestly? Same. Not that I actively want to do that, it's just . . . well, like, if things were different. And he weren't such a weirdly kind jerk. And if he wasn't already planning to fuck another person's brains out as soon as he possibly can. And if he didn't know Josh. And if, and if, and if. Then I would. I definitely, definitely would.

Hollis's eyes are focused directly on me. How long has he been watching me stare at him in this weird half-ogling, half–mind-completely-somewhere-else state? Awkward. I flash him my brightest smile because I'm not really sure what else to do, and get his exaggerated frown in return.

"Hello. Sorry to bother you, miss."

I turn and find a man standing beside me. So maybe Hollis's frown wasn't for me after all. This guy is older, mid-sixties maybe. Probably not a *Penelope* fan (though you'd be surprised).

"Hi," I say. "Can I help you with something?"

"I hope so, miss. I must've lost my wallet at the rest stop about twenty miles back, but I don't have enough gas to get back there, and my phone's dead. I just need—"

I pull my wallet out of my backpack. "I think I only have a twenty. Will that be enough?"

His eyes widen and his thin mouth falls slightly open. I wonder how many people refused to give him anything before he found me. He smiles as I hand him the cash. "Yes. Oh yes. Thank you so much, miss. You're a kind soul. Thank you truly."

"No problem," I say. "I hope you find your wallet."

"God bless you," he says, then turns and goes inside the convenience store. I notice then that Hollis is beside me, frown still in place.

"He swindled you."

I rock back on my heels to see around a window display. "He's paying for his gas at the register." I look back at the gas pumps. "I bet that's his truck parked over at three."

Even though it's not possible to see exactly what the man is doing at the counter from where we're standing, Hollis says, "Or he's buying cigarettes, beer, and a nudie magazine, all on your dime."

I shrug. "So what if he does? Twenty dollars isn't going to make or break me, but if it's the difference between a shit day and a happy day for him, well, whatever."

He runs a hand over his face in clear exasperation, his round tortoiseshell glasses pushed temporarily askew when his fingers slide under them. "I have met babies more worldly than you, Millicent."

The man comes out with a can of Arizona iced tea tucked under his arm. He gives us a nod and another quick thank-you. "You got yourself a good woman there," he says to Hollis. "A real good one."

Hollis absently says, "Yep," and smiles. It's bizarre and grimacey and obviously forced. His real smile *must* be better, and my determination to draw it out rises anew, if only to clear whatever the hell that was from my memory.

"See, he bought something," Hollis says after the man is out of earshot.

"It's a can of Arizona, dude. That's what? Ninety-nine cents? Hardly an extravagance. And look, he's going to pump three, getting his gas. Told you so."

I head back to the car and Hollis follows.

"Still doesn't mean he needed it in the first place. Probably has piles of money like Scrooge McDuck back in his mansion because he tricks nice young ladies into covering his daily expenses."

I roll my eyes. "Mhm. Yeah. I'm sure that's exactly the case, Hollis. Sounds like a super-efficient lifestyle." The man gives me a wave from within his truck's cab as he pulls away.

We're back on the highway before Hollis speaks again. "I don't understand how you go through life this way, trusting everyone to be who they say they are and want what they say they want. Doesn't it ever come back to bite you?"

"Not often. But sometimes." I make a sound that aspires to be a chuckle but mostly comes out a little sad. "It certainly did with Josh."

"Oh," Hollis says. "I didn't mean to . . . We don't need to talk about that."

"It's fine. I feel okay about it now." I really do. I'm still stunned by a lot of the assholery that I somehow missed over the three years we were together, but I don't dwell on it anymore. "There's nothing quite like finding out your boyfriend has been pretending to be you online to increase his own name recognition to make you realize you're better off without him.'"

"Hold on. He did *what* now?"

"That's the reason we broke up, the reason I came out of the party so upset that night. One of Josh's acquaintances told me she just *loved* my Instagram. Except I don't have an Instagram. In fact, I very intentionally stay away from all social media because, as you may have noticed, people have a lot of feelings about Penelope that I, Millie, do not necessarily want to know about. So I confronted Josh, and he confessed that he started an account in my name about six months before. He wanted to get me back into the public eye because he thought it'd help him sell more copies of his book. He felt like I owed him because he 'put up with me' or whatever."

What Josh actually said while he had me pinned up against a wall in the hallway leading to the restaurant's bathrooms was, *If you're going to be fucking weird, Millie, you should at least be fucking weird and famous again so I'm not with you for nothing.* It was in that moment that I knew our relationship was over and that he didn't love me. Probably never had. But despite knowing deep inside that those words say much more about him than they do about me, I don't want to tell Hollis the whole truth. I'm embarrassed. It's like my shame at the airport; sometimes I can't help but feel somewhat responsible when men are shitty to me, but then I feel guilty for falling into that trap. And then the result is the same: me feeling bad about my feelings.

"So he like . . . posted pictures of you? I don't think I understand."

"Yeah. Hundreds of them. Of me, us, our apartment. Most of

which I didn't even know he'd taken. But he captioned them as if it were me posting. Ten thousand people liking and commenting and . . . He gave people access to my life, access to *me*, without me even knowing."

"Wow. That's super scummy." He's not looking at me, since he's driving, and he's still frowning from back when we were at the gas station so I have no idea how genuine the sentiment is.

"Yeah." I don't tell him the worst part: that Josh revealed later that he was going to propose that night in front of everyone at the party. And I would have said yes, not even realizing it was all a big publicity stunt.

There's a pause in the conversation as Hollis focuses on the road. We're getting closer to Richmond. Rush-hour traffic on I-95 is always bad. But combined with the people heading to the beach for the long weekend, we're going about twenty miles an hour. Every once in a while, someone slams on their brakes, just for fun, I guess.

We're at a standstill when Hollis speaks again. "So are you completely anti–social media? Because I saw you take a picture with that prick at the airport. You know he's probably posted it to Insta, Twitter, Facebook, wherever. Right? Or do I need to go track him down and break his phone?"

I can't tell if that's a sweet offer or if Hollis just really hated that guy. Not sure I'd blame him if it's the latter. "Ha, no. It's fine. I don't want to participate, but I don't mind popping up here and there. Besides, I can't really avoid it, not completely. Whether I like it or not, acting when I was a kid means I'm always going to be considered public property in some ways. If I don't pose for the pics, they take them stealthily. I'd rather at least look halfway decent. Choose what parts of me the public gets to consume. That's very important to me. And that's why what Josh did felt like such a huge violation."

"Makes sense," Hollis says, signaling to change lanes.

"I mean, *I* think so. But during the fight Josh said letting other people post selfies with me isn't any different than what he did."

Hollis shakes his head. I hear him mumble something that sounds an awful lot like, "Fucking asshole."

"What was that?" I ask. Because I want him to say it louder, to know if he's really on my side instead of Josh's, even though that's where his loyalty should lie. Probably. I don't know the loyalty code for frenemies.

"I said he's such a fucking asshole." He crisply enunciates each syllable like a grittier version of the NPR correspondents he likes listening to. I can't help but grin. "Your issue is with the lack of control over your image," he continues. "Posing for a picture with someone is one thing. Having someone take pics of you and plaster them online, plus he pretends you're the one posting? He's either the least intelligent human on the planet or simply an asshole. And as little as I think of Josh Yaeger's intellect, it's clear that it's mostly option B in this situation."

A hopeful warmth blooms inside my chest. This is different from Dani reassuring me over and over after the breakup that I was in the right every time I called her in tears at three in the morning. And from Mrs. Nash's endearing anger—after I explained what the hell Instagram is—that Josh would do such a thing. It's different because Hollis doesn't have a horse in this race. He isn't invested in my happiness. I mean, I'm not sure he even *likes* me. So I can only surmise that that little speech and the way his jaw is clenched and his fingers are digging into the steering wheel translate to genuine indignance on my behalf. It shouldn't matter that Hollis cares that Josh hurt me, but it does. It matters so much.

Before I can say anything in response, Hollis's grip on the wheel loosens, freeing his fingertips to tap out a short rhythm. "Hey," he says. "You hungry?"

4

. . . . .

"JOSÉ NAPOLEONI'S RIO GRANDE TRATTORIA?" THAT'S WHAT THE sign says, so I'm not sure why it comes out of my mouth as a question. Maybe just because I'm struggling with the concept of Mexican-Italian fusion, especially housed in what is clearly a former Pizza Hut just off the highway.

"It's either this or fast food," Hollis says. Before I can tease him for being a snob, he adds, "I don't mind fast food, if that's what you want. My tastes are pretty much the opposite of bougie. But I figure we can wait out some of the traffic if we sit down to eat here."

He has a point. Fast food would be, well, faster. But it's not like rush hour is about to magically disappear, and I'll dwell less on the ticking clock if we're eating a decent meal than if I'm sitting helplessly in the passenger seat with nothing to do but wait and imagine the worst.

There are only three cars in the restaurant's parking lot, which isn't the best sign. Then again, this isn't exactly a bustling area—

wherever it is in Virginia we even are—so maybe three cars is an absolute crush for slightly before dinnertime on a Thursday. I look the place up on my phone and find that it only opened within the last month and therefore has a whopping four reviews, one of which is inexplicably in Polish.

Hollis peeks at my phone, then throws his head back against the driver's seat. "Jesus. You are the most . . . the most—"

"The most what?"

"Just the absolute goddamn most, Millicent."

"Thank you," I say, still focused on the reviews. Maybe I will suddenly know how to read Polish if I stare at my phone hard enough. I want to know why they gave José Napoleoni's one star when the other three ratings were comment-less fives, but not enough to bother messing with Google Translate.

"You'll get into a car with any ol' stranger you meet at the airport, but when it comes to trying a new restaurant you're all 'Ah, I don't know, I really better do my research before agreeing to this.'"

"Listen." I turn my body in my seat to give Hollis my full attention, because this is important for him to understand if we're going to be spending a significant amount of time together. "I have never once claimed to make sense as a person. And I would appreciate it if you would stop remarking on my idiosyncrasies as if you've caught me in some continuity error."

His C-on-its-face frown flattens into a contrite straight line. "You're right. I'm sorry."

My head tilts and my eyes narrow in confusion; it's as if Hollis is speaking to me in an extinct language. "Wait. That was an apology. A real one, with no 'but' or 'it's just that' trailing behind."

"Yeah. Do you have to sound so accusatory about it? I did something that upset you. I don't want to do that. I'm not *that* much of a jerk. So I said I'm sorry, and I'm going to stop doing the thing. This isn't exactly rocket science."

"You wouldn't think so, no," I say.

You can always judge a person by the quality of their apology, Mrs. Nash reminds me from inside the memory of when I found out someone in my grad cohort was hosting *Penelope to the Past* viewing parties for the rest of our classmates. I exhale, blowing away the grief that threatens to envelop me like a thick fog. "Also, you didn't upset me. Just annoyed me a little."

"Oh. Well, apology rescinded then. Because you've annoyed me a little for the past two and a half hours, so we'll just call it even."

"Whatever, let's eat."

"Let's," Hollis says, unbuckling his seat belt.

José Napoleoni, ready your spaghetti tacos. Here we come.

I'M NOT SURPRISED BY THE RESTAURANT'S RED/GREEN/WHITE color scheme—I mean, it's the obvious choice, isn't it? But I am surprised by the giant sombrero-wearing taxidermy bear by the hostess stand, which is presumably posed to be mid-roar but looks more mid-yawn. And I suddenly want nothing more than to put my fingers in the stuffed bear's mouth and see what it feels like in there. Even if I stand on my tiptoes, though, I think I'll still be about two inches too short to reach.

Before I can ask Hollis for a boost—which I'm sure would have gone over *great*—a short man with gelled-back black hair and medium-bronze skin appears beside the PLEASE WAIT TO BE SEATED sign. "Hola and buonasera," he says, a large, toothy grin peeking out from under an impressive mustache with the ends waxed into curlicues. "Welcome to José Napoleoni's Rio Grande Trattoria. I'm José, and I will be happy to take care of you this evening. Follow me, please."

Hollis and I slide into opposite sides of a booth, and a young waiter with a few wispy black hairs above his top lip trudges over with two glasses of ice water.

"Focaccia and salsa," José says to him. "My son," he explains with a fond smile as the teenager walks with an impressive lack of urgency to the kitchen. "Now, what can I get you folks to drink?"

"Just water for me, thanks," Hollis says, his face buried in the menu.

Okay, I love this place. First the unexpected sleepy bear. Now I find my favorite drink of all time on the menu, and with *free refills*. "I'll have a Shirley Temple."

"One Shirley coming right up. Ah, thanks, Marco." José takes the basket of bread from his son and places it in the middle of the red-and-white checkered tablecloth. Marco places a dish of chunky fresh salsa beside it. "Rock salt and cilantro focaccia with fresh pico de gallo," José explains. "Enjoy."

"This is certainly interesting," Hollis says, dipping the bread into the salsa. I watch as he brings it to his mouth and his teeth disappear into the pillowy focaccia. He has a really nice mouth when it's not scowling at me. "It's like . . . Mexican bruschetta?"

"Hmm." I take a bite. "It's definitely not bad."

"What are you getting?" he asks, returning to his menu.

"No idea," I say. "I usually panic while ordering anyway, so it's easier not to decide on anything."

He lowers his menu to reveal his dark eyebrows in a V over his eyes. His heterochromia isn't as obvious under the red-and-green stained-glass pendant light hanging above our booth.

"You panic?" he asks.

I nod and use the small spoon in the salsa dish to scoop more tomato and onion onto my bread. "Sometimes when faced with too many choices, I panic when it comes time to commit and I choose something completely different. Like I'll want the chicken, but find myself ordering steak. And it's always fine. I'm not picky or anything. But then I always regret not getting the chicken. So if I never decide to want the chicken to begin with, I won't be as disappointed when I don't order it."

He closes his menu and lays it on the table. "That might be the most ridiculous thing I've ever heard."

"I find that hard to believe considering I told you not three hours ago that I'm on a mission to deliver the human remains in my backpack to an elderly woman in Key West."

Hollis's arm reaches across the table and his long fingers flip my menu back open in front of me. "Figure out what you want," he says.

I let out a huff of a sigh. Great. Another man who thinks he can make me more normal by telling me to *simply do the normal thing* and *isn't that so easy*. "Hollis. I just told you—"

"Figure out what you want," he repeats. "And then tell me what it is. I'll order for you so you don't have to worry about panicking."

"Oh," I say. And there it is again. That kindness. A firefly-like ember of warmth flits around inside my rib cage.

"Don't read into it. It's only because I don't want to hear you complaining for the next three hours about how you wish you'd ordered something different."

"Right, of course," I say, a smile stretching across my face. "You're just being selfish again."

"Yep."

The menu is certainly eclectic. Like the focaccia and pico de gallo, everything is a hybrid of Mexican and Italian classics. My eyes keep returning to the appetizer section, where there's a picture of fried ravioli arranged in a starburst pattern on a large red plate. *Fried Ravioli Sampler: An assortment of cheese, chorizo, ground beef, and shredded chicken ravioli, fried golden brown, with a trio of dipping sauces.* They look like a bunch of tiny empanadas, and I crave them with a burning passion.

"Fried ravioli sampler," I announce, slapping my menu shut.

"Fried ravioli sampler it is."

José brings my Shirley Temple. "I apologize for the wait," he says. "I got a little carried away with the garnishes."

He isn't kidding; the glass he places in front of me has three of those tiny plastic swords protruding from the top, each speared with cherries and orange slices. It reminds me of when Mrs. Nash and I got tipsy on mai tais on New Year's Eve and watched a bunch of YouTube tutorials on how to tie cherry stems with our tongues. She spent hours laughing at my vain attempts while she turned out perfect knot after perfect knot.

"Now," José says, distracting me from the uncomfortable sensation the memory sparks—kind of like hundreds of those tiny plastic swords stabbing me repeatedly in the heart, "are there any questions I can answer for you?"

I'm tempted to ask him about the taxidermy bear's provenance, but I assume he means questions regarding the menu.

"No, I think we're ready," Hollis says. "We'll have a fried ravioli sampler and the fideo with meatballs. Brought out at the same time. Thanks."

We hand our menus over to José, and he passes them along to

Marco before he hurries to the kitchen. Marco stares at the menus in his hands and lets out the most teenagery sigh I've ever heard before plunking them on a random table.

"Thank you," I say to Hollis.

He shrugs but doesn't verbally respond.

I look around the restaurant. We're the only customers here except for two men drinking and watching soccer at the big, U-shaped bar in the center of the room.

Hollis pushes up the sleeves of his hoodie and oh no, I can't stop staring at his forearms. They look as if he writes his books by hand with a thirty-pound pencil. And they've got this dark brown hair all over them that reminds me of the bear out front, and now I can't remember if I want my fingers in the bear's mouth or in Hollis's. He does have a really great mouth . . .

"Millicent," he says, ducking his head into my field of vision. "Are you listening to me?"

My eyes jump to meet his. "Yeah, sorry. What?"

His lips do that thing where they curve only at the edge. "I said you should tell me more about Mrs. Nash and Elsie while we wait."

That sure swats away the rest of my daydreams. My fists clench under the table, wishing they'd taken him up on his offer to let me do him minor bodily harm back at the gas station. For some reason, this man really makes my long-dormant bloodlust bubble to the surface. "Why? Why would I want to tell you more after the way you responded?"

"I'm sorry about that. It wasn't my place to say those things."

"No. It wasn't."

"I promise I won't let my—what did you call it? Lack of emotional fortitude?"

"I believe that is what I said, yes."

His lips curve further. I can't quite decide if I'm insulted or charmed. "I promise I won't let my lack of emotional fortitude intrude on the story this time." Hollis's eyebrows raise and he stares into my eyes. "I promise," he repeats.

"Ugh. Fine. Where was I?"

"They met at the beach. Elsie lured Rose to her room with chocolates."

José brings me another Shirley Temple (less heavily garnished this time) and whisks away the empty glass I have no memory of draining. "Right, right. Okay . . ."

Key West, Florida
December 1944

RAIN BEAT ITS TATTOO AGAINST THE ROOF, A PERSISTENT RHYTHM that made Rose's limbs feel loose and her brain sleepy. She and Elsie worked similar schedules, which seemed like supreme luck until Elsie confessed with an uncharacteristically sheepish grin that she'd arranged it that way. The two women had taken to spending most of their free time together at the beach where they first met, lounging in the sun and staring up at the planes flying low overhead until Elsie's restlessness inevitably steered them into the ocean's waves. On rare poor-weather days like today, when the sky dumped bucket after bucket on Key West as if it forgot it was supposed to be in the midst of the dry season, Rose and Elsie stretched out on the plush carpet in the living area of the nurses' quarters, playing gin rummy. Elsie was an atrocious card player, always too full of energy to focus, yet it did not stop her from beginning each game absolutely certain she would win.

"My bad luck streak is finally ending, I can feel it," Elsie said as she shuffled the cards.

Rose scratched the resident tabby cat, which flopped down beside her. She smiled at the way Elsie's nose wrinkled as she began the next game determined to concentrate harder this time.

Again, Rose was victorious.

"I'm hopeless. You're just too clever," Elsie said. Rose considered employing false modesty to bolster Elsie's ego, but then Elsie reached for Rose and tucked a strand of hair behind her ear with the care of a lover. "I'm just grateful you still choose to grace me with your beauty and brains despite my horrendous card playing."

This was not the first time Elsie had complimented Rose like this, praising her looks and intelligence. While Rose beamed with pride that this fascinating woman found her worthy of her attention and time, it also left her a bit unsettled. Elsie couldn't know the effect of her words and her careless touches, the way it heated Rose's blood and made her want things she couldn't have. It would have been almost cruel if it had been deliberate—which Rose was certain it was not.

Elsie held up a finger, then disappeared down the hallway that led to the bedrooms. She quickly returned with the shoebox in which she kept her candy stash. She held it out to Rose and offered her some of the chocolate-covered peppermint patties a distant cousin had sent from Pennsylvania. Rose grinned as she selected one from the box, and then took another for later; they had quickly become her favorite confection.

Elsie settled again on the floor and popped a piece of bubblegum into her mouth, the pale pink color a perfect match for her lips. "What will you do when the war is over?" Elsie asked.

Rose swallowed the bite of candy, relishing the mint's coolness on her tongue. She licked a crumb of chocolate from the tip of her finger. When she looked up, Elsie's brow was furrowed in a way Rose couldn't read. "I suppose I might go back to Oshkosh," Rose said, omitting how she had cried most nights since arriving in Florida, missing everything and everyone she'd left behind so intensely it felt like an illness. The only time she wasn't homesick, now that she thought of it, was while she was with Elsie. "My parents are there, and most of my siblings."

"Will you marry? Have children?"

That was the plan; Rose had promised her mother—who was an advocate for large families, and was therefore concerned about her daughter wasting some of her most fertile years in the Navy—that marriage and a family would be her first priority when she returned home. It was the only way her mother would agree to give Rose her blessing when she confessed she planned to fudge her birthdate so she could enlist in the WAVES nearly a year before she was technically eligible to serve. Rose was not a dreamer in the way some girls were; in fact, everyone expressed some surprise that she hoped to join up and leave Wisconsin at all. So she'd seen no reason why she would be disinclined to settle down back home after the war, and agreeing had come easy to her.

"I suppose," Rose answered, suddenly uncertain if her promise would be as easy to keep as she assumed when she made it. "I have always hoped to be a mother one day."

As the oldest girl in a family of seven children, Rose spent much of her childhood helping care for her brothers and sisters. She had no aspirations to fill a farmhouse full to bursting with screaming babies, though, and she hoped her future husband would be content with two or three. Her mother would disapprove of such a small family, of course, but Rose thought it more than enough to keep her occupied.

"You'll make a terrific mother," Elsie said. She sounded sincere, though her tone was incongruent with the odd, brittle smile stretched across her face.

"And you? Will you also marry and have children?" Rose asked.

Elsie laughed as if Rose had told her a joke. She shook her head, making her moonlight-colored hair dance along her shoulders. "I don't plan to have time for children. I want to go to medical school, become a surgeon. I want to be in *charge* in the OR instead of taking orders from pompous jackasses. And honestly, I've never seen the appeal of the pitter-patter of little feet when I could be elbow-deep in someone's bowels." She stifled a laugh, well aware by this point in their friendship that Rose was cursed with the combination of a powerful imagination and a weak stomach.

"Perhaps," Rose said once her nausea dissipated, "you could find the appeal in both with the right partner. If you had someone very supportive of your dreams."

Elsie's responding smile looked somehow sadder than any other expression Rose had ever seen on her face in the few weeks they'd known each other. "Yes. Perhaps," Elsie said. She schooled her face back to a pleasant smile and began shuffling the cards again.

5

. . . . .

THE FOOD IS INCREDIBLE. MY RAVIOLI SAMPLER LOOKS JUST LIKE the menu picture—big red plate and everything—and Hollis keeps making these throaty *mmm* noises with each bite of his fideo and meatballs. I'm finding it both incredibly weird and incredibly arousing.

"Do you always eat with such . . . gusto?" I ask.

"What?"

"You sound like you're constantly coming a little over there."

Hollis struggles to swallow his next bite and grabs for his water. "No, I don't."

"Mmm," I say, doing my best impression. "Mmm. Mmm. Ahhh. Mmm." I increase the volume with each iteration. The men at the bar both turn to check out what the hell's going on.

"Practicing my audition for a *When Harry Met Sally* reboot," I explain.

The men nod and turn back to their bottles of Modelo. Bits

and pieces of a conversation about how Hollywood must be out of ideas drift from the bar to our booth.

"For someone who appreciates her privacy, you sure don't mind making a scene," Hollis says in a sharp whisper.

"Me? I'm not the one getting it on with my dinner."

He puts his spoon down in the bowl with a small clang as the metal hits ceramic, leans back in the booth, and folds his arms over his chest. His body language says *two can play this game*, and I feel my skin heat under his stare.

"Been a while since you had a good meal, Millicent?" And shit, he *smiles*. A real smile, not the horrifying forced thing he flashed at the gas station or the nearly imperceptible hints of amusement from the car. This is the genuine article, and it causes these deep parentheses to bracket his mouth. Like the pleasure he's taking in this conversation is an extra bit of information he wants me to note.

"I . . . eat," I say. How is it possible that my throat feels too dry while my mouth feels too wet? I swallow hard, and he must notice because his grin widens.

"But who cooks for you?"

It is entirely unacceptable that he is throwing me off with his handsome face and this convoluted metaphor. Two *can* play this game. Put me in, coach. "Oh, I prefer to feed myself these days. Otherwise I find I usually leave the table still hungry." I consider winking, but that's always a gamble for me since half of the time I full on blink instead. I'm going for playful and sexy, not bewildered or like I have something in my eye. So I pick one of the plastic swords from my Shirley Temple and run the tip of my tongue up the side of the cherries before sliding them all into my mouth.

It has the desired effect; Hollis's Adam's apple bobs. He clears his throat and regroups, the smile returning as he comes up with his next line. "Maybe you just haven't found someone who knows their way around a kitchen."

"Well, we can't all have private chefs waiting for us in Miami," I say, biting into one of my raviolis. And that does it. The smile falls from his face, leaving his mouth in a perfectly straight line, no parentheses in sight. Sure, part of me regrets putting an end to the sexy banter, but most of me is glad it's over because it wasn't going anywhere, and truly I haven't had a good . . . meal . . . since Josh. Before Josh, in truth. His idea of cooking was opening a can of off-brand SpaghettiOs. Half the time he couldn't even get the lid off fully before trying to shake me out into a saucepan.

This is getting entirely away from me. The point is Josh was bad at sex, I haven't been with anyone since we broke up in September, and Hollis's flirting doesn't feel fair when he's on his way to spend a week in bed with someone else.

"Millicent," Hollis says. "I wasn't trying to . . ." He pauses. He squints and his jaw visibly tenses. "Is that a guitar?"

I look up from where I've focused my eyes on my plate to find five men wearing black suits and giant, red-ribbon bow ties approaching us, instruments in tow. Sure enough, the guitarist is strumming the beginning chords to a song. When they reach our booth, the music pauses, and the man in the center takes a deep breath and belts out in a clear tenor voice, "En Nápoles, donde el amor es rey . . ." Hollis stares unblinking at his food as a trumpet joins in, and his jaw tenses further.

As they play, I recognize the tune, if not the words. I don't laugh so much as cackle as a mariachi version of "That's Amore" fills the mostly empty restaurant.

The band comes to the end of the song, and I give them my

fervent applause. "Thank you so much," I say, "for providing something I didn't even know was missing from my life."

The tenor smiles. "Another song, señorita?"

"No," Hollis says, a little too vehemently. "We're . . . we're good here. Thank you, though. Thanks."

The mariachi band strolls over to serenade another table, where José recently seated a family with two small children.

"Let it never be said José Napoleoni isn't fully dedicated to this restaurant's fusion concept," I say.

Speak of the Mexican-Italian devil, the proprietor himself comes to check on us.

"The dessert menu is there, when you're ready," José says, gesturing to a laminated trifold propped between the caddy of sweeteners and the salt and pepper shakers. "We're doing a special right now to celebrate our recent grand opening. If you post a photo of yourselves on social media using the hashtag JoseNapoleonis, dessert is on the house. Trying to get the word out there." He gives a little wink before going to take the other table's order.

Hollis checks out the desserts and his eyes go wide as they land on something he must find particularly interesting. The man appears to have a major sweet tooth. "Sopaipillas with cannoli dip," he says, his voice filled with longing.

"Do you have an Instagram account?" I ask.

He sounds uncertain as he responds, "Yes?"

"Okay, so let's take the picture and have the post ready to show José when he gets back." I slide out of my side of the booth and into his.

He scoots farther in toward the wall so our legs aren't touching. "No, it's fine. We can pay the eight dollars or whatever to buy it. I know how you feel about social media stuff."

"But I owe you. You ordered for me to ensure I got my raviolis, and sugar seems to be your preferred gratitude currency. Besides," I say. "Josh probably follows you, right? If he sees us together, it's going to make him so mad."

"Oh, I see," Hollis says, turning to face me. "Using me to get to Florida isn't enough. You're going to use me to get back at your ex too."

The smile that crept onto my face while imagining Josh's annoyance fades.

"I'm kidding." His words fall out in a hurry, as if realizing how fiercely accusatory he sounded. "Just kidding. Besides, now that I know what Josh did to you, I'm extra into anything that will piss him off."

"Even if it might make you straight-up enemies instead of frenemies?"

"Especially if it might do that."

"Okay. Cool," I say, trying not to let Hollis's apparent allegiance to me make me feel anything stronger than mildly pleased. "Let's earn us some dessert."

Hollis flips the camera on his phone to face us. I take the opportunity to rest my head on his shoulder. To get more of the restaurant's decor into the frame. *Not* because he smells like the human embodiment of the perfect way to spend a day.

"Smile!"

I grin and watch the screen, waiting for him to join me. But he still looks like a kid who got coal for Christmas.

"No," I say through my teeth like a terrible ventriloquist. "You need to smile or it looks like I'm holding you hostage."

"You kind of are, though, aren't you?"

"Ha ha, very funny. Blame your conscience for not letting you leave me at the airport."

"You would've been perfectly happy winding up on a missing-persons list, yeah, I know."

Another photo attempt. Another former TV star smile from me and nothing at all from him. "Hollis. Come on. Smile. Or I'm going to have to tickle you."

"You wouldn't dare."

"Don't be so certain," I say. "You really don't know me very well."

Oh god, there's that awful grimace-smile *thing* again. It's like in medieval times when people tried to draw lions without ever having seen one and created all sorts of un-lionlike abominations. Except Hollis is managing to do it with his lips and teeth. How can such a handsome face morph into something so horrifying so quickly?

"Ah! No. That's even worse. Jesus. Gimme that." I take the phone from his hand, hold it in front of us. "Okay," I say. "Spitfire dad jokes. Here we go. What do you call a pig who does karate? A pork chop." The Hollis on the phone's screen only looks grumpier. "Why do seagulls fly over the sea? Because if they flew over the bay, they'd be bagels." Nothing. Not even the tiniest lift of the corner of his mouth, even though that joke is *hilarious*. "Man, you're a tough crowd. Time to pull out the big guns. Where did Napoleon keep his armies? In his sleevies." There it is! A response, a slight one, but it's good enough. I take the picture in the split second before he wipes all evidence of amusement from his face. "There we go," I say, handing him back his phone. "Now was that so hard, Grumps McGrumperson?"

Hollis ignores me and focuses on typing a caption. "What do you think?" he asks, holding it up for me to see.

Superb dinner with my favorite redheaded time traveler. #JoseNapoleonis

His *favorite*. The word is like a surprise hug—warm and welcome, but briefly disorienting. Except that's an extremely specific category . . . "Oh, I'm your favorite redheaded time traveler, but not your favorite time traveler in general?"

"Well, I mean. There's Scott Bakula. The entire cast of *Hot Tub Time Machine*. And the guy in that short-lived show where he gets with Paul Revere's daughter . . ."

"Yeah, yeah," I say. "I get the message. So this is fine, but . . ." I take his phone again and add *#PenelopetothePast*, *#MillicentWatts-Cohen*, *#roadtrip*, and a row of heart-eye emojis. "Now it's perfect."

"You really don't need to play it up like that. We'll get the dessert with the one hashtag, and I'm sure you don't want the extra attention your name will bring to the post."

"Usually I wouldn't, but . . . I think today I do. It'll give José some extra exposure, and I really like this place. Plus, do you know how jealous Josh is going to be when he sees this? It will absolutely kill him that I'm using my fame to help you. And he knows I love heart-eye emojis, so he'll probably realize I had a hand in writing the post. What he stole from me, I'm giving his competition freely."

Hollis's eyes trail over my body, their difference in color stark again now that we're sitting close together. "I do believe there's a bit of a storm brewin' under all that sunshine," he says. And for a split second there's a different cadence to his voice, a drawl that wasn't there before. Or maybe I'm imagining it. I don't know. I'm too distracted by the fact that I've got him smiling for real again.

AS WE LEAVE, I GIVE THE TAXIDERMY BEAR AND ITS YAWNING
mouth a longing look.

"It's not exactly consistent with the rest of the decor," Hollis
says, following my gaze.

"I want to know what its mouth feels like."

"Sorry, what now?"

"I've been wondering since we got here what it feels like inside
its mouth. Like is that its real teeth, do you think? And are the
insides of his cheeks squishy, or like plastic, or is there fabric in
there? Would it be silk? Felt? I have a lot of questions and I think
a good feel around would answer most of them."

Hollis shakes his head and sighs. "Well, go ahead. I'm not going to stop you. Just make it quick so we don't get stuck explaining
to José why we're molesting his stuffed bear."

"I can't, though," I say, and demonstrate my inability to reach
the bear's mouth. "I'm too short. Like so many things in life, I'll
just have to be okay with never knowing, I guess."

"For god's sake."

Hollis's body is suddenly pressed against mine. Except the
parts are all misaligned—my pelvis is against his chest, his arms
are tight around the backs of my thighs. And oh, my feet aren't on
the ground.

"Now," he says, "hurry it up."

"Are you . . . Did you just pick me up so I can literally poke a
bear?"

"No, I'm training for a petite-woman-lifting competition. Nationals are in Albuquerque this year." I can't tell if he's more

annoyed with me than usual or if his eyebrows just look extra stern from this elevated angle. "Any more stupid questions or are you going to put your damn fingers in that bear's mouth so we can go?"

Hoisted up like this, the bear and I are practically the same height. I have to admit, it's a little uncomfortable looking into its vacant glass eyes. "Sorry for the intrusion, sir. I'll only be a minute," I say as I extend my hand toward it, gently press my fingers against the varnished teeth, run them over the hard plastic tongue and reach deep inside to where the throat would be in the usual circumstances, encountering only a smooth, cool dead end. Equal parts satisfied and skeeved out, I mumble a quick "Thanks for your cooperation," then remove my hand and place it on Hollis's shoulder.

"Okay, I'm done."

Nothing happens. "Hey, I'm done." I look down, expecting to find him staring back up at me. Instead, I find his gaze focused straight ahead, which is exactly where my chest is.

"I hope you're not expecting more desserts for this," I say.

"Huh?"

"I think being in close quarters with my tits for the last thirty seconds straight is payment enough for this good deed."

Hollis's head tilts up and his eyes meet mine at last. He blinks twice. "Fair enough," he says. "Come on, let's get a move on. My friend's expecting me tomorrow, and you have an elderly lady in Key West to bother."

My feet are on the ground again before I can respond. A small part of me was hoping for a long, delicious slide down the front of his body. But an uneventful descent was probably for the best. Hollis is right: I'm on a mission, and I can't let myself forget that time is of the essence.

6

. . . . .

IT TAKES ME ALMOST TWENTY MINUTES TO TALK HOLLIS INTO LET-
ting me play more of my road-trip playlist, then I almost immediately fall asleep to the soothing, repetitive melody of Al Stewart's
"Year of the Cat." My eyes flutter open sometime later in response
to a steady reduction in our speed. Looks like we're pulling into a
rest-stop parking lot. When we left José Napoleoni's, it was still
overcast, but now pink and orange streak the sky.

I arch my back in my seat to stretch out my spine. "Where
are we?"

"Virginia," Hollis says.

"Still?" I whine. "I was asleep for like six hours!"

"You were asleep for like *one* hour."

"Ugh. When did Virginia get so big?"

"I don't know. The eighteenth century? You're the historian,
you tell me." Hollis shifts the car into park. "Are you getting out?"

I'm still a little drowsy, which makes the idea of movement
seem like a major hassle. But then my bladder reminds me that I

had three Shirley Temples back at the restaurant, plus the one José kindly handed me in a to-go cup on our way out the door. "Yeah." I disconnect my phone from the aux, then grab my little leather backpack and swing it over my shoulder as I get out of the car. "Just a pit stop, Mrs. Nash," I say. "Then we'll be back on our way to Elsie."

"I don't know why I'm surprised you talk to her," Hollis mutters as we walk toward the brick building's glass double doors.

"I don't know why you are either."

You might assume she talks back; she doesn't. I hoped when she died that she might continue to exist inside my head, and she sort of does. I can see her vividly, but she never speaks unless it's a replay of a memory. Because I am the one who would have to generate what she says now, and I know that any words I put into her mouth wouldn't be hers. Just mine in disguise. Somehow that's more depressing than her not talking at all.

Hollis isn't there when I return to the car, even though I took an embarrassingly long time trying to get the automatic toilet to stop flushing down the seat covers before I could even sit. Maybe he decided mid-pee that all this isn't worth it and started walking home. Oh, but there he is, over by a copse of trees, staring at his phone again. Probably giving Miami Woman an update. Which reminds me, I never told Dani I'm with Hollis. As far as she knows, I'm still on my way to Charlotte with Mike. And while she's extremely chill about almost everything, she will 100 percent call the cops—or worse, my parents—if she doesn't hear from me. I pull out my phone and shoot off a quick text.

MILLIE: Change of plans. Now driving to Miami with Hollis Hollenbeck, who I sort of know through the dbag. 30ish,

white, handsomely disheveled brown hair, 1 blue eye + 1
brown, about 6 ft, great forearms.

DANI: So you wanna bang him, huh?

My cousin truly has a gift for reading between the lines.

MILLIE: Even if I did, he's on his way to a sex appointment.

DANI: Tell him your vagina has an earlier slot available.

Ha!

"What's so funny?"

My head snaps up in response to Hollis's voice. "Oh. Hey.
Nothing."

"Some advice for you: Never play poker unless you're looking
to lose all of your money," he says. "You're a terrible liar."

I consider responding that I'm a *great* liar, but what a weird
thing to insist. And also I'm honestly not. Which is probably another reason I never succeeded as an actress after *Penelope to the
Past*, now that I think about it; pretending to be someone else
started to feel like nothing but socially acceptable lying by the end
of my showbiz career.

"Your tell is that you blush. Here." His finger pokes into the
side of my cheek, right where I have a dimple when I smile—what
my aunt Talia used to call my "million-dollar divot" when I started
doing commercials at six. "And here," Hollis says. The finger
moves to the very top of my breastbone, right under my throat.
That wet mouth—dry throat thing happens again, but I can't swallow without him noticing. Instead, I let out an awkward whining

sound like a balloon deflating. I probably should have just swallowed because whatever that was was *waaaay* weirder.

The bizarre noise brings Hollis's attention to the fact he's still touching me. He shoves his right hand into his pocket, as if putting it in hand jail as a punishment for its transgression, and raises his free left one to show me his phone. "Josh commented on our post. Thought you might be interested."

"Oh, what'd he say? Let me see." Hollis apparently has more clout than I realized. There are a ton of likes and comments. I quickly scroll through, in awe of the vast number of them, losing Josh's in the process. "You some kind of social media big shot?" I ask, trying to get back to it while not reading any of the others in case they're creepy.

"Uh, on Twitter maybe. I got a bunch of new followers there when I published a piece in *The New Yorker* a few weeks ago that got some traction. I only have like a hundred on Insta, though. I don't know most of these people. They must've found the picture because of the hashtags."

"Oh." I scroll faster because that makes it even more likely some of the comments are stuff I'd rather not see. Even trying not to read anything, I spot several mentions of the notorious yellow bikini, and I'm beginning to regret adding the #MillicentWatts-Cohen and #PenelopetothePast hashtags when I find what I'm looking for. Josh's stupid face stares back at me from the little picture next to his username. He's wearing the cream-colored fisherman sweater he bought after seeing *Knives Out*. *What are you doing?* I asked when I came home from the National Archives and found him at the kitchen table with a pair of scissors, strategically cutting into the wool to make holes like Chris Evans's sweater had in the film. *Authenticity is very important to me*, he said, not joking at all. And now I have zero regrets about anything, including hastily sewing the holes back together with fluorescent-orange thread the day I moved out.

Josh_Yaeger
Is this supposed to be some kind of prank?

Oh, he's mad. And it's amazing. Getting under Josh's skin is like a drug, and I forgot how addicted I am. "Can we post another one?" I ask, bouncing on the balls of my feet.

"Does it get me more sopaipillas?"

"Probably not."

"Then no."

"You're no fun," I say.

"That's right, kid. Best remember it." Hollis takes the phone from my hand and goes around the car to the driver's side.

"Stop calling me 'kid,'" I grumble as I climb back into the passenger seat. "I'm almost thirty. And you're what, thirty-two, thirty-three, tops?"

"Thirty-one. And forgive me if I sometimes forget that even though you're short, naive, and have poor impulse control, you're not actually eight years old."

"Ha ha ha. Aren't you a hoot."

"Yep. A no-fun hoot. That's what I am." Hollis tucks his hands behind his head, giving me a fabulous view of his right tricep, and closes his eyes. And then he stays that way.

It's tempting to stare at him for a while, just to torture myself I guess. But there's really no time. "What are you doing?"

Without opening his eyes, he says, "Power nap. Didn't sleep well last night and it's catching up with me."

"Why don't you let me drive for a while so you can rest?"

"No one drives my car but me."

"You have control issues."

"No, I have very low insurance premiums. I'd like to keep it that way. Give me fifteen minutes and we'll get moving again."

"No," I say.

Hollis opens his eyes to give me a death stare. "No?"

"Sorry. No. Unacceptable. We don't have time to dilly-dally. Every minute counts, and we've wasted too many already."

"Jesus. What's the big hurry? Mrs. Nash isn't going anywhere."

"Elsie is dying!" The volume of my voice is too loud for the enclosed space, and it makes Hollis sit up straight in his seat. Hugging my backpack to my chest, I take a deep breath. "She's at a nursing facility, in hospice. They couldn't give me details because I'm not family, but the receptionist I talked to when I called yesterday morning said she doesn't have long at all. That's why I immediately booked a flight to head down there, even though traveling over Memorial Day weekend is a complete nightmare."

What Rhoda, the woman on the phone, actually said was, *I'm not supposed to say anything. HIPAA, you know? But if you're really determined to see her, the sooner the better. Should I tell her to expect you? Maybe having a visitor to look forward to will help her hang in there.*

She doesn't know me, I responded. *But um, you can tell her . . . Oh. Tell her that Rose is sending her a pigeon. Hopefully she'll remember what that means.*

Her mind's still sharp, Rhoda said. *I'm sure she will.*

Ugh, all the time we've already wasted. That extra half hour or so at the airport, all the crawling along in holiday weekend rush-hour traffic, the almost-hour we spent at José Napoleoni's. God, I stopped to put my hand in that bear's mouth. What was I thinking? How could I have so easily lost sight of how urgent it is that I get Mrs. Nash to Key West as soon as possible so Elsie can confirm that their love story has a happy ending?

Hollis. Hollis is how. I've been too distracted by the shiny bits of himself he keeps hidden for whatever reason. They keep teasing me through the cracks in his facade, making me want to chisel away at him to see if he might secretly be all shine under there. And also I'm distracted by his great arms, and his interesting eyes, and his mouth that is frowning at me again.

"So, sorry," I say, "but fifteen minutes might be the difference between getting to Elsie in time or being too late. You aren't sleeping unless you do it in the passenger seat. And if you think I'm not serious, that you can close your eyes right now and ignore me, well, I seem to remember you reacting pretty strongly to the threat of tickling before." My fingers become clawlike in demonstration of my willingness to inflict maximum discomfort.

"Okay," Hollis says to punctuate an exasperated sigh.

"Okay what?"

"You can drive for a while. But if anything happens to my car, Millicent, I swear—"

"Yeah, yeah," I say, practically leaping out the door to come around to the driver's side. I adjust the seat and mirrors to accommodate my shorter stature, plug the aux cord back into my phone, and wiggle a little as I back out of the parking space to the smooth sounds of Atlanta Rhythm Section's "So in to You."

Hollis groans. "Do we really have to keep listening to this?"

"Yes. Deal with it," I say.

And I guess he does, because he's snoring softly by the time the song ends.

7

- - - - -

OWNING A CAR IN DC IS TOO MUCH TO BOTHER WITH WHEN I WORK
primarily from the efficiency apartment in Cathedral Heights I'm
now subletting, or from libraries and archives downtown that
don't have parking for less than twenty dollars an hour anyway. So
I've forgotten over the eight years since I moved from LA how
much I enjoy driving. It's meditative to listen to my music and get
lost in thought as the road stretches out in front of me. We're sol-
idly in North Carolina—Virginia finally ending a short while after
I took over—and even in the dark, I can tell that the pine trees
lining the highway aren't the same kind I'm used to up north;
these are, I don't know, fluffier? I wonder if Mike's made it home
to Carla and the pugs yet.

Hollis is still snoozing beside me. The moonlight streams
through the window and coats his messy hair and coin-worthy
profile in this really beautiful way that makes me wish I could take
more than fraction-of-a-second glances. His phone is next to mine
in the center console's alcove, the navigation reminding me every

once in a while that we're on I-95 for the next bajillion miles. Otherwise, it's buzzing almost constantly, probably with Instagram notifications. I guess I understood on a theoretical level that when people posted selfies with me on social media they likely got some attention for it, but experiencing it in real time is something else. It's still baffling to me why anyone would care.

Mrs. Nash didn't get it either when I tried to explain why Josh created the Instagram account. *While I am furious on your behalf, I must admit I don't understand why the internet would need so many photos of you*, says my memory of her the night of the book release party, when I showed up at her door with an overnight bag and a plea to sleep in her spare bedroom until I found a new place to live. *You're a lovely girl, Millie, but you're no Carol Burnett.* Which, harsh. But fair.

It's been almost three hours since the rest stop, and my bladder is starting to curse me out again for filling it with so much ginger ale and grenadine. But at close to eleven at night, there aren't many options for a pit stop. Finally, I spot a billboard for a McDonald's with a twenty-four-hour dining room right off the next exit. Thank the bathroom gods I won't need to squat in a bush on the side of the highway.

When I take the keys out of the ignition, Hollis shifts a little in his seat but doesn't wake up. Which is good, because I think I might be staring at him. Okay, I'm definitely staring at him. I can't help it! He might be kind of a jerk, but he's a total snack. And that conversation about "eating" we had back at the restaurant reminded me that I'm an increasingly hungry woman.

His phone yells at me to make a legal U-turn, then to turn left, then to take the on-ramp back onto the highway. This bathroom detour is distressing the lady who lives inside the map app. I grab the phone to pause the trip, but a notification pops up as soon as my finger touches the screen. Everything shifts. And Hollis, the dummy, must not have a lock on his phone because instead of pausing the navigation, a text exchange with someone named Yeva Markarian opens up without asking anything further of me.

HOLLIS: Flight canceled. Driving. Should be there by tomorrow night. Sorry.

YEVA: 😭 😭 😭

HOLLIS: I'll make it up to you.

YEVA: You better. I can't believe I'm all alone on our anniversary.

Anniversary? What? Is it not a sex appointment awaiting him in Miami but a full-scale girlfriend? Why would Hollis lie about that?

The phone vibrates again in my hand, and another text shows up.

YEVA: I guess I'll just have to start without you . . .

Yikes. I am not supposed to be privy to this conversation. I should really put the phone back down, mind my own business—

Oh. Geez. Wow.

The picture that appears on the screen is . . . a lot more of Yeva Markarian than I ever intended to see. It's artfully shot, for sure; the lighting is actually quite lovely. But there is no mistaking what is going on in that photo.

"What are you doing?" Hollis's voice startles me into dropping his phone. It bounces off his leg and falls to the floor.

"Nothing," I say, feeling my face heat. "I think you, uh . . . you have a text from your girlfriend."

"Girlfriend?" He recovers the phone from where it landed between his feet, rubbing the area by his knee where it hit him. "You mean Yeva? She's not my—"

"Well, whatever. None of my business, is it? Pause the navigation, please. That's what I was trying to do in the first place." I sound relatively calm, I think. But inside, my heart is slapping against my sternum. It shouldn't matter that Hollis's friend with benefits is apparently more like a girlfriend with . . . standard amenities. It shouldn't *matter*. It *shouldn't* matter. Except it clearly does for some reason. And before I can unpack the whys—because I extremely don't want to—I slam the car door behind me and march to the side entrance of the McDonald's. The glass door opens more easily than I expect, and the handle hits the brick wall, bouncing the door back into me and pushing me inside like I'm in some sort of vaudeville act. Hollis watches the whole embarrassing scene from the car, his eyebrows raised in what could be either confusion or amusement. I stick my chin in the air and continue through the restaurant's vestibule.

The thing is, when I broke up with Josh, moving next door into Mrs. Nash's apartment was a double-edged sword. No need for movers (or even to put anything into boxes), minimal disruption to my daily routine, easy enough to retrieve any misaddressed mail. The downside was that the sound of Josh having aggressively loud sex with someone new within a few days of our split carried remarkably well through the shared wall. And the feeling was kind of the same as this. This heavy-in-the-pit-of-my-stomach-ness that

I can't reason my way out of no matter how many times I tell myself I have no right to be jealous.

At least that memory, coupled with this unpleasant feeling, makes me remember Mrs. Nash's amazing reaction when the noise carried into our living room. As soon as it became apparent what the sounds were, she scrunched up her nose as if smelling something rotten.

I'm sorry, Millie, she said. *I know you must have cared for him at some point to have stayed so long. But I have to say, that boy fornicates like a gorilla doing an Elvis impression. And this new friend of his sounds like a squeaky door.*

I laughed until I cried. Each exaggerated grunt and high-pitched glissando that reached my ears sent me howling again, while Mrs. Nash continued her scathing commentary on their efforts. It ended after a few minutes, and I sobered as I realized: If we could hear Josh and his mystery woman, Mrs. Nash had probably heard Josh and *me.*

Oh no. Mrs. Nash. Please tell me we weren't terrorizing you with our sex noises for the past two years, I said, clutching her hand.

You silly thing. I never heard a peep from you. Which is one of the many reasons I was relieved to learn you were leaving him.

There's a grin on my face when I come out of the bathroom, but it fades when I see Hollis leaning against the wall in the little hallway, studying the brown wallpaper peppered with large sans serif food words opposite him. He extends my backpack toward me, his index finger hooked through the loop at the top.

"You forgot Mrs. Nash. And your wallet."

I take the backpack and thread my arm through one strap. "Thanks, but I don't want anything."

"Okay," he says. "I'm sorry, by the way."

"For what?" I fold my arms over my chest, waiting for him to admit he lied to me. I still don't understand *why* he would lie about something like this. Why hide an entire girlfriend?

"I presume you saw that picture. It, uh, clearly was not meant for you."

"Right," I say. And then, maybe because it's been a long and weird day and my brain-to-mouth filter is unreliable even under ideal circumstances, everything in my head suddenly turns into actual words I am saying. "Because why apologize for lying to me about Yeva, right? I mean, I'm just some ridiculous girl you're stuck driving to Florida with. You don't owe me the truth. You don't owe me anything at all, really." And that's a pretty thorough accounting of reality, so I don't know why I'm spitting my sentences with such venom.

"I'm starting to think 'ridiculous' isn't the right word for what you are," he says, taking a step toward me. "Weird, absolutely. I'd give you weird. But not ridiculous."

I take a step backward, and my butt hits the wall. "Thanks . . . I think?"

"And I didn't lie to you. Yeva isn't my girlfriend. She's exactly what I said she is: a friend I have sex with sometimes."

"Then what anniversary is she talking about? The first time you banged?"

"Uh . . ." His eyes shift away from mine and focus on the tile floor as he rubs his right earlobe. Is this what Hollis looks like when embarrassed? It's adorable. "Actually, yes. We first hooked up over Memorial Day weekend five years ago, when I was in town for a mutual friend's wedding. The anniversary thing, it's become sort of an inside joke, because I always wind up visiting at the end of May. It's not a . . . sentimental arrangement. It just works well with both of our schedules."

"Hold up. So your sex appointment is . . . annually recurring? Like blocked out on your calendar and everything?"

"Yeah. When circumstances allow, at least. Last year Yeva was involved with someone, so I didn't come until they broke up in July." His lips compress as if rethinking his phrasing. "Didn't come visit," he clarifies.

The tension drains from my shoulders, and my backpack shifts down my arm. "Why didn't you tell me that from the beginning?"

"How was I supposed to know you'd want to be informed of all the logistical details of my sex life?" This is a new expression on his face. It's . . . smug. It makes him look extra-punchable, but also somehow more attractive.

"I don't," I say. "What you do is your own business. And I'm really sorry I violated your privacy. I swear I was only trying to pause the navigation, but the text came through, and the notification wound up where the pause button was, and you don't have a passcode on your phone, which you really should—"

"It's fine. Considering how red you've turned, I think you're adequately mortified. Just be more careful next time. I can't promise I won't get more texts like that tonight."

"Yeva's got a good eye for angles," I admit.

"Never said they'd all be from Yeva." Before I can think too much about that, he claps his hands together. "Now, enough yapping. Let's get back on the road. You still okay to drive?"

"Yeah."

"Good. Then I'm getting an ice cream cone."

"IT MAKES NO SENSE," HOLLIS GRUMBLES FROM THE PASSENGER seat. "If you're open twenty-four hours a day, you should have ice cream available twenty-four hours a day. You can't just decide to arbitrarily shut down the ice cream machine."

It's been fifteen minutes since we got back on the highway, and he's still moping about this. I can't help but smile at his petulance. "I think they said it was off for cleaning. Not exactly arbitrary."

"Don't care. Dirty ice cream would've been better than no ice cream."

"Ew," I say. "Gross. No, it would not have been."

Hollis runs his hands through his hair and makes a gruff sound that's almost a growl. It . . . does things to me. It probably does things to Yeva too. Gah. I can't get that picture of her out of my head. It's not like I'm a prude or anything; I've seen my fair share of genitalia on the internet over the years (sometimes intentionally, sometimes not). But it's one thing to see something intended for mass consumption, and another completely to stumble upon a photo meant for only one person's enjoyment. And now I'm imagining Hollis . . . enjoying it. And oh god. That thought is making me feel like both the perv and the . . . pervee?

"What are you thinking about over there?" Hollis asks.

"Nothing. Nothing at all." My denial sounds way too suspicious even to my own ears, so I grasp around for a lie and find it in the highway sign up ahead. "Just, you know, Eisenhower and the interstates."

"Oh, Eisenhower and the interstates gets you all hot and bothered, does it?"

I glance over at him, wondering for a moment if he might be a mind reader. If so, I'm in a lot of trouble. I have never had very good control over my thoughts.

"Like I said, terrible liar." He shakes his head in mock sympathy. "You're breathing like a caricature of a phone sex operator, and I can see you glowing pink even in the dark."

The breathing I could've passed off as my asthma acting up, but I have no excuse for the blushing. Sometimes it's a real pain being so pale I could be mistaken for a human-shaped bag of milk.

"So why aren't you and Yeva like, together together?" I wanted to change the subject, but that's probably not the direction in which I should've taken the conversation, considering it's basically the last thing I want to think about right now. Oh well. I don't have very good control over my mouth either.

I can see the force of his frown in my peripheral vision. "Because I don't want to be."

"Why? She seems . . . uh . . . fun."

"She is. Yeva's great." Hollis shifts in his seat. "It's not that I don't want to be with her, it's that I don't want to be with anyone. Besides, even if I were capable of something more serious, she lives in Miami, which—as you may have noticed—is not super close to DC. And I guarantee we'd get on each other's nerves if we ever had to spend more than a few hours together with our clothes on."

"Everyone gets on your nerves, though," I say.

He lets out a huff that might be his version of a laugh. "Yep. Which is one of the many reasons I don't do relationships anymore."

"You just do annually recurring sex appointments."

That huff again—though I can't tell if this one is more amusement or frustration. "I really wish you'd stop referring to it that way."

"Hmm. Wait a second. You said 'anymore.' So you used to do relationships? And then you stopped. Oh. Is it because someone broke your heart? Is that why you're so grumpy?"

He bangs his head against the headrest, *thump thump thump*. "I'm grumpy because you refuse to mind your own business." But as exasperated as he sounds, I think I catch an ever-so-slight lift to the corner of his mouth. Like maybe he's enjoying this back and forth between us as much as I am. "Shit," he says, suddenly sitting up straight in his seat and staring out of the windshield to the road ahead.

And as I tear my eyes away from his profile, I see what he sees and slam on the brakes.

I'M NOT SURE I'VE EVER SEEN SO MANY EMERGENCY VEHICLES IN one place. Their lights flash obnoxiously out of sync for what looks like miles. We're part of a short caravan creeping toward the scene of whatever happened. Something massive, apparently. I don't know what else would draw this kind of response.

"Seriously?" Hollis says.

"What?"

When I look over, his face is illuminated by his phone screen. "Found a local traffic Twitter account. Says it's an olive oil spill."

"Is that . . . something other than what it sounds like?"

"No, it's exactly what it sounds like. Apparently, a truck was hauling a metric fuckton of olive oil and sprung a leak. The road's covered in the stuff on and off for miles." He shows me the picture included in the tweet, though it's hard to make out any details since it was taken in the dark.

"Guess the road heard about the purported benefits of the Mediterranean Diet."

"It caused two accidents, Millicent."

Whoops. "Oh. Shit. Well, what should we do? Wait it out?"

"Checking," he says, his fingers tapping at his phone. "Navigation's still telling us to go straight through. Guess it doesn't know about the road closure yet. The time stamp on the tweet was only a few minutes ago. Let me switch to no highways." Hollis changes the settings, and his phone dings before announcing that it's calculating the route. "Drive up the shoulder to that exit up there, then follow the signs for 501."

The detour leads us through an area of illuminated fast-food restaurants and not much else, then we take a turn onto US 501 and go through a town that's mostly banks, funeral homes, and churches long since closed for the night. The streetlights end as the buildings become more spaced out and are soon replaced by alternating tracts of fields and woods interspersed with the occasional one-level prefab home set way back from the road. This is the sort of place people must mean when they talk about the boonies.

Hollis's fingers play on his leg like his jeans are made of piano keys. But he has regular, boring, non-musical pants, so he's only generating barely audible repetitive thuds that are starting to get on my nerves.

"Why are you fidgeting so much?" I ask.

"Helps distract me from how likely it is that you're going to wreck my car on this dark country road."

"Ah, not concerned that we'd be injured or dead. But the car! The *car* might get a scratch on it. I see what's important."

It's hard to tell because it's basically pitch black with the moon now hiding behind a cloud, but I'm fairly certain Hollis's mouth has the same tight shape as a Lucky Charms marshmallow rainbow.

"Here, I'll put on the high beams," I say as if I'm doing it as a courtesy to him and not because I'm getting nervous without the extra light. Except as soon as I do, a car heads toward us from the other direction and I need to turn them off again. "Gah. So much for that."

"Let's switch," Hollis says. "Pull over."

"No."

"Yes. It's my car, and I'm more comfortable driving in areas like this at night. I say we switch."

"And I say we don't. You need to sleep more so you can take over in an hour or two. Then I can sleep a bit, and we can drive through the night and get to Miami by breakfast time. Which means you can make Yeva belated sexiversary waffles as an apology for being late, and I can still get to Key West as originally scheduled."

Hollis grumbles. Out of the corner of my eye, I see his hand slide from near his knee to his hair. "As if I can sleep while I'm worried about you running us into a ditch."

"I can drive in the dark just fine, thanks." I turn on the high beams again, but they seem to be cursed because another car comes toward us. Off they go again. "Dammit."

"Stay right at the fork," Hollis's phone, now balanced on his thigh, says. Except there is no fork; it's only the single road stretching out ahead. "Calculating route," it announces.

"What the heck," I say. "You're drunk, map lady!"

He stares at the screen. "I think we lost signal."

Not super surprising, since this is basically the middle of nowhere. "Well, am I still going the right way?"

"Yeah, I think so. It should come back soon." Hollis glances up from his lap. "Jesus, Millicent, turn on the high beams so you can see more than a foot ahead of you."

"I've been *trying*," I say. "But every time I do, a car comes from the other direction."

"Well, there aren't any cars coming now."

"Yes, thank you, I can see that," I say, flipping on the high beams again. Just in time for the light to bounce off a large, glowing pupil. My foot slams on the brakes, and their loud screech joins the horrifying sound of a scream and shattering glass. Something hits my forehead with the force of a hurled rock. Everything is dark—so, so dark. I'm dead. I must be dead. Oh wait. No, I just have my eyes closed.

Hollis's panicked voice fills my ears. "Mill, are you okay? Are you—"

"I'm fine," I say, fluttering my eyes open. "I'm, I'm—" staring into the eyes of an incredibly freaked-out deer.

8

• • • • •

"THERE'S REALLY NOTHING YOU COULD'VE DONE TO PREVENT this," Officer Shonda Jones from the Gadsley, South Carolina, Police Department reassures me for the third time in the last five minutes. "Nothing at all. Just remember: The deer hit *you*. You didn't hit *it*." She pats my shoulder through the Mylar blanket that isn't keeping me warm so much as making me look like a baked potato that could feed a family of eight.

The police arrived within minutes of the accident. So did the local veterinarian, who hastily introduced himself as Dr. Gupta before injecting the deer in its hindquarters with a sedative. With a bit of help from Hollis and Officer Jones's burly partner, Deputy Anders, Dr. Gupta oh so carefully removed the deer from where it was trapped inside the car and laid its conked-out form in the bed of his pickup truck.

"We havin' venison steaks for dinner tomorrow?" Officer Jones jokes when Dr. Gupta approaches us.

He scratches his graying temple. "Well, I won't know for sure till I can check her out at the office, but I don't see anything obviously fatal. I'm a bit shocked, considering the damage to the car, but I think she's likely to make it."

"Great news. Thanks for coming out this time of night, Dev," Officer Jones says. "Really saved us the hassle of trying to get someone from Nat Resources on the phone."

"Always happy to help. After all, I am an animal doc, all 'round the clock." Dr. Gupta chuckles and holds up both hands in farewell as he climbs into his truck. I adjust the cold pack Officer Jones gave me for my forehead, pull the Mylar blanket tighter around my shoulders, and watch as the veterinarian and the unconscious deer disappear into the darkness.

A hand lands on my shoulder, and I ready myself for Officer Jones to repeat the script. Nothing I could have done to prevent this, yadda yadda. But then my leather backpack dangles in front of my face.

"Found this in the back seat," Hollis says.

I drop the cold pack and grab for my bag. Inside, the wooden box that holds the baggie of Mrs. Nash's ashes as well as the bundle of letters nestled beside it appear undamaged. "Thank you," I say.

"How's your head?" His fingers brush against the giant lump above my right eyebrow. The pleasure of his touch almost makes me forget the throbbing pain.

"I haven't had any complaints yet," I quote dutifully, even though my heart's not really in it.

"Huh?" Hollis pauses as he drops to sit beside me on the police car's hood. I can almost see his mind rewinding and replaying the exchange, trying to make sense of it. He runs his hand through his hair, not out of exasperation this time, but to shake some of the glass pebbles from it. "Oh. Cute."

I dip my chin toward my chest and whine, "I can't believe a deer punched me in the face."

"It could have done a lot worse. I felt its hoof while I was helping haul it out of the car. Sharp as a knife. Surprised you're only bruised and not sliced and diced."

"Maybe she didn't punch me then. Maybe she like . . . elbowed me. Do deer have elbows?"

Hollis doesn't answer—and, I mean, I doubt he knows much about deer anatomy, so that's fair. He stares at his car, pulled off to the side of the road. It's definitely not drivable. Shattered windshield and a cracked window. Side mirror dangling from its wires. Broken headlight. And a massive dent on the hood that makes it unable to fully close.

"I'm really sorry about your car," I say softly.

Hollis shrugs.

"I think this is where you're supposed to say, 'Oh, it's not your fault, Millicent.' 'There's nothing you could have done, Millicent.' Maybe even 'I'm just glad you're okay, Millicent.'"

To my surprise, an arm wraps around my shoulder and eases me closer, the Mylar blanket crinkling a little with the movement. Hollis's cheek rests on the crown of my head, and it makes his voice sound strange and echoey inside my skull. "It's not your fault, Millicent. There's nothing you could have done. And I'm just really glad you're okay."

"Oh," I whisper. "Really glad?"

"Really, really," he whispers back.

I tilt my head to look at him, and I know it's a mistake as soon as our eyes meet. Our faces are too close, our mouths *especially* are too close, and it's turned this moment up to eleven; eleven intimacies, which is at least seven too many, and—

And then he's gone. Not *gone* gone, obviously. But he's standing and much farther away from me than before. "Tow truck just arrived. I better go talk to them. Probably stuff for me to sign."

I salute him with two fingers. His eyes narrow in confusion as he turns and walks away. I consider informing Officer Jones that I might be concussed and need her to call the ambulance from two towns over after all, but let's be real: None of this is exactly outside the realm of ordinary behavior for me. So I'll just sit here on the hood, awaiting further instructions, trying not to read into that *really, really*.

"THIS IS THE FIRST TIME I'VE BEEN IN A POLICE CAR," I SAY TO HOL-lis beside me. As a former child star, any misstep automatically becomes tabloid fodder—just ask Justin LaRue, who played Penelope's little brother on the show but is now best known for his appearances on "15 Celeb Mugshots That Could Double as Headshots" internet listicles—so it's always been an easy decision for me to stay on the straight and narrow. And, again, being an almost-famous, small, redheaded bag of milk, no one's exactly champing at the bit to find reasons to arrest me.

"Congratulations." Hollis folds his arms across his chest.

Sure, he's bummed for the obvious reasons—primarily that his car is busted up and has deer fluids smeared all over the upholstery—but I'm not exactly pleased about this unscheduled layover either. Chip Autobody (probably not his real last name, but the one my brain has helpfully assigned him) told Hollis he'd work as quickly as possible to get us back on the road but said to plan to be in town for at least three days. I don't know if Elsie *has* three days. Plus, a deer elbowed me in the skull. If anyone has reason to be grumpy right now, it's me.

Officer Jones and Deputy Anders are taking us to a bed-and-breakfast. It was either that or a one-star motel on the other side of Gadsley. Considering the motel's latest review on Tripadvisor mentioned that the "roach situation is somewhat better than last year," we were beyond relieved when Deputy Anders called the B&B and confirmed they have a room available. Just one, though. Probably with only one bed. I'm trying not to think too much about it.

As we reach the center of the tiny town, Hollis frowns more deeply at me.

"What now?" I ask.

"It's just . . . You've got some . . ." He points to his right cheek.

I try for what feels like forever to wipe away the problem with my finger but make no progress. Hollis's "no"s and "not quite"s sound increasingly impatient.

"You do it then," I say, my voice a frustrated screech.

He licks his thumb and drags it across my cheek. "Blood," he says, holding it up for my inspection in case I didn't believe him, I guess.

"Did you just—I can't believe you put your spit on my face. That's so gross, dude." I rub at the spot with the back of my hand, but somehow it only feels wetter and cooler.

"Doesn't look like you have a cut there, so it must be the deer's."

"Great," I say as the police car comes to a stop in front of a large Victorian house just off the town's Main Street. "Try to keep your DNA to yourself from now on."

"Weird way to say that," he says as he gets out of the car.

"It was weirder to *do*, Hollis."

"Well, look at y'all, bless your hearts," the gray-haired white woman who answers the door says as soon as she sees us on the wraparound porch. Based on my limited knowledge of southern turns of phrase, I assume Hollis and I are looking a little worse for wear. At least I'm no longer streaked with deer blood. Presumably. "Please, come in, come in. Welcome to Gadsley Manor Bed-and-Breakfast."

I wave goodbye to Officer Jones and Deputy Anders to let them know we're good. The police car drives away as we step into a cozy, wood-paneled foyer. A staircase takes up the entire left side, and I'm suddenly desperate to climb it and fall into a bed. Any bed. Just the first one I encounter. Don't even care if it's occupied by another guest.

"My name's Connie," the woman says. "I run this place with my husband, Bud. You'll meet him at breakfast in the mornin', I'm sure."

Somewhere in the house, a clock chimes once. God, it's late. And Connie is wearing slippers and a robe. "We're so sorry to wake you," I say.

"Oh, no apologies necessary. I'm just glad we could help. We were supposed to be completely booked tonight—the festival this weekend, you know—but we had a last-minute cancelation because of this business with the airlines. So when Drew Anders called and told me what happened, well, I was pleased as punch to have something available for you. God sure does work in wonderful ways," she says. "And it's such a gift when we get such a clear reminder that He always has a plan."

Hollis and I exchange glances.

"Um," he says. "Yeah. Definitely. So, we'll be staying only for tonight—"

"Huh? Chip Autobody said it would take at least three days to fix the car," I remind him.

"I did a quick search on the way over here, and there's a rental car place the next town over. I'll call them first thing in the mornin'." Hollis turns back to our host. "So just the one night, ma'am, thank you."

That slight accent of his has slipped through again. And it sounds a lot like Connie's as she says, "Well, we'd love to have you stay with us longer, but I'm sure you're eager to get on your way to . . ." She pauses, smiles, raises her chin a bit. "Wherever you're goin'," Connie finishes, sensing that we're not in the mood to chat. "Oh. Just one thing before we go up. If you could write down your info for me and sign here. And then you can pay Bud when you check out."

Hollis follows Connie to a small desk by the stairs to fill out the paperwork. He stops writing at one point and stares at me as if trying to figure something out. Maybe he doesn't know how to spell my name. "What?" I mouth, but he ignores me and returns to the forms.

After she reviews the information, Connie tucks the papers into the desk and claps her hands together. "Great. Now let's get you to your room. I'm sure y'all're exhausted."

"Extremely," I say. With my little backpack slung over my shoulder, I start hauling my suitcase up the stairs. I bang the backs of my ankles with the wheels five times before Hollis lets out a huff and orders me to hand it over.

Thankfully, Connie unlocks the first door in the upstairs hallway and pushes the heavy oak panel open. "We call this the

Mustard Seed room," she says, beaming with as much pride as anyone can at one in the morning. "It's our smallest, but I like to think its abundant charm makes up for the size. I hope you'll find it comfortable."

I walk in and am immediately met by dozens of eyes. The room's golden-yellow walls are covered in paintings of . . . Jesus. That's definitely Jesus. White Jesus. Black Jesus. Brown Jesus. And he's doing all sorts of stuff. Holding a sleeping child. Pledging allegiance to the flag. Rescuing a drowning man. Building a table. Cuddling a corgi. And those are just the ones above the bed.

"Wow," I say.

"Yes. 'Wow' is . . . 'Wow' is a good description of this room," Hollis says. "The art particularly is . . . wow."

"Oh, I'm so glad you like it," Connie says. "I just love doin' paint-by-numbers. Not so often lately, what with bein' so busy and my hands not always cooperating, but . . ."

"You painted all of these?" I ask.

"Well, if you count fillin' in bunches of little spaces with the right color paintin', I suppose I did."

My lips part to ask her where she found a paint-by-numbers Jesus in space, but Hollis subtly shakes his head. He's probably right. I don't exactly *need* a space Jesus painting in my apartment. But boy, do I *want* it. I mean, he's *in space* and also cupping *the entire galaxy* in his hands!

"Breakfast is from seven to nine in the dining room. That's the room to the left when you first came in. You've got all your toiletries in the en suite, and there's extra pillows and a quilt in the chest at the end of the bed should you need 'em. Is there anything else I can get you?"

"No, this is great. Thank you, ma'am," Hollis says.

"You're very welcome, dear. Mine and Bud's apartment is up-stairs if you need us. Good night, Mr. and Mrs. Hollenbeck."

"Oh, we're not—"

Hollis cuts me off, throwing an arm around my shoulders and pulling me toward him. "We're not sure what we did to be blessed with such graceful hospitality. Good night, Miss Connie."

She hands Hollis two room keys, then shuts the door behind her. When the sound of her footsteps recedes, Hollis drops his arm. The heat of his body disappears from alongside mine as he strides across the room and throws his duffel bag onto the emerald-green velvet armchair in the corner.

"Let her think we're married," he says. "She seems pretty religious. Might not be cool with us sharing a room if she knows we're just friends."

Pretty religious is an almost comical understatement considering all of the Jesuses staring at us, but that's not the part of what he said that captures my attention. "Aw. Hey. You said we're friends."

Hollis rubs his temples. "It's been a long day, Millicent. Don't make a big deal of it. I'm really not in the mood."

His gruffness doesn't distract me from the fact that he doesn't try to deny our friendship. That's . . . progress?

My eyes drift from Hollis to the bed. I gaze longingly at the fluffy pillows and the sage-green-and-mustard-yellow floral-print comforter.

Hollis must notice where I'm looking. "Do we need to Rock Paper Scissors to see who's going to be sleeping in the chair, or can we be extremely tired adults about this?"

"I'm okay sharing the bed if you are."

"Fine with me." He tucks a gray T-shirt under his arm and digs around in his duffel bag for whatever else he needs.

"Hollis," I say, and wait until I have his attention. "I am really sorry, you know. About the car."

He says, "It's not your fault." But the tone in which he says it and the grumbling under his breath certainly makes it seem like he actually believes otherwise.

"Then why are you mad at me?"

A sigh so heavy it could fall right through the floor escapes him. "I'm not mad at you, Millicent."

"But you're . . . huffy."

"That's just my personality."

"Well, what can I do?" I ask.

Hollis chuckles, but there isn't much humor in the sound. "To change my personality? Nothing. Many people have tried, none have succeeded. I'm like a haunted house. They go in very brave and confident, but they always run away screaming."

If he's a house at all, he's a gingerbread one that's been baked a few minutes too long but still has plenty of sweetness to offer. I'd tell him that, except his scowl is a great reminder that he's already annoyed enough at the moment.

Hollis mentioned his low premiums before, and he wanted a thousand dollars for letting me come along with him to Miami. Maybe it's about the money. "I'll pay for the repairs. I know I won't be with you when you pick up the car from Chip Auto-body, but—"

"Insurance will cover it," he says, hanging his hoodie on a hook beside the door. "Now, I would like to get to sleep before anything else terrible happens. Do you want the bathroom first or second?"

I hang my head in defeat. Whether Hollis actually blames me or not, the result is the same: I'm going to have to share a bed with a hot grump who probably wishes I would disappear. "First, I guess."

"Fine. Go ahead, but make it quick. I'm completely beat."

The small pink bag that holds my toiletries is still right on top inside my suitcase, despite the thing getting jostled throughout the day's adventures. I'm already inside the bathroom with my jeans halfway off when I realize the problem. "Um. Hollis?" I call through the door.

"What?"

I open it just enough to stick my head out while still hiding my underwear-only lower half. "Uh. Do you happen to have an extra T-shirt or something? I didn't pack any pajamas. I don't . . . I don't usually wear them."

He looks at me wide-eyed for what feels like forever, then blinks a few times as if trying to catch up for the ones he missed while staring. "You don't . . . wear . . . ? You've got to be kidding me."

"I sleep hot," I explain. "So the fewer layers . . ."

"You sleep hot." Eyes wide again, lips pressed together, Hollis turns to the painting hanging by a large oak dresser. "She sleeps hot," he tells the portrait of Jesus shaking hands with Elvis. Okay, I *have* to find out where the hell Connie is finding these ultra-specific kits.

"Do you have a spare or not?" I reach my arm out, waiting.

Hollis goes to his duffel in the chair and riffles through. He pulls out an old, faded blue Bookstore Movers T-shirt and tosses it toward my outstretched hand. I fail to catch it, and it falls to the hardwood floor outside the bathroom. Before I can reach down to pick it up, Hollis is in front of me, balling it up and pushing it into my palm. "Here," he says. Our eyes meet and his look . . . lustful.

Or maybe just annoyed. Perhaps one is lustful and one is annoyed. It's hard to tell with them being different colors. Regardless, it's making me feel like I ate some static, so I slam the door shut in his face.

When I'm stripped to nothing but underwear, I pull the T-shirt over my head and down my body. It falls to mid-thigh—short, but it covers what it needs to cover. I pee, brush my teeth, wash my face (only accidentally poking at the painful lump on my forehead three times in the process), and secure my hair into a messy bun on the top of my head.

"All yours," I say to Hollis as I slip back into the room.

As he passes me, his gaze hastily sweeps my body. He murmurs something unintelligible and disappears into the bathroom.

After throwing my dirty clothes into the designated plastic CVS bag in my suitcase, I pull back the covers and climb onto the absurdly high-off-the-ground mattress. Even though I haven't shared a bed with someone else since Josh, I notice I've automatically claimed my usual side. Old habits die hard, I guess. The bedding smells like lavender, which is one of my favorite smells. When Hollis comes out of the bathroom in his gray T-shirt and plaid pajama pants, I'm rubbing my face all over the comforter like I'm a cat in a patch of catnip. He doesn't acknowledge it, only turns off the overhead light. How quickly he's grown accustomed to—or maybe completely fed up with—my eccentricities.

The weight of his body settling into the mattress makes me feel like I'm a piece of space trash getting pulled into his planet's orbit. I shift a bit farther toward the edge, trying to resist snuggling up beside him. The bedding is nice and warm, but I bet he's warmer. And I might sleep hot, but right now I feel chilled to the bone.

"Hollis," I say to his back since he's turned away from me. "I know things aren't going as planned, but—"

"Ha, you think?" His sarcasm is harsh, cutting deeper than anything else he's said to me over the last few hours. Throughout the day it's been easy to tell myself he's actually a really nice guy inside. That the snark and rudeness is only a mask he wears for some reason, and that I shouldn't take it personally. But right now, with the weight of everything at stake heavy on my brain and my heart, it's not so easy to let it roll off me. I get the message loud and clear. I'm going to let it go, stop trying to get him to drop the facade and let me in. Maybe he's right; maybe people aren't as good as I want them to be. Maybe *he's* not as good as I want him to be.

I close my eyes tight against the pressure building behind them, but open them again as the mattress bounces in response to his shift in position. He's facing me now. It's dark, but I can see his frown. His default, I already know, so it tells me nothing.

"I should be in Miami right now, sweaty and inspired after round six with Yeva. Instead, I'm stuck in the middle of nowhere with a damaged car, twenty-five Jesuses staring at me—and yes, I counted while you were in the bathroom, there are twenty-five of them—and *you*." He spits the word "you" as if I'm the worst part of it all. "So no. Things are not going as planned."

"Hollis—"

"Go to sleep, Millicent. It'll all be equally miserable in the morning. We can discuss it then." He turns away again and pulls the covers over his shoulder.

He's right. This is miserable. If Hollis likes me at all, it seems like he resents me more. We're losing valuable travel time that might mean the difference between delivering Mrs. Nash to Elsie and being too late. And the deer! Oh no, the poor deer. What if

Dr. Gupta was wrong and it's dying, or it's already dead? Officer Jones said it wasn't my fault, and that the deer hit the car, not the other way around. But I feel terrible about it anyway, and extremely guilty, and oh god, all the blood, and it was on my *face*—I'm not sure whether to puke or cry. Cry. That'll involve less cleanup. So I'm going to turn away and cry. Go ahead, eyeballs, release the floodgates. Stomach, please standby.

"Mill." It's a whisper, Hollis's breath hot against my ear. "Are you okay?"

I sniffle and try to wipe away evidence of my tears with my forearm, but I'm still crying so it's kind of like using windshield wipers during a monsoon. "Peachy," I manage.

Hollis lets out a soft, emphatic *dammit* before his hand settles on my upper arm, heavy and warm through the cotton of the T-shirt. "Mill, I'm sorry. I've been a complete bastard all day, and I'm so sorry. You didn't deserve any of that. Tell me what to do to make it better. I'll do it. Whatever it is. I hate it when you cry. It makes me feel . . . panicky."

"When have you ever—" I manage before the congestion in my sinuses forces me to swallow, cutting me off.

"That night at the party, when you came out of the restaurant. You were crying pretty hard then."

"Oh. Right."

"I barely knew you—we'd only met in passing a few times— but I could tell that you were this bright, sunshine sort of person. Seeing you cry . . . it's like watching the sun flickering out. Like I'm getting a preview of the apocalypse. A horrible glimpse into a world that's colder and darker—"

"Yeah, yeah, we get it. You're a writer," I say through my tears.

A chuckle rolls through his chest and I can almost feel it

against my back. He's so close, but only his hand connects us. "Please don't cry. I'll do anything. Anything to make it up to you, to make it better. I'll even . . ." He pauses as if thinking something over. "Ha. Sure, why the hell not." Hollis makes a small, resigned groaning sound and I sense him leaning closer. And then a quiet, familiar melody floats into my ear. "Don't let the sun . . . go down on me . . ."

Laughter rises up in my throat, but I push it back down, settling on a huge grin instead. Hollis is singing Elton John to me, and I'm pretty sure he's doing so in an unironic effort to cheer me up. The last thing I want to do is spook him, which I will definitely do if I burst out laughing like I want to.

"I just realized . . . I don't know any of the other words . . ." he continues, still loosely clinging to the tune.

I can no longer keep my amusement hidden behind just a grin, and permit what I can only describe as a childish giggle. To my relief, Hollis sighs and says, "A single ray peeking through the clouds, but I'll take it."

Finally, there's a break in my tears. I reach for a tissue on the nightstand and blow my nose into it. "The live version with George Michael is my favorite." I sniffle.

"Yes, I know. You mentioned that several times when it came on in the car."

"Wait a second." I roll onto my opposite side to face him. I'm full of regret when his hand slides off my arm and he shifts a few inches away to give me more space. "You did remember me from that night at Josh's party. At the airport earlier, you acted like you didn't."

He raises his right shoulder in a shrug that presumably would be joined by the left if it wasn't buried in the mattress. The corners of Hollis's mouth shift ever so subtly into a smirk. "Maybe I did. Maybe I didn't."

I give him a shove, but despite the force of it he doesn't move. Instead, I'm just pressing my hand against his chest until I realize the thumping against my palm is his heart. Suddenly, the moment feels like it's turning into a *moment*, like the one on the hood of the police car, so I pull my hand away and let it fall to the mattress between us.

"I am sorry, Millicent," he says. "I meant what I said about us being friends. I don't want to do anything to hurt you. I'll try to be less . . ."

"Of a dick?"

"Yeah."

"Thanks." I stare at my hand, counting the chips in my nail polish to keep from having to make eye contact. "Though, while I'd appreciate that immensely, that's not why I was crying. I mean it was, but it wasn't the whole reason."

"Elsie?"

I manage a nod.

"Ah. Right." He bites his thick bottom lip and looks to the side as if contemplating the problem. Hmm . . . I wonder if that lip would feel good between *my* teeth. No. This is not the time to get distracted by his lips. Not at all the time. Elsie is dying. Elsie is *dying*.

"What if she's gone before I get to her because of all this?"

"Then . . . I guess you did the best you could."

"That doesn't feel like enough," I whisper.

"It'll have to be."

I sigh. "And the deer. What if it doesn't make it? What if I killed it? What if it *haunts* me?"

"Then we'll call an exorcist. With the amount of deer that die of unnatural causes, I bet they're extremely used to taking care of this kind of thing."

"And by 'this kind of thing,' you mean deer hauntings?" My words come out deadpan, but I can't help but grin. I can never keep a straight face when something's funny—reason number ten thousand I wasn't a very good actress.

"Yes. I bet we could even find a two-for-one coupon." His face remains completely serious at first, then slowly cracks. The full-blown smile that hits me is so powerful it's amazing it doesn't light up the room. I'm so dazzled that it takes me an embarrassingly long time to notice I'm staring at him the same way he stared at the sopaipillas at José Napoleoni's—like he didn't want to wait another minute to find out what they tasted like.

The realization that dinner was less than twelve hours ago reminds me that I'm way too exhausted to be unproductively lusting over this strange, sweet jerk. "Well, we should get some sleep," I say.

"Yeah. Good night."

We both lay in the dark on our backs, our arms parallel to each other, separated by the smallest amount of space. I feel the heat rolling off his skin, like standing in front of an open oven. And even though the thin material of the T-shirt is already making me feel like I'm suffocating, when Hollis's breathing slows and becomes interspersed with the soft snores that already feel so familiar, I press my arm against his and bask in the warmth of our connection as I drift off to sleep.

Key West, Florida
December 1944

STRICTLY SPEAKING, IT WASN'T ALLOWED. BUT IT WASN'T AS IF
N.A.S. 42 55 K.W.—also known as Bertie—had anywhere else to go. He certainly wouldn't remain in the loft much longer; he was a nervous bird with a tendency to pluck out his feathers, which meant that he was barred from flight a majority of the time. Even when he did fly, he delivered his messages with only 20 percent accuracy, and at the abysmal speed of thirty miles per hour. After two years of training, it was clear that Bertie was not cut out for service in the Navy.

Maybe it was because Rose wasn't so sure she was cut out for it either—her frustration with her menial duties and yearning for home still plagued her whenever she was alone—that she decided not to log Bertie's return to the loft one day. She instead carried him to a small nearby shed she'd noticed no one seemed to use. "This is your new loft," she told Bertie. "Welcome home."

Kinship explained why Rose stole the pigeon, but she couldn't quite put a name to the thing inside her that urged her to train

Bertie to fly to Boca Chica Beach. It was a mere mile away—which even a pathetically slow messenger like Bertie could manage—and the simple exercise was good for the bird, Rose told herself. She refused to admit that it had anything to do with Elsie; it was only a coincidence that she could use the tree under which they always rested as Bertie's destination. And if he was flying to the tree anyway, he might as well deliver a message . . .

On a cloudless Monday in mid-December, Rose hid within a clump of trees, watching Elsie Brown sitting in the warm sand. Bertie cooed above, then fluttered to the ground beside Elsie's outstretched legs. He strutted around, bobbing his head and periodically pecking at the sand for food, and Elsie squinted as she noticed something wrapped around the bird's leg.

"Come here, little fella," she said in her sweet singsong voice, slowly easing forward so as not to frighten the pigeon. When Bertie did not fly away as Elsie reached for him, Rose saw the moment understanding unfurled in Elsie's mind like a banner, and she had to stifle a laugh. Bertie allowed Elsie to pull the end of the red thread around his sticklike leg. Along with the tie, a folded piece of paper fell to the ground.

Will be a few minutes late today. —R

"So what do you think?" Rose asked, coming from the tree line to sit beside Elsie.

"You sent me a pigeon!" Elsie said in the way someone else might talk about being gifted a diamond ring.

"I did. I figured it would be a good way to be in touch with you if I can't meet you for whatever reason. And also it was an easy training exercise for Bertie, here. He's not a good distance flyer, are you Bert?" Rose captured the bird with skilled hands and ran her thumb down the pigeon's neck.

"I can't believe they let you train a pigeon to come to me." Elsie shook her head, her smile still wide and beautiful.

Rose bit her lip, looking guilty. "Well, he doesn't come to you exactly. He comes to the beach, this spot specifically. And also, it's possible that my superiors are unaware of this particular training exercise. And that I . . . liberated Bertie from the loft. They think he never returned from his last flight."

"Oh, you naughty girl," Elsie said. The sensuality of her voice and the way her pale blonde eyebrows raised, creasing her forehead, made Rose's heart leap. "I didn't realize you were such a rebel, Rosie."

For the first time in her life, Rose did feel rebellious. She felt like someone who could steal a pigeon that was property of the US Navy and teach it to fly to the woman she had dreamt of kissing every single night since they had first met. For a moment, Rose almost convinced herself she truly was the rebel Elsie believed her to be. Her fingers loosened around the bird in her grasp, ready to release him and take hold of Elsie's strikingly square jaw so that she could bring their mouths together.

Bertie's wings hit the air with a quiet whooshing sound, reminding Rose that she wasn't brave, just homesick and confused and avoiding replying to Dickie's latest letter. She should go back to her quarters and reread the pages he'd sent until she felt more like Rose McIntyre of Wisconsin instead of this reckless, fantasizing fool trying to get herself into all manner of trouble, trying to lose the only friend she had here.

"I should probably return to base," Rose said. "Make sure no one notices his coming and going."

"Of course." Elsie stood and reached down her hand to help Rose. The heat between their palms felt like a warning. "I'll see you soon?"

"Yes, yes. Soon," Rose muttered, already taking steps backward.

But Elsie kept hold of her hand for a moment, preventing her from running even though Rose's brain told her she must leave, she must, before she forgot again who she was.

"I really do need to go," she heard herself say. "I left the shed open and someone might notice, or he might try to fly back to the old loft and . . ."

"Yes, of course, go. Go," Elsie said, releasing her.

As she walked through the airfield, back toward the shed-cum-loft, Rose caught sight of Bertie in the air, slowly making his way back as well. Home would be much easier for her to find after the war if it remained a place, and not a woman who swam like a mermaid and made her feel braver than she had any right to be.

9

• • • • •

I AWAKE TO THE SOUND OF A SLAMMING DOOR AND THE RATTLING of twenty-five Jesuses in their frames.

"Mother*fucker*." Hollis smacks his palms down on the low dresser.

My forearm swipes over my eyes, urging them to open wider. The lids feel swollen and achy from last night's tears. My head is throbbing. "And good morning to you."

"Ah, sorry."

I sit up against the wooden headboard. The way Hollis's gray T-shirt stretches over his back in this position highlights the definition of his shoulders. Not that I'm checking him out or anything. Just, you know, taking in my surroundings—getting my bearings.

"Bad news, I take it?"

"Rental car place is out of cars," he says.

"How can— I mean, it made sense at the airport with everyone clamoring for one, but why wouldn't they have any here?"

Hollis straightens and walks toward me, then turns and walks the other way. He's pacing. I did not have him pegged as a pacer. "Because of the flight shitshow yesterday, they shipped all their cars to Charlotte Douglas to meet demand there. I checked this morning, and planes are finally in the air again. But like, hundreds of flights were canceled, so there are thousands of stranded passengers. Impossible to rebook them all immediately. People are still trying to find other ways to get where they're going."

"Maybe someone will return a car today?" I venture.

"Not according to any of the reservations in their system, no."

"Next town over?"

His frown does the impossible and droops further. "This was the next town over, Millicent."

"The next town over from the next town over then. Maybe they have a larger rental car place, one that's more central, and—"

"Called them. Same deal."

"Well," I say. "Shit."

"Shit indeed." Hollis throws himself backward onto the end of the bed and lets out a sigh as he stares up at the ceiling fan.

"Okay. So what now?" I ask.

"I guess we'll wait. Chip will have the car ready in a few more days. I don't see what other choice we have right now."

I shake my head. "No, no. There's got to be some other way. What if we get a ride to a train station, or a bus station, or . . . I don't know. But we have to do something. I have to get to Key West before—"

"Yes, I'm aware." His voice is too loud and too harsh. But he must remember last night and his promise to be less of a jerk, because he sounds penitent when he speaks again. "I know this is important to you. But this isn't exactly DC. You can't just hail a taxi. I mean, I checked Lyft when I thought I'd need to go pick up the rental car and it basically laughed at me."

It's not that I doubt Hollis. I'm sure he's done his best to find a solution to our problem. But maybe there are avenues he hasn't explored, ones we haven't thought of yet. "I'll figure something out," I declare.

"Oh, great," he says. "I'm sure your solution is going to involve us hitchhiking or sneaking onto a cargo ship or something."

"That's absurd. We're not even near a large enough body of water to find a cargo ship. And that scene where Pee-wee gets a ride from Large Marge really messed me up as a kid, so definitely no hitchhiking."

"What are you even talking about?"

"In *Pee-wee's Big Adventure*, when— Oh right. You haven't seen that movie. A lot of things about me would make more sense if you'd seen it."

"I seriously doubt that," he grumbles.

"Hey," I say, and nudge his leg with my foot from under the covers. "Thanks for trying."

"Yeah, well, lotta good it did. At least Connie and Bud said we can stay another few nights if we need." Hollis gets up from the bed and pulls something that looks like a ball of napkins from his hoodie pocket. "Breakfast ended fifteen minutes ago," he says, laying whatever it is on the dresser. "But I brought you this." The napkins fall away to reveal a lemon poppyseed muffin, the glaze drizzled on top glistening in the sunlight pouring in through the thin lace curtains.

"Thanks," I say, practically falling out of the bed when I try to get up. Maybe I should suggest to Connie she get one of those tiny staircases they make for elderly dogs to put beside this skyscraper of a mattress.

When I emerge from the en suite showered and dressed, Hollis is scribbling away in his notebook. Seeing him totally absorbed is fascinating; the way his eyes look at the page with single-minded focus and his pen moves with the speed and precision of an Olympic ice skater. As I break apart the muffin over the trash can and pop pieces into my mouth—Connie is a truly gifted baker—I wonder if that's what Hollis would be like in bed. Focused and precise, I mean. Not gifted. Except that too. Might explain why he's getting nudes on the reg, and from multiple lady friends. Not that he's not attractive enough for women to want him. Like, clearly *I* want him plenty and— Damn, I really need to cut this out. I clear my throat, and croak out, "What're you working on?"

"Something new," he says without looking up. "I think it has more promise than what I was stuck on."

"Oh, that's good. What's it about?"

"A small redhead who asks too many questions and gets deserted at an extremely religious bed-and-breakfast."

"Sounds boring," I say. "I'm going to see if there's a coffee shop or something nearby. Put out some feelers in case anyone in town can help us somehow. Wanna come?"

"No. Going to stay here and write. I need to get this on paper before I forget it."

"Writer's block gone, I take it?"

"It wasn't a block. It was a—"

"Minor clog. Yes, I remember. Guess you unclogged yourself then, huh? Didn't need Yeva to . . ." I make a fist and gesture how I imagine one would clear a pipe. But by the way Hollis's eyebrows raise, I'm pretty sure it looks like I'm miming something quite different.

He clears his throat. "Yeva's pretty open-minded, but I don't think she'd be up for that."

"I'll leave you to it. The writing, not the . . ." I repeat the gesture. *Why*.

But he's not looking at me now anyway, his pen busy skating over the page again.

I slide my backpack's straps over my shoulders and leave the room. Hollis is completely absorbed in what he's writing, so I don't want to interrupt by saying goodbye. Besides, I'm fairly certain that if he even notices my lack of farewell he's not going to dwell on it.

At the bottom of the stairs, I cross paths with a deeply tanned bald man with a pink, triangular scar on his forehead. "Oh, hello. You must be Millicent," he says.

"My friends call me Millie," I say. "Nice to meet you."

"I'm Bud, Connie's other half. So sorry to hear what happened to y'all last night. Those deer have been a real menace lately. And I know your husband ran into—oh, pardon the expression—some disappointment with the rental car company this mornin'."

It's so difficult not to correct him. Every part of me wants to blurt out, "He's not my husband. He's just a friend. I think. It's all very new." But Hollis is clearly more familiar with the type of people who have a room filled with Jesus paint-by-numbers than I am, and now that we might be here awhile, I really don't want to risk getting kicked out of Gadsley Manor and having to stay at the horrible motel. Except a lie by omission is still a lie, and Hollis was right before: I am a terrible liar.

Thankfully, Bud saves me by marching the conversation

forward. "Though all said, suppose it worked out all right. Least now you'll be in town for the festivities."

"Festivities?"

"Oh, guess it was too dark when you arrived to see the banners. This weekend is our Broccoli Festival."

"Broccoli . . . Festival?"

"The Alston farm just outside of town is the largest broccoli producer in the state. Been around for near a hundred years. They had a bad crop a few years back, so we did some events to raise money for them. Keep them from havin' to sell. People came from all 'round the area, and it was such a good time that we decided to make it an annual celebration. Each year it gets bigger and bigger. The parade is tomorrow at noon, and then later in the day we have the pie-eatin' contest, live music, vendors of all sorts, fireworks. It's a great time."

"Wait," I say. "*Broccoli* pie?"

Bud sticks out his tongue. "Blech. No. Normal pie, normal. Apple usually, I think. Gosh." He shivers dramatically. "Boy, I don't think most people could stomach a bite of a broccoli pie, much less eat a contest's worth of 'em. Guess it would be okay if it were quiche, though. I could probably eat my weight in that." His laugh is deep and boisterous, which I was not expecting from such a short, slender man.

I clear my mind of the broccoli pie image and replace it with apple. Based on what I've seen of his food preferences so far, I would bet a lot of money that Hollis is a fan of apple pie. My brain can picture the scene as vividly as if I were watching it unfold in front of me: him sitting at a long table on a stage in front of an eager crowd, a starting pistol cracking into the air. (Do they use those for pie-eating contests? Doesn't matter, they will at this one.) I'm sitting in the front row to cheer him on, and he gives me a look that says *imagine if this pie were you*. Then he takes it in his hands, and licks over the lattice crust without breaking eye contact, and he's already lagging extremely behind the other contestants, but he doesn't care, because he knows just how easy it is for me to imagine his tongue is caressing *my* lattice crust and—

"Millicent?"

I jump—literally jump!—at the sound of Hollis's voice behind me. "Holy sh—" My mind has just enough time to recall that, given what I know about his wife and their B&B's decor, Bud may not be cool with swearing. I manage to course correct enough that it comes out as "Holy shoooooooes," which the two men thankfully ignore.

"Mornin' again, sir." Hollis gives Bud a polite nod, which Bud returns. "Everything okay? I thought you were going out," he says to me.

"I was. I am."

"Oh gosh," Bud says. "I'm sorry. You were on your way somewhere and here I am waylayin' ya."

"No, no. I wasn't in any hurry. Thanks for the information about the festival. Sounds like a lot of fun. Oh, but, um, Bud. Could I ask a favor before I head out? Do you have a book I could borrow? Maybe something about the local history, or . . ."

Bud's face lights up like a kid's when school lets out for summer vacation. "Got just the thing. One second."

"Writing break?" I ask Hollis when we're alone in the foyer.

"About to get on a call with my agent to discuss the marketability of my new idea, but wanted to grab a bottle of water first." He frowns at me deeper than feels warranted, even for him. "There's a mini fridge in the kitchen with drinks, by the way.

Connie gave me a quick tour of the house after breakfast. And you? You're . . . doing what, exactly?"

"Absolutely *not* thinking about you eating a pie," I say. My hands clap over my mouth like I'm in a cartoon, then slide to my cheeks. Because maybe if I cover how much I'm blushing he will not register the strangeness of what I've said.

"I'm not going to ask," Hollis says. But then as he turns to leave, the whisper of a smile appears. "Mm. Pie does sound good right now, though." He bites his lower lip before disappearing into the dining room, and I swear my kneecaps tremble even though the rest of my legs are standing still.

The book about the town of Gadsley that Bud provides me—written by John Edward Gadsley V, who I was somewhat surprised to learn is Bud himself—winds up being the perfect thing to read at the little diner around the corner. It's interesting enough that I don't zone out and forget to turn the pages, but undemanding enough that I can keep an ear on the conversations around me. Just in case someone's like, "I sure am excited to fly my private plane down to the Florida Keys today!" Or like, "Wow, I wish I had some nice folks who'd be willing to test out the amenities of my new yacht as I sail it down the East Coast."

What? It could happen.

So far, though, all I've learned is that the town is extremely divided concerning the local high school marching band's deviation from its usual John Philip Sousa medley for tomorrow's Broccoli Festival parade. There's a new band director this year, and he's either a "hepcat with no regard for tradition" or "just the young new perspective this town needs" depending on which diner customer is currently providing their opinion. Also, someone named Karen is doing much better, though someone named Peggy is doing much worse. Someone named Gary is doing about the same as he was last week.

"Can I get you more coffee?" the waitress asks, balancing a tower of empty dishes from a nearby table on her tray.

"I think I'll actually switch to iced tea, if you've got it."

"This is the South, darlin'," she says with a smile.

My empty mug is whisked away, and a large, red, plastic Coca-Cola tumbler filled with crushed ice and tea appears in front of me. A momentary silence falls over the restaurant. Everyone is suddenly looking in my direction. Did I do something weird without realizing? Is the iced tea spiked with something and they're watching to see if I notice I'm being poisoned?

Oh. They aren't looking at *me*, just at the man who is suddenly standing beside my table. He took the waitress's place so seamlessly I didn't even notice his approach. But now, as I look up, I understand the silence: He's *gorgeous*. Tall, blond, green-eyed, strong-jawed, golden-beige skin. A supermodel of a man, right here in this tiny diner in Gadsley, South Carolina.

"Hi," he says, flashing an easy, brilliant smile. "Sorry to interrupt your reading."

"What reading?" I ask, staring up at him with the same slack-jawed expression I probably had when I met John Stamos.

"I just assumed, since you have a book . . ." I follow the direction of his gesture.

"Oh! Yes. The book. I am reading it, yes. Hello. Don't worry about it. It's not very good." My face goes tomato red with embarrassment and also a bit of shame that I've undeservedly insulted Bud's hard work.

"May I join you?"

"Join me in reading?"

The man chuckles. "Join you at your table. I'd like to chat with you about something, if you have a minute."

"Oh. Sure." My mental database tries to bring up the search results for "topics about which a hot stranger might want to chat." Error: No results found.

"Millicent Watts-Cohen. *Penelope to the Past*, right?"

Ohhhh. Right. I *am* ever so slightly famous, and this Adonis is the exact right age for having watched the show when it originally aired. A fan. I know how to talk to fans. In fact, I can pretty much go through this script in my sleep—assuming my scene partner doesn't start ad-libbing like that creep at the airport—so I can probably get through the rest of this conversation without making a further fool of myself.

"Yes. That's me."

He smiles again, and my brain goes completely offline. Uh-oh. It takes me a while to respond after he says, "I saw you coming in here this morning on my way to work. Really glad you're still in town. Heard about what happened with the deer."

"Wow. Word got around quick, huh? Guess it's true what they say about small towns."

"You don't know the half of it," he says. "When I got here last August, I already had parents lined up outside my house the day I moved in, wanting to inform me of Aiden's desire to switch from trombone to trumpet, and Chloe's severe peanut allergy, and how Elijah and Hailey P. should never sit near each other on the bus to away games."

"Wait! You're the hepcat!" Hmm. That actually explains the silence and the staring more than every single person in the diner being in awe of his good looks.

His eyes dart in the direction of the group of older men sitting at the counter. "You've met Barney, I take it?" Before I can admit that I haven't met Barney so much as eavesdropped on his and his friends' conversations for the last three hours, the hepcat continues. "I'm as big a Sousa fan as the next band geek, but the kids are so tired of playing the same thing for the parade every year. This would be the fourth time for the seniors, and their last performance before graduation. No idea why some people are so opposed to changing it up. It's just Fleetwood Mac, for Pete's sake."

I clutch the edge of the table in my excitement. "You're having the marching band play Fleetwood Mac?"

He smiles. "'Tusk.'"

"I *love* 'Tusk,'" I say.

"Me too. It was between that and Paul Simon's 'You Can Call Me Al.' But 'Tusk' has a part where the kids get to run around and yell a bit, so it won in a landslide when we put it to a vote." He lets out a charming, almost dorky laugh that only makes him more attractive. "Ha. 'Landslide.' Get it?"

Boy do I ever. "I know we just met," I say, "but I think we should be best friends."

He laughs again. "In that case, you should probably know that my name is Ryan."

"Nice to meet you, Ryan the hepcat," I say. And then I maintain eye contact with him as I wrap my lips around my straw and take a sip of my iced tea. The intense sweetness comes as a shock to my tongue. "Holy shoes, that's like straight-up simple syrup that might've brushed against a tea leaf a few years ago."

"Ha, yeah, they take their sweet tea very seriously in these parts. I grew up in Vermont and I prefer my tea unsweetened, which might be the real reason half the town hates me. Um, so, Ms. Watts-Cohen—"

"You should call me Millie if we're going to be best friends."

"Millie," he repeats with that easy smile of his that momentarily pauses my brain. "I'm here to ask a very big favor of you, but I think I can make it worth your time."

Oh, right. He came over here to chat about something and presumably it was not the speed with which information spreads around Gadsley or his excellent taste in marching band music. "Sure, I'm listening," I say.

"Our mayor went to this small-town tourism convention last month and now he's obsessed with getting 'younger' people to think Gadsley's hip and fun. And by 'younger' people, he apparently means millennials. So he started this Young Residents Advisory Council, which is really just me and his daughter. Which . . . now that I think about it, maybe the council is all just an elaborate matchmaking attempt?" His jade-colored eyes drift away for a moment, considering, before refocusing on my face. "Anyway, he asked me to find a grand marshal for the Broccoli Festival parade who would match our new hip and fun millennial vibe. And, uh, I procrastinated on it because I've been busy with the band, and because his daughter told me that he'd probably change his mind anyway and want to be the grand marshal himself like every other year but . . . parade's tomorrow, he hasn't changed his mind, and I'm completely screwed."

"So you want me to help you find someone who will appeal to millennials and is willing to be your parade grand marshal with twenty-four hours' notice?" Does he think I have a phone full of contact info for celebrity thirtysomethings who just happen to live within driving distance of Gadsley, South Carolina?

"No. I want *you* to be the parade grand marshal with twenty-four hours' notice. You're exactly the person we need. I don't think I could've found anyone better had I actually put effort into it."

"Thank you?"

Ryan's eyes drift upward, looking somewhere over my head, and his smile droops like a flower arrangement on the fifth day in its vase.

"Hey. Sorry to interrupt," says a familiar voice that doesn't sound even a little sorry.

I tilt my head back until I'm staring up at the stubbled underside of Hollis's chin. He's focused on Ryan until I say, "Hey, what are you doing here?" Then his head bows so he can meet my upturned eyes, and his glasses slide a fraction of an inch down his nose. For some reason, when he pushes them back up with his index finger, I feel the need to take an extra deep breath.

"Needed a break. Figured I'd get some lunch." Without waiting for an invitation, he pulls an empty chair over and sits beside me. "Have you eaten yet?"

"I had an egg and some toast," I say. "But that was hours ago now. I wouldn't mind something else."

Hollis is looking at Ryan again and there's an odd tension in the air. It's momentarily broken when the waitress comes over to take Hollis's and my lunch order—Hollis ordering for me, reluctantly this time because I insist on the kid's mac and cheese, which is topped with a hot dog sliced to look like an octopus. Ryan doesn't order anything since he won't have time to eat before he has to get back to the school.

"Oh, introductions," I say once the waitress leaves. "Hollis, this is Ryan. He's the high school's band director and he's just proposed something very interesting. Ryan, this is Hollis." How does Hollis want to be introduced? Am I supposed to keep up the Mr. and Mrs. Hollenbeck nonsense here, or just at the B&B? "He's my . . . uh . . . Hollis."

Ryan's friendly smile can't hide his confusion, but I give him points for trying. "Nice to meet you," he says.

"Likewise. So what's the proposition?"

Ryan repeats his explanation about the mayor and the parade. Hollis sits with his arms crossed, nodding, as Ryan gets to the point. "So I've asked Millie to be our grand marshal."

"Okay, and? What's in it for her, exactly?"

"Oh, right. Yes. That part's important, isn't it? So I heard that you're in a bit of a hurry to get back on the road. If you do this for me, I'd be happy to lend you my car for as long as you need it."

At that, Hollis's spine straightens and his arms unfold, literally opening himself up to the idea. "We're going pretty far, and don't plan to pass back through this way again for about a week."

"No problem," Ryan says. "I bike or walk almost everywhere. The car's just sitting in my driveway doing no one any good right now." He turns his attention toward me. "I'd really like to help you, Millie."

"But she has to help you first," Hollis says.

"Well, yes. I'm in a real jam here. And I'm already not the most popular person in town at the moment. If I don't deliver a parade grand marshal, the mayor won't hesitate to make sure all of Gadsley knows I was the one who dropped the ball."

Hollis slumps back in his chair again, recrossing his arms. "That sounds like a you problem."

"Hollis," I say, a warning note in my voice. "Ryan's trying to help us."

He sighs and pastes on one of his grimacey smiles, which makes Ryan lean an inch or two away from him.

"When do you need to have my answer?" I ask.

"Let's say five o'clock?" Ryan says, rising from his chair. "You can come over, discuss any questions or concerns, figure out logistics."

"Sure," I say.

Ryan clutches his hands together in gratitude. "Great. Think about it, talk to your . . . your Hollis. And then I'll see you at my house at five." He looks up at the clock on the wall above the diner's counter. "Whoops. My prep period's over in ten. Gotta get back to it. Connie and Bud can give you my address. I mean, probably anyone in town can, but Connie and Bud are likely the most convenient."

"Small towns, huh?" I say with a smile.

"Exactly. See you later, Millie. Hollis."

"Later," I agree. I wave, then nudge Hollis with my elbow until he gives Ryan the most perfunctory wave I have ever seen.

"He just offered us a way out of here," I snap at him. "You better be nicer when we go to his house tonight."

Hollis's huff-like laugh makes a reappearance. "Oh, I'm not going to Ryan's house tonight."

"Don't be like that," I say.

"I'm not being like 'that,' whatever 'that' is. I'm not going because I'm fairly sure I wasn't invited."

"What do you mean? You were invited. I was right here when he said it. He said 'You can come over . . . '"

"*You.* 'You' was the key word in that sentence. Otherwise, he would've said 'y'all.' Like 'y'all can come over.'"

"Ryan's not from around here, so no, he wouldn't have. But I'm starting to suspect you *are* from around here. You have the accent. Or a similar one, at least."

Hollis stares at me, neither confirming nor denying my allegation.

I prop my elbows on the table and rest my chin in my hands. "Why would Ryan want me to come over without you? We'd both be borrowing his car."

Hollis laces his fingers together in front of him. He leans in closer to me. "Well, Millicent, sometimes when people find each other attractive, they choose to spend time alone together on something called a date, often with the goal of engaging in an act known as sexual intercourse."

I groan and let my arms collapse on the table, burying my face in the dark little cave they make.

"Now," he continues. "It is true that, while two is the most common quantity of people for this transaction, it's not the only possible one. But that man did not seem interested in a threesome. He only had eyes for you."

My brain immediately latches on to the image of me, Hollis, and Ryan in some tangled conglomeration of limbs. *Oh my.* I'll never be able to raise my head again, or Hollis will know exactly what I've been thinking. The nest of my folded arms and the grain of the wooden table will be the only things I see for the rest of my life, and I'm going to have to make peace with that.

Hollis's hand settles on my back. It moves slowly up and down, making my face burn even hotter. "You don't have to do it, you know." His voice is soft and close.

"Yes, I am aware I do not need to have sex with everyone who is interested. Thank you." I venture a peek over my arm and find Hollis's lips quirked up in the corners and only a few inches away from mine.

"I meant about the parade. I know how you feel about the spotlight, about not having control over where it shines. If you don't want to be the grand marshal, you shouldn't do it."

"But the car," I say.

"Screw the car." His tone is surprisingly emphatic. "We'll find another way. I don't want you to do anything you don't want to do, Millicent. Mrs. Nash wouldn't want that either."

Our eyes meet, and for a moment my heart squeezes. One time, early in our friendship, I told Mrs. Nash that I was considering getting my nose pierced, but that I didn't think Josh would like it. She said, *Who cares what he thinks? You must always do what is right for* you*, Millie. What is right for anyone else doesn't matter, because you are the one who will live with your decisions.* My fear of needles made the decision for me in the end, but Mrs. Nash's words have stayed with me.

Just as the wave of grief that sometimes crashes into my heart begins to recede, I remember that Hollis knows almost nothing about Mrs. Nash. His words might be correct, but they're nothing but empty assumptions; other than her and Elsie's love story, the only things I've told him are that she loved York Peppermint Patties and used to have a male dog named Lady. "You just don't want me to be in the parade because you don't like Ryan."

His hand pauses, heavy on my shoulder blade. "No, I don't like Ryan. But I don't like most people. It's nothing personal. So do the parade, don't do the parade. It's your decision."

"It affects you too, though."

"I'm not going to ask you to do something that makes you uncomfortable just so I don't have to wait as long to get laid." The hand on my back gives me a light pat, then withdraws. "The choice is yours, kid. I'm behind you one hundred percent."

"Not a kid," I grumble as our food arrives at the table.

"Says the woman who insisted on ordering off the children's

menu." He removes the frilly toothpicks from the triangular tow-
ers of turkey club on his plate.

"You're just jealous that your lunch didn't come with a hot dog
octopus."

"Right. I'm sure it's actually that."

Hollis *mmm*s his way through his sandwich, and I make fun of
him because, come on, how can I not? But the entire time, I'm also
trying not to think too hard about what Hollis said about Ryan's
intentions tonight and why exactly I'm not more interested in the
prospect.

10

• • • • •

"I'M GOING TO DO IT," I DECIDE.

"You're going to have sex with Ryan?" Hollis asks, his tone distracted. He's been writing for the last hour at the desk in the corner of our room at Gadsley Manor, while I've been sprawled out on the bed, debating the repercussions of a public appearance in a small southern town.

"No, the parade." I've been thinking about the sex thing too, let's be real. Maybe it's just what I need. Like a palate cleanser. A scoop of sorbet to clear out the slightly metallic taste Josh left behind. Casual sex seems to work out well enough for Hollis. And Yeva, I imagine. Also, I know that Dani has had her share of satisfactory no-strings-attached hookups. Why shouldn't I give it a try? "I might or might not do the sex. Haven't decided yet."

This gets Hollis's attention. He drops his pen and shifts to look at me. "So you're going to do the parade?"

"Yes. I looked it up, and all a grand marshal really has to do is sit in a convertible and wave and smile. I excel at all of those things. So why not?"

"You won't mind the attention?"

I shrug. "The crowd itself is no problem. I might make the papers or trend on social media or whatever, but if we can get back on the road tomorrow afternoon instead of in a few days, get to Elsie sooner, it'll be worth it. Besides, this is something I'm choosing to do. I know there will be photos, and I know they'll be out in the world. I don't have to read any of the comments. So it's fine."

Hollis nods. "Okay. Sounds good." He picks his pen up again and continues writing.

I try to pay attention to Bud's book, but after rereading the same sentence six times, I give up and let myself watch Hollis's profile as he works. When he's particularly focused, he bites his bottom lip. Occasionally he pauses and stares into space for a minute before bobbing his head ever so slightly and returning his attention to his notebook. His concentration is both fascinating and maddening. I have this impulse to test its limits that is probably not very nice but sounds like an excellent way to spend my time.

"Working pretty hard there, aren't you?" I ask.

Silence.

"This book is great, by the way. Bud's a decent writer. Should I read you a few select passages? Maybe it'll inspire you." I flip back toward the beginning and read aloud a paragraph about the town's founding, then jump ahead to one about the Alston broccoli farm's history.

Silence.

"Going to borrow your toothbrush. Hope you don't mind."

More silence.

"Might clean the toilet with it. I noticed a rust stain this morning that I bet Connie would love to get rid of."

Nothing.

"But first, do you mind if I jump up and down on the bed naked, singing 'The Battle Hymn of the Republic?'"

He turns in his chair, draping an arm across the back and resting his chin on it. "No, I don't mind. Go ahead."

A fierce blush blooms on my cheeks, then spreads all the way to the tips of my fingers.

"Well," he says. "What're you waiting for? Surely you weren't just *saying* things to try to distract me from my work." Hollis's expression is that of someone two moves away from checkmate. "That would be childish. And you are, as you've reminded me on several occasions now, not a kid."

"On second thought," I say, searching for an exit that doesn't involve admitting I was screwing with him for the purposes of my own entertainment, "probably not a good idea to break out the ol' 'Battle Hymn' in these parts. They still haven't forgiven Sherman for his March to the Sea, you know."

"Oh, I don't think Bud and Connie will mind. Bud surely isn't into that Lost Cause nonsense with his great-great-granddaddy and the founder of the town a former Union colonel. An officer in the US Colored Troops even. No, I'd say you're good to go there. Might even be appreciated. A tribute to his family, and to Gadsley, South Carolina's illustrious and surprisingly progressive history."

Of course he was listening while I read the passages from Bud's book. Hoisted by my own petard yet again. And it's clear by the look in his eyes behind his glasses, equal parts self-satisfied and predatory, that he knows that I know I'm in a pickle here. Sure, I could back down. But what if . . . Well, what if I just do it?

What if I call *his* bluff? Hollis is such a know-it-all, thinking he knows me, thinking he knows Mrs. Nash, thinking he knows the truth about love and people and the entire universe. It might be nice to knock him off balance, show him how little knowledge he actually possesses.

My fingers hesitate for a moment at the hem of my chartreuse shirt, then close over the fabric and slowly lift. Hollis's mouth opens to say something but freezes with his lips slightly parted as he catches the motion.

Oh.

It's not just bravado, is it? Hollis's antagonistic flirtation isn't about flustering me for his amusement. Or at least, it's not completely about that. He wants me like I want him. I see it in the way his eyes follow my leisurely movement, how his shoulders rise and fall as he takes a deep breath.

Six inches of paste-white stomach are sandwiched between the bright yellow-green cotton of my bunched-up shirt and the light-blue denim of my jeans. Any higher and Hollis is going to get an eyeful of boobs. The fact that they'll still be mostly covered by my bra and it's not all that different from what he'd see if he googled "Penelope to the Past bikini" doesn't make it feel any less like we're standing on the edge of a precipice. His eyes connect with mine in a silent dare: *Jump.*

I'm going to do it. I'm going to. Because I don't want to do this with anyone else if Hollis is an option, and it's starting to feel like he might be. If I'm going to jump, I might as well do it from the highest point possible so I have more time to enjoy the fall.

My brain doesn't even have time to tell my hands to act before a knock sounds at the door, and I pull my shirt back down in a panic. Hollis's body whips around to face his desk again. The heat that's been flowing like lava under my skin turns into burning-hot embarrassment, as if the door is transparent and we've actually been caught doing something naughty. Then the knock comes again, a little louder this time. Hollis clears his throat as he stands and marches the few steps to the door.

"Miss Connie," he says as he opens it a crack and sticks his head out. "Good afternoon, ma'am."

"Oh, Hollis darlin', I hope I'm not interruptin' your work," she says in a hurry. "I only wanted to let you and Millie know that we're doin' tea and scones downstairs, if y'all are interested. Didn't think to mention it earlier, since we thought you'd be leavin' today, but since you're stickin' around after all . . ."

"Thanks so much," he says. "I'm afraid I've still got a lot to do here, but I'm sure Millicent will be down shortly."

"Wonderful," she responds. "And how are y'all on essentials? Towels and whatnot?"

"Just fine. Thank you."

"Great. You'll let me know if there's anything we can get y'all to make you more comfortable?"

"Of course. Goodbye, Miss Connie."

"Goodbye now," she says. Then hastily adds, "And sorry again to disturb—"

"No problem. Have a nice evening, ma'am."

After he shuts the door, Hollis leans his head against it. "Tea and scones," he says on a weighty exhale.

"Tea and scones," I repeat. It feels like we're speaking in some sort of code, but I'm not exactly sure of the translation. "So, I . . . I think I saw a Chinese place when we came in last night. We could go get some takeout. I'm sure Connie has Ryan's number, I can just text him and tell him I'm good to do the parade."

"No, you should go to his place. Have a good time." He pushes off from the door and settles back down at the desk, immediately reabsorbed in his writing.

"I don't mind skipping it," I say. "So you don't have to eat alone." I'm suddenly aware of the double-meaning of my words, and I flush a bit even though that's exactly how I meant it anyway.

"No. I think it's probably best if you eat with Ryan tonight," he says.

The rejection pinches my pride, especially when he seemed so game a minute ago. But . . . tea and scones. Tea and scones. Perhaps I read it all wrong. Maybe he wasn't excited so much as horrified by the prospect of me naked. Too horrified to stop what was unfolding. Maybe Connie didn't interrupt so much as save Hollis from the terribly uncomfortable situation in which he found himself.

"Okay. Well, um, I'm supposed to be at Ryan's at five, so I'm probably not going to come back up to the room before I head out. So . . . bye."

"Wait," he says, standing abruptly.

I freeze midway through threading my arm through my backpack's strap. My heart is thumping in anticipation of Hollis changing his mind, asking me to stay. "What?"

"Let me give you my phone number. Just in case things go bad. I mean, you're going to a stranger's house in an unfamiliar town, and you completely lack evolutionary survival instincts."

I sigh and my heartbeat calms. "Fine." I add Hollis Hollenbeck as a new contact and enter the numbers as he says them.

"Text me so I have yours too?"

"I will," I say. "When you least expect it."

His frown deepens. "Please don't forget."

"Okay, *Dad*."

A few of the B&B's other guests are enjoying the tea and scones when I go downstairs. I listen to Connie and a lady from Alabama chat about baking for half an hour, nodding every so often as if I know enough about the subject to agree with some point or another. *Yes, yes, I too find I have more success with my muffins if I put them in the oven at a higher temperature then turn it down after a few minutes.*

Mostly my mind keeps drifting to Mrs. Nash (who never met a baked good she didn't love), and then to Elsie and the miles that still separate us. Part of me wants to call the nursing facility to see how she's doing, but another part of me is so terrified it might be bad news that I decide I'd rather not know right this moment. Schrödinger's Elsie is a lot easier to cope with while I have all this other stuff floating around my head. Like why Hollis's disinterest in me is so disappointing when I never expected him to be interested in the first place. And whether sleeping with a hot guy who likes Fleetwood Mac might make up for some of that disappointment or somehow exacerbate it.

OUTSIDE, ON GADSLEY MANOR'S WRAPAROUND PORCH, I STUDY the rough map of town Bud sketched on a piece of scrap paper for me. Connie seemed a bit suspicious that I was headed to a bachelor's private residence while my "husband" remained behind until I explained who I am and that I'm going to be the parade's grand marshal. After a few minutes of flustered excitement about not knowing she was hosting a celebrity, she had no further qualms.

Ryan's place is a ten-minute walk from the B&B, but I've left a bit early so I can take my time. Stop and smell the roses—maybe literally, if I find some in bloom. Perhaps because of her name and preference for heavily floral perfumes, it's an activity that never fails to make me feel like I'm wrapped up in a Mrs. Nash hug. And I could really use one of those today.

I'm about to step down onto the meandering stone path to the sidewalk when I remember that I never texted Hollis.

MILLIE: Thanks for signing up for Broccoli Facts! 🥦

MILLIE: Broccoli is part of the species Brassica oleracea. 🥦

HOLLIS: UNSUBSCRIBE.

MILLIE: Thank you for your interest in receiving MORE Broccoli Facts! 🥦

MILLIE: Did you know? Broccoli contains almost 90% water. 🥦

MILLIE: 2018 survey results show that broccoli is America's favorite vegetable. 🥦

HOLLIS: Millicent. I'm trying to work.

MILLIE: 🥦🥦🥦🥦🥦🥦🥦🥦🥦🥦🥦🥦🥦

HOLLIS: Giving you my number was an immense mistake.

I'm smiling down at my phone when I realize I've already reached Ryan's house. Damn. Hollis made me forget to look for roses along the way. Also, now I'm early. I guess it doesn't matter, because Ryan sees me through the bay window and opens the door before I can decide whether to ring the doorbell or run away.

"Hey, Millie," he says. "No trouble finding the place, I take it?"

"Ryan," I say, my decision finalizing as soon as I see him. "You are super attractive, but I don't think I want to have sex with you."

His eyes go wide, and he's silent for a moment. "Sorry. What was that now?"

"I know what you're thinking. I barely know you, so how do I know I don't want to have sex with you yet? But for me, that's how it is. I think I should know a person first, a little at least. See, I've only ever had sex with men I'm in a relationship with. I do think I'd like to give casual sex a shot. But I don't think it's smart to do it with someone I *just* met, considering my issues. Oh, uh, I guess I should explain. I have trust issues. The opposite type of most people, though—I trust almost everybody. So it's probably not a good idea for me to do the deed with you. I'm sorry if you're disappointed." I didn't mean to say all of that, especially not the part where I referred to having sex as "doing the deed," but now that I did, well . . . I guess it's better that he knows at the outset.

"Okay, um. Well, thanks for letting me know . . . your feelings on that." A woman's choked laughter floats out to the porch from somewhere inside the house. "So. Everyone except the mayor is already here actually, so, uh, why don't you come on in?"

Unless this was supposed to be an orgy with Ryan, the mayor, and whoever is waiting inside, I believe I have made a very big, very embarrassing mistake here. My laughter sounds robotic and my face is so hot with mortification that you'd need pot holders to touch it. However, this is hardly the first time my lack of filter has conspired against me. I know I will recover. The all-consuming desire to be mistaken for a rabbit and swallowed whole by an enormous bird of prey fades as soon as I'm inside Ryan's house (which is good, because the likelihood of encountering a hawk that size indoors is quite low).

The next two hours are filled with pizza and last-minute Broccoli Festival parade logistics. Ryan, the mayor, the mayor's daughter (who shows me pictures of her dressed as Penelope for Halloween in 2002), a local florist, and Officer Jones are all ecstatic to have me as grand marshal. Ryan's cat, Shako, is ambivalent about it, and about my presence in general despite how clearly desperate I am for his approval.

"Thank the good Lord that deer stranded y'all here," the mayor says to me with a laugh that reminds me of our string of bad luck and makes me want to vomit pepperoni and mushroom onto his scuffed oxfords. Listening to the timeline of tomorrow's events, all I can think about is how many hours we'll be wasting with this instead of getting back on the road to Florida. If we left right now and drove all night, we could get to Miami by sunrise. It would only be a few more hours of driving after parting with Hollis before I'd reach Key West. But tomorrow, instead of holding Elsie's hand while she tells me about what she's been up to for the last seventy years, I'll be sitting in a shiny convertible from a local car dealership, waving and smiling to the citizens of Gadsley and the broccoli fans who've flocked here for the weekend's events. The only thing that keeps me from crying in frustration is that this is absolutely ridiculous and will therefore make an excellent story that I can tell Elsie when I meet her. I'll tell her about the canceled flight, and Hollis, the olive oil spill, the deer, being grand marshal in a small town's Broccoli Festival parade. And I'll make sure she understands that it was truly nothing compared to what Mrs. Nash would have happily endured to see her again.

"I'M SORRY ABOUT BEFORE," I SAY AS RYAN SHOWS ME OUT AROUND seven. "When I said I don't want to have sex with you. Obviously I was under the wrong impression about why you asked me to come over."

He purses his lips and closes one eye, still somehow being model-level attractive even while looking like he drank straight lemon juice. "No, it's my fault. I should have been clearer that it would be the entire planning committee, not just you and me. I guess I assumed that you and Hollis are . . . somehow involved? So it never crossed my mind to clarify that I didn't intend for it to be a date."

"Oh no, we're not—I mean, Hollis is just a . . ." A guy I'm stuck on a road trip with who is kind of rude but also very sweet, and with whom I shared a *moment* last night (and also a queen-sized bed but nothing sexual happened except I really wish something sexual would happen because I find him extremely attractive)? No, that won't do. ". . . a friend. Just a friend."

"Oh," Ryan says. "Well. Honestly, if I'd known that . . . maybe I would have tried to make this a date."

"Really?"

"Duh. You're gorgeous and funny and a Fleetwood Mac fan. How could I not be into you? Alas. You're only passing through, and you've already decided you don't want to have sex with me." Ryan bumps my arm with his. His carefree smile stretches across his handsome face, and I'm annoyed with myself for not wanting him when everything about him is so wantable. "Thanks again for saving my butt with this grand marshal thing," he says.

"No problem. It should be a lot of fun. Thank you in advance for the car," I say. "I promise we'll get it back to you in one piece. Assuming we don't encounter any other kamikaze deer."

Ryan chuckles. "See you at the parade, Millie."

I stand on my tiptoes and give him a peck on the cheek. "Yeah. Have a good night."

When I get back to the B&B and key into the Mustard Seed room, I find Hollis laying back on the bed with his tablet propped on his stomach. He jumps slightly, startled, and slams the tablet closed in its case.

"You're back early," he says, feigning calm. But even from here I can see his pulse fluttering in his neck.

"Orgies don't last nearly as long as one might think." I step out of my sneakers and grab the Bookstore Movers T-shirt I left balled up on top of my suitcase. From the bathroom, as I change out of my clothes, I add, "There were twice as many women as men. We made do, of course, but I think your presence actually would have been welcome. The mayor has a bad shoulder, so Ryan had to pull most of the sexual weight in the more acrobatic positions." The mirror above the sink shows that I've turned vermillion saying this aloud; it's a good thing Hollis can't see me.

"Not really my scene," he says. "But I'm glad you had a good time."

Once my color fades to some semblance of normal, I stroll out of the bathroom in my borrowed pajamas. "It was a last-minute parade and festival logistics meeting. And of course, thanks to you, I rolled in all 'Hey, Ryan, I'm not interested in having sex with you.' I wanted to die."

Hollis's eyebrows shoot up. "Don't blame me. I never told you to do that."

I stuff my dirty clothes into my suitcase and sit on the end of the bed. "Oh, I definitely blame you. Because he said that the reason it wasn't a sex thing was because he thought you and I were together. You cockblocked me, dude."

"It sounds to me like you cockblocked yourself. You're the one who turned him down before you even crossed his threshold."

"Because you psyched me out, telling me Ryan wanted to cross *my* threshold."

"Except it sounds to me like if he knew you were single he would have wanted to . . . cross your threshold? God, that's a stupid way to say that. Besides, I wasn't wrong, was I?"

I don't want to admit that once Ryan realized sex could have been on the table he told me he would've been game. Hollis is not allowed to be right. "That's not the point," I say. "What were you doing when I got back here, anyway?"

Hollis glances away and rubs his ear. That's his embarrassed gesture, so I definitely don't believe him when he mumbles, "Nothing."

The possibility hits me that he was watching *Penelope to the Past*. The thought makes my stomach roil a little, and I almost regret asking at all. But now I have to know. "You were clearly watching *something*. Something you didn't want me to know about."

"A movie. I was watching a movie. Okay?"

Relief quashes the pizza rebellion inside my digestive system. "Oh. Which movie? Is it pornographic?" I crawl up the bed, swiping the tablet from where it rests beside him before he can react. He makes a half-hearted grab, but I hold it out of his reach. If it is porn, things are about to get either a lot more interesting or a lot more awkward between us. The tablet turns on with a press of the small button on the side, and—like his phone did in the car last night—the screen lights up without requesting any kind of passcode or pattern swipe from me. "You really need to protect your shit better," I admonish as the page for the movie reloads.

Resume watching, the screen says above a still of Pee-wee Herman holding handfuls of snakes with fire raging behind him.

"Oh my god. You were watching *Pee-wee's Big Adventure*!"

"I needed a break from writing, and you said it was good. So."

"It's not good, Hollis. It's *great*. It's basically my entire philosophy of living. My cousin Dani and I watched it pretty much every day when we were kids. Scoot over." I tuck myself under the covers beside him. "Now. How far in are you?"

He sighs but adjusts to allow me to move closer until I'm practically in his lap. "Not far. He just finished breakfast."

"I'm so glad I came back early from that orgy," I say.

"Yeah. Me too," Hollis says. It sounds strangely genuine. But before I can question if he means it or if his sarcasm tuner's just broken, he pushes play.

Key West, Florida
New Year's 1944/1945

IT WAS ELSIE'S IDEA TO SPEND NEW YEAR'S EVE AT BOCA CHICA Beach. "It's quiet and beautiful," she said. "Best of all, there won't be pickled petty officers making passes at us all night."

"Should we invite some of the other girls?" Rose asked. She had been trying to spend more time with Elsie in a group instead of just the two of them, theorizing that the other women's presence would keep her from acting on the intrusive thoughts that were becoming increasingly explicit as her and Elsie's emotional connection grew.

She watched familiar lips stretch ever so slowly into a sly smile, and suddenly the past weeks of not allowing herself to hope—of brushing off Elsie's compliments and suggestive jokes as within the realm of normal female friendship, of telling herself that her desire was as one-sided as it had been with her best friend back in Oshkosh—all disappeared as reality transformed into the dreams Rose never believed could become anything more.

"I was hoping to ring in the new year with you," Elsie said. "Only with you."

Here was Elsie, with her sultry mouth and her chocolate-brown eyes that traveled conspicuously over Rose's body. It seemed impossible that Elsie had never looked at her this way before; the heat in her gaze was too familiar. Could it be because it mirrored Rose's own so exactly? It was like waking up and finding herself not in her cot on base but floating among the glimmering incandescence of a thousand stars.

At midnight, stretched out beside each other on an olive-drab Navy-issue wool blanket, Rose discovered that Elsie's mouth was salt and sun. It kissed her in sweet, lapping ripples and great crashing waves. Did all mermaids taste so deliciously of the sea or only hers?

"I have wanted to do that since the moment I saw you here, sitting so primly in the sand," Elsie whispered. "And I've wanted to do a lot more than that. Lately, I've thought of little else."

Joy and desire allowed Rose to smile, but her nerves reminded her that her knowledge of "more than that" was relatively limited. She had given her virginity to Dickie before he left for the Air Force—a hasty affair in his grandparents' hayloft, "like some sort of country girl cliché," she'd later joked—but that must be different than this. "I've never with a . . . I don't . . . You'll have to show me what to do," Rose said.

Elsie kissed her again, and Rose lost herself in the way the wet heat of their mouths matched the sensation between her legs.

Later they would laugh together at the way Rose made love as if training one of her birds—slow movements, touches both gentle and firm, ensuring she had documented every detail before finally allowing release—but in that moment, Rose felt much more like the pigeon: at peace in Elsie's embrace yet yearning for flight. Every touch lifted her higher into the air, urged her to take to the sky, to soar. And when her limbs grew heavy and her heart satisfied, she returned to the place—the person—she knew instinctively as her home.

As the sunshine unfurled from its slumber, shooting sparkles over the undulating sea, Rose and Elsie strolled along the beach, hand in hand. Rose never cared much for the way people spoke about New Year's. The passage of time didn't work so precisely, so tidily; a celebration couldn't do anything to prevent the problems and sorrows of the previous year from rolling over into the next. Yet on New Year's Day 1945, the air itself felt different. The year seemed alive with possibility and clarity in a way that all of her previous years on earth had not. Love surged through Rose's blood like a drug that made even the most absurd fantasies feel within reach. Maybe this year the war would end. Maybe this year would be the beginning of her new life—one with Elsie always by her side.

11

. . . . .

I AM HIGHLY SUGGESTIBLE WHEN IT COMES TO DREAMS, SO IT'S
not exactly unexpected that I'm dreaming about playing Penelope
again, but as an adult. And instead of my companion in my time-
traveling escapades being a CGI lizard named Newton, it's a sen-
tient crown of broccoli. We are touring the Alamo. Considering
I'm lying beside him and wearing his T-shirt, I was kind of hoping
to dream about Hollis. But you can't win them all.

Except now I'm not dreaming about anything, because I'm
suddenly awake thanks to a loud boom. As my sleepiness recedes,
I become aware of sheets of rain smacking against the window
like someone pleading to be let in. The boom must have been
thunder. What time is it? It seems way too dark in here for it to be
morning, even with a storm raging outside. There's an alarm clock
on the nightstand, but its digital display is black. Power must
be out.

I roll over as lightning flashes, lighting up the room in time for me to see Hollis close his eyes and grip the edge of the comforter tighter.

"Hollis?"

"Hm?"

"You okay?"

I can just make out his eyes opening cautiously, as if unsure what might await him. "Everything's fine," he says. "I'm fine. Go back to sleep."

Another deafening clap of thunder. It's so powerful the whole house trembles. Hollis's eyes snap shut again as he flinches. I lay my hand on his arm under the covers, and the tension in his muscles makes it feel like he's turned to granite.

"Hey, tell me," I whisper.

"Ahh," he says as if he's not sure he wants to say anything at all but it's coming out anyway. "I don't like thunderstorms at night. But it's fine. I'm fine. Let's sleep."

"Is it the noise, or . . . ?"

Hollis shakes his head. "When I was ten, our house was struck by lightning during a late-night storm like this. Whole place went up in flames."

"Oh god. That's terrible."

"Everyone made it out, but we lost almost everything. So I just have some . . . residual anxiety. About . . . about that. It's not a big deal."

It sounds like a big deal to me. The vulnerability in his voice and the way he's clutching the comforter as if he's debating diving beneath it and hiding makes him seem so young. Like a little boy who happens to have a really intense five—or whatever-the-hell-o'clock-it-is—shadow.

"Does anything help?" I ask. I guess I assumed fear was some-

thing he didn't believe in, like lasting love or the inherent goodness of others, so seeing him scared like this feels wrong. So
contrary to how he presents himself. If I'm sunshine, he's a constant low rumble of thunder. It's ironic, really, since that's probably
the last thing he'd want to be.

Even with his eyes closed, his muscles stiffen further as the
lightning flashes. "Not that I know of. I usually just have to ride it
out if I can't sleep through it."

"Okay. Well. I'm here. So I'll ride it out with you." I slide my
hand over his arm until I locate his fist. He doesn't put up a fight
when I pry the comforter from his grasp and intertwine our fingers. In fact, he squeezes hard when the next round of thunder
rolls through the room. Shifting closer, closer, until my body is
pressed flush against Hollis's side, I run my free left hand over his
hair. No idea what prompts me to do this except that my childhood dog, King Velociraptor—I saw *Jurassic Park* for the first time
the day before we got him—used to hate storms too, and petting
him usually kept him from whimpering and trying to burrow into
the couch cushions.

"It's okay," I whisper. "You're safe. I've got you." Which is
also, now that I think of it, what I used to say to my dog.

When the lightning next flashes, I begin to count aloud.
"One hippopotamus. Two hippopotamus. Three hippopotamus.
Four—"

"What are you doing?" he asks, staring up at me. I've adjusted
our joined hands so I can prop myself up on my right elbow and
lean over him for a better view of his face. I want to be able to
watch his expressions, monitor the tide of tension that flows in
and out of his jaw. And in this ultra-dark room, I have to be close
to see anything at all.

"Figuring out how far away it is. That way you can know when it's almost over."

"And? How far away is it?"

"I don't know. You interrupted me." I smile down at him, and to my surprise, he returns it with a small one of his own. Not the beautiful full-teeth one when something's really amusing, and not the begrudging one that only reaches the very corners of his mouth, but something fascinating in between. Something spontaneous and natural.

Hollis's fingers brush against my cheek. They find a strand of hair that's escaped from my messy bedtime bun and tuck it behind my ear, careful to avoid the bruise on my forehead—he must remember its location, because I doubt he can see the purple-and-blue splotch in the dark. Then his fingers drift to the nape of my neck. Feather-light, leaving goose bumps in their wake as they travel along my skin. If Thursday night on the police car was eleven, this has to be around thirty-five intimacies. But his jaw is relaxed now, his face no longer frozen in psychic pain, so thirty-five intimacies don't seem like too many. They may not even be enough, because Hollis's fingers have ceased their wandering and are now threaded into my hair, warm against my scalp. And they're pressing, gently, so gently, easing me down until our mouths meet. My eyes flutter shut as the next bolt of lightning illuminates the room. The thunder, when it comes an indeterminate number of hippopotamuses later, is even louder than before. It rattles the windowpanes. Yet Hollis's only response is to hold me tighter, to kiss me deeper, to—holy shit, to suck on my tongue.

This moment started sweet, but it's taking a swift turn toward dirty. And I am so here for it. Getting physically involved with Hollis is probably a terrible idea. A total mistake, considering, well . . . everything. Though it's not like my track record with casual sex is *bad*. Mostly because it's nonexistent. But if I can eat a fantastic slice of cake without wanting to grow old with it, I can do this. How different could it be?

I uncouple my right hand from his left, then lift myself to straddle his hips. My fingers are in his hair, and his are in mine. Except now they're not. I'd worry he was about to put an end to this if he wasn't kissing his way down my throat, which doesn't seem like something someone coming to his senses would be doing. Finally, he's touching me again, working his fingertips up my thigh at a leisurely pace that's driving me mad. They're creeping under the hem of my borrowed T-shirt, and then they're at the lace trim of my underwear, and then there's a flash of lightning and they freeze. Apparently, this is where their journey ends. It was fun while it lasted.

"Fuck," Hollis breathes against my neck. "God, Mill. I want . . ."

"What, what do you want?"

"I want to touch you. Please. Can I touch you?"

"Yes. Oh my god, yes."

"Where? Where can I?"

"Anywhere. Everywhere. Just touch me. Please. Or I'm going to . . . going to melt. And then I'll have to evaporate, and turn into a cloud, and Hollis, please, please just touch me so I don't have to be a cloud."

He smiles and it's another new one—an achingly soft one that makes me extra aware of every place on my body I want to feel him. "You are so strange and beautiful and . . . and *good* . . . and I don't know why you make so much sense when you shouldn't make any sense at all but, Mill, I need you so much."

It's probably mistaken in its lust-addled state, but my brain thinks that's the loveliest thing anyone has ever said to me. I crash my mouth back down onto his, where we ride out the next thunder boom, his left hand on my hip and his right one now cupping my breast under the T-shirt, thumb stroking my nipple until I gasp. He repeats the action on the other side, and I'm grateful for the symmetry, even if I'm increasingly eager to feel his fingers elsewhere.

"Please," I beg. "I need—"

"Hmm, I know. You need me here, right?" A fingertip traces down the front of my underwear, making me shiver. He looks up at me, waiting. "Not a rhetorical question, Mill. Talk to me."

"Yes. Yes, there."

Hollis's hand dives under the lace waistband. His fingers easily find the place where I need him, as if they've been here before and know the area well, like they're returning to a favorite vacation destination. Pleasure zings through my nerves, and Hollis's lips brush against mine, a whisper of a kiss as he slides his hand deeper into the front of my underwear and buries two fingers inside me. My breath hitches, and it makes him smirk.

"Ride my hand," he orders. "Show me how you like it."

It feels so good and so right having some part of him filling some part of me that I'm almost reluctant to move. But when he kisses me again, it changes the angle of his hand, and his fingers slip out a fraction of an inch, and my clit drags across his thumb. My body is now fully convinced of the possibilities. I move myself up and down his fingers slowly, aware even in the dark that his eyes are fully focused on me. He's become immune to the storm that's still raging outside. And oh god, this is the most gloriously powerful I've ever felt in my entire life.

"So you like it slow, huh?" He suddenly plunges his fingers deep again without waiting for me. They move back out, keeping my pace from before, and I focus on the sensation, which feels different somehow, better even, with him controlling it. Maybe because of the way he's crooking his fingertips so that they drag against every sensitive nerve on the way back out. "Is this what you want?"

"Yes. Yes."

"Is this all you want? Because I am happy to finger fuck you till kingdom come, Mill, but—"

"Your cock," I gasp. "I want your cock inside me."

"God, yes," he groans. "I was really hoping you'd say that."

I'm desperately aware of how empty I feel when he removes his hand from inside my underwear and rolls out from under me. His dark silhouette hurries to the armchair, where his duffel still sits. "It's really freakin' dark in here," he says absently as he digs through his bag. "But I have an entire box somewh—ah-ha. You best be naked for me by the time I get back to that bed, Millicent."

"Way ahead of you." My voice comes out breathy, and I'm pleased at how sexy I sound when I'm pretty sure I'm just hyperventilating a little.

I hear him tear open the box, cursing under his breath when it initially resists, and the barely-there sound of the foil ripping. It's impossible to see him shed his clothes and unroll the condom onto his erection, but just the thought of it is enough to make me ache with need. The mattress dips, and Hollis's warmth returns beside me. "You're sure about this?" he asks.

I nod.

"Millicent, it's very dark. I need words."

"I'm sure. I want you. I've wanted you for . . ." I have no idea if it's currently Friday or Saturday, so I settle on the less specific but still accurate "for days."

"Good, then we have something in common. Come here." His arm snakes around my waist, and he grabs a handful of my bare ass. My mouth finds his again after a brief detour along his shoulder and up his neck, and Hollis rolls on top of me. He threads our fingers and presses our joined hands into the pillow. When a bolt of lightning gives the room a momentary glow, I watch for him to tense up, for his eyes to clamp shut like before. But they remain open, trained on my face.

"You're gorgeous," he says. "So gorgeous." And he kisses me deeply as he slides inside me, inch by incredible inch.

When I've taken him in completely, he bites his lower lip and groans as he makes a few exploratory movements. "God. You feel good. So damn good."

Josh used to say things like that to me before he drilled his dick into me with absolutely no regard for what I wanted or needed. *You're so warm and tight, how do you expect me to hold back, Millie?* Or *I can't slow down when you feel this good, Millie.* As hard as I try to banish my ex-boyfriend from my head, I wince at Hollis's words. My body tenses out of habit, preparing itself to take whatever's given.

Hollis stills above me. "Hey," he says. "You good?"

I'm speechless for a moment as I register his question. Hollis is paying such close attention to my body that he can *feel* my thoughts? "Yeah, I just . . . I haven't done this in a while."

"Don't worry. I'm a pro."

I want to laugh, to joke about how "pro" is probably not the right word here unless he's got a side hustle he hasn't told me about yet. But before I can make a sound, he ducks his head and sucks my nipple into his mouth at the same time he withdraws almost all the way. I gasp instead.

His grin is devilish when he looks back at me before moving to the other nipple. Just enough of his cock is still inside me to make me aware that I want it all, and I grab his ass to pull him back, urging him closer.

Hollis's hot breath skims over my neck and tickles my ear. As he looks into my eyes, seeing me through the dark—really *seeing* me—I wonder if casual sex is always so . . . romantic. Maybe all good sex is on some level, and I just haven't experienced enough of it to know. I'll have to ask Dani later; she has more experience with these things. Right now, I need to focus on the way Hollis is hitting just the right spot with each slow thrust and retreat, lighting me up like an expert pinball player going for the high score on his favorite machine. This needs to be about sensations, not about feelings. I know that much at least.

I'm still clutching his ass, and digging my nails in a bit, which he seems to like since he moans when I do it harder. I explore up his back, testing different pressures and places until I find a spot on his shoulder blades that makes him momentarily falter. "Shit," he says.

"Good or bad?"

"Good. So good."

"You can go faster," I say, a bit annoyed with myself for how much I enjoy his praise. "If you need to. I can take it."

He stares down at me for a moment. "I would love to take you hard and fast, Mill, don't get me wrong. If *you* want me to go faster, I will. But . . . but I can tell you like it like this, the same pace you set when you fucked yourself with my fingers. This is how you like it tonight, isn't it? This is what's going to make you come for me?"

He thrusts back into me and drags out again, slow enough for me to savor the friction.

All I manage is a little whining sound in the back of my throat.

"I love the way you whimper a little every time I move into you, like you were losing your mind waiting for me. In fact . . ." Hollis stops moving his hips, refusing to thrust deeper. "I think you might like being teased a little."

"No," I protest. "I want . . . I want you to . . . Dammit. Please."

"Wrap your legs around me," he whispers.

And I obey. Of course I obey. Because Hollis is turning out to be the exact opposite of Josh in bed. I know I'm too trusting in general so it's not saying much, but I trust him completely, and I want to go anywhere he'll take me because I'm so certain he'll only take me places he knows I'll like.

My legs pull him deep and restrict his movement enough that he can't leave me again. He sets a new pace, faster but not hard, his fingers working between us and his cock stroking that perfect spot over and over and over while his lips press against mine until I come hard, trembling, gasping into his mouth. I tighten my legs around his back and dig my nails into his shoulders. He comes deep inside my body, muttering a long string of profanity that certainly has all twenty-five Jesuses glaring at us (if they weren't already).

As soon as he's recovered his wits, Hollis reaches between us to ensure the condom remains in place as he pulls out and topples over beside me on the bed. My heartbeat is loud inside my skull, the only thing I hear except our heavy breathing.

"I think the storm's over," I say.

"Oh. Right. I . . ." He releases a small huff of laughter. "I forgot all about it. Thanks for . . . God, thanks for that." His hand finds my hip and gives me a light pat of appreciation, then settles into a hypnotic back-and-forth rhythm over the skin there.

"Well. Now you know that there is something that helps. For next time."

"Mm," he says.

"Guess I'll have to sleep with you every night for the rest of your life, just in case the weather turns." As soon as the words leave my mouth, all of the tension Hollis helped me shed jolts back into my muscles. His hand stills on my hip. "That was a joke," I say in a hurry. "Not a funny one, though. Don't worry. I understand—that is, I know that you—that I—we aren't—"

His mouth is on mine in the next instant, sweet and warm. He kisses me until my body goes languid again, forcing my mind to follow suit.

"I had fun," he says. "Did you have fun?"

"Yes." Actually, "fun" seems like an incredible understatement for what I had, but it's impossible to formulate a more accurate description at the moment.

"Good." He makes a quiet, throaty sound as he removes the condom. "Do you want the bathroom first or second?"

"First." My toes find the rug and my feet drop the extra inch with a thud. After I locate my discarded T-shirt and underwear pretty much by feel alone since the power still isn't back on, I move to the bathroom door, tripping over the rug on the way.

Inside the windowless bathroom, I stare into the mirror, even though it's much too dark to see my reflection. I wonder what this version of myself looks like, the Millie who has spontaneous sex with her gruff traveling companion. Based on what I can feel, all I can tell is that she has really disheveled hair.

I'm relieved Hollis didn't let me keep rambling on, making everything worse. At the same time, I'm aware that the reason he knew how to keep me calm is because he's probably been in this exact situation countless times before. He knows how to maintain his postcoital cool. Because what was earth-shattering for me was just another Friday night for him. In fact, if luck were on his side, he would have been with Yeva tonight instead of with me. I'm sure Yeva is never awkward after sex. She seems so self-possessed and sophisticated.

Shit. Yeva. Have I broken some part of the unwritten Lady Code by sleeping with Hollis when they had a sex appointment on the books? Another thing I have to run by Dani. Then again, Dani was the one telling me to go for it in the first place, so maybe this is within the bounds of acceptable. And if it wasn't, Hollis is the one who should have known that and not started kissing me in the first place. Right?

Ugh. I thought the point of keeping things casual was that it was supposed to be *less* complicated.

"Hey," I say, pointing to the mirror in reproach even though I can only make out a vague outline of my head. "You knew what you were getting into. This is what you wanted. Now stop freaking out and go pee so you don't get a UTI."

When I leave the bathroom, Hollis is a shadowy figure sitting on the edge of the bed. He grabs my wrist as I pass by and pulls me over.

"You okay?" he asks.

"Yeah, I'm . . . I'm great." Especially great now that his warm skin is against mine again and the wiry hair of his thighs is tickling my bare legs.

"Are you sure? I heard you talking to yourself in there."

"I wasn't talking to myself," I say.

"Who were you talking to then?"

"Uh. Someone else?"

"Someone else is in our bathroom?" His hand finds my jaw and his thumb brushes over my bottom lip. "Hmm. You're awful calm about that."

"You know me," I say. "Friendly to a fault."

He stands and kisses me softly. "Nothing's changed between us, Millicent. You don't need to overthink this."

"I know. I know."

"Good." He plants a kiss on my palm before releasing my wrist. The sweetness of the gesture only confuses me further.

Once he's in the bathroom, I tuck myself into the lavender-and-sex-scented sheets and reach for my phone. It's 2:42 AM, which means Dani is definitely still awake. Probably just finished up her shift at the New York City hotel bar where she works.

MILLIE: I had sex with Hollis.

DANI: Get it giiiiirrrlll.

DANI: How was it???

MILLIE: Sort of . . . amazing.

DANI: 😻😻😻😻😻

MILLIE: Except I don't know what to do now. I've never done the casual thing before.

DANI: What you do now is him, as often as possible until the end of your trip.

MILLIE: He's on his way to have sex with someone else though.

DANI: Aren't many of us when you truly think about it?

MILLIE: Are you high?

DANI: Extremely.

High Dani's advice tends to be too philosophical to be immediately useful. Besides, I hear the bathroom door opening, and I don't need Hollis to know I'm panic texting my cousin about what we did. I shove the phone under my pillow, turn onto my side, and channel all of my long-dormant acting skills to feign sleep until it actually arrives.

12

. . . . .

I'M ALONE WHEN THE ALARM ON MY PHONE GOES OFF AT SEVEN.
There's no sound from the bathroom, no sound anywhere in the
room really, except for the steady hum of the air conditioner. Hollis must be elsewhere already this morning. The lace curtains do
little to block out the sunlight, which floods the room and illuminates all of the Jesus paintings. Really, how the hell did we do what
we did last night with all of these eyes on us? I've never been so
retroactively thankful for a power outage.

As I sit up and stretch, I become increasingly, painfully, aware
of how sore my limbs are. Not from the sex, but because I kept my
body rigid as I slept, balancing on the edge of the mattress to
avoid accidentally touching Hollis. The last thing I wanted was
him thinking I was trying to cuddle. I might not know much
about how this is supposed to work, but I know it's *wham, bam,
thank you ma'am*, not *wham, bam, thank you; now do you want to be the big
spoon or the little spoon?*

My phone has a handful of work emails that can wait a few days and a text notification from Dani that she sent a few hours after our brief conversation. It says: It's only complicated if you make it complicated, cuz. Dani's straightforward advice is so different from the way Mrs. Nash helped me navigate the gray areas of my problems that the grief that sits dormant inside my heart like a daffodil bulb in winter threatens to send up a tender green shoot. I try to conjure in my head an image of my best friend, sitting in her favorite palm tree–patterned chair by the apartment's picture window. But while I can imagine her in perfect detail, she only smiles back at me, not saying a word. I'm as lost as I was all those times I came to her seeking advice, except now I can't even hope that she'll help me find my way.

I glance over at my backpack, slung across the back of the desk chair. Mrs. Nash can't help me anymore, but I can still help her one last time. That's why I'm going to ride two miles per hour in a convertible and wave to people later this morning. So I should probably shower now because it's going to take a good three hours to locate an outfit worthy of a parade grand marshal.

Except I guess while I was blow-drying my hair, Hollis snuck back into the room, because there's suddenly a Kelly green sheath dress hanging from the front of the armoire. I clutch my towel tighter around my body as I approach it. The tag inside is faded, like it might be vintage. It looks close to my size, but the only way to know is to try it. My underwear and bra are sitting on top of my suitcase where I left them before my shower, so I drop the towel and put them on. Then I gently remove the green dress from the hanger and step into it.

The door opens when the dress is covering only my bottom

half. For a second I startle, trying to cover my chest with my arms. But Hollis appears in the doorway, leaning on the frame as his eyes sweep slowly from my bare feet up to my eyes.

"I've seen you naked, Millicent," he says. "You don't need to hide your bra from me."

"You've *felt* me naked. You couldn't *see* much of anything last night."

"Semantics. The point is, I already know what's going on under there." He latches the door and pads over to where I'm standing by the armoire. "Turn around."

When I do, he coaxes the dress up until my arms are through the holes. Then he zips me up. But none of it is especially sensual. His movements aren't slow and deliberate so much as efficient. It's more reminiscent of how one would dress a toddler than seduce a lover.

"Hollis," I say, deciding honesty is the only way I'm going to get through this, "I don't understand how this works."

"It's a dress. It covers your body. There's not much more to it."

"No. Not— I understand clothing, thanks. I do not understand how this works between us now."

"Oh. I told you last night. Nothing's changed."

"Maybe not emotionally, but *something* has changed. You didn't dress me yesterday morning."

"I would have if you asked."

"You know what I mean. Like you said, you know what's going on under here." I gesture wildly in the direction of my chest. "You stroll over and touch me in a way you never would have done before we . . ."

"Before we fucked. It's okay to say it, you know."

"Before we fucked," I say, trying to say every syllable as precisely as I can to show I'm unafraid. "I understand how to talk to you. But I don't know what the rules are for the physical parts of this. How do we know if or when we're going to do it again? Who can touch whom and in what contexts? I've never done the casual-sex thing. And you do it constantly. I need guidance so I don't get it wrong and do irreparable damage to our friendship."

"I do it *constantly*?" He huff-laughs. "Just how much game do you think I have?"

"Hollis. Please. Tell me the rules."

"The rules?"

"Yes."

"Okay." He dips his head to position his lips close to my ear. His voice is low, intimate. "Rule one. Open communication—always. For example, if I want to get you out of this nice dress that Connie thought you might want to wear for the parade today, and then make you come on my tongue, I will communicate that to you and ask if that's something you're up for. And then you will say yes or no or maybe propose something different. Consent is never assumed, and we can each change our minds at any time and for any reason."

"W-what's rule two?"

"Rule two is be safe. And rule three is have fun. That's about it." He lightly nibbles my earlobe. "So what do you say, Mill? Can I find out how you taste?"

I squeeze my eyes closed, overwhelmed by the liquid heat pooling between my legs. "Oh. Shit. I thought that was hypothetical."

"No, I meant it as an actual right-now proposition."

"Oh." *It's only complicated if you make it complicated.* Dani's text flashes in my brain. I wait for Mrs. Nash's words to do the same, my memory searching for some past advice that might apply enough to act as the angel to the devil Dani on my shoulder. But the only thing I find is *always do what is right for you.* And what is right for me at this moment—according to my body, if not my brain—is Hollis's mouth. I reach back and grab his wrist, then turn it so I can read the time on his watch. Hours and hours still before I have to be ready for the parade. "Yes, I am amenable to that."

The dress's zipper slides back down, this time with Hollis's lips on the back of my neck and his other hand caressing my exposed skin. With a little shimmying, the green fabric puddles at my feet.

"Is this you finally being nice?" I ask.

"No," he whispers into my ear. "This is me being extremely, extremely selfish."

I'm fully naked with little fanfare, Hollis pausing only long enough to confirm that yes, those are dogs wearing sunglasses printed on my underwear. He guides me toward the bed, gently pushing me onto my back before dragging me by the hips to the edge of the mattress. After setting his glasses on the chest at the foot of the bed, his tongue skims along my inner thigh and makes my legs turn to jelly in anticipation. But inches from his ultimate destination, he pauses and stands abruptly.

"What's wrong?" I ask. This is really not the reaction you want someone having when confronted with your vagina.

"Sorry. I was raised Southern Baptist and I . . ." Hollis mutters as he climbs onto the bed behind me and reaches up. "Can't with the . . . them staring." He flips the Jesus paintings over, then moves on to the next grouping of them, and the next, until all twenty-five have been forced to avert their eyes.

I laugh the entire time, deep belly laughs as he frowns in his very Hollis way as he encounters each one. "Now," he says when he sinks to his knees beside the bed again, "let's make that worth the trouble it's going to be to flip them all back around again."

13

· · · · ·

MY TWO FAVORITE THINGS ABOUT THE GADSLEY BROCCOLI FES-
tival parade are that the procession is short, so I will be able to
hear the marching band playing "Tusk" behind me the entire
time, and that someone has given me a silky PARADE GRAND MAR-
SHAL sash and a flower crown with broccoli florets tucked into the
arrangement.

"Look!" I call to Hollis from my place in the back of the white
convertible as we wait in the staging area. I point to my head. "Do
you get it?"

"No," he says. He's standing a few feet away on the sidewalk, his
arms crossed over his chest, frown firmly in place. For a man who
got laid not two hours ago, he sure looks grumpy again. It's actually
kind of impressive how dedicated he is to being a curmudgeon.

"It's a *broccoli crown*!"

He shrugs as if to say *so what?*

"The way broccoli is harvested, you know, like the bunches.
That's called a crown. So it's a pun."

Hollis rolls his eyes.

"Maybe you'd have known that if you hadn't unsubscribed from Broccoli Facts," I say just as the car dealership owner driving the convertible turns the key in the ignition. That at least tugs at the corners of Hollis's lips.

No doubt he's remembering this morning. After he brought me to orgasm with his mouth, he told me not to worry about him even though it was obvious he was hard. So when he began turning the paintings above the bed back around, I grabbed for my phone and texted him that California is the United States's primary producer of broccoli. He read the text and got the stormiest, sexiest look on his face.

"No. No more broccoli facts. No more."

"Had a feeling you might say that," I said. And then I hit send on a draft I prepared just for this moment:

The heaviest broccoli on record was grown in 1993. It was 35 lbs. 🥦

"Millicent," he said through clenched teeth as his phone buzzed on the nightstand. "If that's another broccoli fact, I swear to god."

"What are you gonna do about it?" I asked, daring him with my smile.

Suddenly, he was over my naked body, kissing me hard. "Gonna block your number, first of all," he mumbled against my lips. And then I felt him smile.

"What's second of all?"

My face heats at the memory of what Hollis proposed and proceeded to do to me. I fan myself with my hand, hoping the cool air will dissolve the flush of my cheeks.

"Little hotter down here than y'all're used to up north, huh?" the mayor says beside me.

"Ha, yeah." Gadsley is currently a balmy seventy degrees. But I'm too grateful for the excuse to mention that I'm originally from Southern California or that DC is technically south of the Mason-Dixon line and gets a lot hotter than this (with way higher humidity) once summer hits in earnest.

The parade should last about twenty minutes—which is the amount of time it takes to travel the length of Gadsley's Main Street at a leisurely pace on foot—and I bask in the warmth of the midday sun and the crowd's attention as we go. Because as much as I value my personal privacy, I always did love an audience. The only other time I was in a parade was when I rode on the Pringles float in New York on Thanksgiving Day 2003. Now that was a throng. But this is a much more manageable four hundred or so people, all lining the sidewalks and waving back at me like we're neighbors. Ryan the Hepcat did a great job with the band, and even after hearing the same song on repeat for a quarter of an hour, I'm not at all tired of it.

Still, I keep catching myself wishing we could speed up, get to the end already, because we're wasting too much time. In the shower this morning, I thought again about calling the nursing facility before we get back on the road. But like the last time I considered it, the idea left me a little nauseated. Then Hollis distracted me from giving the matter much more of my attention, for which I was grateful. Hey, maybe I could get Hollis to call. It's cowardly, but it also feels less insurmountable than having to ask the question and hear the answer myself.

Hollis is waiting for me at the end of the parade route, typing on his phone.

"How'd you get here?" I ask. "You were at the staging area before."

"I walked," he says, sliding his phone back into his pocket. "Y'all were going like two miles an hour. It wasn't exactly difficult to keep up."

"Were you watching me the whole time? That's kind of creepy, dude."

"I was sending an email, if you must know." Hollis frowns one of his very deepest frowns as he holds out a hand. "Are you going to get out of that car so we can get going, or are you going to keep interrogating me?"

I lay my palm against his, and my warm skin turns hot at the touch. Hollis wraps an arm around my waist and lifts me down from the convertible. Our faces are close together when he sets my feet on the ground. He looks like he wants to kiss me, and I definitely want to kiss him. But he lets go of me and takes a step back.

"There are newspaper people here," he says. "And I saw a few local TV news vans."

"Yeah? Well, good. Then Ryan and the mayor are getting the publicity they wanted."

"I just meant that I probably shouldn't be seen with you. In case the media thinks we're together. That's not the kind of attention you signed up for."

I smile and fiddle with the zipper of his hoodie. "Well. That's very considerate of you. But I'm nowhere near famous enough for anyone to care who I'm involved with. That was kind of Josh's whole point in doing what he did."

Hollis crosses his arms over his chest, cutting off my zipper access. "Still. I don't think it's a good idea."

"Wait. Is this about Yeva?" I slap my palms against my forehead, wincing when I hit the bruise strategically hidden under a swoop of hair and fifty layers of concealer. "You don't want her to see you with me. That's the real reason, isn't it?"

How do I keep forgetting about Yeva? If cutting in front of someone to ride a roller coaster is bad, cutting in front of someone to ride their sex friend is probably like a hundred times worse. "I knew this was a terrible idea," I groan. "And I'm a terrible person."

"What? No. There's no need to freak out. Don't—" Hollis steps toward me again.

"Do I need to apologize to her? Send her like . . . some flowers or something? Maybe an Edible Arrangements? Does she have any allergies?"

"What are you even— Mill. Look at me."

I squeeze my eyes closed in defiance, refusing to be talked down from my panic.

"Millicent." His voice is a low, frustrated growl, the kind that turns me on a little. He snakes his arms around my waist and draws me against him. "Open your eyes and look at me."

I open a single eye to find Hollis staring down into it.

"Don't worry about Yeva," he says. "This has nothing to do with her."

"You're just trying to make me feel better about cutting in line."

"Cutting in line?"

"Yeah. If you were a roller coaster—"

Hollis cuts me off with a grumbled "For god's sake." His hands come to my face before his lips press against mine with enough pressure to communicate that this is mostly about getting me to shut up and stop spiraling. But soon the kiss shifts to a leisurely, soft exploration of mouths. And whoops, we're making out in the middle of Main Street, surrounded by dozens of people.

A wolf whistle from someone in the crowd brings us back to reality some indeterminate amount of time later. I try to jump back from Hollis, to put space between us as if it will make any difference now. But he holds me against him, and says softly into my ear, "Guess we'll find out if you're right about not being famous enough for anyone to care."

I'M NOT FAMOUS ENOUGH FOR ANYONE TO CARE. OR RATHER, I wouldn't be. Except it turns out that when someone takes a video of two people sharing a passionate kiss at the end of a parade route, and one of them is the parade's grand marshal who is wearing a flower crown that includes raw broccoli florets, it gets a bit of traction online. Because apparently, even though Hollis and I are not a couple, we are somehow still *hashtag couple goals* and *so obviously in love.* The slack-jawed freckled kid in the background who drops his ice cream cone when Hollis squeezes my butt cheek only added to the speed with which the thing went viral.

A half hour after the original post on Twitter, the grand marshal thing got lost in the absurd game of telephone that is the internet. So thanks to the crown on my head, I've been dubbed the Broccoli Princess (although one retweet called me the Green Goddess, which I thought was inspired). Anyway, someone finally put two and two together and figured out Broccoli Princess equaled Millicent Watts-Cohen. So now social media is filled with *Penelope to the Past* hot takes and stills of my awkward teenaged body in the infamous yellow bikini.

"Stop looking at it," Hollis says for the third time from the driver's seat of Ryan's lime-green Kia Soul. "You're just going to get upset or skeeved out."

I go deeper down the rabbit hole of retweets and quote tweets and—oh geez, there's already a parody of it with two guys who have a comedy podcast or something. The bearded one is playing me and their dog is the kid in the background. It's actually pretty hilarious.

"How did you wind up using my phone for this anyway?" Hollis mumbles.

"You have the app. It's easier to use."

"You can get it on your phone too, you know."

"Then I'd need to make an account. No thanks, I'll just keep using yours," I say.

No one's figured out Hollis's identity yet, as far as I can tell. I hope that means Yeva won't see the video. Hollis may have told me not to worry about her, but I can't help wondering if my horniness is going to cause her distress. I'm about to bring it up again, to ask if Hollis is sure Yeva won't be upset, if their arrangement explicitly accommodates this sort of thing, when Hollis's phone buzzes in my hand.

Please don't be Yeva again. Please don't be—

Well, it's not Yeva. But someone's figured out the man in the video is Hollis Hollenbeck.

JOSH YAEGER: What the hell do you think you're doing, Hollenbeck?

Seeing my ex's name makes my stomach dip. "Uh. Hollis. You have a text from . . ."

JOSH YAEGER: I know you want to be me and have whatever
I have but this is taking it too far.

"From . . . ?" Hollis coaxes.

"Josh."

"Oh." He huff-laughs. "What does that asshole want?"

I watch the phone's screen, my hand trembling as I wait to see
if another message will come through. "He must've seen the video.
I think he's pretty upset."

"Good."

JOSH YAEGER: If you want to stick your dick in crazy, be my
guest. She's a terrible lay anyway.

The words shoot fury into my chest at the same time they
make my self-assurance feel like peeling wallpaper that could
come down with one good tug. I've already become so used to the
way Hollis makes me lean into the strongest parts of myself that I
forgot how easy it is to be stripped down to something faded and
fragile.

JOSH YAEGER: You should know she's only using you to get
back at me. Must've heard that's all you're good for.

Between reading the comments about the Broccoli Festival
parade video and now this, I think I've punished myself enough
for one day. I put Hollis's phone in the empty cup holder and stare
out the window as we travel down the highway. Hollis is focused
on the road, his exaggerated arch of a frown curving more se-

verely as the opening notes of "Sister Golden Hair" come through the speakers. If we weren't in a completely different car and I didn't now have a bruised forehead and a thorough mental map of Hollis's naked body, it would be as if the last two days never happened. But they did, and we're now twenty-four hours past my original intended arrival time at the nursing facility. We're not even through South Carolina yet.

"Hey," I say. "Will you do me a gigantic favor?"

"Depends," he answers.

"On?"

"If I want to do it."

I roll my eyes but honestly appreciate this evidence that nothing really *has* changed between us.

"What is it?" he asks.

"Would you call the place where Elsie is and check if she . . . if she's . . . Would you see how she's doing? I can't seem to make myself do it. I'm too afraid of what they'll say."

"Oh," he says. "Yeah. I can do that. Next time we stop?"

I exhale, relieved. "That'd be great. Thanks."

We're silent for a moment, and I can almost hear his brain formulating the question that eventually comes out of his mouth.

"What will you do if—"

"If I'm too late?" I finish.

"Yeah."

I shrug. "I don't know. I've been trying not to think about it."

"Will you still go to Key West? Or head home?"

The part of me that will be crushed will want to turn around and go home. But the other part of me, the one that needed to take this trip in the first place, will demand I continue to Key West anyway. Then I can at least find a place there to lay my three table-spoons of Mrs. Nash to rest. I mean, it'd be silly to take her back to DC after we've come so far.

"I'll still go," I say. "Just for a few hours. To scatter the ashes, at least."

"And if Elsie is still around? What's the plan then?"

"Reunite her and Mrs. Nash, of course. Talk to her, if she's able and willing. I have so many questions. I want to hear everything about her life. I know the basics from the research I did to find her, but there's only so much government records and a few news-paper articles can tell you."

There were US Navy reports about what happened in Korea, though they were too official to go into detail about the situation beyond stating there was an "administrative error." After that, Elsie Brown popped up in the *Yale Daily News* in an article on women students at the medical school, and then in the acknowl-edgments in a few surgical medicine journal articles. From there, I figured out that she spent most of her career as a trauma surgeon at a hospital near Fort Lauderdale, and that she retired in the early '80s. I thought that was where the paper trail ended, and it wasn't exactly easy to find any relatives, with her last name being so com-mon. Then this past Wednesday morning, I came across a brief feature in the *Key West Citizen* acknowledging her recent 101st birthday, which is how I learned she's been living at The Palms at Southernmost for the last five years.

Oh my god. I think I've found her, I said to the box of ashes sitting beside my laptop when I got to the last line of the article. The Mrs. Nash in my head responded with a beatific smile.

"Right," Hollis says absently as he changes lanes to pass a slow station wagon in front of us.

"But I'll probably stay until . . . until the end if I can. I don't know if she has any remaining extended family. So I want to make sure she has a friend there with her at least."

"I'll need to get back on the road by Saturday," Hollis says. "I'm teaching a summer writing class that starts the next Monday."

I can't understand why he's telling me this unless . . . "Oh! Don't worry about me. I figured you'd keep Ryan's car, take it back to Gadsley to pick up yours whenever you're done in Miami. I'm just going to get a rental car, then fly home as originally planned. Easier than trying to align our itineraries, especially since I have no idea when I'm heading back. I wouldn't ask you to leave Yeva early or hang around extra days waiting for me."

"Millicent, I'm not—"

"Fuck." The thought of Hollis with Yeva sends a little pang of jealousy through me that has me wanting to hold my backpack to my chest like a shield. But when I search the floorboard by my feet, it isn't there. "Fuck," I repeat. "I lost my backpack. I must've— shit. We have to—we have to go back. I have to find it."

"Are you sure it's not in the back seat, or in the trunk with the suitcases, or—"

"Yes, I'm sure. I must've left it at the B&B. Shit. Shit. What if it's not there? What if Mrs. Nash is in a dump somewhere or halfway to Canada, along with my phone, my money, my driver's license . . . my National Archives researcher card! Oh god, Hollis, this means I don't have any ID. If we die in this borrowed car there'll be no way to identify my body except dental records, and I haven't been to the dentist in so long. What if my teeth have changed too much and my family never knows what happened to me? They'll search and search for me, thinking I'm just missing, never knowing—"

"Millicent," Hollis says, laying his hand on my thigh. I think it's supposed to soothe me, but his touch sends an inconvenient flare of electricity through my leg. "I am sure your backpack is safe and waiting for you at Connie and Bud's. And if it isn't, it's somewhere else in Gadsley. We'll find it. Okay?"

I force myself to take a deep breath to subdue both the panic and the arousal now competing for my attention. "Okay."

"And I have my wallet in my pocket. So if we die, they'll be able to ID me. Enough people know we're traveling together at this point that they'll know who you are."

"Well, that's a relief."

The dashboard clock reads 1:21. We've been on the road for almost an hour; driving back to Gadsley, finding my backpack, and getting back to wherever we currently are is going to add over two hours to our travel today. "Dammit," I whisper. "Dammit, dammit, dammit."

Hollis takes the next exit and immediately gets back on the highway heading in the opposite direction. "Hey, at least you noticed now and not when we were halfway through Florida."

My head snaps up and around to stare at this alien in the driver's seat. His eyes shift over to glance at me for a split second before they return to the road. "Who the hell are you?" I ask. "And what did you do with my super-hot but absurdly pessimistic travel buddy?"

"Just because I usually choose not to focus on silver linings does not mean I don't have the ability to find them when I want to."

"Well, stop it. The role reversal's making me uncomfortable." I try not to focus on how finding the silver lining to make me feel better is apparently something Hollis *wants* to do. "You should be extremely annoyed with me right now. I've just delayed your sex appointment with Yeva by at least another two hours."

Hollis's frown deepens. "Enough of this. Get my phone."

"Why?"

"I need you to look at my texts with her. Scroll up to last night's."

I've already grabbed his phone, but now I lay it facedown on my leg; I have zero desire to see any more of Yeva than I already have. "Sorry, but I really do not want to read your sexts with another woman. I'm trying to be chill about this stuff, but I cannot be *that* chill."

"Oh my god, Millicent, they aren't—just read the damn texts."

I sigh, brace myself for any explicit pictures that might be waiting for me, and navigate to the conversation with Yeva Markarian.

YEVA: Updated ETA?

That text arrived yesterday evening. Probably what made his phone buzz on the nightstand right as Pee-wee arrived at the Alamo. Hollis glanced at it and set it back down without responding. But apparently he did send something back eventually, because there's a reply with a time stamp of 10:12 PM.

HOLLIS: Hey. Really sorry to do this to you, but I'm not going to make it after all.

YEVA: ☹ Everything ok?

HOLLIS: Yeah mostly. A friend has to visit someone in hospice and I'd like to be there for her.

YEVA: Oh wow all right. Sorry to hear that . . .

HOLLIS: Yeah. Sorry again. Hope I didn't screw up your week.

YEVA: No worries, we'll catch up some other time. It's important to be there for your friend xo

HOLLIS: Thanks xo

The first thing my brain latches onto is the exchange of "xo"s and how I wish they weren't there. But it quickly shifts to the bigger picture, that Hollis canceled his sex appointment to come with me to see Elsie. And he made that decision post–*Pee-wee*, pre-intercourse.

"Hollis . . . this is really sweet of you," I say.

"I'm not trying to be sweet. I'm trying to get you to stop worrying about me and Yeva because there is no me and Yeva. There's only me and you right now."

I know he doesn't mean anything romantic by that, but my too-soft heart does a tiny pirouette anyway. "You may not be trying to be sweet, but you're still succeeding," I say. "And Yeva didn't seem all that surprised by you doing a nice thing for someone. Total secret cinnamon roll. I knew it."

Hollis lets out a heavy sigh, and his right hand moves from the steering wheel to his earlobe. "Why did I agree to spend more time with you?"

"Because I'm delightful."

"That's debatable."

"Are you sure you want to come to Key West?" I ask, wanting

to give him an out in case he's actually regretting his decision. "I'll be okay alone if you'd rather—"

"Yes, I'm sure. I want to be there when you reunite Mrs. Nash and Elsie."

"But why? You don't believe in any of this lasting love stuff." Is he really going to come to Key West with me just to rub it in my face if it turns out Elsie doesn't care? That seems cruel, and Hollis can be a jerk for sure, but he's given no sign of being intentionally sadistic.

He glances at me for a second, then returns his attention to the road. "Maybe I'd like to be convinced that I'm wrong."

Key West, Florida
March 1945

ONE WARM MORNING IN MARCH, ROSE AND ELSIE CLIMBED INTO A small rowboat. They had borrowed it from the local fisherman Elsie befriended at a local bar when she drank him under the table. Rose told her friends when she returned to her quarters that the fish weren't biting that day, but she had no way of truly knowing since neither she nor Elsie ever cast their lines. Instead, they spent hours anchored in the Boca Chica Channel, southwest of the air base, letting the gentle sway of the placid water lull them into the illusion that they were alone in the world. Rose would look back on those first few hours in the boat, with hers and Elsie's legs tangled together as they kissed and laughed and touched, as some of the very best moments of her life.

Elsie twisted Rose's dark hair in her fingers. "Do you have anyone back home?" she asked, and Rose started at the way the question cracked the protective shell of the moment.

"What do you mean?"

"A fella, maybe? Someone you like. Someone you . . . love?"

Elsie wrapped her arms around Rose's shoulders in response to the sudden tension in her lover's body. She kissed the side of her neck as if in apology, though she continued, "It's all right, you know. I don't mind."

Perhaps it was wrong, but it had been easy enough for Rose to keep Elsie and Dickie in separate compartments in her heart and in her head. Examined apart, her love for Dickie and her love for Elsie seemed so different: Dickie was safe contentment, shared history, and an uncomplicated future. Elsie was all wild joy and passion, the here and now, the thrilling and terrifying full spectrum of possibility. Speaking of her love for Dickie as if it could compete or compare with her love for Elsie somehow cheapened her feelings for both of them. She resented the way Elsie forced her to tear down the dividers and confront her love as a murky, indiscriminate, traitorous thing.

"Tell me about him," Elsie whispered, and it was something like shame that made Rose comply.

Rose let her eyes flutter closed to better summon the image of the petite boy that years of farmwork had transformed into the broad-shouldered and handsome man with whom she had once been eager to share her body and spend her life. "His name's Dickie. Dickie Nash. His grandparents own the farm beside our house in Oshkosh. We were very close growing up, and everyone used to joke we'd marry one day. But . . ."

Elsie raised her blonde brows, summoning Rose to continue.

"The war started and Dickie joined the Army Air Forces. He's stationed somewhere near Palermo."

"You don't keep in touch?" Elsie asked, her fingers brushing up and down Rose's arm in a hypnotizing rhythm that Rose presumed was supposed to be comforting.

The sun came out from behind a cloud and exacerbated the heat taking over Rose's face. "He writes to me. Sometimes. When he can."

"And do you write him back?"

"I don't know why you want to know this," Rose said, shifting until she was no longer in Elsie's embrace. She wrote Dickie weekly at least, even writing of Elsie on occasion—not the truth of what they did together and were to each other, of course, but it was impossible to leave Elsie out of her letters completely when she took up so much of Rose's days and thoughts. "You know how I feel about you."

"And you know I feel the same." Elsie's hand reached for hers, and Rose let her take it though her guilt made her feel unworthy of touching and being touched. "But I think you should still consider marrying Dickie Nash."

"You want me to marry someone else?"

Perhaps Elsie heard the heartbreak in Rose's voice, because she gathered her close again and spoke hurriedly as if trying to get to the end of something painful. "Well, it's not as if I can marry you. Rosie, I would love *nothing* more than to spend the rest of our days together, just like this. But I know you want other things out of life. You've told me how much you want children."

Rose had feared the moment she would have to choose between traveling the expected path with Dickie and the unknown one with Elsie, but she saw now that she'd been naive to believe that choice would ever be hers to make. Still, she desperately attempted to fight her way through the panic tightening her chest. "I do want children, yes. But we could have children together. You wouldn't have to give up your dreams of becoming a doctor. You could still work while I care for them. I'm sure there must be some way women . . . women like us . . . there must be a way for us to be together. To have everything we both want."

"Of course there are ways. Women who love women and men who love men have existed forever, formed families of their own. But society isn't eager to embrace them. It doesn't hand them their dreams on a platter. They have to fight for their happiness. And what I want for you is happiness you don't have to constantly fight for."

Rose thought back to the night shortly after New Year's when she confessed to Elsie that she joined the Navy in part to escape town after a disastrous and less-than-subtle attempt to determine if her best friend felt the same physical desire toward her. Joan's rejection left Rose embarrassed and convinced she was some sort of anomaly—like a midnight-colored kitten born of two orange tabbies. Not *wrong*, perhaps, but certainly not *right* either. Elsie asked her a few other questions—though thankfully had not asked for details when Rose admitted to having sex with a man and rather enjoying it—then explained to her that some people desired both men and women, and that her previous lover was such a person, as was her first. Instead of jealousy toward these other women Elsie had kissed and stroked in the dark, all Rose felt was the surging excitement of knowing she wasn't such an anomaly after all.

"What about you?" she had asked Elsie. "Have you ever been intimate with a man?"

"No," Elsie had said with a little laugh. "Nor have I ever wanted to."

Rose shifted again in the rowboat so that she and Elsie were sitting face-to-face. "But you . . . You'll have to fight, won't you?"

"I have no choice if I want to be true to myself."

"So let me fight with you. We'll fight together."

"You don't understand." Elsie's voice was so uncharacteristically forceful that Rose flinched. She flung out her arms, gesturing to the sea, sending the boat rocking. "This is not the real world, Rose. Here, we can float along and enjoy each other, and if anyone should notice, they'll turn a blind eye just like they did with those girls at Fort Oglethorpe. They're too desperate to keep the manpower to go through the trouble of discharging us. But after this is over, when the Navy doesn't need us and we're forced back to reality, the tide is going to turn against love like ours. So if you marry Dickie, you'll have the opportunity to live the life you always dreamed of. I cannot let you give up that opportunity. I'd rather you have happiness with someone else than be miserable with me."

Rose wanted to argue that the only way she could ever be happy was to be with Elsie, but before she could open her mouth, Elsie pressed her cheek to Rose's. "If he's a good man and you have warm feelings for him, if you love him even somewhat, say yes if he asks you to marry him. I'm begging you, Rosie."

As her lips parted to protest again, Elsie cut her off with a kiss. "You are my everything," she whispered. "But I cannot be yours."

14

• • • • •

WE'RE HALFWAY BACK TO GADSLEY WHEN HOLLIS'S PHONE RINGS. The number isn't in his contacts, but when I tell him it's an 843 number, he asks me to answer for him. It's Connie, who found my backpack while she was cleaning our room. When I tell her we're already on our way back to town, she insists on meeting near Florence to save us some time. She's such a lovely, selfless woman. Although maybe not completely selfless, because she's chosen a mall parking lot as our rendezvous point. I suspect she'll be heading into the Belk she told us to park in front of as soon as she's returned my bag.

"So," I say when Hollis turns off the engine. "You hide it well, most of the time. But your accent kept slipping out in Gadsley. And you know the local area codes. You're from around here, aren't you?"

He sighs and rubs his hands down his thighs. "Not here exactly. A bit over an hour west. Near Columbia."

"Do your parents still live there?"

His huff-laugh sounds less laugh and more huff this time. "No." For a moment I think that's all he'll tell me, but after he runs his fingers through his hair and clears his throat, he continues. "My dad's a lit professor. He got a new job at a university in Florida and moved there when I was thirteen. And my mom died the summer before my senior year of college."

"I'm sorry," I say.

"Yeah, well." Hollis frowns so intensely as he stares out the windshield that when a woman holding a bunch of shopping bags passes in front of us, she practically sprints past to escape his glare.

"Your parents were divorced then?"

"No. Though that certainly didn't stop my father from acting like they were."

I don't get a further explanation.

"You mentioned you have a sister," I say. "Is she still in South Carolina?"

"No. She married a Belgian guy she met while doing her PhD and moved to Bruges a couple years ago."

"Oh. My brother's in Europe right now too. But just until the end of summer. Study abroad—he's in college for engineering. He's ten years younger, so we aren't super close." I search for a way to further this conversation that will give me more information on Hollis without it being obvious how curious I am. "Are you close with your sister?"

"Close enough for her to guilt me into doing things I probably would never do otherwise," Hollis says cryptically. He heads me off before I can ask what he means. "I don't really want to talk about this right now."

"Okay. Well, what do you want to talk about?"

"Why do we have to talk at all?" he asks, banging his head

against the headrest. His tone comes out sharp, and he winces as if he notices. But he doesn't apologize.

I slide off my sandals and prop my feet on the dashboard. "We don't. Just figured it'd help pass the time."

His eyes travel over my legs, stopping at the hem of the green dress, which Connie insisted I keep. "There are plenty of other ways to pass time that are a lot more fun than talking about my dysfunctional family," Hollis says.

I can tell exactly what he's thinking—there's no mistaking that look—but decide to play coy anyway. "I guess we could play Twenty Questions. Ooh, or I Spy! I'm good at I Spy."

"I was thinking about getting each other off, but if you'd rather play games—"

"I spy, with my little eye . . ." I give him my best wolfish grin as my eyes travel over his body. "Something sexy."

"Your dirty talk needs some work," he says. But his breath hitches when I reach over and gently run my palm over the front of his jeans.

"And yet you're already hard as a rock and breathing like you ran a mile. How odd." I trace the seam of his fly with my finger. "You know, I don't think I've given a hand job in a borrowed car since I was in college."

"Hmm," Hollis hums, distracted. "I'd imagine it's a lot like riding a bike, though?"

I pause with my fingers pinching the pull of his zipper. "I think you've been riding bikes wrong."

The tension in his face as he waits for my next move—his eyes shut tight, lips pressed together, the deep line that forms between his furrowed brows—reminds me of last night, before we kissed. Except this time it isn't fear or anxiety, it's pure desire. And this isn't some fantasy of fooling around with a childhood celebrity crush for him. He is extremely aware, after all we've been through, that I am not Penelope Stuart, but an actual real, live, weird human being. Hollis isn't hard for Millicent Watts-Cohen, former Screen Actors Guild member and notorious yellow bikini wearer. He's hard for Millie—the awkward woman who makes references to '80s comedies and can't order her own food. He's hard for *me*.

The urge to test the boundaries of this power makes me abandon his zipper and stroke him lightly through his jeans instead. Considering how frustrated and hot it's making me, I know it must be torture for him. Which only makes it better.

"You're the worst." He groans. But the tiniest hint of a smile shows at the corner of his mouth.

"Oh, well, if I'm the worst . . ." I stop moving my hand, making it a heavy, stationary weight in his lap.

He chuckles in this incredulous way that I find oddly adorable and tilts his head back. His eyes dart to the side until they hold mine, and it's the same look he gave me at José Napoleoni's. The two-can-play-this-game look. It makes me blush so intensely that even my toes turn pink.

"I loved it when you came on my tongue this morning," he says matter-of-factly, as if talking about stock prices or the weather. "Do you know what you taste like, Mill? Like cherry tomatoes, straight from the garden. Sweet and bright and like an endless summer day. You taste like a memory. One I want to revisit again and again and— Ahhhh! Jesus Christ!"

Hollis clutches his chest, his gaze directed just above my shoulder. My first instinct is ghosts. This mall parking lot is probably haunted by some cool rebellious teens who busted their heads skateboarding here in the '90s. But then Hollis exhales and says, "Connie." Which makes a lot more sense, I guess.

I glance behind me, and sure enough, there she is. Connie gives me a friendly smile and a wave. When I try to lower my window, it doesn't budge since the engine is off. So I unlock the door and get out of the car instead. I am aware I'm still blushing furiously, but there's not much that can be done about that. Still, I mumble something about it being surprisingly warm in the car in an effort to explain it away.

"Sorry to sneak up on y'all," she says. "Thought this looked like Ryan's car, then saw the Gadsley High Marching Band bumper sticker and figured it had to be." She hands me my backpack. "Hope y'all weren't waiting long. There was a bit of traffic gettin' through town 'cause of the pie-eating contest."

"Oh, not at all. We just got here and were . . . we were . . ." Shit. The only thing my brain is generating is a replay of me running my fingers over Hollis's erection and him saying I taste like cherry tomatoes, and I can't tell Connie *that*. "Talking about gardening. Anyway, thank you so much."

"Well, you are very welcome. Now, I hope y'all have a safe and uneventful rest of your trip."

"Me too. Thanks again for everything."

I smile at her. She flashes me one in return, but it fades after a moment.

Connie hesitates as if unsure whether she wants to say something. If it's about how Hollis and I should probably not engage in heavy petting in parking lots, I'm okay with skipping that conversation.

"Can I ask you a question?" she says, apparently making up her mind. "It might not be any of my business, but I would like to know if it's something about me, something I need to change to make Gadsley Manor feel more welcoming . . ."

"Of course," I say, trying not to reveal just how simultaneously nervous I am about where this is headed and relieved that it's likely not about her seeing my hand on Hollis's crotch.

"Why did you and Hollis register under his last name and let me think y'all were married?"

"Whaaaat?" I aim for bemused, but it sounds absurdly fake even to my ears. Again, I was never actually good at acting.

Connie folds her arms over her ample bosom, covering the embroidered monogram on her pullover. "I might be old, darlin', but I know how to use Wikipedia. I looked you up after you told us that you used to be on TV. Didn't say anything about you ever havin' a husband, or even a fiancé."

I'm about to say that's probably because I'm not important enough for anyone to care about documenting my relationship status on the internet, which is the truth (barring the Broccoli Festival make-out session video, but that's only coincidentally about me). Except before I can articulate my response, Hollis appears by my side. My eyes dart to the front of his jeans to check on that situation; it seems to be under control. Which, of course it is. He's thirty-one years old. This is not his first inconvenient boner rodeo.

"Hi, Miss Connie. That whole thing was all my fault. Millicent sometimes has issues with people being invasive of her privacy, and because we arrived so late at night and without knowing anything about y'all or the town, I thought if I put her name as Millicent Hollenbeck she might have a better chance of going unrecognized. I was just trying to look out for her, but because I was tired and a bit rattled by the accident, I went about it in a sorta silly way." He hangs his head, his eyes tilting up toward Connie like a basset hound puppy's, so cute and innocent. "I am very sorry I lied to you, ma'am." Based on this performance, you'd think Hollis was the one who used to be on TV.

"Oh, now that is sweet," Connie says. "And I must say I was fooled for a while, what with the way y'all look all googly-eyed at each other and bicker like old married folks. Maybe it won't be long till we have a Mr. and Mrs. Hollenbeck stay with us for real, hmm? We book out Gadsley Manor for weddings, you know . . ."

Hollis's usual light-olive complexion drains of color when Connie gives him an exaggerated wink. I hug her tightly before she makes any comments about our future children and frightens the rest of the blood from his body. "Thank you again for bringing my bag. We appreciate it so much. But we better get going before we get even more behind schedule."

Connie hugs Hollis, and he murmurs a quick thanks. As predicted, Connie heads for the entrance to Belk.

Hollis gestures to the driver's side, his face still unnaturally pale. "Uh, you mind driving for a bit? I'd like to get some more writing done."

"I didn't think you'd trust me behind the wheel again after what happened."

"The deer really wasn't your fault. Also, this isn't my car, so what do I care?" He opens the passenger-side door and slides inside.

Once I'm settled in the driver's seat, I riffle through my backpack to make sure Mrs. Nash, the letters, and everything else is there and undamaged. Not that I don't trust Connie, but I feel a lot better after I take inventory and a few deep breaths.

"All good?" Hollis asks.

"Yeah." I pull out my phone from the front pocket and find notification after notification. "Except I have about a thousand texts and missed calls from my parents. They must've seen the video. I'm fairly certain they have a Google Alert set up for my name in case I ever get into trouble. My parents go a little overboard with the worrying sometimes."

"Do they? Your high school superlative should've been 'Most Likely to Voluntarily Assist with Her Own Kidnapping,' so I suspect they worry just the right amount."

I read through the messages from my dad and respond as reassuringly as possible without actually explaining myself; the full truth—that I'm traveling to Key West in a borrowed car with a man I only kind of know (yet am sleeping with) to meet an elderly stranger before she dies—will not ease my parents' concern in the least. The text from Dani that's just a bunch of clapping-hands emojis requires no response.

"Hey," I say, putting my phone down. "Those same decision-making skills you're criticizing are the ones that very nearly led to me stroking your salami in a mall parking lot."

Hollis cringes. "Please never ever call it that again."

"No promises."

"And just because your poor choices sometimes work to my advantage doesn't mean they aren't also deeply concerning to those who care about you."

With Herculean effort, I manage to restrain myself from asking if that includes him. Instead, I hug my backpack one more time before tucking it beside Hollis's foot. "That was some quick thinking with Connie. You're a frighteningly good liar," I joke, grasping for a change of subject as I turn the key in the ignition.

"Yeah, I can be," he says, turning his head to stare out the window. "But I wasn't lying to her."

"Huh?"

Whatever he was watching must disappear, and his attention returns to me. "What I just told her? That was the truth. I registered us under my last name to keep people from knowing who you were. That it helped cover our asses in case she was super conservative was an added bonus. I was extra glad I did it when I saw all those Jesuses."

"So what you said about her not being cool with us—"

"I mean, the only other person I've ever met who decorated like that was my maternal grandmother, who definitely wouldn't have been cool with unmarried people sharing a bed under her roof. But when I talked to Connie and Bud Friday morning about staying a few more days, they mentioned they didn't have anyone booked until Wednesday, when their nephew and his boyfriend are coming to visit. They requested to stay in the Mustard Seed room—god knows why. Anyway, Connie and Bud apparently don't give too much of a shit about unmarried people rooming together. Seems they're actually pretty open-minded."

The thought of someone *choosing* to sleep with all of Connie's Jesuses staring at them throws me until I realize that I would absolutely want to stay in the Mustard Seed room again if given the option. How could any of the other rooms top it?

"Why didn't you just tell me the real reason you registered us that way from the beginning?" I ask, trying to get myself back on topic.

"You would've been convinced I was being nice to you, and I was too exhausted to try to convince you that I wasn't. The Jesuses were a surprise, but they made an excellent excuse."

"But you were being nice. That was a nice thing to do. Why would you need to convince me it wasn't?"

He shrugs.

"You have issues, Hollis."

"Well, yeah. Clearly." Before I back out of the parking space, Hollis grabs his phone from where I left it in the cupholder. "Oh. I promised I'd call Elsie's nursing facility for you. Want me to do that now?"

Although the sinking feeling I get imagining possible outcomes of that call makes me want to put it off even longer than I already have, I force myself to nod.

My hands tremble as I look up the number for the place and hit call before handing him my phone. "Use mine."

"Speaker?" he asks, finger hovering above the symbol on the screen as the faint sound of ringing comes through.

I shake my head. My stomach feels like it's getting tossed around by a choppy sea. I don't want to hear this directly. While bad news won't magically turn good if it comes out of Hollis's mouth, something tells me it will be easier to take from him than some stranger who doesn't know what all this means to me.

My eyes instinctively go to the backpack on the floor, wanting to hug Mrs. Nash to my body again. It's as if some part of me thinks this might be difficult for her as well. The truth is, though, she was way better at dealing with disappointment than anyone I've ever known. *There are a lot of things that don't go your way over ninety-some years*, she told me once when I asked how she remained so unaffected by it. *You learn to take it in stride and be extra grateful for the things that do.* Of course, that was about our favorite sub shop closing. But I'm sure it applies to bigger stuff too.

Even trying not to listen, when the ringing stops and something like a muffled Charlie Brown's teacher voice replaces it, my muscles freeze up like they're bracing for impact.

"Hello," Hollis says. "I'm calling for a status update on a resident. Yes. Elsie Brown. She's in hospice care. Yeah. Sure. Thanks."

There's an endless pause that feels like it's for dramatic effect but is probably the receptionist looking something up on the computer. The *womp-womp* voice returns, and Hollis responds, "No, I'm a friend, on my way to see her, and I wanted to— Right. Right. I do understand that but— Yes, but when my— I see. Yes. Yes. Okay. I understand. Thank you, anyway."

He hangs up the phone and stares at me. His lips are pressed together in an odd expression, and I brace for the worst.

"Got a different receptionist than you did, I guess. One with a lot more qualms about giving out patient info to random people over the phone. She wouldn't tell me anything. Just kept repeating 'I'm sorry, sir, but we cannot discuss our patients with anyone not listed in their file.'" He says this last part in a high-pitched nasally voice that would probably be funny if I weren't on the brink of vomiting.

I take a deep breath, trying to navigate the tangle of relief, frustration, and disappointment resting in the pit of my stomach. Part of me wants to believe that if Elsie were already gone, the receptionist wouldn't have bothered being such a stickler for confidentiality. But her lack of cooperation also might not mean anything at all.

Hollis's hand closes around mine on the steering wheel. "Are you okay?" he asks.

"I'll feel better once we're on our way again."

He nods and lets go, leaving my hand feeling cold and naked. "I'll start the navigation. Now that you've finally relinquished my phone."

The map lady in Hollis's phone resumes telling me what to do in her commanding robot voice, and I intend to let my playlist lull me into a pleasant state of meditation that keeps me from further analyzing the receptionist's response to Hollis, or Hollis's confession to Connie, or his apparent genuine investment in this trip, or well, anything that isn't Carole King's "It's Too Late."

But Hollis cuts into my reverie before it can really begin. "Is it true? What Josh said in this text?"

I glance over and see his red notebook still closed on his lap. He's staring at the phone in his hand with a mixture of anger and disbelief, as if it just sucker punched him—which is basically how I felt when I first read Josh's messages too.

"Because I know you're new to this sort of arrangement," he continues, "but there's a difference between casual sex and using someone. And I'm not okay with being used, Millicent. So if that's what this is for you—"

"What? How could you even—" Except I know exactly how he could think that. I was all in on that Instagram post, knowing how Josh would feel about seeing his ex-girlfriend with his frenemy. "I am not having sex with you to get back at Josh," I reassure him. Honestly it's not even an added bonus anymore; reading those texts brought me zero joy.

"Okay," he says. "If you say so."

"If I *say so*?"

"It's just that you seemed pretty insistent that we make out in front of all those people at the parade. Like you knew this is what would happen."

"Are you kidding me? *You* kissed *me*. In fact, you started all of this with your 'Ahh! I'm so scared of thunderstorms' act last night." I'm vaguely aware I've said something super mean, but all I can think is *Wow, was that really only last night?*

"Go fuck yourself," he says, turning to look out the window. The coolness of his voice is worse than if he'd yelled.

Okay. I know I went way too far. I'm still used to fighting with Josh, I guess. Going for the jugular ends the actual conflict as quickly as possible and gets to the cold-silence part, which, in my opinion, is preferable to actively arguing. The method is harsh yet efficient. But I know Hollis's fear last night was no act, and neither of us planned for it to turn out how it did. Still, the accusation that I'm using him when he's the one who initiated everything rankles.

Then Josh's stupid voice pops into my head: *If you're going to be fucking weird, Millie, you should at least be fucking weird and famous again so I'm not with you for nothing.* Of course. Why would Hollis choose to stay with me unless he thought he'd get something out of it? And if it isn't my fame he wants, and it isn't sex, what exactly is he after?

Goddamn Josh, stirring up shit. This is exactly what he wanted to happen. And yet now that we're going down this path of anger and suspicion, it's too easy—almost a compulsion—to keep twisting the knife. Except I'm not sure if it's stuck in Hollis's chest or in mine.

"I think this is what happened," I say, my deepest insecurities wrapping around the hilt, prepared to inflict maximum damage. "Tell me if I'm close. You decided to tag along with me to find Elsie because you're so certain you're right, that she won't care about Mrs. Nash anymore. And you couldn't pass up the opportunity to be there to tell me you told me so. So you canceled with

Yeva, because I guess giving up your sexfest seemed like a small enough price to pay for the possibility of watching goofy, naive Millie's heart shatter into a million pieces and rubbing the shards in her face."

"Millicent." He says my name as if it's a warning.

The hair on my arms stands on end, like I'm walking into an electrical storm. I trudge on ahead anyway. Too late to turn back now; the words are already lining up to march out of my mouth. "Except you didn't even have to give up your sexfest, not really. I'm sure you could tell I was interested and figured you could still get some if you wanted, easy-peasy. Is that why you kissed me last night? God, and you were probably thinking the whole time, 'Hey, she's no Yeva Markarian but you can't beat the convenience!' I understand that sex with me was nothing but a consolation prize to you, Hollis. So don't you dare accuse *me*—"

Hollis smacks his fist into his leg. The gesture is dramatic, but the sound it makes is an underwhelming, muffled *thud*. "Stop, dammit! Stop." He runs his fingers through his hair and growls in that frustrated way of his that makes me want to jump his bones.

And then there's silence between us. It stretches and stretches, lasting the entirety of ELO's "Telephone Line." I didn't remember that song being five billion minutes long. Finally, Hollis's lips part, and I ready myself for whatever he's going to say. Which is apparently still nothing. He's gone back to staring out the window. Cold silence with Hollis isn't the relief it was with Josh. It feels like being slowly pecked to death by a gang of bloodthirsty crows. I try to figure out something to say, because this is killing me, but nothing feels quite right. The opening bars of "Tusk" fill the car, and I realize I'm the tiniest bit tired of that song just as Hollis reaches over and turns off the stereo. I almost object, figuring another argument about Fleetwood Mac might be preferable to this terrible state of ignoring each other's existence. But then he opens his mouth again, and this time he actually speaks.

"I kissed you because I wanted to," Hollis says with a calmness that I doubt he feels. "Because I've wanted to since the first moment I saw you at Cheryl Kline's terrible poetry reading at that coffee shop in Alexandria. I wanted, more than anything in the world, to find out more about the redhead in the cobalt-blue dress who was knitting a hideous scarf and beaming while Cheryl butchered iambic pentameter." He huffs out a laugh. "You know, despite what he thinks, I've never once been jealous of Josh Yaeger, never had any desire to be him. Except for that night, when he strolled in late and took his seat beside you."

Oh. Right. I knew Josh's book release party wasn't mine and Hollis's first encounter, but I had somehow forgotten about that chilly February evening in Alexandria two years earlier. It seems so strange now that I didn't remember that Hollis was one of a group of MFA students who schlepped to Old Town to support their lovely but syllabically challenged classmate. Josh and I moved in together the month before; my new neighbor, a lively nonagenarian named Rose Nash, was teaching me how to knit. I guess the more recent and emotion-fueled memory of the night I broke up with Josh drowned it out, but now that first meeting comes rushing back with surprising clarity. Hollis's hand might have been just another in the sea of them I shook as Josh introduced me to the other members of his cohort. Except I remember a warmth spreading up my arm as I looked into mismatched eyes, thinking "Wait a second . . ." And at that very moment, Hollis was wanting to kiss me? He's been wanting to for *years*?

I tuck away this development, not knowing what to do with it

yet. Surely it means something—something important, maybe—
but I don't have the emotional energy to puzzle it out. I'm too
baffled by the possibility that all Hollis wants from me is . . . me.

"It wasn't all terrible," I say eventually. "Cheryl's reading, I
mean. I remember liking the poem about the daffodil."

My eyes are focused on the highway, but I suspect Hollis is
raising his eyebrows as if to say *really?* His voice is soft when he
speaks again. I can tell he isn't angry anymore; his forgiveness is
baffling. I'm not used to immediate de-escalation. Fights with Josh
lasted *days*. A week or more, on some occasions. There was one
time I crashed at Mrs. Nash's for ten nights because of a disagreement over whether the guy behind us in line at Trader Joe's was
Bernie Sanders (I swear it was).

"Sex with you is not a consolation prize," Hollis says. "It's not
a prize at all."

"Wow, that was unpleasantly blunt."

"No, I mean . . ." He lets out a frustrated huff. "Being with you
isn't about adding some shiny trophy to my collection. It means a
lot more than that to me. Despite your terrible taste in music and,
apparently, poetry, I happen to really like you, Mill."

"Oh." Can your heart beat strong enough to bruise your
breastbone? Because my chest aches all of a sudden. "I happen to
really like you too," I say. And I do. I'm kind of amazed actually at
just how much. If someone asked me to describe Hollis Hollenbeck after our interaction at the airport, the word "likeable"
wouldn't have been within the first hundred adjectives that sprung
to mind. Maybe it's because he makes me feel like my blood has
turned to rocket fuel whenever his lips meet my skin, or because
he doesn't try to argue or manipulate me out of my weirdness. In
fact, he seems to look for ways to make me more comfortable in

it. And I like him so much right now that it feels wrong that there was ever a time—especially one so recent—when I barely knew him.

"Okay then," he says, and flips open his notebook. "Glad that's settled. Back to work." He begins writing, the point of his pen bursting the bubble of emotional intimacy forming around us before it grows too big and we get carried away.

Key West, Florida
July 1945

BEING IN A PROPER BED WITH ELSIE FELT LIKE AN INCREDIBLE IN-dulgence after months of making do with stolen moments on the beach and pressed against each other on narrow cots.

"I can't believe you spent so much money on this place," Rose said for the third time since they had arrived at the bungalow Elsie rented them downtown for the long weekend. "It's too much."

Elsie kissed Rose's shoulder. "Oh Rosie, don't fuss. Let me spoil you for your birthday."

"It's not even until next week."

"Well, this is when we could both get away from base. Your birthday celebration will just have to last for the next seven days. Is that really such a hardship?"

Elsie slid out of the bed, as graceful in her nakedness as she was swimming in the ocean. Rose watched the way the sun played on her tanned skin and turned her hair into strands of gold. She'd only seen Elsie completely nude one other time before, on New Year's at Boca Chica Beach. They'd abandoned any attempt at cau-

tion that night, telling themselves that anyone who might stumble
upon them at such an hour would likely be too soused to notice.
That was Elsie at night, though, the moonlight emphasizing
shadows instead of highlighting all of the places she glowed. So
distracted by the way the light streaming through the window ha-
loed Elsie's subtle curves, Rose barely noticed the small package
in her hands when her lover returned to the bed.

"Els, what is this? You've already spent so much—"

"Happy birthday, darlin'," she cut her off. "Open it."

Rose made a show of peeling back the brown paper wrapping,
revealing a white rectangular box with an elaborate black *R* em-
bossed on the center of the lid. "Is this my own candy stash?" she
asked with a grin. "I hope not. I much prefer having the excuse to
come visit yours."

Elsie bit her lip as Rose lifted the box's lid. "Do you like it?"

Rose gazed down upon a sheet of stationery—a stack of it, she
assumed based on the depth of the box. In the top-left corner was
a watercolor illustration of a pigeon holding a red rosebud in its
beak.

"It's beautiful. How did you find something like this?" Rose
asked.

Elsie shifted beside her, oddly nervous. "I had it made. One of
the other nurses is dating an artist who lives beside Pepe's on
Caroline Street."

"It's beautiful," Rose repeated, her fingertips sweeping over
the image.

"They're saying the war will end soon now that Germany's
surrendered. I hope when we go our separate ways, you'll still send
me a pigeon on occasion."

The reminder that their time was limited—and that Elsie had

unilaterally proclaimed it so—tugged at Rose's nerves. Bitterness twinged with guilt made the secret she had been keeping for the past week spill from her mouth. "Dickie's tour of duty ends next month. He decided he's going to begin school in the fall. In Chicago. He's asked me to marry him as soon as the war is over and move there with him."

It was clear that Elsie's responding smile was an act, but her insistence on this mask of happiness only heightened Rose's frustration. Some foolish part of her thought that Elsie would change her mind about spending their lives together once the risk of losing her became real. Yet Elsie threaded her fingers into the hair above Rose's ears, cradling her head in her hands. She brought her lips to her forehead for a long, gentle kiss. "That's wonderful news. I wish you both all the happiness in the world."

"How can you say that?" Rose snapped, pulling away from her. "How can you sit there and condone me marrying someone else? Unless you never really—"

"*Don't.* Don't you say it, Rose McIntyre. Don't you even *think* about saying it." Elsie's face crumpled, pain flashing in her deep brown eyes. "Knowing I'm going to have to let you go . . . I feel like I'm dying the world's slowest death. My desire to survive fades a little each time I touch you, but I can't stop, even though I know one day—one day soon—there will be nothing left of me. But I'll be able to go on as long as I know you are happy. So please, Rosie, give me that one small consolation. Promise me you'll try to be happy with Dickie. Forget about me if it makes it any easier. Just forget—"

Rose's lips crashed into Elsie's with silencing hardness. "How dare you. How dare you suggest I forget you. I couldn't even if I wanted to," she muttered against the smooth skin of Elsie's jaw.

As a girl, Rose had always imagined true love as something that would open the world so wide its spine would crack with the abundance of possibility, and she was furious to find that it instead seemed to be nothing but an illusion that she had any freedom at all.

"Even if you aren't brave enough to let me choose you, you can't stop me from loving you every single day of my life." Rose kissed Elsie one last time, then stared into her eyes as she delivered her parting shot. "But as much as I love you, I resent you more right now."

She climbed out of the bed and collected her clothes, hoping Elsie would stop her from leaving and returning to base. Instead, when she opened the bungalow's front door, Elsie called out, "I'd rather you resent me now than in ten years, when you realize that the things I can't give you are the ones you truly want after all."

And those were the last words between them until a single sheet of the custom stationery arrived, trifolded in an envelope addressed to Ms. Elsie Brown, in September 1946, announcing the birth of Richard Wayne Nash Jr.

15

. . . . .

LIKE IS NOT LOVE. I KEEP HAVING TO TELL MYSELF THAT AS WE cross the South Carolina–Georgia border. Why I feel the need to issue constant reminders of that fact, I don't care to contemplate. Hollis said he likes me, but of course he doesn't love me; we've only been traveling together for three days. Even I, die-hard romantic that I tend to be, will admit that no one falls in love after three days—not really. And then a little voice in the back of my head that sounds suspiciously like Mrs. Nash's questions if it's been three days for Hollis or if it's been two years. But I put the kibosh on that because I'm fully aware that the sentiment might have that quiet, slightly raspy quality that I miss hearing so much, but it's still being generated by my own brain. And my brain needs to cut it the hell out.

Besides, I barely said more than two words to him before the night he drove me home from Josh's book release party. Even once I was in his car, I'm not sure we discussed anything beyond my address and maybe the weather. If he does love me—which he *doesn't*—it would be based on nothing but watching me across the room at a handful of events. That might sound romantic in theory, but in practice it's delusional bordering on creepy. Now, wanting to kiss me, get me naked? That I could see being a persistent desire from afar. I mean, didn't I feel that exact way about Hollis almost immediately after we started traveling together? And now that he's gotten to know me a bit, he likes me. As a person. A friend. A friend-person. That is all very normal and rational and *not* love.

But what if . . . ?

This repetitive cycle has been going through my head now for over an hour. I went to this restaurant once that had a whimsical vintage travel theme, and the centerpiece of the place was a toy train that chugged along on an oval-shaped track suspended from the ceiling. If you missed it passing by your booth, no big deal— wait a minute and it would come around again. That's the way my thought process feels right now. It would take something pretty major to derail it.

I'm vaguely aware of the guitar opening to Hall & Oates's "Sara Smile" coming through Ryan's (impressively high-quality) car stereo. My shoulders roll slowly, my upper body absentmindedly swaying to the tune the way it has for every song that's played as I've been lost in my stupid thoughts. It's halfway through the first verse when I notice that Daryl Hall is not performing vocals solo.

Hollis. Is. Singing.

Thought train successfully derailed.

He isn't belting out the lyrics by any means; his head is still bowed, eyes focused on his notebook. But when I sneak a glance, he's undeniably moving his lips. Considering his objections to my music up until now, I am never going to let him live down this little singalong. I wait until the end of the song to say anything (is he even aware that he's doing it?), but as soon as the last note ends, I pounce.

"Ah-ha! You like Hall & Oates," I say.

The way he startles at the accusation gives him away, even though his voice reveals nothing. "I don't know what makes you think that."

"You know every word to 'Sara Smile.'"

"It's a fairly popular song. I guess I might know some of it through cultural osmosis."

"And you sang it!" I hit my palms against the steering wheel in triumph.

"Hmm," he says, still managing to sound way too chill for someone who has been caught enjoying something he insists he can't stand. "I'm pretty sure I didn't."

"Hollis, I saw your mouth move."

"I was talking through a wording issue with myself."

"I *heard* you singing."

In my peripheral vision, I see him look up from his notebook. "Maybe you heard *someone* singing, but it was not me."

I let out a muted scream of annoyance. "Who was it then?" I demand. "If it was not me, and it was not you, who was singing along to Hall & Oates?"

"Probably the same person you were talking to in the bathroom last night."

I don't even need to look to know that the corners of his mouth are trembling as he fights off a full smile.

"We should stop for gas up here," Hollis says, peering over at the dashboard's fuel indicator.

I exit the highway, wondering if the offer to punch him once we arrive at the gas station was exclusive to the Wawa back in Virginia or if I can redeem it now.

"That song's okay," he admits at last as I pull up to a pump and shift into park. "I will even acknowledge that most of your music is fine. All of it except for—"

"I swear, Hollis Hollenbeck, if you start talking shit about Stevie Nicks again I'll—"

"You'll what?" he asks, his voice deep and husky.

"I'll . . . I'll . . ." For all the dirty thoughts my mind has constructed in Hollis's presence, it's really letting me down right now. So why on earth am I talking anyway? "Do stuff to you. Stuff you'll like a lot. Too much even. And then you'll be so overcome by the pleasure you'll explode into a million pieces. I won't bother to gather them, so all the bits of you will be at the whims of Mother Nature. A seal might eat you."

"Wow. Can't say I predicted that twist at the end."

"Yeah, well. Being sexy is not my forte."

"Could've fooled me."

He clears his throat and adjusts in his seat. My eyes spot the return of the long, hard ridge in his jeans.

"Dude! Are you turned on because I said I'd explode you with sex and then a seal would eat you?"

"It's not because of the seal," Hollis grumbles.

"Did that actually awaken something in you?"

"You awaken all sorts of things in me." He sounds extremely annoyed about it, which gives me a buzz of satisfaction.

Like is not love, I tell myself. Like is not love. Sex is not love. Sex is not like. Except sometimes it is. It is now. But like is not love.

This is getting too confusing.

"Yeah?" I say. "Things like your dormant passion for classic soft rock?" I reach over and give him a light squeeze that makes his breath catch.

"As much as it almost literally pains me to say this, I don't think we have time right now." Hollis lifts my hand away and drops it onto my own lap. He moves to get out of the car and sharply inhales at the movement. "Can you buy me a bottle of water while I pump the gas, please? I'd go in myself, but uh . . ."

I sigh dramatically. "Since you asked nicely, I suppose I can save you from having to wave your seal-fantasy hard-on all over the 7-Eleven."

"I told you, it's not because of the seal!" he calls out as I head for the entrance.

Inside, I head for the cases of beverages along the back wall and grab two of the biggest bottles of water they have. Then I walk up and down the aisles collecting various snacks until we have enough to hunker down for nuclear war. We'd split some fries from a food truck after the parade while we waited for Ryan to finish with his students and hand over the keys, but that was hours ago. Hopefully this assortment of cookies, chips, pretzels, trail mix, and candy will keep us from having to stop for dinner.

I pile everything on the counter. The clerk starts scanning, not glancing up until he reaches the waters. He has stringy green hair and an eyebrow piercing, which raises in recognition. "Hey, you look familiar," he says. "Where do I know you from?"

The clock on the wall says it's after four. I don't exactly have time—or, honestly, the inclination—to go through the entire *Penelope to the Past* fan interaction script right now inside this convenience store. Even my extroversion has its limit, and I think I hit it several hours ago, when I rambled on about how lovely of a town Gadsley is for what felt like forever as reporter after reporter found me after the parade.

"I do porn," I say. "Penelope Alameda." I know it's not the standard first-pet-plus-street-you-grew-up-on formula, but something tells me King Velociraptor Alameda wouldn't be as believable a stage name.

He nods as he runs my credit card. "Oh, right. Cool. You're the one with the . . ." The clerk makes a gesture with his fingers that I'm either too tired or too sheltered to understand. "I'm a big fan of your stuff. Thanks for making it."

"Thanks for enjoying it," I say, taking the bag from the counter. It's an automatic response that I've said to countless *Penelope to the Past* fans, though I guess it means something a bit different in this context. Still works, though.

Now I guess I'm going to need to do some major searching for my porn actress doppelganger. And then watch enough of her videos until I figure out what that gesture represents.

When I return to the car, Hollis is back in the passenger seat, scribbling away in his little spiral-bound notebook. He shuts it and tucks it between his thighs as I open my door. I put our bottles of water in the cupholders and hand him the bag of snacks.

His eyebrows shoot up as he peeks inside. "Wow. Did you buy one of everything?"

"Pretty much. Except Cheez-Its. I had a college roommate who ate them pretty much nonstop and now I can't deal with the smell." The memory makes me gag. I attempt to recover with a super casual, "So, how's the writing coming along?"

Hollis shrugs as he combs through the bag. "Fine. Good. I mean, it's not good quality-wise, but words are on the page, and that's the goal of a first draft."

"Cool. So what's this book going to be about?"

"Hmm?"

"The book. What's it about?"

"It's not going to be about anything if you don't stop distracting me." His fingers tap against his leg as he seems to reconsider his brusqueness. "Sorry, it's just that I don't really like telling anyone except my agent what I'm working on until it's finished. I'm . . . superstitious like that, I guess."

I have to admit I'm strangely pleased by this further evidence of how different Hollis is from Josh. If you asked Josh what his book was about when he started writing it, he said stuff like, *It's a modern take on Dostoyevsky, exploring the nature of suffering and attraction in a post-industrial society.* Which it turns out is pretentious literary bro for: *It's about an accountant whose melancholia is eclipsed only by his desire to bang the barista at the coffee shop near his office, and it takes place in 2009 for some reason.*

"Interesting," I say slowly, peeling off the wrapping of a Reese's Cup and shoving it whole into my mouth. "And don't pretend you don't like it when I'm distracting." The words come out as an unintelligible string of vowels—aa oo e e oo o ii ii ee i iaoi.

"Just drive, Millicent."

We're several miles farther south and two candy bars, one bag of chips, and a small box of mini donuts down when my phone vibrates in my backpack. It continues on at a steady beat that announces a phone call. And then another, and another. My first instinct, even after two months, is that it must be Mrs. Nash calling from the old rotary phone in her living room. My stomach dips at the thought that I'm too far away to help her if something's wrong, then bottoms out when I remember that both she and the rotary phone are gone now.

But someone sure is eager to get in touch. "Check that for me?"

Hollis reaches down to the bag beside his foot and finds my phone in the front pocket as it begins to ring again. "Your dad," he says. "Want me to answer for you?"

"Oh god, no. Do you know how freaked out he'll be if a strange man picks up my phone? Put it on speaker."

Hollis complies, and my dad's voice is already shouting, "Hello? Hello?" before I can say a word.

"Hi, Dad," I say. "Is everything okay?"

My father's thick Long Island accent that somehow never faded despite thirty years of not living there now fills the car. "Is everything okay? You tell me, Millie. What on earth is going on?"

"Not much. Just driving."

"Your mother has been sick with worry."

"Oh, don't blame Millie just because I've been practically bed-ridden wondering if she's all right," my mother says. Bubbe—my paternal grandmother—could've guilted a fish into walking on dry land, and I've always found it fascinating that she somehow managed to pass some of her talent on to her daughter-in-law.

"There's really nothing to worry about. I'm fine. Like I said in my text."

"Nothing to worry about?" Dad says halfway between question and exclamation. "We don't hear from you for days and then see you sucking face with a stranger, wearing broccoli in your hair in the middle of nowhere. And then you ignore our multiple inquiries—"

I don't understand why my father starts sounding like a bill collector whenever he's concerned. "Again, like I said in my text, I didn't have my phone on me." To be precise, I didn't have my phone at all. But they don't need to know that.

"You didn't tell anyone where you were going, who you were with—"

"I told Dani."

"You could've been dead in a ditch for all anyone knew, Millie."

"I wasn't, though," I point out. "You can tell by the fact that you are currently having a conversation with me."

"But you *could've been*," I hear Mom say from farther away. Based on the loud whirring noise in the background, she must be using the blender.

"Well, I'm definitely not now," I say. "I'm just on vacation."

"A vacation?" Dad sounds incredulous. "A vacation is lounging on a beach, Millie. Exploring a national park. Not taking part in some produce parade and doing the PDA with a stranger."

"Doing the PDA?" Hollis mumbles. "Now I see where you get your way with words."

"Who was that?" Dad asks. He's a bill collector with the hearing of a bat, apparently. "Who's that with you?"

"That's Hollis," I say. "He's the guy in the video. And he's not a stranger. We're friends."

"Oh, friends, huh?" Dad says. "Maybe I'm too old-fashioned, but in my day a man didn't kiss a woman like that if he thought of her as just a friend."

"Welp, that's what we are. So." I bite my lip, knowing my face must be beet-like at this point. Part of me wishes Hollis would jump in and save me somehow, but I also know if he did I'd be annoyed that he thought I couldn't handle my own parents. Besides, what could he even say to get them off my back? Something like "You're right, sir. I was balls deep inside Millicent this morning, so 'just friends' may not be the most accurate representation of our current relationship?" That would go over well. Besides, based on what I know about Hollis, having sex with someone and being just friends with that someone aren't mutually exclusive in his view.

"Are we on speakerphone?" Dad asks, startling me out of my thoughts.

"You are," I confirm.

"Good. Hollis, tell us: Why should we trust you with our daughter?"

"Oh my god." I groan. If I weren't driving, I would cover my face with my hands. This is worse than when my father gave my prom date a brochure on proper condom usage. Like then, I know he means well, but . . .

Hollis clears his throat and sits up straighter. "You don't have to—" I begin, but he lays his hand on my thigh and says, "You should trust me with Millicent because she's decided she trusts me. That should be enough."

"I understand what you're saying," my father concedes. "And Millie is a wonderful girl, don't get me wrong. But she's too kind-hearted, easily manipulated—"

"She's an adult who can make her own decisions," Hollis says. "She knows what she's doing."

"Ha." Somehow all of Dad's intense disagreement with Hollis's claim manages to fit inside that tiny word. It feels like someone tugging down on my heart, testing to see how much it can stretch before it tears. "If she knew what she was doing," he continues, "she wouldn't have wasted three years on that schmuck Josh."

Hollis's fingers curl into a fist against his leg, and I have a sneaking suspicion he's about to say something really rude to my father. I know I need to end this conversation right now before it gets even more out of hand. So why am I instead on the metaphorical edge of my seat waiting to hear my new friend with benefits defend me?

But before Hollis can give Dad the dressing down he probably deserves, blue and red lights appear in my rearview mirror.

"Sorry, gotta go," I say, throwing on the turn signal.

"Oh shit," Hollis says, seeing the police cruiser behind us at the same time its sirens let out a *woop woop*. He gives my thigh a squeeze. "They've found us. Floor it, Millicent."

I whack Hollis on the arm with the back of my hand. He smiles at the rising panic in my mother's voice as she asks what's going on, and I can barely contain the bark of laughter building in my chest.

Hollis holds the phone closer to his mouth to ensure my parents hear him. "Faster, honey, faster. I can't go back to prison."

"Millie!" my parents shriek in unison.

"Talk to you later, loveyoubye!" I say in a hurry as I pull over. And I'm pretty sure the last thing my parents hear as Hollis ends the call is me cackling like a cheap, animatronic witch decoration.

16

· · · · ·

"NICE OF YOUR PAL RYAN TO GIVE US A CAR WITH A BURNED-OUT taillight," Hollis says.

"I'm sure he didn't do it on purpose."

Whether Ryan knew or not, this little chat with Trooper Rodrigo on the shoulder of I-95 has cost us forty-five minutes of travel time so far. About ten of those minutes were spent unloading everything from the tightly packed glove box trying to find the registration and proof of insurance, which it turns out was attached to the passenger-side visor all along. Since I had no idea where the documents were, have an out-of-state license, and didn't know Ryan's last name until I read it off the registration, Trooper Rodrigo decided to give him a call to confirm we have permission to drive his car.

"My parents usually worry I'm about to be the victim of a crime, and the police think I might be committing one," I muse as we wait for the trooper to return from his cruiser.

"Oh, I don't know. Thanks to me your parents might now be convinced we've decided to Bonnie and Clyde it."

I cover my face as I laugh. "I cannot believe you did that. They're probably calling every southern state highway patrol as we speak to find out if I've been arrested."

"Sorry if I overstepped, by the way," Hollis says. "I hope it didn't seem like I was trying to mansplain you to your own mom and dad."

"No, *I'm* sorry that my parents put you on the spot like that. I appreciate you sticking up for me. Even if you didn't really mean what you said."

"I did mean it. I know I tease you, but I've realized over the last couple days that you have some sort of system to calculate risk. Even if I don't always understand it, I have to admit that it's mostly worked for you for the last twenty-whatever years."

"Almost thirty," I say. "But aren't you the same person who decided to let me come with him to Miami because he was convinced there was a one hundred percent chance that I'd get murdered and dismembered if left to my own devices?"

"Not one hundred. Maybe ninety-five percent. Also, I didn't know about your system then," he says. "You just seemed like a happy little boat floating along in the middle of a hurricane, completely unaware that you were dangerously close to being dashed upon the rocks."

I smile at the analogy. "Please. If anything, I'm the hurricane."

"As I have discovered. And I'm starting to suspect that *I* might be the boat." He lets out a hefty sigh.

"Don't worry," I say. "I'll use my awesome power to guide you safely to shore."

The corner of Hollis's mouth lifts. "I'm not sure you know anything about how hurricanes work."

Trooper Rodrigo is still sitting inside his cruiser, phone to his ear. I really hope he can get in touch with Ryan (whose last name I now know is Dubicki). Otherwise my second time in a police car could be less than forty-eight hours after my first.

"Have they always been so overprotective?" Hollis asks.

"Police cars?"

He narrows his eyes in confusion. "I'm talking about your parents."

"Oh. Right." That makes a lot more sense. "No, not always. I mean, they were always attentive. But the excessive concern started when I was on *Penelope to the Past*. Fame, even minor fame, brings the creeps and weirdos out of the woodwork. Then, even as the creeps and weirdos went back into the woodwork for the most part after I was off TV for a while, Mom and Dad remained on high alert. And there they've been for the last fifteen years. They mean well, but it gets old."

"How did you even wind up acting anyway? I'm assuming it wasn't your parents' idea. And you weren't exactly talented."

"Wow, thanks," I say.

He holds up his hands. "I'm only repeating what you yourself have said multiple times."

"Yeah, yeah, sure." Let's be real, I can't even pull off convincing fake indignation. "Nepotism. Nepotism is how I got my start. My aunt Talia is a Hollywood casting director. She convinced my parents to let me do a few local commercials when I was six. Someone at the network saw one I did when I was ten for a furniture store in Burbank and thought I had the right look for the role of Penelope, so they asked me to audition. My parents weren't thrilled about it—my mom was pregnant with my brother, and it meant a lot of changes for our family all at once—but I enjoyed doing the commercials and hadn't realized yet I was getting by on my cute face alone. I hoped *Penelope* would show everyone how great I was, lead to bigger and better things. I wanted to be a movie star. But a funny one. I'd just seen *Clue* for the first time, and I was a little obsessed with Madeline Kahn." I give Hollis a rueful smile. "I memorized scripts easily, but I discovered that actually delivering all those lines was another story. I had no illusions of stardom by the time I stopped acting. Puberty shattered the last few remaining ones."

"What do you mean?"

"You've seen the screenshots. The yellow bikini. That's why the show ended."

"I don't understand."

"After that episode, some people at the network were absolutely aghast that I dared to develop breasts. Didn't I know Penelope was supposed to be a *wholesome* character?" I roll my eyes, hoping it will help hide the way that memory still hurts a little when I press on it, not unlike the dull ache of the bruise on my forehead.

"Wow, fuck them," Hollis says.

"Well, there was also a not-insignificant contingent that was thrilled that Penelope now had sex appeal. They figured my new tits would do great things for the ratings, open up new marketing opportunities."

"Okay, I've changed my mind. Fuck *them*."

"The whole thing was terrible for my mental health. I was

self-conscious enough about my body at that age. My contract was up for renewal at the end of the season, and Mom and Dad told me I wasn't going to be on the show anymore. I pretended I was mad at them for making the decision for me, but I'm sure they could see through my feigned anger. I was actually incredibly relieved to be done with it."

Filming those last few episodes was a nightmare; trying to say my lines and move just right while feeling disoriented in my own skin. Knowing with absolute certainty that people were having discussions about my every new jiggle and curve. I force a smile, close my eyes, and let out a long sigh. Hollis's hand blankets mine, warm and reassuring, but he pulls it away when Trooper Rodrigo appears beside my window.

"I spoke to the owner," he says. "He confirmed you have permission to drive this vehicle. I made him aware of the taillight issue, and he promised to fix it as soon as you return the car, so I'm not going to bother with a repair order. But please do remind Mr. Dubicki when you see him."

"Thank you," I say, taking our proffered documents from him.

"Have a good one now." Trooper Rodrigo knocks twice on our roof before walking back to his cruiser.

It's after seven, and the assortment of gas station snacks feels piled against one side of my stomach, leaving me half nauseated, half hungry. Without either of us saying a word, I take the next exit and pull into a Taco Bell parking lot. Hollis and I switch seats so he can take care of ordering when we go through the drive-thru; I try not to make a big deal about how much I appreciate that his doing this for me has become automatic, just another part of our routine. A bean and rice burrito evens out the asymmetrical feeling into something heavy but more fully distributed at least. I'm glad I'm not driving now, because the only destination I can see up ahead is Zzztown.

I go to plug my phone back into the stereo, but Hollis grabs my hand mid-reach for the aux cord. "Hold on," he says.

"Hollis, please. I'm tired," I say in a voice that's much whinier than I intend.

"We've gone through your whole playlist twice already during this trip. And it'll drain your phone battery." Hollis turns on the radio and flips through the stations, probably looking for the local NPR affiliate.

"But—"

Before I can complete my objection, he lands on the station he wanted. It's not the news, though. It's the Doobie Brothers' "What a Fool Believes."

"I saw a billboard for a classic rock station a few miles back," Hollis explains as if anticipating my question. "I took note in case I suddenly snapped and threw your phone out of the window in real life instead of just in my daydreams."

"Oh," is all I manage. Michael McDonald's soulful vocals wrap me in a cozy embrace. I stare at Hollis's profile through drowsy eyes, not even trying to hide my examination of this grumpopotamus who keeps surprising me with his kindness. As I replay the day's events, starting with the dark and stormy early hours of the morning when he first kissed me and ending with this moment, my chest aches with something like affection. Something almost like—

No. Not going there. I don't want to be like the fool in the song, falling hard for someone who will barely think of me at all once we part.

The startling realization that the only thing standing between me and future heartbreak is my own infamously weak willpower should probably keep me awake, but somehow my exhaustion wins out. I dream of Michael McDonald wearing a reflective vest and my broccoli flower crown, holding a large, orange construction sign—CAUTION: DANGEROUS CONDITIONS AHEAD.

17

· · · · ·

THE THING THAT WAKES ME IS THE LACK OF NOISE. NO HUMMING engine, no whooshing of passing cars. No radio on or road-trip playlist picking out banger after banger. There's only Hollis's breathing in the driver's seat.

"What's going on?" I ask, my words stretching along with my body.

He pulls the key from the ignition and clutches it in his palm. "We're stopping for the night."

"What? No. Hollis, we can't—"

Hollis takes my hands in his. At first I think it's sweet until I realize it's just to keep me from continuing to flail around in panic. He ensures I'm looking him straight in the eyes before he speaks. "Listen, Millicent. We have a while to go still before we reach Key West. If we keep driving tonight, we're going to arrive at four something in the morning. But if we stop here, we can get some sleep, do a load of laundry, and still leave early enough to be at the nursing facility soon after visiting hours start."

My brain flitters awake enough to notice that we're parked in a residential driveway in front of a white stucco ranch with a Spanish-style clay roof that's flat except for a steep diagonal over the two-car garage. "Where are we?"

"Boca Raton. Come on." Hollis gets out of the car before I have the opportunity to request he be more specific. He grabs our bags from the trunk and heads to the wooden double doors, my legs too stiff from several hours of upright sleep to follow with any haste.

"Wait," I say, these events proceeding too quickly for me in my still-drowsy state.

Hollis fiddles with an outdoor thermometer mounted near the door. It pops open to reveal a key.

"Are we breaking and entering?" I whisper.

"Just entering. No breaking required," he says, gesturing to the way the key turns into the lock and the door cracks open.

I cross the threshold into a large room with a tiled floor. When Hollis flips on the overhead light, I can see that we've entered a living room decorated in beige and chocolate brown with pops of butterscotch yellow. We slip off our shoes before going any farther, and the cool tile feels nice against the bare soles of my feet. "Is this an Airbnb?" I ask.

"No, it's my dad's house," he says, setting our bags on the floor.

"He isn't here?"

"He's at a conference in Paris."

"And he doesn't mind us staying overnight?"

Hollis shakes his head. "Nah. I texted him when we stopped for gas to see if we could crash if needed. He said we should make ourselves at home."

I walk over to a built-in bookcase and run my fingers over the leather-bound tomes lining the shelves. The gilt letters on their spines appear to be Cyrillic. "Is this Russian?"

"Yeah. My dad specializes in Russian lit. He's one of the foremost Dostoyevsky experts in the United States."

"Bet he loved Josh's book then."

"Huh?"

"Josh's book. It's supposed to be some sort of modern take on *Notes from Underground*."

"Oh. Is that what he was going for? I thought it was just a lot of navel-gazing through the perspective of a horny, depressed accountant."

A laugh originates deep inside my stomach, weaves over and under my ribs, and barges out of my mouth.

Hollis looks perturbed by the sound I'm making; it must seem to him like an absolutely bonkers amount of laughter in response to what he's said. "What?"

How many times did Josh claim I just didn't *understand* his work? But Hollis can see through his bullshit, which means I'm not alone. That's what I like best about Hollis: He makes me feel like there's nothing wrong with me. For all his fussing about my perhaps worryingly high tolerance for risk, he makes me feel like I can trust myself. And maybe I didn't realize it until he made me start again, but that's something I haven't been doing nearly as often in the last few months.

"That made me very happy is all," I say. My grin is beginning to hurt my cheeks, but it refuses to fade. Something deep inside me feels like it's glowing, and this goofy smile seems to be the only way to safely let out some of the light and heat before I burst.

Hollis stares at me like a cat sizing up a mouse. He stalks over and wraps his arms around me from behind. He's never touched me like this. Then again, he's only been doing it at all for a couple days, so there still must be countless ways he hasn't touched me.

The intimacy between us is dialed way up again, not only physical but something else I can't name as well, and that glow inside me is growing with the encouragement of his warmth—both literal and metaphorical. Then it fizzles out as I remember that we're just friends. Friends who have had sex and may continue to. But still just friends and nothing more. Like is not love. I can't let myself forget that.

My eyes search for something in the room to comment on, to break the silence and get my feelings back on track. I find a framed photo sitting on one of the shelves in front of me. It's of a middle-aged man and a young woman. The man is definitely Hollis's father; they look almost identical except for his father's hair being a handsome salt-and-pepper instead of dark chocolate, and his eyes are both identical in color—the blue-gray of Hollis's right one. "Who's this?" I ask, pointing to the frame. "Your dad and your sister?"

"No, that's Fiancée Number Four. Madison, I think her name is."

"Oh. She's . . . um . . . young."

"Twenty-three." In this position, Hollis's breath tickles my earlobe as he talks. "My father ages, but his girlfriends never seem to."

"Oh. Well. She looks . . . nice."

"She probably is. I haven't met this one yet. Dad didn't start seeing her until after I was here for Christmas, and then he proposed a few weeks ago."

I turn my head to try to meet Hollis's eyes, but instead wind up almost headbutting him. "They got engaged after dating less than five months?"

"It was a record for Dad. Three months from first date to proposal is his usual modus operandi. Guess he's getting more circumspect in his old age." There's a twinge of bitterness in Hollis's sarcasm that I'm tempted to press him on, but I don't get a chance before he says, "Come on, let's get a load of laundry started so we can go to bed."

He slides his hand to my lower back and guides me down a hallway. We stop at a door that looks like it'll open to a linen closet but actually holds a stacked washer and dryer. Hollis fishes my bag of dirty clothes from my suitcase and empties it into the machine, then adds his own collection from his duffel.

"Strip," he orders.

The idea of getting completely naked in the hallway of a stranger's house makes me pause for a moment. What if Hollis's dad isn't in Paris, France, but in like, Paris, Mississippi, and he decides to come home early? But once Hollis is standing in front of me with nothing on except his glasses and watch, it feels almost more uncomfortable not to undress. Walking in on your son and his friend naked might be awkward, but finding him naked and the friend still fully clothed probably raises more questions.

"I need help with my dress," I say.

He pulls the zipper down, his breath warm against my neck but his mouth never touching the skin there. I recall earlier in the morning when he trailed kisses over my shoulders and ran his hands over my body as the dress slipped to the floor, and I'm slightly disappointed he's not initiating a repeat performance. Then again, two orgasms in the last twenty-four hours is already an extremely admirable quantity.

Should I be worried that Hollis somehow makes me go with

such speed from shy about undressing in his dad's house to wanting him to take me on the floor?

The dress turns out to be dry-clean-only (no wonder Connie didn't mind getting rid of it), so I shove it into my suitcase while my bra and dogs-with-sunglasses underwear get thrown into the washer. Hollis adds some detergent and presses the button to start the cycle.

"Onward and upward," he says, guiding me down the hall, his hand returning to the small of my now-naked back. His touch makes my spine feel like undercooked spaghetti. At the end of the hallway, we climb a small staircase, which leads to a bedroom. By the angle of the ceiling, I can tell we're over the garage.

"This was my bedroom over summers and holidays," Hollis says. "And during college, whenever my roommate's long-distance girlfriend came to visit. She snored like a freaking buzz saw."

The room is clean despite its disuse; the bed is made, the dust is minimal, and there aren't any funky smells. But otherwise it's a time capsule. A museum diorama with an interpretive sign reading: MALE TEENAGER'S ROOM, MID-AUGHTS.

"This is a nice space. I'm surprised your dad didn't turn it into a guest suite or a library or something by now. It looks like he hasn't touched a thing in here." I shuffle through a stack of video game cases. "Oh shit, you have a PS2? I'm super good at Guitar Hero."

"I would absolutely obliterate you," he says. It's not a very menacing threat since he sounds like he might fall asleep at any second.

My attention jumps to a framed high school diploma. "'This certifies that Frederick Hollis Hollenbeck has completed'— Wait. *Frederick*?"

"Yep. Named after my father."

"You're a junior?"

He throws himself onto the full-sized bed in the corner. "No. We have different middle names."

"You're telling me this whole time I could've been calling you Freddie? Or Fred? Ooooh. That's even better."

"I am very much *not* telling you that."

My fingers sweep over the spines of the books on a narrow shelf beside his ancient CRT TV. *To Kill a Mockingbird*, *1984*, *The Catcher in the Rye*. Probably his assigned reading for high school English. I spot a few textbooks from college science gen eds, some of Shakespeare's greatest hits, a worn copy of the New Testament. It's interesting seeing what was deemed unworthy of the thousand-mile journey to the bookshelves in his studio in Arlington.

"Stop caressing my books," Hollis says. He has his arms folded over his chest, and with him naked and relaxed on the bed, he looks like he's posing for a life drawing class.

"Jealous?" I ask, yawning halfway through the word. My suitcase is on the end of the bed, and I move toward it to search for my toiletries bag.

I find it but get distracted again before I make it to the bathroom. There's just so much interesting stuff in this room. Little League trophy. Blue and orange CO_2 dragster. Picture of a teenaged Hollis in a baseball uniform (shaggy hair, grimacing, awkwardly cute).

"Really, dude?" I hold up a DVD of *Showgirls* I find beside the TV, sandwiched between *Zoolander* and *Super Troopers*.

"Big Kyle MacLachlan fan," he says.

"Riiiight."

I pick up a tiny, hand-painted wooden turtle bobblehead from his nightstand. I attempt a reenactment of the "Bohemian Rhapsody" scene in *Wayne's World* with it, but it slips out of my hand. It winds up rolling under the bed, so I drop to the floor. The oatmeal-colored Berber carpet is rough against my bare skin as I wiggle myself half under the metal frame and rescue the turtle.

"Hey, did you know you have a baseball bat under here?" I ask. "And a flashlight? At least I hope that's a flashlight."

"I'm not sure what else you think it could be," Hollis says in a faux-innocent tone that makes it clear that he does indeed know what I'm talking about. "Now, as captivating as it is to watch you dig around under there with your bare ass in the air—"

"Hold on . . . what's this?" I slide a slender, forest-green book out from under the bed and read the cover. "Walt Whitman. Did you know this was under there?"

"Wait," Hollis says, almost falling off the bed as he reaches for the book. I dodge his hand and open to the title page. Someone inscribed this copy: *To Hollis—I love your every multitude. Forever yours, Vanessa*

Hollis tears the book from my hands, his face drained of all color.

"So, Vanessa," I say, trying to sound casual. "Who's she?"

"No one worth discussing," he says, and flings Walt Whitman into the empty trash can by the door.

"Wait a second. The other day, when I was joking about you not doing relationships anymore because someone broke your heart—Hollis, is that actually what happened?"

I'm about to laugh when he turns away from me, the muscles in his back hard and tense. Oh. This isn't another remnant of his youth that stayed behind in this room when he moved on to adulthood. It's something he still hauls around with him.

I wrap my arms around his waist and press myself against him. This is my chance to figure out if whatever turned him off love is something he'll ever be willing to cast aside. "What went so wrong with Vanessa that you never want to try again?"

Hollis doesn't respond.

"Will you tell me if I guess correctly?" I ask into his shoulder blade.

He lets out a humorless huff. "Pretty sure you won't."

"Did she cheat?" It's too obvious, but I'd be remiss not to start there. I wait a beat but am met with silence. "Okay, so not that. Did she not actually love your every multitude and disapprove of your aspirations to become a writer?"

Nothing.

"Okay. So what then? She turned out to be a flat-Earther? Ate your goldfish in front of you? Tried to frame you for tax evasion? Don't tell me all this 'lasting love doesn't exist' nonsense is because you ultimately wanted different things."

Hollis flashes one of his horrible, gritted-teeth fake smiles. "If by 'wanted different things,' you mean I wanted to marry her and she wanted revenge on my father, then yeah, I guess we wanted different things."

"What."

His shoulders sag as he exhales, like he can no longer hide the way this weighs on him. "Can we at least have this conversation sitting down?" Hollis takes my hand and leads me to the bed. He sits on the edge and pulls me onto his lap. The skin-on-skin contact lasts about ten seconds before he says, "God, your ass bones are sharp," and knocks me off. I yelp as I fall backward onto the comforter. Hollis sprawls beside me and drapes an arm over my hips, tugging me closer. His eyes dart around as he observes my face. My determination to get some clarification must be apparent, because he asks wearily, "Is there any way I get to go to sleep tonight without talking about this?"

"No. Because I don't think *I* can sleep without talking about this. You can't just say something like that and then not elaborate."

"Fine," he says. "Short version: I was a senior in college, I met a second-year lit PhD student at a lecture, I fell completely and stupidly in love with her way too fast, thought she felt the same way, took her home to meet my dad and sister. Turned out she was my dad's ex and was only with me to get back at him for dumping her."

My eyes go wide and it takes me a while to remember to blink. "I have . . . so many questions. I mean, how did you not—"

I'm not sure if the frown on Hollis's face is deeper than any other he's ever given me, or if laying so close and side-by-side is somehow exaggerating the curve. Still, I get the message: This is the sorest of subjects. Figuring question time is limited, I readjust my strategy to make the most of it. "So clearly things between you and her ended. What happened with you and your dad?"

"We had a huge fight. About how his selfishness had hurt so many people—which I still stand by, actually. I said some unnecessarily terrible things to him, though. Like how I'd always be disappointed to have a father who wasn't a better man."

I'm so tempted to try to dig deeper into what he means by his father's "selfishness," because the way he emphasizes the word reminds me of how adamantly he insists he's ruled by nothing but his own selfish impulses. Like maybe Hollis has convinced himself that his father's choices are a symptom of something genetic, something inescapable that's also embedded in his own DNA. But all I manage to say is, "Ouch."

"I was only twenty-one," he explains. "Young. Impetuous. I did know on some level that I couldn't blame him for what Vanessa did, and I actually agreed with his reasons for breaking up with her once he explained. For all his flaws, my father's always been weirdly ethical in his philandering—that was the first and last time he dated a student in his own department. But I was so angry and heartbroken. And my mother had just died. I needed to be mad at someone. Blame someone. He understood, I think. Understands. But it definitely made our already somewhat-strained relationship a lot worse for a while."

"Considering we are currently staying in his house, does that mean it's better now?"

"We're back on speaking terms, at least. Mostly thanks to my sister. She insisted we patch things up before her wedding. So for the last couple of years, I've been coming here for Christmas and whenever else she and Jan decide to visit. And it's . . . it's all right."

Josh's text to Hollis flashes in my mind. *You should know she's only using you to get back at me. Must've heard that's all you're good for.* "That bastard," I say.

"Pardon?"

"Josh. He knows about this, about what happened with Vanessa, doesn't he? That's why he said what he said in that text. About me using you. To dredge up all those bad memories."

"Yeah. When we were doing memoir stuff in one of our classes, I wrote a bit about it." He brushes my hair from my face, still careful to avoid the bruise from the deer. "I'm sorry I let his stupid texts get to me, by the way. You're nothing like her. You're pretty much the anti-Vanessa, actually."

"And I *swear* I've never even met your dad."

Hollis playfully pushes my shoulder until I'm on my back.

"Not funny," he says from his sudden new position on top of me. But there's a slight lift to the corner of his mouth.

"I'm sorry she hurt you," I say, removing his glasses and placing them on the nightstand. He has that one lusty eye, one annoyed eye thing going on again. But they shift as my words sink in. Now there's vulnerability and some sort of warmth that I haven't seen there before.

"I'm sorry she did too."

It's such an odd and unexpected response that I grab hold of it before it can zoom past unexamined.

"Why are *you* sorry?" When he doesn't immediately respond I nudge him with my elbow. "If you need to apologize for anything, it's your terrible taste in movies as a kid." His eyes follow mine as they drift over to a poster for the 2004 version of *Catwoman*.

"You found my DVD of *Showgirls* and yet you think half-naked Halle Berry was in my room because I was a fan of the movie? You of all people should know how gross teenage boys are about beautiful celebrity women."

"Ew," I say.

"Yeah, well, if it's any consolation at all, I would rather die than walk up to Halle Berry at an airport and reveal that I used to jack it to her on the daily."

"Chivalry isn't dead after all," I say.

Hollis kisses me with a suspicious intensity. He's trying to distract me. But it's not going to work. At least not for more than like . . . a few minutes.

"Why are you sorry she hurt you?" I repeat, turning my head to dodge the next kiss when my need for his words finally overrides my need for his mouth. I know we're already at like a thousand intimacies. I know this was more than Hollis ever meant to share with me. But I'm greedy for whatever is past this. I'm finding that I'm becoming greedy for everything when it comes to him.

Hollis pauses for a moment, letting out a slow sigh.

"Because," he whispers against my skin as his fingers comb deeper into my hair, "if I still believed in happily ever afters, I think I would've begrudgingly enjoyed having one with you."

Hollis stares down at me. If he's waiting for a verbal response, we're going to be here a very long time. I cannot form a coherent thought, much less put one into words. Hollis's declaration is like an eraser scrubbing frantically at a chalkboard, except the chalkboard is my brain and it's now pretty much blank except for some dust to remind me there was once something there.

I take his face in my hands and pull his mouth back to mine. It's the coward's way out, I know. But my affection for Hollis is growing so rapidly that I can hardly keep up with it (much less outrun it). And I don't know how to put that into words without it also sounding like a lament that he can't offer me anything beyond what we're doing right now.

I'm surprised and also somehow not surprised to realize that I am disappointed. Him acknowledging that we might have had a future under different circumstances seems to have pried open the little hope-filled treasure chest that I've kept buried deep inside my heart lately, then plundered its contents in one fell swoop. Kissing the pirate feels easier than confronting him over the theft.

Our nakedness hastens things along, and soon Hollis moves down my body and rests his head on one of my breasts while he cups the other. His thumb brushes over my nipple, back and forth, back and forth. I close my eyes to savor the way the sensation pulls at some intricate knot low in my stomach, threatening to unravel it. My fingers thread into Hollis's hair, and he lets out a barely audible moan as I mimic his rhythm over his scalp. Soon his movements slow. The initial frustration I feel as his hand comes to a rest is eclipsed by the expectation that he is going to switch sides, or maybe use his tongue. Except he doesn't. Because he's fallen asleep.

"Hey," I say, nudging his shoulder. "Wake up."

"Sorry," he mumbles. "I was just . . . taking a short break."

"Yeah, yeah, sure you were."

"Where was I?" He plants a kiss on my breastbone, then gives a yawn so big that I can see the dangly thing in the back of his throat.

I slept something like five hours in the car, but Hollis has been up since early this morning. And last night wasn't exactly restful. "Bedtime," I decide, rolling out from under him.

"But, Mill, I want you—"

"I'm going to be incredibly offended if you fall asleep inside of me, and there's a not-insignificant chance of that happening if we keep going. Sleep, Hollis."

As he drowsily navigates to the pillow, he mumbles a reminder about the laundry and something about how he's cursed to never make it past second base in this room. He's out before I can even ask him for the Wi-Fi password.

Chicago, Illinois
September 1950

ROSE PICKED UP THE TELEPHONE ON THE SECOND RING. THE OP-
erator requested she please hold for a long-distance call from
Miss Elsie Brown in Los Angeles. Her heart knocked against her
ribs in a way that made her breathless as she waited for Elsie's
voice—so familiar, yet rarely heard since the war—to come over
the line.

In that first letter in 1946, Rose had confessed that she regretted the way things had ended between them. Elsie had responded,
"Then let's not allow that to be the end." They had since carried
on a steady correspondence. With Rose married and over a thousand miles separating them, their relationship transformed into
something more akin to friendship than passion. Still, the words
that they could not put on paper outright were ghosts haunting the
spaces between each line; their love for each other lingered even
as it was forced to take new forms.

"Who is it?" Dick asked from the sofa, his face buried in a
book for one of his graduate classes.

"My friend Elsie Brown. From the Navy. She's calling from Los Angeles."

"Los Angeles? I thought Elsie still lived in Florida."

Elsie, joking that she could never again live in a landlocked state, had rented an apartment in Miami after her discharge instead of returning home to Oklahoma. Rose frowned as she adjusted the telephone's receiver in her palm. "So did I. I've no idea what she's doing in California."

"Well, give her my regards," Dick muttered around his pipe stem as he noticed an ink stain on his pant leg. He looked every bit the librarian he was studying to become.

"I will," she said. Of course, Rose had never told Dick that Elsie was so much more than a friend. Sometimes Rose wondered if her husband would be jealous if he knew. She wondered if he would understand the magnitude of her love for Elsie, and if it would make him feel fury, or maybe pity, or—perhaps worst of all—if he would write it off as a silly little wartime peccadillo that warranted no strong feeling from him at all.

Though letters arrived with regularity, she and Elsie had only spoken on the phone a handful of times: once in 1947 a few days after a terrible hurricane hit Florida and Rose couldn't bear waiting around to receive a letter reporting on how Elsie had fared, and last New Year's Eve, when Elsie called after a few glasses of whiskey and slurred whispered memories of making love on the beach, while the din of boisterous conversation, clink of champagne glasses, and Mel Tormé's "Careless Hands" in her living room competed for Rose's attention.

"Rosie." Now Elsie's voice came through the receiver like an exhale, and Rose knew today's call wasn't courtesy of some alcohol-fueled bout of nostalgia.

"Els. Is anything the matter?"

"I've been recalled from the Reserves. The Navy's been caught with their pants down in Korea. They need all the medical personnel they can get."

Rose's words caught in her throat, which was perhaps for the best because all she could think of was how Korea was so far away—even farther than Elsie already was from her.

"Rosie, darlin'? Are you there?"

"Yes, yes. Sorry. The Navy is sending you to Korea then?"

"Thereabouts. A hospital ship. The USS *Haven*. We sail next week."

Rose fought through her rising panic—Elsie, across the world, close to the front—and searched for some concrete action she could take to alleviate the worry that squeezed at her throat. "Shall I . . . shall I fly out there to see you off?"

Dick peered over his book with sudden interest.

Elsie's musical laugh traveled through the telephone wires and tickled Rose's ear as if she were just beside her. "No, Rosie. No, it would be terribly expensive, and you've got your family to care for. How are Dick and the boys?"

"They're fine, but Els—"

"Besides, if you show up here and I hold you again, I don't know if I can make myself get on that ship." Her voice sounded thick with emotion. Rose's own tears threatened to spill from her eyes. Not right now, she thought, not in front of Dick.

"Speaking of things that are terribly expensive," Elsie continued, her tone light again in an artificial way that only made everything worse, "this call is long-distance, and I'm back to being a meager Navy surgical nurse. Even with the nighttime discount, the minutes are adding up." She paused. "Listen, I know

you probably can't say it back—I'm sure you aren't alone—but . . .
I called because I needed you to know before I leave that I love
you, Rosie. You are the love of my life. No matter what happens,
or where I am, or who I am with, it will always be you. And just in
case—"

"No, please don't—"

"Just in case," she repeated more slowly, "something should
happen to me, I need you to know that my final moments—
whether they come tomorrow or a hundred years from now—will
be spent thinking of you. Of your smile, and your laugh, and holding you close in the warm sand."

Rose glanced at her husband. Dick's full attention was now
upon her.

"Elsie, please be careful over there." She hoped everything
else she wanted to say would somehow make it into Elsie's heart
through those words alone.

"I will. I promise. But I do really have to go now. Someone else
is wanting to use the phone and they're starting to get impatient."

"All right."

"All right." There was a brief silence, and Rose worried they
had already been disconnected. Then Elsie's voice came over the
line again, so soft and sweet. "Send me a pigeon, darlin', if the
mood ever strikes."

"I will, Els. I will."

"Goodbye, Rosie."

Then the call ended, and Rose's tears finally fell. She blinked
and Dick was beside her, taking her hand in his. "You forgot to
give her my regards," he said softly, planting a kiss on Rose's palm
before going to check on their sleeping sons, leaving his wife to
her thoughts.

18

· · · · ·

I'M WRAPPED IN HOLLIS'S ARMS WHEN MY PHONE ALARM GOES
off. Night two and my self-imposed no-cuddling rule is already
shattered. After the washing machine buzzed, I turned over the
laundry, then used the bathroom and climbed back into bed. I
watched Hollis sleep just long enough to feel creepy. Then I
thought, why the hell not, and kissed him goodnight on the cheek.
He stirred enough to gather me in his strong arms and, despite not
having felt all that tired a moment before, I was dead to the world
in no time.

I reach over and silence my phone. I don't remember setting it,
but I'm grateful I did. Today is the day. We are going to reunite
Mrs. Nash and Elsie. There are so many ways this could go awry.
But I refuse to think of a single one of them. Because as blank as
my brain was last night, this morning it's buzzing like a hive of
caffeinated bees. I'm starting to understand that even though like
is not love, it's dangerously close to it on my end. Maybe the only
thing keeping it from being mutual is Hollis's need for proof that

forever is something that exists in real life and not just in fairy tales. Didn't he tell me in the car that he wants to be convinced he's wrong?

So we are going to need to get moving. I have to give Mrs. Nash and Elsie their happily ever after. Because I think maybe, if I can make that happen, I might get one too.

I grind my ass into Hollis's crotch. "Wake up, wake up, wake up," I say in a robot voice.

"You are the most annoyingly arousing alarm clock," he mumbles, his hand sliding over my stomach toward the copper-colored hair between my legs.

"Nope. No time to waste." I slide out from his arms and step over to my suitcase.

He groans. "I don't see how it would be a waste of time. I've been hard four times since yesterday afternoon without actually getting to come. If my balls were any bluer they could take the place of Uranus and Neptune in a solar system diorama."

Don't laugh because he said Uranus. Don't do it.

"Sorry," I say. "All these false starts haven't exactly been a walk in the park for me either." I open a dresser drawer and find a collection of old, balled-up socks. "Now, get up in the next thirty seconds or I'm going to pelt you with these. Don't let their softness fool you. I have a great arm. I played softball like . . . twice. And my team almost won one of those times. So don't test me, Frederick Hollis Hollenbeck."

He sighs and rolls his eyes like the teenager who used to live in this room, but gets out of bed anyway. I take a quick shower in his dad's large master bathroom while Hollis does the same in the smaller hall bath so we don't get sidetracked. We barely speak as we fold the laundry and gather the handful of items we bothered unpacking. I don't know if it's because of what he said last night and how I didn't acknowledge it with anything except my tongue in his mouth, or if it's because today is effectively the end of this journey. But an odd nervous energy has settled heavy over our interactions like a weighted blanket that's increasing my anxiety instead of easing it.

Once we're in the car, I open the fig bars we found in the pantry. It's not necessarily my ideal breakfast—figs weird me out ever since I learned how they're pollinated—but unlike his taste in women, Hollis's dad's culinary preferences are decidedly of his age, and fig bars won out over a box of cereal that looked like tiny twigs.

"Fig me," Hollis says, and holds out his palm. I lay a cookie in his hand and watch him bite into it, teeth sinking into its softness as he backs out of the driveway.

"Did you know that for figs to grow at least one wasp has to die inside of it and be absorbed into the fruit?" I say.

He stops chewing for a moment. "I did not. What a delightful fact to share with me mid-bite."

I nibble at my cookie but find I don't have much of an appetite. Not because of the wasps. But because each minute, each fraction of a mile we get closer to meeting Elsie, the more nervous I become. My knee bounces. My heartbeat thuds like a heavy object falling down several flights of stairs. I'm a ball of terrified energy. For an absurd moment, I ponder getting out of the car and running all the way to Key West. Flying like a bird, or a rocket. If I shook up my bottled anxiety, opened its cap, and let it explode, it would probably propel me the rest of the way to our destination.

And to think, this is only a small fraction of what Mrs. Nash would have felt had we been able to visit Elsie together—with

Mrs. Nash alive and not in my backpack, I mean. What must it be like to see the person you love after decades and decades apart? My heart did a sort of drunk version of the "Macarena" this morning when Hollis reappeared after his shower, and he was only out of my sight for twenty minutes. Not that what I feel for Hollis is anything like the enduring love Mrs. Nash felt for Elsie. What we have isn't love at all, it's just like. Extremely strong like. Now my knee is bouncing half because of today's mission and half because I'm nervous Hollis will somehow see through all of my faux cool and know that I hope to change his mind about lasting love for reasons other than wanting to be right.

"Did Mrs. Nash know you found Elsie?" he asks.

"No. I didn't find her until after Mrs. Nash died." I shift around in my seat, suddenly aware of everywhere I'm not comfortable. "I was going to start looking right after she told me about her, but I agreed to do some fact-checking for a War of 1812 drama, and that wound up taking up most of my time for a while." I fidget with the zipper on my backpack. "I wish I'd prioritized it. Sometimes I wonder, if I'd found her earlier, maybe Mrs. Nash would have lived longer. Like if she knew Elsie hadn't been killed in Korea after all, the prospect of getting to see her again might've been enough to keep her around."

"It's not your fault Mrs. Nash died, you know," he says in a warm, low voice that caresses my guilty conscience. "I don't think anything you did or didn't do had any effect on the timing."

I do know that on some level, but it's one of those things that's easy to know but difficult to make myself feel. "You're pretty good at absolution. Maybe you should've been a priest."

"One, I'm not Catholic. Two, should I be offended you'd prefer me celibate?"

"Oh. Right. Not a priest then." My mind has lost the thread of this remarkably fast, devolving into me mentally dressing Hollis in different occupational uniforms. "You'd make a really hot car mechanic," I say.

"Do those grant absolution?"

"No, but they do wear coveralls. I think you would look really good in those."

Hollis shakes his head, a small smile at the corner of his mouth. "Such a weirdo," he says with the same affection I used to hear in Mrs. Nash's voice whenever she called me a *silly thing*.

"You know you love me," I counter without thinking. An awkward silence descends. I reach to turn on the radio, hoping to find a way out of it, but the new classic rock station Hollis found us when we lost the last one is currently playing an endless queue of commercials. "So . . . late-stage capitalism. Not great, huh?" I say, grabbing onto the first change of subject that pops into my head.

A small huff-laugh comes out through Hollis's nostrils. "I bet you're great at parties."

"I am. I am great at parties." If I wasn't sitting, I would put my hands on my hips. "I'll have you know, most people find me charming."

"I'm sure they do. Why are you assuming I was being sarcastic?"

"Because you have two modes, Hollis: sarcastic and Cormac McCarthy."

"I think I'm supposed to be offended," he says. "But I'm going to choose to take that as a compliment."

Yet another commercial—this one for a car dealership in Miami—prompts Hollis to reach over and turn the volume down.

His eyes dart over to me for the briefest moment. Oh no. He

wants to talk about something; I can tell by the way he bites his cheek. I really hope it isn't my "You love me" comment. There's really no need to emphasize that he doesn't.

"I'd like to ask you something personal," he says. "You don't have to answer."

"Oh. Um. Okay?" I say.

"Josh Yaeger. Why?"

"You mean like why did I date him?"

"Date him, share a bed with him, move in with him. Yes. All of that. Why?"

Given what I've said about Josh's and my relationship, I can see why someone would question the appeal of a sneaky, self-serving asshole who couldn't even get me off most of the time. And yet the question hurts. It feels like Hollis is asking how I could have been so stupid. While I have to admit I asked myself that same thing a million times after the breakup, it has a different sting when it comes from him.

"He wasn't always such a douchecanoe, you know," I say, unable to keep the defensiveness from my voice. "It's not like I met him as he currently is and was like, wow, what a catch. He used to be . . ." My lips purse and shift to the side as I try to remember the good times. The breakfasts in bed and the surprise trip to New York City to see Dani and celebrate me finishing my master's (or was that all just for Instagram too?). "He was handsome. Ambitious. A little uptight, yeah, but in a charming, starchy way. It was fun to unravel him a bit. Keep him from taking himself too seriously. But then during the second semester of the MFA he won an award for a short story, and some big-deal author he met at a conference blew smoke up his ass about how he could be the next great American novelist. That's when he changed. His ambition stopped being attractive. He became obsessed with success and people thinking he's brilliant and—well, you know what he's like now. Other people are either competition or a means to an end."

Hollis doesn't say anything as he reaches for my hand. His thumb brushes back and forth over my open palm. The motion grounds me while also sending sparks of pleasure into my bloodstream.

"Josh told me once that the reason he loved me was because I could always rescue him from the dark moods he fell into while writing. That I reminded him of the importance of living in the light. I thought it was romantic. I didn't realize until the end that he was just *Garden State*-ing me."

Hollis removes his hand from mine so he can navigate around a pokey RV, and I miss the contact immediately. This is going to be such a problem if I have to quit him cold turkey.

"So you were his manic pixie dream girl?" he asks.

"Yeah. Hey, you understood that."

"It helps that sleeping in my old bedroom apparently pushed your references into the current century."

"Eh, don't get used to it," I warn.

"Right. The early aughts are much too recent for an old soul like you."

"Blech." I stick my tongue out.

"What?"

"The term 'old soul.' Almost every person who has ever called me that was a man twice my age trying to explain why it wasn't actually creepy that he wanted to get in my pants."

Hollis's frown stretches. "Noted."

"Anyway," I say, "once it became clear that I had my own ideas and dreams and wasn't his salvation or some fun accessory to make his shitty personality pop, I think Josh started to resent me. He did a good job of hiding it, though. I didn't notice until the Instagram thing. In retrospect, there were clues, but . . . I don't know. I thought he loved me. There wasn't reason to question it."

"Yeah. I know how that is," Hollis says.

I guess he does. Maybe his relationship with Vanessa wasn't that different from mine with Josh—just shorter-lived and longer ago. We were both used by the people who claimed to care about us. Except Hollis looked at his parents' fractured marriage, his father's tendency to jump from coed to coed, and Vanessa's deceit, and saw evidence that lasting love is a lie; while I put three tablespoons of my elderly best friend in my backpack and booked a flight to Florida to prove that it isn't foolish to keep believing someone might genuinely care for someone else for a lifetime.

As the water signaling we've reached the Keys appears outside my window, sparkling in the morning sun, I know it's not much longer until we discover which of us is right.

19

* * * *

"YOU HAVEN'T SAID ANYTHING FOR A WHILE. IT'S MAKING ME NER-
vous," Hollis says as we travel across yet another bridge.

"Sorry," I say. "I don't really feel like talking."

"That's okay. We can just listen to music." We gave up on the
radio an hour ago after the supposed classic rock station played
Nickelback. Surprisingly, Hollis was more upset about it than I
was and insisted we listen to my road-trip playlist again. So I imagine hell has reached record-low temperatures.

"Never Going Back Again" comes on, and I automatically
reach out to guard the on/off button for the stereo. "Okay, I know
you don't like Fleetwood Mac. But this one's super short and it
isn't even Stevie Nicks singing, so please can we just—"

"Millicent," he says. "I wasn't going to turn it off. I don't mind
this song, and I know how much you like it."

"Wait," I say. "No. Stop that. Stop *not* being rude about my music.
It makes me feel like you feel sorry for me, and there's no reason for
you to feel sorry for me yet. Don't act like I've already failed."

"I don't feel sorry for you, but sweetheart—"

"*Sweetheart?*" I react to the term of endearment as if he reached over and pinched my arm. "What the hell is going on with you? Why are you calling me that? Stop it."

Hollis's eyes dart to the side for a second and his frown shifts from his standard one to the medium-deep one that means he's frustrated. "No, you stop it."

"Why don't you make me," I grumble.

"Because," Hollis says. "I don't make monkeys, I just train 'em."

"Oh yeah, well— Wait. Was that— Hollis, did you just quote *Pee-wee's Big Adventure*?"

My eyes blink rapidly like they're trying to clear a speck of dust, unable to believe what they're seeing. Hollis's mouth is slowly transforming, the corners stretching and lifting, his lips parting and exposing teeth. But it doesn't end at that gorgeous, genuine smile. No! The teeth part a bit and a loud, joyful sound comes from somewhere deep inside of his body. Holy shit. Hollis is laughing. Not exhaling a huff of amusement, but full on *laughing*.

It hits me in the chest like a massive and unexpected wave, made more unexpected because I somehow convinced myself my feelings for him were a bathtub instead of an ocean.

"Pull over." My voice comes out scratchy. Maybe my heart is clawing my esophagus as it tries to climb its way out.

The laugh fades into its more familiar, less destructive version. "What? Why?"

"Pull over," I repeat. "Please."

I've lost awareness of our surroundings, so it's pure luck that I've made this demand while on one of the islands and not in the middle of a long stretch of road over the water. Hollis turns into an empty parking lot for a gift shop called The Sea+Shell, which isn't open this early in the morning.

"What's wrong?" he asks. "Do not tell me you left Mrs. Nash at my dad's—"

"No, no. I have her. I just needed, I need . . ." I bury my fingers into my hair, hard against my scalp.

"What do you need, Mill?"

I need you. Now and after this is all over. Because I think I'm falling in love with you, and I'm sorry. I'm so sorry. I know that's not how this arrangement is supposed to work, and that you don't do relationships. I don't expect you to feel the same way, I just . . . shit. I'm sorry. I promise I didn't mean to do it.

That is what's going to come out of my mouth in about three seconds if I do not take immediate action. With getting to Elsie in time (and then actually meeting her) already claiming every available square inch of my anxiety—not to mention that Hollis and I will still be stuck in this car together for another hour—I know this is not the time to take this leap. I lean toward the driver's side, trying to close the distance between us, but the seat belt protests my sudden movement and locks, pulling me back against the seat.

"I need you—" is all that manages to slip past my lips before Hollis pushes the button to free me from the belt.

He pulls me to him, his kiss saving both of us from my inability to keep anything to myself. My right foot is twisted in the strap of my backpack, and the gear shift is digging into my hip. But it's the most right I've felt since I left his arms this morning. Hollis releases his own seat belt so he can adjust the angle, and his hands are in my hair, gripping, gently pulling to tilt my head back more.

"Good," he says against my lips. I have no idea if it's commentary on my needing him or my kissing performance; either way, I'll take it.

I practically throw his glasses onto the dashboard, then reach for the hem of his T-shirt and slide my hand inside to touch the warm skin of his stomach. Hollis's tongue leaves my mouth, and I whimper in protest until it reappears against the sensitive skin under my ear.

"Condom?" I gasp.

His response is either a nuzzle or a head shake. "Buried in my bag in the trunk," he says.

For the briefest of seconds, I imagine declaring that I don't care, that I want him inside me right now and Rule Number Two be damned. Even though the madness is extremely fleeting and I am almost certain I haven't said anything aloud, Hollis freezes. "No. We . . . No, Mill. We can't."

Rule Number Two might be discarded in a fit of passion (or, let's be real, stupidity). But Rule Number One is nonnegotiable. Besides, I know that the heat and tension twisting through my body is more emotional than physical. Sex isn't going to ease it—not completely. And do we really want to have to pay to get Ryan's car detailed before returning it to him?

I cradle Hollis's stubbled jaw in my hand and turn his head until our lips match up again. Our kisses are slow, soft. A cooldown stretch after an ill-advised sprint.

"I'm nervous not knowing how this ends," I whisper against his mouth.

"Me too," he responds as he retrieves his glasses. His full attention shifts to removing a fingerprint from one of the lenses with the hem of his shirt. "But let's go find out together."

We're pulling into the nursing facility's parking lot by the time I realize we might not have been talking about the same thing.

Chicago, Illinois
August 1952

COVERED IN SO MANY STAMPS AND MARKINGS, THE ENVELOPE
looked more like something Richie had practiced his writing upon
than a returned letter. Rose had sent Elsie many over the last two
years, and all of them had reached her promptly and without inci-
dent (except the one a few months ago where Walter had pried off
one of the stamps without her noticing). The postage was intact
on this one, but perhaps she had made some other silly mistake.
At least it came back just in time; by tomorrow they would no
longer be living in Chicago. They were headed to Washington,
DC, where they were staying with a buddy of Dick's from the
army until they could find an apartment. It was wonderful that her
husband had been hired at George Washington University, but the
logistics involved with the move itself were proving to be a bit of
a test of their marriage.

She stared down at the envelope in her hands. If only she could
read through the bold red lines and faded black and maroon
ink declaring this and that to determine which one held the

explanation for why this letter hadn't made it to Elsie. At least she could focus better now with Richie and Walter finally asleep.

She stood in their living room among dozens of moving boxes, stacked three high in some places, trying to navigate the envelope's cluttered markings. Then finally, on the front, under the address and the several lines striking it out, she saw it—dark pinkish gray and worn from travel, the type blunt and offensively nonchalant in its message.

VERIFIED DECEASED

Rose fell to her knees, clutching the letter to her chest as if putting pressure on a mortal wound in a futile attempt to keep from bleeding out. That's how Dick found her when he arrived home half an hour later—kneeling on the carpet behind a tower of boxes, her eyes painfully swollen, the skin of her cheeks uncomfortably tight as her tears evaporated, her body reft of its moisture and left trembling.

"Rose? What's happened? Are the boys all right?" he asked, dropping to the floor beside her.

"She's gone. Elsie. She's . . . she's dead."

Dick swept Rose into his arms and carried her to their bed as he had on their wedding night. She sat on the edge of the mattress and allowed her husband to remove her shoes, her stockings, to unbutton the eleven buttons on the front of her dress and slide the fabric away. Her underthings posed a slight challenge, but Dick coaxed his wife to cooperate enough to relieve her of the constricting brassiere and girdle. He dressed her in one of his pajama shirts, since it was one of the few articles of bedclothes they hadn't yet packed. As he pulled the flannel over her arms and shoulders and buttoned the front, Rose felt like a small, helpless child. Then Dick tucked her under the covers and slid into the bed beside her.

He pulled Rose against him, and for a split second she resented the sound of his heart, beating so strong inside his chest when Elsie's was forever stilled. The shame she felt at the thought managed to unbury some previously unknown store of tears, and she sobbed against her husband's strong, warm chest.

"Shh," he whispered into her hair. "I know, sweetheart. I know."

Rose very much doubted that. How could he know what it was like to lose someone who felt like part of you when he didn't even know that his wife had never been wholly his?

"Dick, I . . . I . . ." She couldn't say she loved Elsie; it refused to come out after all these years of practice keeping it to herself. The shame washed over her again, this time because she suspected that Elsie knew all along that Rose wasn't brave enough to love her aloud.

Dick adjusted Rose until he could cup her face in his hands. "Elsie was more than a friend to you, wasn't she?" His voice was quiet, and his eyes glistened as if he too were on the verge of crying.

Rose managed to dip her chin, the smallest nod.

"You loved her," Dick said. It wasn't a question.

"Yes," Rose whispered, squeezing her eyes shut, trying to alleviate the ache settling into every crevice of her body. "So very much."

"Oh, sweetheart. How I wish I could bring her back for you."

Dick tucked Rose's trembling body against him again and pressed his lips to her temple as she cried herself to sleep.

20

· · · · ·

FROM THE OUTSIDE, THE PALMS AT SOUTHERNMOST LOOKS LIKE A
hotel—three stories, buttery-yellow stucco with emerald-green
shutters that match the tropical shrubbery around the perimeter, a
one-story annex that could house an indoor pool. But inside, there's
no denying that this place isn't a Hilton; it's a hospital in disguise.
Fluorescent lighting, scuffed linoleum floors, the rhythmic beep of
a machine somewhere down the hall. The smell of cheap maple
syrup from the breakfast trays stacked on a nearby cart clashes with
some sort of bleach-based disinfectant and the lingering scent of
human waste. A nurse with supplies piled in her arms cuts through
the lobby at a power walk. A resident sits at a table working on a
puzzle, and his eyes narrow as he pretends not to be eavesdrop-
ping on two nearby women in wheelchairs.

"Hey," Hollis says. "You okay?"

"Yeah, why?"

He runs a hand down my arm. "You're shaking."

"Probably low blood sugar. All I had for breakfast was half a fig bar," I say.

Hollis looks entirely unconvinced but doesn't argue. His fingers intertwine with mine as we approach the large half-circle reception desk in the center of the lobby.

The woman is on the phone, cradling it between ear and shoulder like a pro. She gives us a smile to let us know she'll be with us shortly. When she speaks into the receiver, I recognize her slight Jamaican accent. So this must be Rhoda, the receptionist I spoke to when I called the other day.

"Hello," she says, placing the phone in its cradle when her call ends. "How can I help you?"

I glance at Hollis, begging him with my eyes to talk for me. He gives me a subtle shake of his head and squeezes my hand. He's right; this is what I came all this way to do, and I need to be the one to do it. For myself. And for Mrs. Nash.

"We're here to see a resident. Elsie Brown," I force myself to say. "I'm not sure of her room number, but I believe she's in . . . in hospice care."

The receptionist's kind smile collapses, and I know. I just *know* what's coming. It's as if I'm standing in the middle of a worn-out bridge, and the rotten wood and frayed rope preventing me from plummeting into the dark, watery chasm below is rapidly disintegrating before my eyes.

"You're the young lady who called on Wednesday, aren't you?" Rhoda asks.

I nod. I can't speak with this lump in my throat. My nose burns as the tears gather, ready to spill.

"I'm so sorry, honey. I wanted to let you know, but I didn't have a way to reach you. Miss Elsie passed away Thursday morning."

"No," I hear myself say. "No, that can't be right. My flight was scheduled for Thursday *afternoon*. I was supposed to get here first thing Friday. So she couldn't have . . . She has to be . . ."

Suddenly, I'm not inside myself but out. Hollis has his arms wrapped around a small redheaded woman's waist, holding her to his body so she doesn't collapse into a crying heap on the cold linoleum floor. His low "shhh"s and "I've got you"s in her ear are surprisingly audible for how far away I'm standing from them. *It must be so nice to be comforted like that*, I find myself thinking before I remember I *am* being comforted like that. And then all of the sensation comes rushing back. Strong arms that squeeze almost to the point of pain against my slack body. Hollis's lips against my ear as he attempts to soothe me with a flood of words my brain can't process. Hot tears streaming down my cheeks. One extremely gross snot bubble that keeps inflating and deflating in rhythm with my erratic breathing.

"Millicent," Hollis says.

I lift my face to meet his eyes. Is that moisture glistening in the corner of the blue-gray one, or does it only seem like that because I'm looking through a curtain of water myself?

"I'm going to take you back to the car, okay?"

An attempt at a nod turns into a new, stronger bout of crying. I bury my face into his chest, turning the cotton of his T-shirt damp on contact.

"Hold on to me," he says.

As if I could ever let you go. Thankfully my grief-drunk brain thinks the thought but can't direct my mouth to say it. Which is good because he apparently meant it literally; he hoists me into his arms, carrying me like a bride. I wrap an arm around his neck and fist his shirt in my hands.

There's a metallic clunk as Hollis kicks at the automatic door button positioned low on the frame, followed by the quiet whir and woosh of the door opening. The light breeze feels like ice on my wet face, just like that night outside the restaurant in George-town. But here in Key West, Hollis's lips press against my temple to summon the warmth to return.

"I'm going to put you down now," he says.

He bends until the soles of my sandals reach the asphalt, loos-ening his grip incrementally to ensure I won't crumple to the ground as soon as he releases me. Finally, I'm on my feet, standing of my own accord.

"I'm sorry, Mill," he says, cupping my face in his hands. "I'm so sorry."

"No," I say. "This is a mistake. It has to be a mistake again."

"Millicent." Hollis's voice is filled with so much pity that it tears apart my sorrow and repairs it with anger.

I push him away. "No! This isn't the first time she's done this, you know. She isn't actually dead. We just need to find her. I found her before, I can find her again—"

"Mill, she's gone. I'm sorry, but she's really gone."

I'm rewrapped in Hollis's arms, his hand on the back of my head. I know deep inside that he's right, and my shoulders heave with every sob.

"I'm going to put you into the car, and then I'm going to go back inside. Will you be all right for a minute?"

I don't understand why Hollis is going back in there, what he hopes to accomplish. We're too late. And I would have been too late even if everything had gone according to plan. I never even had a chance, did I?

I give a weak nod as I'm guided into the passenger seat, and Hollis drops my little leather backpack onto my lap. "I'll leave you two to chat," he says in a way that sounds like he's surprised he doesn't find that statement absurd. He squeezes my knee before closing the door.

It's good that he left, because I'm becoming aware of how much of a wreck I am, and oh no, it's mortifying. He had to *carry me out* of there. I'm sure The Palms at Southernmost has seen its share of grieving friends and family, but something tells me the residents and staff are going to be talking about the hysterical little redhead for weeks to come.

"Oh, Mrs. Nash. I'm sorry. I'm so sorry. I made such a scene. I know I have no right to be so upset that she's gone—I never even met Elsie—but . . ." I choke back another sob. "I really wanted to. And more than that, I needed to do this for you. I failed. I failed you."

I know Mrs. Nash wouldn't have blamed me. Ninety-eight years on Earth means you lose a lot of people you love very much; she outlived a husband, a son, her parents, most of her siblings, countless friends, and—she believed—Elsie. She understood better than most that death doesn't care about things like flight schedules. But knowing that doesn't mean I can make myself believe it right now.

Hollis returns to the car sometime later to find me half-asleep, clutching my backpack to my chest.

He leans over to press a kiss to my temple, then brushes my hair behind my ear with his thumb and plants another, feather-light, on the edge of my plum-and-gold bruise. "Let's go to the hotel," he says. His over-the-top sweetness feels too much like pity—a reminder of my failure—and it makes me want to start crying all over again.

The hotel—which was extremely accommodating each of the three times I called to change my reservation while we were on the road—isn't far from The Palms at Southernmost. Before I know it, I'm standing red-faced and swollen-eyed in front of a large, whitewashed check-in desk while Hollis takes care of everything.

How would I have managed this if he weren't with me? I want to believe I would have done all right alone. I am a competent adult woman who can handle whatever life throws at me. But I'm so glad I don't have to prove it right now.

In our hotel room, I sit on the edge of the bed in a sort of here-but-not-really state, vaguely aware of the sound of running water in the bathroom. Time stretches and contracts, and I'm unsure how much of it has passed when Hollis appears again, kneeling in front of me.

"Bath's ready," he says. "Let's get you out of your clothes, okay?"

I manage a nod but don't have the energy for much else. Hollis removes my shoes and socks first, and presses a light kiss to my ankle before taking off my shirt, shorts, bra, and underwear while whispering requests to hold up my arms, lift my hips, stand. His touch is gentle and warm, intimate without demanding anything. That's how he washes me too; the way he runs the washcloth over my skin is thorough without feeling clinical, caressing without veering into sexual. At some point, his sweetness stops rubbing me the wrong way, no longer seeming forced or pitying but like a secret part of him I've unlocked. I feel cared for. Adored.

Reuniting Elsie and Mrs. Nash was supposed to remind me

that love can last a lifetime. That forever is a possibility for me too, if I only keep believing. But when Hollis wraps me in one of the fluffy white robes on the back of the bathroom door, leads me to the bed, and cocoons me in his arms, I suddenly understand that forever isn't the part that I almost lost faith in. It was the millions of right-nows along the way.

21

• • • • •

AFTER A FEW HOURS, I BEGIN TO FEEL LIKE MYSELF AGAIN. THE world stops cutting in and out like a poorly edited movie and just . . . is. We're sitting on the bed, propped up on like a dozen fluffy hotel pillows, my head resting against Hollis's shoulder. He turns on the TV and pushes the button for the guide.

"What do you want to watch?" he asks.

"Don't care," I mumble into his shirt. It comes out croaky and congested, like I'm a toad with severe seasonal allergies.

"Oh, here we go," he says. "*The Blues Brothers*. This is the movie you were joking about with Mike, right?"

Wow. Mike and the airport feels like a distant memory, but it was only four days ago. Four days is how long I've been traveling with Hollis. Four days is how long Elsie has been dead. How can so much change in less than a standard workweek?

I try to pay attention to Jake and Elwood Blues with their filthy mouths and bad attitudes. Hollis chuckles at a few lines, and the eye that's closest to me—the blue-gray one—sparkles in response to the gratuitous car chases. I would usually be thrilled that he's enjoying it, but it's a challenge to feel anything right now without it leading back into the deep, dark grief that left me sobbing against Hollis's chest again after my bath. Instead of risking a repeat performance, I force myself to focus on Hollis's fingers, the way they brush up and down my arm with just enough pressure for me to feel his touch through the thick terry cloth of my robe.

"I'm sorry," I say.

"For what?"

"Being such a mess."

He moves so his lips rest against my head. It feels like little kisses along my hairline as his mouth moves with his words. "You're allowed to be a mess. You're grieving."

"There's no reason for me to be this upset. I didn't even know her. Not really."

"You can definitely grieve someone you don't know," Hollis says. "But I don't think you're grieving Elsie."

"I'm . . . not?"

"No. I mean, maybe a little. But that's not what has you this upset."

"What is it then?"

"I think you're grieving Mrs. Nash," he says.

"That doesn't make any sense," I protest. "She died over two months ago."

"Yeah. And what did you do when it happened?"

"Well, when she wouldn't wake up, I called 9-1-1—"

"No, I don't mean immediately. What I'm asking is did you ever take the time to properly mourn her? All the things you lost?"

"She was really old," I say. "It was her time, and I know she wasn't afraid—"

"It doesn't matter if it was somewhat expected or if it was a freak accident. You were so close with her." In response to my blank stare, he continues, "Millicent, you broke up with your long-term boyfriend, moved out of your shared apartment, lost your best friend, and had to find another new place to live all in the course of like six months. That's a lot for anyone to deal with. A lot of loss and change. And did you? Did you actually process it?"

Unless carrying around Mrs. Nash's ashes while doggedly tracking down the woman she loved to reassure myself that wanting someone to want me back for the rest of my life isn't pointless counts, then, no. No, I did not.

"It's okay," he says when I still don't respond aloud. "I'm not criticizing. As far as coping strategies go, occupying yourself with all this was one of the better options. When my mom died and then Vanessa . . ."—he waves his hands in a gesture that I guess is supposed to represent *completely destroyed me in her quest for revenge*—"I tried to avoid feeling anything by drinking too much and being a dick to everyone."

"You're still a dick to everyone," I say with as much of a smile as my tired face can manage.

"What can I say? I found it suited me. A lot more than the drinking, anyway. You probably won't believe this, but I'm an extremely affectionate drunk."

My skull feels like it's filled with concrete that's starting to dry as I lift it from Hollis's shoulder to get a look at his face. "You are not," I say. "There's no way."

"It's true. Tequila in particular makes me absurdly insistent on group hugs. Friends, enemies, acquaintances, strangers. Anyone and everyone who's around must join in."

"That must have been difficult. All that hard work keeping

people away with your gruff personality undone by your enjoyment of a good mass squeeze."

"A mass squeeze," he repeats with the smallest of smiles. "That's a Millicentism if I ever heard one."

I stretch my arms around Hollis's neck and rub myself against his jaw like a cat needing attention. He wraps me in a tight embrace. "I'm only one person," I say against his throat. "But is this doing it for you?"

"Needs more arms."

"Sorry I'm not an octopus," I say.

His breath ruffles the hair near my temple as he sighs. "Nobody's perfect."

I shuffle onto his lap, wrapping my legs around him too. "Is this any better?"

"I don't have any complaints."

We remain like this for a while, me clinging to his front as if I want to be absorbed into him and Hollis holding me tight like he might not mind that so much.

"If I haven't said it yet, thank you for taking care of me during my embarrassing public breakdown."

"Anytime," he says.

Hollis's chest rises and falls against mine. His pulse beats against my ear. This is a hundred thousand intimacies, so many more than I've ever experienced before—with Hollis or with anyone. It doesn't feel like too many. It doesn't feel like not enough. It feels like exactly the right amount for this moment.

"What happens next?" I ask.

"Probably food soon. You've barely eaten today."

On cue, my stomach rumbles long and loud like an oncoming avalanche.

"I gave Rhoda your phone number to pass along to Elsie's next of kin," he says, acknowledging what he knows I was really asking. "I told her we'd be in town for a day or two. Figured maybe we can at least meet with someone who knew Elsie, get some answers for you that way."

"Thank you. Thanks for thinking of that. For doing that."

I expect him to try to explain it away as another selfish action, but he doesn't say anything except "You're welcome."

Like is not love, my brain reminds me. But all of this has been an awful lot to do for someone he only really likes.

"Hollis," I whisper, tilting my face so I can see his eyes. They're back on the TV, boyishly enthralled by another car-chase scene.

"Hmm?"

"Why are you here?"

He shifts his arms so they're lower around my back as his gaze refocuses on me. "I'm assuming you don't mean that in like an existential way."

"No. Why did you come to Key West with me?"

"So you wouldn't be alone," he says.

"But why did you care?" I ask. The past tense feels wrong, though, considering the last few hours, so I amend it to, "Why *do* you care?"

He looks at me like I'm a particularly challenging crossword puzzle and he's running out of easy clues so now must revisit the harder ones he's been saving for later. The blue-gray eye looks frustrated. The brown one bemused. Taken together, though, they appear gently curious.

Maybe he won't answer me at all. Maybe his reasons for everything he does are as selfish as he claims. But something inside me, the thing that wants to tell him that I'm falling in love with him, believes there's more to this. More to *us*. And I want him to admit it.

Instead, he says, "My sister's name is Rhiannon."

"What?"

"My parents had a deal. Dad got to pick the first name for any boys. Mom got to pick for any girls. So, Dad named me after himself, and Mom named my sister after her favorite song."

"Fleetwood Mac," I whisper.

Hollis gives me a tiny smile, a new one that I can only describe as rueful. "It's been over ten years now, and I still . . . Look, I don't listen to songs that make me miss my mom, okay? I don't talk to my father about anything except baseball and books, and I don't have sex with anyone who wants more from me than a fun time and a superficial friendship."

This last one feels like a rebuke. Like he can tell that I'm developing serious feelings for him and he's pushing back against it, reminding me that was not the deal we made when we got involved. I'm just another friend he sometimes sleeps with—a less voluptuous, much paler, redheaded Yeva Markarian. "I don't expect anything," I say in a hurry. "I know you don't—that you aren't—but, Hollis, you're right. I've lost so much lately, and I didn't really deal with it. Now, soon, I'm going to lose you too, and I don't want to pretend I don't feel anything about that. Because if I pretend like it doesn't hurt and bury myself in work or something, it's only a matter of time until I completely lose my shit inside the Library of Congress, and they really frown upon wailing in the reading rooms. Wailing like crying, I mean. Not whaling like . . . with boats and whales, although that would also—"

"Millicent," Hollis whispers. "Stop talking. Please."

His lips brush over mine, once up, once down before settling in. The kiss isn't the cowardly kind I gave him in his childhood bedroom; it isn't an attempt to change the subject so much as a conversation without words. But I'm not sure if my translation is accurate. Because it feels like he's saying he understands, that he's falling in love with me too, and that cannot be right. Hollis doesn't do relationships. He doesn't believe in lasting love, and nothing that's happened over the course of this terrible day gave him any reason to reconsider that belief. And yet . . . *I'm feeling what you're feeling,* his mouth tells me. *You won't lose me,* it claims. Maybe I'm not mistranslating so much as willfully misunderstanding. Or buying into a lie. If that's all it is, it's extremely convincing. Then again, Hollis is a much better liar than I am.

My limbs are still wrapped around Hollis's torso, like I'm a koala and he's a tree. Except the koala and the tree are making out, so I guess it's not like that much at all. His arms release me, and his hands slip between us. They slide into my robe, following my curves. His touch leaves a trail of heat, and the effect lands somewhere between comforting and sensual.

"My point is that I don't like big feelings, Millicent," he says. "My whole adult life—my whole personality—has been built around avoiding even the possibility of encountering them."

I open my mouth to apologize for slathering my big, messy feelings all over him. But he presses another kiss against my lips. A preemptive shush that shows how well he knows my brain despite the short amount of time we've spent together. I'm tilted backward, backward, until I'm parallel with the mattress and Hollis is above me. My arms and legs give way to gravity, and I fall onto the bed. The coolness of the air conditioning blowing against my skin where the robe is open emphasizes the sudden distance between our bodies. Is this how it ends? The point where he tells me sorry, but this is too much and not at all what he bargained for, best of luck with my future, so long?

He stares down at me with that look of sweet bewildered frustration. "But there's no avoiding you, is there? I tried at first. I really did. I was actually *in* my car at the airport, key in the ignition, before I had to go back inside to find you. I mean, shit, I even tried sending you off to have sex with someone else, hoping it would help me keep my distance."

His face changes, as if the last answer has come to him and the puzzle is complete. "I'm starting to realize that you're inevitable, Millicent. It's like you tied my shoelaces together the moment we met and the knot's only getting tighter the longer I try to outrun you. It's just . . . I have no idea what to do with all of this intensity, this longing, this . . . sort of painful thing in my heart that feels like hope and fear and *need*. The muscles to carry these sorts of big feelings atrophied a long time ago, and the weight of it is crushing me."

I don't even realize that my mouth has fallen open as I attempt to process these unexpected words until Hollis's touch draws my attention to my bottom lip. The pad of his thumb traces the curve of it as he says, "You want to know why I'm here in Key West with you? Because watching you exist in the world, trusting and loving and beautifully strange . . . it makes these feelings even heavier, yet somehow easier to bear."

Holy shit. Hollis has big feelings for me. He might not want to, but he *does*. Of course, him saying he's tired of fighting it isn't a promise we'll be together forever (or even an admission that he believes that forever is a possibility for anyone). But what do promises really mean in the grand scheme of things? When it comes down to it, a promise is little more than an earnest intention; I've learned that the universe tends to laugh at those and do its own thing anyway. Maybe that's why I'm so willing to think the best of people. I don't want to assume malice when mostly we're all just victims of the universe's whims.

"Did I freak you out?" Hollis asks in response to my silence, his thumb stilling.

My smile spreads slowly across my face as I look up into those mismatched eyes. "No. I'm just thinking that we're all just doing our best in the face of a fickle universe."

"Right," he says. "That makes sense."

"And that you shouldn't be wearing so many clothes."

This time, when his mouth presses against mine, there's no need to translate or second-guess. He couldn't be clearer if he hired a skywriter to zip about until big puffy letters spelled out his intentions. I'm feeling it too, this compulsion to turn words into actions. After he takes off his glasses, I grab the back of his shirt and lift it over his head, forcing him to break away from me long enough to sit up and maneuver his arms out of the sleeves. My hands slide over his chest, and I bury my nose in the place where his neck and shoulder meet, where the rainy-day-with-a-favorite-book scent of him is strong and comforting. His fingers on my skin generate a sort of fizzy yearning sensation that circulates through my bloodstream and makes me clumsy as I attempt to help him out of his jeans and underwear, which are still around his ankles when I reach for him.

Hollis lets out a small huff of amusement as he moves his hips away and grabs my hand. There's a whimper of protest in response that must come from me, although I don't remember my brain telling my vocal cords to do that.

"Hold on," he says, pushing the robe from my shoulders so

we're both naked and on our knees. "There's no hurry. We have all the time in the world."

It probably doesn't mean anything. *We have all the time in the world* that's a thing people say all the time without intending it to be taken literally. But I want so badly to believe right now that forever might be an option, that Hollis could change his mind about lasting love and decide whatever this is between us doesn't need to end when this trip does. Despite the lack of concrete evidence, I want to believe that Mrs. Nash and Elsie loved each other until the end, and I want to believe that Hollis is saying he'd like to give us a chance to start. And so I acknowledge him with a slow, leisurely kiss, and I let myself believe. The frenzied need driving me toward the finish doesn't disappear, but it exits the highway and ambles along down a scenic back road.

Hollis whispers that he'll be right back and leaves the bed to find the box of condoms in his bag. When he returns, he rolls one over his erection, then summons me back to his lap. I sink down onto him and wrap my arms around his neck and my legs around his waist so that as much of my body is surrounding his body as possible. He tilts his head, resting his forehead against mine and for a long time, neither of us moves. This is the maximum number of intimacies. I don't know how to quantify it—twenty-seven katrillion, maybe?—but it's gotta be the limit because I cannot fathom how we could feel any closer than we do right now.

Hollis's hips nudge forward and up. I follow his lead, rocking against him in a languid rhythm reminiscent of the tide sweeping over the sand. The movement is so subtle that there's space to gather every sensation, be fully aware of every detail of each breath and fraction-of-an-inch slide and kiss pressed against sweat-coated skin. Tension builds slow and steady, which I'm now fully convinced is the best way to win this particular type of race. Except at the moment, I don't want to win at all; I never want it to end.

"You can let go, Mill. I have you. I'll always have you," Hollis whispers.

It sounds enough like a promise that I take it as the permission I didn't even know I needed to shatter apart, and it's like all of my grief and worry scatter to the recesses of my brain to make room for one blissful moment where nothing exists but joy and love and release. Hollis holds me tighter as he keeps rocking into me, whispering every sweet and dirty thought that crosses his mind, and my heart thump-thumps in time to his movements. The spasms of his climax feel like someone setting off heart-shaped fireworks that explode in my chest. The embers rain down, sizzling, and I'm not even surprised when a quiet, slightly raspy voice in my head says, *You love him, you silly thing.* Because I know.

I already know.

Washington, District of Columbia
October 1953

IT HAD TAKEN OVER AN HOUR, BUT BOTH CHILDREN WERE FINALLY in bed and quiet, if not asleep. And quiet was really all Rose could ask for after a day like today. First, Richie had woken up complaining of a sour stomach. Then Walter, jealous that his mother's attention was focused on his older brother, claimed to be suffering from the same ailment, which he proceeded to demonstrate by rolling around on the floor, clutching his gut and howling so effectively that the family dog, a male mutt the boys had inexplicably insisted on naming Lady, joined in. Then Dick had come into the room—apparently undeterred by the already-unfolding chaos—to ask Rose if she had seen his favorite tie. Which meant that she had to remind him that he somehow managed to dunk a good quarter of it in tomato sauce last week when he leaned in to kiss her at the stove and it had yet to be picked up from the cleaners. That caused Dick to relive the memory, getting upset all over again at his clumsiness—which Rose found quite endearing, actually—but that made him late for work, and the entire day had continued in much the same fashion.

Now Rose sank into her favorite chair—beige upholstery patterned with rust-orange palm trees that reminded her of the sunsets and warmth of Key West—and slipped off her flats. Dick would be home any minute, as long as his bus didn't run into too much traffic downtown, and she looked forward to sitting down to dinner together, then sharing a drink, and perhaps making love if he wasn't too tired. They had been discussing the possibility of a Baby Nash Number Three, but with Richie and Walter already running amok and Dick teaching this semester, they never seemed to have the time or energy. Besides, another child would require more space than they had, and Rose and Dick had agreed that they would rather die in their two-bedroom near Dupont Circle than deal with the stress of moving again.

Rose's thoughts drifted to Elsie, as they often did during rare moments of quiet. Mourning her over the last year had been a process. Through all of the anger, the grief, the guilt, Rose kept returning to that day in the bungalow in Key West when Elsie asked her to promise that she would try to be happy with Dick Nash. *Keep trying to be happy with this life for her,* she reminded herself whenever everything felt too heavy. But tonight, as Rose looked around her living room and noted the errant toy soldier lying defeated atop the coffee table, Lady snoozing beside the sofa, and the latest Sears catalog with half its pages dog-eared to indicate items under consideration for Christmas, she found herself sighing contentedly. Somewhere along the way, Rose realized, she stopped having to try—and now she simply was.

22

• • • • •

I MUST HAVE FALLEN ASLEEP. IT'S NOT SURPRISING CONSIDERING we woke up before sunrise this morning. And also that I cried my eyes out in a public place, cried more at the hotel, coaxed Hollis into confessing he's feeling something like what I'm feeling, then had the most transcendent sex of my life. It's been a long, exhausting, roller coaster of a day.

Hollis isn't in bed with me. There's no noise coming from the bathroom, though he must've showered; slightly humid air and the citrusy smell of the hotel's complimentary shampoo have drifted into the room. I call for him, but he doesn't answer. There's a small part of me that panics. What if he got freaked out by all of this new intensity between us and left? But then I see the note on the desk, sitting beside my phone and Hollis's notebook. It's a slip of hotel stationery with a message sprawled across it in a loose, hurried cursive.

Picking up dinner. Back soon. —H

The flatscreen TV beside the desk reflects the massive smile taking up most of my face. It feels strange to look so happy while still harboring so much disappointment and grief, but there's also this spark of joy inside me that fans into a bonfire whenever I think about Hollis and the things he said. The annoyance in his voice when he called me "inevitable" shouldn't have been sweet, but from him it was like a peach straight off the tree at the height of summer.

God, he's really rubbing off on me, isn't he? I'm practically smeared with his tendency toward purple prose. And so much dried sweat. I smell like a pile of fried onions got boinked by a grapefruit.

The shower pressure is on the weak side, like a lazy drizzle instead of the promised waterfall effect, but I enjoy it nonetheless. It feels like I'm cleaning off the day's sadness but also its small triumph. I'm a little reluctant to lose the salty grime of making love, but I tell myself there will be more where that came from. What would be the point in everything Hollis confessed if he planned on ending this as soon as we get back to DC?

There has to be more. This might be the end of the road for Mrs. Nash and Elsie, but it's a beginning for me and Hollis. If it isn't, all that we've been through is meaningless. And I can't accept that at all. Even the universe's notoriously fickle and cruel whims wouldn't do me like that.

We're going to have to have a real conversation at some point. One where we both make ourselves vulnerable enough to state in plain language what we want and need from each other and for how long. Kissing and touching is great, don't get me wrong. But this will never work if we don't stop relying on our bodies to speak for us. That's a problem for later, though. Maybe in the car on the way home. Right now, I'm going to enjoy the possibility that my streak of losing everything I want to keep may finally be at its end.

My phone vibrates on the desk as I'm organizing my wet hair into a braid. I haven't been in touch with my parents since yesterday, so it's probably them freaking out. I'm not sure I have the energy to explain everything to them right now. But when I reach out to send the call to voice mail, I see that it isn't my parents calling. It's a Florida number. Remembering what Hollis said about the nursing facility giving my number to Elsie's next of kin, I snatch the phone and manage to answer it on the last ring.

"Hello?"

"Hi, is this Millicent?"

"Yes, hi. Who's this?"

"My name's Tammy Hines. I'm Elsie Brown's great-niece. I got your number from Rhoda at The Palms at Southernmost. She said you were hoping to talk to me. Are you still in town?"

"Yes! Yes. Hi. Yes."

"Oh, great. Good. I actually think I have some letters to give you. Assuming you are the . . . uh . . . parrot was it?"

"Pigeon," I correct.

"Yes. Right. Aunt Elsie did say pigeon. Sorry, my brain is fried. Anyway, I just finished with a client, but I should be free in about, um . . ." There's a pause. "Twenty minutes. Oh, where are you staying?"

"Um . . . we're in New Town at the—"

"Oh, good. Close to my office then. There's a Starbucks at Seventh and North Roosevelt. Can we meet up around six there? Or would you rather wait till tomorrow?"

"No, six tonight is perfect," I say. Hollis and I will need to eat quickly when he gets back, but there's no way I'm waiting longer than I need to. Letters! I have Elsie's letters to Mrs. Nash in a bundle, tucked next to the wooden box that holds her ashes. So these letters are presumably Mrs. Nash's letters to Elsie. The idea of seeing Mrs. Nash's beautiful, swooping handwriting again makes tears well in my eyes. No time for that, though—Tammy is saying something.

"Sorry, what was that?" I ask.

"Do you have a pen and paper? This is my office line, so let me give you my cell number in case something comes up."

"Oh, okay. One sec." I flip Hollis's note to the blank side. Paper, check. "Pen, pen, pen," I mumble to myself. My eyes search for the cheap plastic pen usually found alongside the hotel-branded notepad, but it isn't there. "Sorry," I say. "Looking for a pen." There must be one somewhere, because Hollis used it to write this note and—bingo. It's not the hotel pen (who knows where that went), but Hollis's clicky black one, which I found tucked into his notebook like a bookmark. I'm careful to use my pinky finger as a placeholder while I scribble down Tammy's phone number and the intersection of the Starbucks.

"See you at six," she says after we confirm I have the correct details.

"Yeah. Thanks so much. See you soon."

I flip open Hollis's notebook to replace the pen. My heart does this little excited wiggle, kind of like a corgi butt, at seeing the page filled with his hastily written words. But as my eyes stop seeing it as a whole and narrow in on the actual letters, the spaces, my heart free-falls through my chest cavity and lodges somewhere stomach-adjacent.

Because Mrs. Nash's name is on this page. Her sons, her husband, her *dog*—their names are here too. Why are they in Hollis's notebook? I read the passage in a hurry, at the same speed he probably wrote it. And then again, slowly this time, hoping it says something different.

Washington, District of Columbia
October 1953

It had taken over an hour, but both children were finally in bed and quiet, if not asleep. And quiet was really all Rose could ask for after a day like today. First, Richie had woken up complaining of a sour stomach. Then Walter, jealous that his mother's attention was focused on his older brother, claimed to be suffering from the same ailment, which he proceeded to demonstrate by rolling around on the floor, clutching his gut and howling so effectively that the family dog, a male mutt the boys had inexplicably insisted on naming Lady, joined in. Then Dick had come into the room—apparently undeterred by the already-unfolding chaos—to ask Rose if she had seen his favorite tie . . .

23

• • • • •

PAGES AND PAGES. IF I WEREN'T SO BEWILDERED BY THE DISCOVERY that Hollis has been writing about me, about us, and about Mrs. Nash and Elsie, I might be impressed by it. There must be thousands of words in this notebook, all written in the last four days. They're framed as vignettes, I guess, and they leap through time and space, past to present and back again.

I read the first sentence of each one, hoping somehow the reality of what I'm reading will change. But no matter how much I flip through, it's more of the same. Some of the dialogue in the Mrs. Nash and Elsie parts is based on what I've told him or pulled from the letters in my backpack; he must have read through them at some point while I was asleep or in the shower (which feels like its own separate violation). Some of it, though, is his best guess at how the conversation would have gone. I'm not sure if I'm more upset that he put words in Mrs. Nash's mouth and thoughts into her head, or that someone who didn't know her at all managed to capture some of her spirit when it feels increasingly elusive to me with each passing day.

And then there are the parts about me. About us.

It feels like Josh and the Instagram account all over again. This notebook is filled with our private moments packaged for public consumption, and it hurts so much more than a bunch of photos on the internet because, unlike Josh, Hollis has apparently been using me from the very beginning. At least with Josh it started out real. But with Hollis . . .

I flip back to the first pages.

We're just north of Richmond when I realize Millicent isn't crazy. She's just a romantic.

It's easy to mistake one for the other, especially when the tiny redhead in your passenger seat has a box full of her elderly friend's ashes tucked into her backpack. But the more Millicent talks, the more I pick up on the subtle differences. Crazy moves erratically, a drunken bee moving through the air. Romantics like Millicent, though, move with purpose toward their goal, following an endless trail of hope. Optimistic breadcrumbs that promise to end with a happily ever after. And Millicent's breadcrumbs, she's informed me, lead to Key West.

She stares into the distance, as if the windshield is a portal to another time. And then finally her wide, full lips part and she begins to tell me a love story:

Being stationed in Key West felt like some sort of cosmic reward. Rose McIntyre had suffered through eighteen cold, dark Wisconsin winters, but in late November 1944, the US Navy gifted her more sun and warmth than she knew what to do with . . .

I turn to another section, further into the notebook.

Sex with Millicent is like strolling through a garden at the height of summer. Her minty mouth claims every inch it can reach. She is green and sweet on my tongue, like cherry tomatoes enjoyed straight from the vine. And when she comes apart, it's like watching a rose bloom in fast motion, her velvety pale-pink thighs falling open like heat-dazed petals. The sweat that dampens my hair and drips down my back might as well be from an endless July day in the sun, running around my grandparents' backyard until the fireflies signaled dusk. Touching Millicent, tasting her, being inside her is like every ambrosian memory I've ever collected replaying inside my soul all at once, and—

"Oh, shit," Hollis says from the doorway. He's cradling a brown paper bag in his arms. "Mill, I—"

"Don't," I say.

He walks over to where I'm standing and sits the bag of food on the desk. "I didn't want you to find out like this. I was going to tell you, and soon. But with everything—"

"I said *don't*." My words come out quiet but fierce, and he visibly shivers. Good. Cold is good. Cold creates distance. "This is the new project you called your agent about, isn't it? You intended to publish it?"

There's a split second where I think he might lie, his eyes darting to the side as if he's contemplating it. But he must realize he's already in a deep enough hole. "Yes, but—"

"I trusted you," I say, pressing my index finger into his chest. "And I know it seems like I trust everybody, so maybe having my trust doesn't feel like a big deal to you. But it's still a big deal to me."

Hollis's brow furrows. "Of course it's a big deal. I never meant to—"

"You never *meant* to? You don't accidentally write a book, Hollis!"

"It's not—it's more like a fifth of a book. A quarter, tops."

"Yes. *That's* the important part of this. That you still have a lot of words left with which to betray me."

"Millicent, please let me explain."

"Okay, fine, go ahead," I say, throwing out my hand to give him the floor. His lips part, and I wait. But nothing comes out.

"Right. It's pretty simple, I think. You've been using me," I continue. "You've been writing down what I've told you about Mrs. Nash and Elsie's story so that you can profit from it."

"I'm not just writing about Mrs. Nash and Elsie. It's also about you. Mostly about you, it turns out."

"Amazing. So you're exploiting *three* women instead of two. That makes it so much better."

He runs both hands through his hair, making it stand on end, and groans. "I'm not saying this right."

"No. You're not."

"It doesn't help that you're looking at me like you want to stomp on my balls. Can we just . . . Could we eat and talk about this later, when you're less emotional?"

I narrow my eyes. I cannot believe . . . "What did you just say to me?"

"The wrong thing. The wrong thing is what I said." He sits on the end of the bed and buries his face in his hands. "Jesus, I hate fighting," he mutters. "This is exactly why I don't do relationships."

"Well, it's a good thing we're not really in one then, huh?" I grab the slip of paper with Tammy's number and shove it inside my backpack. I swing the strap over my shoulder and march to the door.

"Millicent, wait. You don't—"

"I have somewhere to be. Goodbye, Hollis."

The door makes a loud click as it closes and I look down at my bare feet on the hallway's low-pile carpet. Ah, shit. I'm not wearing anything except that damn hotel robe. That last "You don't—" was probably going to be "You don't have any clothes on." The door opens behind me and Hollis stands there, looking me up and down in a way that makes me want to either kick him in the shins or kiss him senseless. So much for my dramatic exit.

"Don't say *anything*," I warn, pushing past him to go back inside.

"Did you even read the parts about you?" he asks. "About how you make me feel?"

I let the robe fall from my arms into a fluffy white lump on the floor. Fighting while naked should make me feel exposed and vulnerable, but instead I'm like some sort of badass lady warrior charging unencumbered into battle. "You mean like how you thought I was crazy until you realized I'm just stupid?"

"That's not— Millicent, that's not what I wrote. I would never say that. Don't go putting words into my mouth."

"Oh, like you did to Mrs. Nash and Elsie?" I'm so pissed off that the tower of clothes I'm compiling on the bed keeps toppling over in my fury and haste. My balled-up underwear falls onto the floor. I pick it up and toss it back onto the bed, where it promptly tumbles off again. "Goddammit," I grumble and give a frustrated groan that's more of a restrained scream.

Hollis picks up the underwear and gently sets them on top of the clothing pile. I know he's trying to help, but the way the underwear heeds his command is infuriating. He is so calm, and my emotions are chaos incarnate. Tears of frustration and hurt spill over my cheeks before I'm even aware of their presence. I am naked, I am crying, and I am *furious*.

"Stop helping me!" I yell. "I never asked you for help. I never asked you to pretend that you care about any of this, or about me."

"I do care! How could you think I— Millicent, I meant every word I said earlier. If you read the rest of what I wrote, you'll see that I—"

"The jig's up, dude," I say, putting on my underwear. Thankfully my legs go into each hole without issue; now is absolutely not a good time for almost falling over while getting dressed. "So you can stop pretending that I'm more than a source of information and a convenient lay."

I hook my bra, then slip into my maxi dress. My dress is too long, and I have to tie the bottom so it doesn't drag on the floor. It takes me three tries to knot it correctly, my brain unable to coordinate my actions and my emotions at the same time.

"Dammit, Mill, listen. You know that's not what you are to me." He takes my upper arms in his hands and stares into my eyes. It would be so romantic if I didn't kind of want to headbutt him and then knee him in the groin. "In the last four days, you've dragged me down paths I haven't been brave enough to explore for almost a decade. You make me feel like I can go anywhere as long as you're there beside me, lighting the way."

"How cliché," I say. I shake my head, *tsk*ing. "Not your best work, Mr. Hollenbeck. But maybe you can come up with something better when you write this scene in your stupid book." I slip out of his grasp and walk over to my suitcase. I don't really need anything from it, but sifting through it gives me something to do and a way to avoid eye contact. "See this, this is the problem. I'm not your damn lantern. I didn't exist to fix Josh, and I don't exist to fix you. I didn't stroll into your life to inspire your goddamn art or make you feel free or whatever bullshit you want to tell yourself."

I spin to face him and throw my hands to my sides as another guttural scream escapes through my gritted teeth. "I am weird, Hollis. That is who I am. A weird person. And it has absolutely nothing to do with you. When I am alone, I am exactly the same. I don't power down like some sort of toy robot, waiting until the next time you want to play with me. I am not the quirky girl whose sole purpose is to add whimsy to the tortured writer's sad, dull life. I have my own shit going on, and in this story the tortured writer is the one who's just along for the ride."

"Really? You're going to claim I'm treating you like a manic pixie dream girl?" Hollis puts his fingers to his temples, like *I'm* giving *him* a headache. "Jesus Christ, stop throwing all of your Josh Yaeger baggage at me, demanding I unpack a bunch of bullshit I didn't pack in the first place."

Damn, he's right. I am doing that. I'm projecting so much of my past hurt onto him. Maybe because it's easier to repeat something I already know I can survive than explore if this new pain might actually tear me apart. My voice comes out as a whisper. "Like I said before, I have somewhere to be. I really have to go or I'll be late."

Hollis grabs my wrist as I walk past. His hand is warm and strong, and it gently tugs me over to him like it did in a dark room at a bed-and-breakfast in South Carolina two nights ago. "Wait, Millicent. Please."

His eyes plead with mine, and it triggers a countdown inside me. It's ticking along, marking the seconds until I let myself forgive this betrayal and beg him to please love me. *Don't leave me*, is what I will say. *I don't care if you've only been using me, as long as we can keep pretending it's more.* It's what I feel in some shadowy corner of myself, and I hate it. I hate that my instinct is always to take less than I deserve. To let a man's inability or unwillingness to fully accept and respect me transform into a shame albatross around my neck. How many times did I do that with Josh, not fully aware of the compromise I was making with my own pride? No more. I can't do that ever again. Especially not with someone who's become so important to me in such a short time.

The countdown is in the single digits now. I can feel my heart softening, making itself pliable, eased along by Hollis's supplicating stare and comforting grip on my wrist. There is only one way I get out of this before it becomes too easy to stay: I'm going to have to hurt him back so he'll want me gone.

All of those stupid fights with Josh prepared me for this moment. *Go for the jugular. End it.*

"Do you know what Josh said to me right before I came out of that restaurant crying that night? He said that if I was going to be fucking weird, I should at least be fucking weird and famous again so he wasn't with me for nothing." The words sting even more with the realization that I was so desperate to believe Hollis could want me with no ulterior motive that I fell for the exact same tricks—the feigned kindness and affection—all over again.

"That piece of shit didn't deserve you," Hollis says. "But I'm not him."

"No. You're not. Because at least when Josh got caught screwing me over, he did me the courtesy of not pretending to be a better man than he was."

I can almost see the moment he clocks my repackaging of the words he told me he said to his father ten years ago. With a few more strategic sentences, I know I can tip that anger over into pain as easily as a metal spoon in an empty yogurt cup. And if it hurts me a little too, well . . . it's just another drop in the ocean at this point.

"Yeah, I know," I continue, "I shouldn't be so surprised. Everything you do is selfish. You warned me of that from the very beginning—warned me repeatedly—and it's my fault that I didn't listen. I should have taken you at face value instead of letting myself believe there was something more under the surface. At least now I see that you are exactly who and what you've always claimed to be. You're self-serving and callous. You're your father's son. You're burnt toast with nothing under it except more burnt toast."

Hollis's nostrils flare as he attempts to regulate his breathing. His eyes burn into mine—blue-gray furious, brown also furious. It's a relief to find our anger levels competing. I'm not alone now in my hurt. We're both going to leave this place a bit destroyed, and that's perversely reassuring. He releases my wrist, dropping it like it's a piece of fruit he's just realized is covered in fire ants.

"Are you coming back tonight?" he somehow manages to say with a jaw so tight that his top and bottom molars must be in danger of fusing together.

"I doubt it," I say.

"Good. I'll leave your suitcase at the front desk then."

"That would be great, thanks." I hesitate for the briefest moment when I reach for the doorknob. Partially because I'm checking my feet to make sure I'm wearing my sandals this time, but also because I know it's still not too late to apologize and talk this out. There might be a way we can move forward as friends at least if not as . . . whatever we were these last few days. Whatever I *thought* we were. But I need to meet Tammy. I don't have time to sift through the wreckage for anything salvageable right now, and I'm not even 100 percent sure I want to anyway.

"Well, see you in the funny papers," I say, not glancing back as I walk out the door and slam it behind me. I'm pretty sure that sentence has never been said with such rage before. It admittedly sounds pretty ridiculous, which is probably why it is not well regarded as a parting shot.

I'm halfway down the hall when I hear a door creak open behind me. I don't turn, but I can feel Hollis's approach. It's a physical thing; the air becomes charged when he gets near me and all of my ions perk up.

"What do you want?" I say, whipping around. He's so close behind me that the tail of my heavy, still-damp braid smacks him. Which, *good*.

"You forgot Mrs. Nash again," he says, holding out my backpack with one hand while his other presses against the spot on his shoulder where my hair assaulted him.

"Thanks." I instill the word with as much anger as possible, and pull my bag from his grasp with more force than is necessary. It may seem petulant, but I know I cannot give an inch or my poor, foolish heart will insist on giving him twelve hundred miles.

Hollis steps closer and frames my face in his hands. My desire to pull away is overruled by my instinct to nuzzle into his palm. I think he knows that my anger is like one of those fake fireplaces—a whole lot of heat but no real flame. I can make him sweat, make him want to keep his distance. But I won't actually burn him if he's brave enough to get close. And he is. His lips press against my forehead. "I'm sorry," he says. "I'm so sorry, Mill. I know that's probably not enough, and I understand why you don't want to stay. But please, at least tell me where you're going?"

I shake my head, and his hands fall to his sides. "You don't get to know how this ends," I say, and walk away.

24

. . . . .

IF I WERE IN A BETTER MOOD, I MIGHT FIND THE HUMOR IN HAVING traveled all the way to Key West to wind up waiting around for Elsie's great-niece in a generic strip-mall Starbucks. But I'm obviously in the worst mood, so I'm mostly resentful. Tammy is fifteen minutes late. That might not be egregious under normal circumstances, but I've had a really rough day. Shortly after I arrived, I shoved a slice of banana bread into my mouth and gulped down a grande iced mocha in record time. I'm now running solely on sugar, caffeine, anxiety, and the pain of betrayal. It's not exactly an ideal recipe for patient waiting.

A willowy woman in a mauve linen pantsuit strolls in and moves her sunglasses to the top of her head, inadvertently pulling a few strands from her blonde French twist. Her skin is almost as blindingly white as mine; I wouldn't peg her as a local except that she's otherwise the spitting image of Elsie. Bake Tammy in the sun for a few days and it would be difficult to tell the difference between a picture of her and the one of her great-aunt that I found in the Naval History and Heritage Command archives. Which is extra impressive considering Elsie was in her early twenties in that photo, and Tammy must be close to fifty.

Her eyes meet mine across the room, and I give her a little wave.

"Millicent?" she asks.

"Mhm. Hi, Tammy."

"So sorry to keep you waiting. I was finishing up an offer—I'm in real estate—and I was trying to wait for the clients to send some info, but it wound up taking a lot longer than I thought it would and, anyway, I'm here now."

I force myself to smile, even though I don't feel very smiley. "No problem," I say.

"So you're Rose's . . . great-granddaughter?"

"No, I—"

"Sorry, hold that thought. Let me just go order quick. Do you need anything? No?"

She hurries away to the counter. I let out a sigh. This isn't going how I imagined. Then again, nothing today has, so why should this be any different?

"Okay," she says, sitting across from me once she has her coffee. She takes a sip from her venti iced double shot, which I overheard the barista warn her is made with *five* shots of espresso. My heartbeat is erratic even looking at that much caffeine. Apparently, Tammy is made of stronger stuff. "You were saying about your great-grandmother?"

"Oh, no, there's no relation actually. I lived with Mrs. Nash at the end of her life. Sort of a caretaker." If Mrs. Nash heard me refer to myself this way she would have a conniption. She hated any insinuation she couldn't care for herself; if I hadn't needed to move out of the apartment I shared with Josh, I doubt she ever would have agreed to let anyone live with her. I was always introduced to doctors, relatives, and whomever else we encountered while in the world together as either Mrs. Nash's "good friend Millie" or "roommate" (or once, when she was mad at me for getting oat milk instead of her preferred almond, she referred to me as her "temporary tenant"). But Mrs. Nash can't protest now, and I did care for her in all the ways, so caretaker is the easiest explanation.

Besides, I'm starting to suspect Tammy isn't that interested in these details. My suspicion is confirmed when she gives me a tight-lipped smile and says, "I have to be honest with you, Millicent. When Aunt Elsie said I needed to deliver letters to Rose's pigeon, I thought the pain meds they had her on were making her loopy. It wasn't until Rhoda called and told me you stopped by The Palms to see Elsie that I realized what she meant. It's just, well, she barely spoke of Rose."

I swallow the lump in my throat. Tammy must see because she lays a hand briefly over mine in an attempt to be comforting. Instead, it's mostly awkward.

"Then again, she didn't like talking about the past," she says. "Aunt Elsie was very private. Growing up, I honestly thought she was just an old spinster, married to her career. Then when she retired from medicine in '83 and no longer had to worry what anyone would think, she started volunteering at a clinic for AIDS patients and living openly with Martina. I was a teenager then, staying with them here for the summer, and I remember being like *ohhh*." Tammy lets out a little laugh.

"Martina?" I ask. It's not that I expected Elsie to be alone for the rest of her life—Mrs. Nash had Mr. Nash, of course. But the idea that there was someone else who meant something to Elsie gives me this shameful pang of jealousy on Mrs. Nash's behalf.

"Martina was a surgical nurse at the hospital where Elsie worked. They were together for almost thirty years."

"What happened to her?"

"She moved back to Bulgaria to be closer to her family. That was in . . . '05 maybe? Elsie didn't want to leave Key West, so they broke up. It was all very amicable from what I understand. They kept in touch. Martina wanted to come for the memorial service, actually, but she's too old for that kind of travel." Tammy looks off into the distance and her lips move without making a sound, as if she's doing some calculation in her head. "She was a bit younger than Aunt Elsie, but she's probably in her late eighties now."

This talk of Elsie loving someone other than Mrs. Nash feels dangerously close to Hollis being right. And Frederick Hollis Hollenbeck is the last person I want to be conceding anything to at the moment.

"You mentioned the memorial service?" I literally cross my fingers under the table, hoping that it hasn't happened yet.

"Yeah. We did a thing yesterday afternoon at The Palms. Just a small gathering of close family and her friends at the facility."

"Oh. Is she buried nearby?" Maybe if I visit her grave I'll find some sort of closure. That's all Mrs. Nash and I had originally planned to do anyway.

Tammy leans back in her chair and crosses her legs. "Aunt Elsie donated her body to science. Apparently, they might use it for up to two years, then they're supposed to cremate whatever's left and scatter the ashes over the Gulf."

"That's nice," I say, trying to convince myself. "I know she loved the water."

"Did she?" Tammy looks doubtful.

Did she even know her aunt? Or is the little I know not even true? I clear my throat. "Do you know anything about what happened while she was serving in Korea? When she was declared deceased?"

"Now *that* she talked about. Aunt Elsie loved to tell everyone how she was dead for a short time. It was one of her favorite stories."

"Maybe you can fill in some blanks for me then," I say. "I figured out from my research that it was some sort of clerical issue, but do you know how it happened?"

"There was a helicopter accident. Aunt Elsie and some other nurses were flying to help out at an understaffed hospital near . . . what's that place called? Inky . . . Inchy . . . Incheon! That's it. Anyway, she broke her leg and a bunch of ribs in the crash, but the pilot and another nurse were killed. The nurse who died, her name was Elise Bruhn. So Elise Bruhn and Elsie Brown both on the same downed helicopter, one dead and one injured—some wires got crossed somewhere along the line, and Elsie was administratively deceased for a week or so, until someone noticed the error."

Elsie Brown and Elise Bruhn, both Navy nurses, serving on the same ship, traveling in the same helicopter when it crashed. Geez. In college, I knew three Andrews who all lived in one dorm room and I thought *that* was confusing.

Tammy smiles politely. "Does that solve the mystery?" she asks.

I nod. "One of Mrs. Nash's letters to Elsie was returned to sender with a stamp that said deceased. She never knew that Elsie was still alive." That familiar guilt creeps up on me again. If only I looked into this sooner. If only I found Elsie before Mrs. Nash died, then maybe . . .

"I don't understand. Wouldn't Aunt Elsie have written to her to let her know what happened?"

"The letter that was returned said that Mrs. Nash's husband got a new job, and they were moving from Chicago to DC. So Elsie never got their new address. She probably had no way of finding out what happened to Mrs. Nash. No way of knowing where she went."

"How sad," Tammy says, turning her cup a few degrees clockwise. "Well, if they were as close as you seem to think."

I guess when she called and seemed so glad to catch me before I left town, I hoped Tammy might want to cry and reminisce with me, mourn our respective yet mutual losses. I hoped she would be eager to share everything about Elsie that I wanted to share about Mrs. Nash, and that we could use each other's memories to form a more complete picture of the love story that inadvertently brought us together. But Tammy is apparently not the crying-and-reminiscing type. She isn't all that curious to learn about the woman who loved her great-aunt so much and for so long. Our interaction feels businesslike and stiff, no matter how much she smiles and nods.

I want to get out of here. I don't know where I'll go since I can't go back to Hollis. Another hotel I guess, somewhere else on the island.

"You said you have letters for me." I mean to pose it as a question, but it comes out as a statement that sounds kind of rude. Honestly, my emotions are thoroughly shot; there's not much energy left for pretending to be polite anymore, and Tammy isn't making me particularly inclined to care.

Luckily, she doesn't appear to care either. "Right, yes," she says, pulling a large, yellow, clasp envelope from her briefcase.

"Here you go. This is everything Elsie told me to give to Rose's pigeon."

The packaging makes me feel like we're spies performing the world's least-covert handoff of confidential information. My fingers tremble as I pinch the metal clasp together and open the flap. I stare blankly at the contents, trying to figure out what I'm looking at. I expected a stack of beaten-up opened envelopes, or a bundle of folded, aged paper like the one I have in my backpack. But there's just one sealed standard envelope and a small book with a worn brown leather cover.

I pull out the envelope, which is crisp and white. It looks brand-new. Like taken straight out of an office supply closet this morning. "I don't understand," I say. "I thought you said letters, plural. I assumed you were going to give me the letters Rose wrote to Elsie."

"Oh, sorry, no. I don't think Elsie kept those. At least, I never saw them."

"Oh," I say. "Okay. And um, what's this thing?" I hold up the brown leather book.

"The letters," she says. "The ones she wanted you to have."

This is making about zero sense to me, and I'm getting more and more annoyed with Tammy. Which is probably not even her fault.

If it's anyone's fault, it's Hollis's. If he hadn't used me, betrayed me, he'd be here with me right now. We'd be doing this together. That's the worst part, I think. The part that is making me extra grumpy. I thought I wasn't going to have to face any of this alone. But here I am. Alone. More alone than I've ever felt in my life.

"Well, thank you," I say, rising from my seat. "I appreciate this, but I have to get going now."

"No problem. I hope you have a safe trip back home."

"Thanks." I turn to leave but suddenly remember what brought us here in the first place. I've been so wrapped up in my own grief I forgot I'm not the only one who lost someone I loved. "Um, I'm really sorry for your loss, by the way. From what I know about Elsie, she was an amazing person."

"Thank you," Tammy says. "She really was." She gives me a brittle smile that feels like the most genuine thing we've shared in the last ten minutes. "And you too. I mean, I'm sorry for your loss as well."

For the briefest moment I think she's talking about Hollis. That loss is the most fresh and at the forefront of my mind. But no, that doesn't make sense. Mrs. Nash. She's talking about Mrs. Nash.

I hurry away from the Starbucks to avoid awkwardly running into Tammy again and find myself sitting on a curb outside of a nail salon. A pigeon lands beside me and bobs its head toward a piece of old gum on the sidewalk. Determining it's not the tasty morsel of food it expected, it struts around in disappointment.

"I know how you feel, pal," I say, looking down at the yellow envelope balanced on my knees. "It's been that kind of day for me too."

It coos a trilled response.

One gorgeous spring Friday right before she died, while people-watching in Dupont Circle, Mrs. Nash explained to me the best method of grabbing a bird, honed during her pigeoneering days. "Both hands, and come at it from above," she said. "That way if it takes flight, you'll still catch it." The memory replays in my mind as the pigeon approaches, and I cup my hands over it. But it ducks and runs along the sidewalk, then flies away.

I DON'T KNOW HOW LONG I'VE BEEN WANDERING AROUND THE shopping center's parking lot like it's my own personal meditation labyrinth. I'm considering going back to the hotel to see if they have another room available. Or maybe I'll retrieve my bag and find somewhere else to stay. Maybe I'll pay some Lyft driver an exorbitant amount to drive me to Miami so I can hop on the next flight to DC. I consider—for longer than I probably should—the possibility of befriending some rich old man with a sailboat and making a long, leisurely journey up the East Coast, postponing a return to real life while still getting the hell away from here as soon as possible.

I wonder if Mrs. Nash was this eager to leave the Keys. All she said about her discharge from the Navy in late summer 1945 was that she was still hopelessly in love with Elsie despite also blaming her for the end of their affair. That she had a fiancé and a new life in Chicago waiting for her initially only exacerbated her heartbreak.

The morning she first told me about Elsie, I sat on the floor in front of her chair with my legs crossed like a kindergartener at library story time. "Please don't think I didn't love my husband," she said. "I always had extremely warm feelings for him growing up, and I grew to love him very much during our marriage. Dick became a wonderful partner, and my dearest friend in the world. But when I married him, it felt like he was snatching me away from the life I wanted to live. The one with Elsie. For a long time, I believed she might have allowed me to stay with her if I hadn't had any other options after the war, and I had a good bit of resentment toward both of them for a while. But I think now that Elsie was never fully convinced of my love, and nothing could have changed that. She didn't know how to believe that I would have chosen her out of everyone, no matter the cost. From what she told me about her childhood in Oklahoma, I'm not sure anyone had ever made her feel worth it before. I hope some lucky woman eventually did, and that Elsie let her."

I glance down at my phone. It's buzzing with an incoming call. My heart flutters until Dani's name pops up.

"Hey," I say. "What's up?"

"You need to call your parents, Millie. They won't stop checking in with me every hour to see if I've heard from you. For some reason they think you might be in jail?"

"Sorry, I'm sorry. I'll tell them to chill. I've just been busy."

"Yeah you have," Dani says with a verbal wink.

"Not that. We're actually . . . that's done now. He was just using me."

"Oh shit. Give me an address and I'll come kick his ass, cuz."

"You're even smaller than I am," I point out.

"Hey, I've been taking kickboxing classes. But if you need the big guns, I'll have Van come down there. The man's built like Jason Momoa, and I'm covering his shift tonight, so he owes me a favor."

"No, I'd much rather forget everything and go home."

"Seriously, though. Are you okay? You sound . . . sad."

"I am sad. I'm sad and disappointed."

"You know who else was sad and disappointed? Pee-wee, when he found out the Alamo didn't have a basement. But that wasn't the end of his big adventure, and this isn't the end of yours." I hear Dani slapping the bar in emphasis of each word. "Uh-oh, the boss man just came in and he looks *pissed*. Gotta go. Love you, cuz. I have every faith that you'll find your bike."

She hangs up before I can thank her. Count on Dani to know how to get through to me without me ever even explaining to her what I'm doing in Florida. As I shoot off a quick text to reassure my parents I'm alive and neither imprisoned nor on the lam so they'll leave my poor cousin alone for at least a few hours, I realize that the issue isn't that my bike is lost; it's that I've lost track of what my bike *represents*. Or rather, what is represented by my bike. This is getting confusing already, and the passive voice is not helping. The point is, I need to remember what I was searching for in the first place when I asked Geoffrey Nash for some of his grandmother's ashes. It wasn't proof of love's endurance to win an argument. It definitely wasn't my own chance at a happily ever after.

It was the trust I lost in myself.

I came here to find confirmation that it's still worthwhile to be guided by my optimism. I wanted reassurance of my inherent belief that lasting love is worth the pain and false starts it takes to find it isn't stupid. That I'm not naive to keep trying. To keep hoping. This was never supposed to be about meeting Elsie, or starting a relationship with Hollis, or being handed a stack of letters by a highly caffeinated real estate agent. All of those would have been welcome bonuses, but they were not my metaphorical bike.

So Dani is right—I can't give up the search yet. And I think I know where to look next.

25

• • • • •

BOCA CHICA BEACH ISN'T THE KIND OF BEACH I'M USED TO. FOR
one, it's apparently clothing optional, as I discover when I pass
two sun-toasted old men, smoking cigars while both buck naked
and sitting upon overturned five-gallon buckets. They give me a
friendly wave, and I return it. As I walk along the shore to find a
place that feels right, I encounter elaborate driftwood and rock
structures and sculptures. An intricate mural is painted on a small,
paved area of ground that looks like it was once a road. Small
boats bob along the horizon. Two dogs roll around in the surf at
the far end of the strip of sand, their presumed owners practicing
yoga nearby.

I find a place under a large tree that reminds me of the stories
about Mrs. Nash and Elsie's spot here, and I twist my dress around
my legs to keep the sand on the outside of my butt as much as possible when I sit. For a long time, I do nothing except stare out at
the ocean and let my mind retell me Mrs. Nash's stories—about
her love for Elsie, but about other parts of her life too—in her

voice. It's difficult to imagine Mrs. Nash as I knew her—plump, a bit hunched over, crepe-skinned and slow-moving, wearing elastic-waisted pants and bright-pink lipstick—at this nudist beach in the Keys. But I've seen pictures of her during the war, and it's so easy to imagine *that* version of her here. Young Rose McIntyre, away from home for the first time, and so very in love with a woman who didn't know how to believe in the possibility of for-ever. She would have fit on this beach as much as I do now. And considering no one is paying me any mind, I think I fit all right.

I slide my backpack from my shoulder and sit it in my lap. I discarded the bulky, yellow, clasp envelope back at the strip mall, tucking the bright-white envelope into the brown leather book and stuffing it in my bag. Now the edge of it sandwiched between the book's pages greets me as I pull the zipper to open the main compartment.

Here goes nothing.

I pinch the corner and pull the envelope free. It resists a little, like it's asking if I'm sure. Well, I am.

Because I'm realizing the contents can't tell me anything I don't already know deep inside my heart. I feel it in the way it keeps thumping despite the faded bruises left by Josh's callous-ness; despite the deep incision that appeared when my beloved best friend died, that heals and reopens anew at least twelve times a day; and despite the fresh, chasmic gash of Hollis's betrayal, which might never fully mend. I'm not naive enough to think I'll never get hurt again on my way to happily ever after, but no matter what Elsie's letters say, I know I'll keep believing. My heart can take it. I am, fundamentally, a person who clings to hope, and trusting that—trusting myself—is worth everything.

My nail drags over the top of the envelope, tearing until it splits open. Inside is a piece of printer paper, equally crisp and white. The handwriting is a loopy print—more like mine than the familiar cursive of the old letters in my backpack. Perhaps she could no longer hold a pen at the end and someone else took down her dictation. Rhoda the receptionist, or a young volunteer perhaps.

My most darling Rosie, it says.

They tell me you're sending me a pigeon. What took you so long?

I like to believe you're still alive, though I admit I don't know for sure. I tell myself I would've felt the moment of your death somewhere deep inside my bones. Perhaps I did, but mistook it for the same sharp ache I've felt every day since I lost you.

My years of experience agree with the baby-faced doctors here that my own time is coming. In case I'm gone or incapacitated by the time your pigeon arrives, I write this letter as an introduction to the others.

Though it's simple: Even though my letters to you began returning unopened, I couldn't seem to stop writing them. I always believed that one day I might find you again and perhaps we would lay in bed for hours and I would rest my head on your shoulder while you read about what I did with my time while you were gone. You would laugh at my melodrama and I wouldn't mind, because it would be rather funny just how much I suffered without you now that my suffering was over and you were with me again.

I suppose I never gave up hoping that day would come. So I kept writing, and I keep writing.

I know I won't get to lay beside you while you read this. But feel free to laugh if the mood strikes, sweet Rosie. My suffering is over, and you are with me again at last.

With all of my love, in this life and the next,
Elsie

I hold back the tears that threaten, knowing I won't be able to read the brown leather book with my vision blurred.

I flip through Elsie's life, learning about her in the pages of the journal formatted as letters but never sent.

———

My last letter was returned unopened, an angry red little hand pointing and declaring RETURN TO SENDER. It seems to say that you have moved and left no forwarding address. I cashed in some favors to call you, but the operator says the line has been disconnected. Perhaps you were so furious that I got myself killed that you got on a plane and are coming to Tokyo to tell me what's what?

———

It's been over a month now without a word from you, and I think you must think me dead and gone. That or you have decided you no longer care for me. I would rather be dead, I think, than no longer have (at least) your friendship.

———

I've been medically discharged and am stateside once again, yet feel as far from you as ever . . .

———

I am freezing my tits off here in New England. Why didn't I choose a medical school somewhere much warmer?

———————

Sometimes when I walk about town, I see a woman with your dark hair, your graceful stride, your curved and perfect body. I imagine I've found you only to have her turn and be a stranger. But New Haven is as good a place as any for you. Maybe one day it will be your smile that greets me . . .

———————

Fort Lauderdale is treating me well. I have a house right by the beach, and I swim every morning the weather allows. The only thing missing in my life is you, sweet Rosie . . .

———————

I lost a patient today. A child, the same age as your Walter must be now.

———————

I've been spending time with a nurse from my hospital. Her name is Martina. We have a rather strong affection between us, made stronger by the knowledge that we aren't each other's true loves. M knows that you will always be my heart and soul. She lost her own sweetheart last year to cancer. We both walk around missing a part of ourselves, but we make each other feel closer to whole. I wonder if this is how you feel about your Mr. Nash, this love that's so different from what we felt for each other but so special nonetheless . . .

———————

Today your absence struck me anew, as it does on occasion. I wish I hadn't been too much of a chicken to choose you back when you tried to choose me. More than that, I wish I were brave enough to try to find you now.

———————

M and I have retired and moved to Key West. I visited Boca Chica Beach today for the first time in over thirty years. You'll think it ridiculous, I know, but I half-expected you to be there by our usual tree, your face glowing and your skin sun-warmed and sand-covered. You weren't, of course. But maybe one day I will find you waiting for me there again.

26

· · · · ·

MY BELIEF IN AN AFTERLIFE ISN'T BASED ON ANY SORT OF RELI-
gious teachings. It's more like a feeling that's crept up on me over
the years as I've experienced more life and more loss. Somehow,
I know that Mrs. Nash and Elsie are okay. Probably not literally
lounging on clouds while an angel plays a harp, but they are at
peace and happy. And they are together. Or they will be—I don't
know the mechanics of it, exactly. So I might as well make it as
easy as possible for them to find each other.

I grab a nearby stick and dig a hole. After a few minutes, I become impatient with my progress and claw at the moist sand with
my fingers. A tiny crab emerges and gives me a dirty look. I apologize to it as it scuttles away. At last, I have a deep enough well to
house precisely three tablespoons of human remains.

The small wooden box that now holds the baggie of Mrs.
Nash's ashes used to sit on her nightstand. When her sons were
school-aged, she worked part-time as a secretary to a professor of
Eastern religions. He brought her the box as a souvenir from one

of his trips to India, and she kept her daily-wear jewelry and hand cream inside. I would bury the whole thing, except it's the only thing I have besides Elsie's letters to remember her by. Also, to be honest, I am tired and don't want to dig a bigger hole. I open the box, and the scent of lemons and jewelry cleaner wafts up before mixing with the ocean air and disappearing completely. Taking in a deep breath, I cradle the box closer in my lap.

"Hey, Mrs. Nash. It's, uh, it's Millie. But you . . . you probably know that." I talk to the bag of ashes, but I know she's not in there, not really. That's not Rose McIntyre Nash. Those might be her remains, but her essence is somewhere and something else. Still, I'm sure she's listening.

"I wanted to deliver you directly into Elsie's hands. But that didn't quite work out. So I think this is probably the next best thing. Elsie will find you here, if she hasn't already. I'm pretty sure. If not, you can haunt me as revenge. Feel free to be spooky about it. I probably deserve it for taking a bit of you away from the rest of yourself and dragging you all the way down the East Coast. Anyway . . ." I choke a bit on the painful lump in my throat. "I'm delaying. I know. It's just . . . it's hard to say goodbye."

I wait for the wind to whisper some secret wisdom in Mrs. Nash's voice. Of course it doesn't. So I laugh at myself, allowing a few tears to slip free from the corner of my eye. They fall with greater frequency as I slowly open the baggie and carefully pour its contents into the hole.

"You were my very best friend," I say as I cover Mrs. Nash's ashes with sand before the sea breeze gets a chance to blow them away. "And I love you so, so much." When the hole is filled, I notice a fairly large brown and white spiral seashell near my foot. There doesn't seem to be anything living inside it, so I lay it atop the small mound of sand as a lovely little makeshift headstone and whisper, "Goodbye, Mrs. Nash."

I sit for a long time, just existing in this place. After hearing so many stories about Boca Chica Beach, it feels almost sacred— nude locals and everything. My efforts to wipe away my tears with my forearms are futile; more keep replacing the ones I clear, blurring everything around me. The men smoking cigars on buckets are russet blobs, the dogs in the water are black smudges in a large streak of faint turquoise. All of it's tinted by the pinkish orange of dusk. The hazy column that approaches me could be anyone on this planet, as far as my bleary eyes are concerned. But the way my heartbeat races and every nerve in my body prickles, I know it can only be one person.

"I hoped I might find you here," Hollis says, sinking down onto the sand beside me.

The faint echo of Elsie's words is enough to make me cry even harder, and as angry as I am with Hollis, I can't manage to be anything except grateful when he puts an arm around me and guides my head to rest against him. His hand runs up and down my back, soothing me with his touch as I sob into the crook between his neck and shoulder.

"She's gone," I say when I run out of tears at last. "She's really gone."

Though that could mean many things in this context, Hollis doesn't ask who "she" is or what kind of gone. All he does is kiss the top of my head and hug me tighter against him.

I loosen myself from his grasp after a few minutes and turn to face him. My anger returns, both over his betrayal and the way he doubted this endeavor from the beginning. "I'm still mad at you," I say.

"I know, and you have every right to be. But I do want to talk. Whenever you're ready."

"I don't know what there is to talk about. You were planning on profiting off two dead queer women. And off your . . . involvement with me." I fold my arms, hoping they'll form a barrier to keep whatever he says next from reaching my heart and settling there like sediment.

Hollis lets out a sigh. "I'm not going to lie to you, Millicent. The book did start out as that, yes. I found the stories about Rose and Elsie interesting. Traveling with you and learning about them was the first thing in a long time that made me feel excited about writing again. I started working on it Friday morning, and the words just spilled out onto the page. And I checked in with my agent, and he agreed that the editor I'm working with on my first book would probably be interested. Except the more I wrote, the more I realized I wasn't writing Elsie and Rose's story. Or, I was. But I was also writing ours. Including you in it might have started out as a kind of framing device, but then you . . . well, you became everything."

Hollis pulls the red notebook from his back pocket and smacks it against his palm.

"On Saturday, while I was walking down Gadsley's Main Street as you rode agonizingly slow along that parade route, I realized I could never publish this and emailed my agent to tell him the project wasn't feasible. I knew I cared too much about you to betray you like that."

"But you kept writing," I say. "I saw you. And there's . . . so much in there. Stuff I told you later. Stuff we did later."

"Yeah. I did keep going. The words were still flowing, and it's not like I had another idea. Producing something, even if it wasn't destined to be my second book after all, felt better than falling back into stagnation." Hollis rubs his ear, his expression sheepish. "When I started, I did truly believe this was about Rose and Elsie. That their story was the perfect example of the bittersweetness of love's inevitable end. I found myself trying to tell it in a way that made it seem like Elsie had no choice but to let Rose go. But I was really just trying to convince myself so that I could let go of you at the end of this trip and tell myself it was necessary too. And I could take solace in the idea that transience—not endurance—is what makes connections between people special." He absently drags his fingertips through the sand, leaving a wave-like pattern in their wake, then meets my eyes again. "But the further I got into writing their story, and the more time we spent together, I started to see that the end isn't always inevitable. I don't know—and I realize now that it's probably not my place to guess—whether Elsie felt that she could have made a different decision, at the time or in the future, or if she ever regretted—"

"She did. Regret it, I mean. Regretted not letting Rose choose her. She said so in her journal."

"Journal?" he asks.

"Yeah. I met with Elsie's great-niece. I'm not sure I liked her very much, but she gave me this." I show Hollis the brown leather book. "Elsie kept writing letters to Mrs. Nash in it, all of those years. Kept hoping they'd find each other again."

"Well, there's your proof," Hollis says. "Elsie and Rose loved each other this whole time, just like you said. Lasting love exists."

"I think you were the one who required concrete proof of that," I say, crossing my arms again. "*I* knew it all along."

"You're right. And even if Elsie hadn't left all of those letters behind, I know you would have found a way to keep your hope alive. Because that's who you are—an optimist. But I'm a pessimist, Millicent, and I always will be. A selfish, grumpy pessimist who can't believe in things without proof. That's why I kept writing. I went from wanting to prove myself right to needing to prove myself wrong—to convince myself that sometimes, if we're lucky, beginnings and endings are choices we get to make. I thought I might find what I needed in Rose and Elsie's story, but it turns out I was looking in the wrong place." Hollis hands me his notebook, his fingers marking a page. I lay it open on my lap, pull my blinking eyes from his face, and read.

I began this trip as a skeptic, and I will end it as a skeptic. Four days of domestic travel   even ones as eventful as ours have been—cannot change anyone so completely that they are no longer the fundamental thing that they were before. I'm grateful for that. I am grateful that, when we return to DC, Millicent will still be a person who believes in things like lasting love, no matter the disappointment we've found in Key West. Me, though, I will still be somebody who needs proof in order to let myself embrace such a terrifying and wonderful possibility. But now, as I look over at Millicent, asleep beside me in this hotel room, I realize that proof won't be found at the end of someone else's story; I'm going to find it in ours, and in every moment of every day I manage to spend by her side.

"Hollis . . ." I say, my voice trailing off as I realize I have no actual response.

"I wrote that right before I left to pick up dinner. The guilt of what I did, of keeping it from you, was starting to eat me alive. So I planned to tell you everything and give you the notebook tonight. Then—assuming you forgave me—in forty, fifty, eighty years, we wouldn't have to send some poor woman to Key West in search of reassurance that she isn't a fool to believe that love can last a lifetime. She could just stay home and read about the happy, frustrating decades I spent with you, compiling my proof."

Did he just say "decades"? Hollis wants to spend decades with me. That's like, multiple tens in a row. My heartbeat thumps extra fast, as if it's trying to add up how many days and nights and smiles and orgasms we can fit into that much time. How many parties will end with me not in tears, but with Hollis still taking me home.

"I came here to find you because if all of this has taught me anything, it's that we are lucky to have a choice, Millicent. We can still decide whether this is a beginning or an ending," he says. "And maybe it's just me being selfish again, but I want a beginning. I want you. I want us." He runs one hand through his hair and stares at the notebook. "But you were right. Even though I realized early on that I can't publish this, it's still a huge violation of your trust that I wrote about the stories you told me and the things we did without your permission. And I'm sure you've realized I went through your backpack Friday morning while you were in the shower and read the letters Elsie sent Mrs. Nash, which is another massive breach of your privacy." Hollis slowly gets to his feet. "I am so incredibly sorry, Mill. And here is the only way I can think of to prove that." He grabs the notebook from my lap, raises it over his head, swings his arm back, takes a few gigantic steps forward, and *chucks the damn thing into the ocean.*

"What did you do that for!" I shout, springing up.

He tilts his head and looks at me like the answer is obvious. "I might be selfish, but I don't want you to ever think I care more about myself and my career than I care about you. And you didn't want me to publish it, so now you don't have to worry—"

"But you just spent all this time convincing me it was actually a romantic gesture! You made me want to keep it and then you *threw it into the goddamn ocean*!"

"Oh. Right. Shit. Fuck. Maybe I can—" Hollis is out of his clothes in what must be a world record. He and his gorgeous bare ass run into the water, aiming approximately where the notebook landed.

"Wait!" I yell as he dives under and disappears. He doesn't resurface. "Hollis!" I call out over the water.

Goddammit. If he dies trying to recover that stupid notebook that he hurled into the ocean like a freaking Olympic discus thrower I am going to be so mad at him. My sand-filled sandals come off, then my dress, underwear, and bra. I toss them on top of my backpack. If all those people with such strong opinions on Penelope in her yellow bikini could see me now. Thank you, approaching dark, for masking all my jiggling as I run into the water.

The sea is a shock to my landlubber system at first—it's been years since I swam in anything but a heavily chlorinated pool. But I soon adjust to the way the waves playfully push me around, and make my way out as far as I can go while still able to bounce along the sandy bottom on my tiptoes. "Hollis!" I yell again. "Hollis! Where are you?"

Something splashes and brushes past my legs. Oh god. This is it. Somehow I always knew I would die at the hands (or rather, fins) of a shallow-dwelling, embarrassingly small shark. Except this shark has strong man arms and is hugging me against his wet chest?

"Can't find it," the shark says into my ear. "I'm sorry."

(Hollis is the shark.)

"Why the hell did you do that?"

"I don't know! It was impulsive and I just wanted you to know that I was sorry." He groans. "I hate this. Loving you is making me so damn stupid."

I turn in his arms to face him, and I can almost taste the briny air with my mouth hanging open like this. "Sorry, what? What is making you stupid?"

"Loving you," he says, sounding super frustrated about it.

"Loving me."

"Yes. If it isn't extremely obvious by now, I'm in love with you, Millicent."

"You're in love with me."

"Yes," he says. "I love you. I know that sounds ridiculous after four days but—"

"Two years," I correct, even though I'm probably focusing on the wrong part of this declaration. "We've known each other for two years."

"You don't even remember meeting me at the poetry reading."

"I do. I remember getting a little lost in your eyes when we shook hands. Which is more than you remember about me from Josh's book release party."

"I remember everything about you from that night. Which is why when I saw you at the airport I pretended I didn't remember you at all."

"Mm, yeah, I think we're going to have to unpack the logic behind that later. But the point is, two years," I say. "We've technically known each other for two years. So it's not too soon."

His fingers run through his wet hair, brushing it back and out of his face. "However you count it, it was only over the last four days that I realized I love you."

I laugh at the way he says it as if it's a huge inconvenience. "You don't have to sound so annoyed about it."

"I am annoyed about it, though. Because if you love me back, my life is going to be awful. You're going to drag me to record stores on the weekends, and I'm going to have to keep pretending I only kind of like Hall & Oates even though I'm secretly *extremely* into Hall & Oates. Like I already bought tickets for us to see them in concert later this summer, and I'm going to have to act like I'm not looking forward to dancing beside you in the arena like a total dork—"

My lips skate across the smile that's slowly fighting its way through his frown. His mouth is salty from the sea.

"I'm sorry to tell you this," I say. "But your future looks pretty bleak."

"Oh no," he says, his beautiful, rare, genuine smile winning out. "I'm going to have to watch so many more '80s comedies, aren't I?"

"Have you seen *Ghostbusters*? If not, that's definitely next on the list."

I know that I don't have to say that I love him too. He understands without the words, because he understands *me*. But I still wrap my arms around his neck and whisper into his ear all of the things I've been holding inside since this morning: I love yous, I need yous, I want you forevers that he eats up with little *mm* sounds like they're ooey gooey airport cinnamon rolls.

When I pull away, he brings me right back. His voice is low and mischievous. "Say, Millicent Watts-Cohen. What are you up to for the rest of the night? I have a box of chocolates back at the hotel, and I've been dying to share them with someone before they melt."

Wow, he was right; that *is* a great line. But before I can respond, a wave crashes something into my hip. "Ow, what the hell?"

Then I see what it is. Hollis's red notebook. It starts to float away, but Hollis grabs it by its metal spiral binding just in time. We look at each other as if both wondering if Mrs. Nash and Elsie had something to do with this immense stroke of luck. I flip it open and, well, if Mrs. Nash and Elsie did somehow summon this back to us, they did it for laughs because it's absolutely soaked through and the ink has bled so much that the words are illegible.

"I knew that was too good to be true." I sigh. "And I barely even got to read any of it."

He kisses a drop of water off my shoulder. "Maybe I'll write it again for you," he says. "You'll have to be patient, though. It might take a while."

Oh, right. Hollis is no closer to a finished manuscript for his second book than he was when we ran into each other at the airport. "I guess you need to get working on something new now that this turned out to be a bust, huh?"

"Well, yeah. But I mostly meant that I don't foresee our story ending anytime soon."

The sweetness is almost too much to bear. So I kiss him on the tip of his nose, which I can tell he secretly loves, and say, "I know you are, but what am I?"

"That doesn't even make sense," he says.

"I know you are, but what am I?"

He growls in that way that makes me feel like my body is made up of butterflies. "Millicent, if you're going to quote Pee-wee, it should at least—"

I stare into those mismatched eyes and give him a daring smile. "I know you are. But. What. Am. I?"

"Getting thrown into the ocean like that damn notebook," he says, lifting me high against him.

My laughter turns to an embarrassing screech as he moves like he might actually toss me into the waves. But instead I'm held tighter, and kissed everywhere that isn't currently underwater, and I know, I already know: Annoying him forever is going to be so much fun.

Washington, District of Columbia
January 2021

THE SONG DRIFTING INTO ROSE'S LIVING ROOM BROUGHT HER BACK to 1973. When she heard the first few lines of Hall & Oates's "She's Gone," the memory was so strong she had to stop herself from going into the boys' bedroom to plead with Walter to please, for god's sake, listen to something else already. Of course, Walter wasn't in the apartment, freshly returned from Vietnam and mourning the recent marriage of his high school sweetheart to another man; Rose's youngest had long since married a different girl, moved to the suburbs, and had children—and now grandchildren—of his own. The old song must be coming from next door.

How odd, thought Rose. The small glimpse of her new neighbors she had caught as they moved in yesterday revealed a couple—a stiff-moving young man with Buddy Holly glasses who was in dire need of a haircut in her opinion, and a petite redhead with a luminous smile and an intriguing aura of chaotic energy about her. Rose estimated them to be in their mid-twenties perhaps. Certainly not old enough to have been alive when this music was popular.

As another track came through the wall—something by Elton John (and, oh, she had always enjoyed that man and his flamboyant glasses)—Rose began to wonder if she had a time traveler living next to her.

And it turned out that, in a way, she did.

ACKNOWLEDGMENTS

I keep thinking about a scene in the 1987 film *Roxanne*. It's one of my absolute favorites. I'm not going to bore you by describing the entire thing (because you could—and should!—just watch it), but Steve Martin's character has this little monologue about the inadequacy of words when trying to express big feelings.

"They've all been wasted on the shampoo commercials, and the ads, and the flavorings," he says (though I'm paraphrasing a bit, because the reality of the scene is actually quite chaotic). "Hollow, beautiful words. I mean, how can you love a floor wax? How can you love a diaper? How can I use the same word about you that someone else uses about a stuffing?"

And that's kind of how I feel as I sit down to write these acknowledgments. Like, how can I hope to convey the enormity of my appreciation using the same words that are printed on grocery bags and signs hoping you'll come back soon?

But the thing about "love" and "thank you" is that, though perhaps trite and insufficient, they are also *concise*. So while they cannot possibly communicate everything I feel, I'm embracing them in order to maximize available real estate. Therefore:

Thank you to my agent, Taylor Haggerty, for making my dreams come true and then some. Because of you, my life has changed in the most incredible ways, and I am forever grateful. Thanks as well to Jasmine Brown, and to my foreign rights agent, Heather Baror-Shapiro, and my film agent, Alice Lawson.

Mrs. Nash's Ashes would literally not exist without my wonderful team at Berkley, especially my amazing editor, Sareer Khader. Sareer, the list of things for which I owe you my gratitude is possibly infinite, but it's your unflagging enthusiasm at the heart of it all. Thank you for loving this book and for oh-so-gently guiding it into the very best version of itself. Big thanks as well to: Jessica Mangicaro, Kim I, Kristin Cipolla, and Stephanie Felty, without whom only about ten people—all related to me—would be reading this; Erica Horisk for truly brilliant copyediting; George Towne for making this book beautiful on the inside; and Anthony Ramondo and Vikki Chu for making it beautiful on the outside. I also must thank Ivan Held, Christine Ball, Jeanne-Marie Hudson, Claire Zion, Craig Burke, Cindy Hwang, Christine Legon, Megha Jain, Jessica McDonnell, Emilie Mills, Tawanna Sullivan, and everyone else at Penguin Random House whose hard work behind the scenes helped get this story into readers' hands.

My critique partners, Amber Roberts and Regine Darius, know my process better than I do at this point and remain my friends even when I'm at the most insufferable parts of it. Thank you for cheering me and this book on every step of the way, for making me laugh so hard I snort, and for the privilege of reading all of your incredible words over the years.

My immense gratitude also to Sarah T. Dubb, Nikki Hodum, Alexandra Kiley, Ambriel McIntyre, Elissa Petruzzi, Stephanie Ronkier, Jenn Roush, Angelina Teutonico, and Amanda Wilson for their feedback on earlier drafts. More thanks to: Meredith Schorr, who read the first chapter before anyone else and told me to keep going with it; Stephanie McKellop for answering my long-term care facility/HIPAA questions; Sarah Hogle for being my wise owl; India Holton for being the loveliest soul; O. Dada and Melissa Scholes Young for sage advice when I first started on this journey; Jessica Joyce for sharing the debut weirdness with me; Jessica Payne, Sara Read, and all of #MomsWritersClub for their support; the Berkletes who generously shared their knowledge and experiences; and the members of SF2.0 for being there whenever I need help determining if what I'm writing is hot or just weird actually.

Mrs. Nash's Ashes is my debut novel, but it was my third completed manuscript. To those who read or workshopped now-shelved stories of mine, and to everyone who's answered my questions about extremely random things (i.e., proper Welsh translations, Civil War cavalry horse allotments, how to commit a white-collar crime, whether a magic trick I made up is actually possible) over the years that will likely never make it into a published book—please know I very much appreciate you too!

Booksellers, librarians, and all of the people who put in the time and effort to share their love of books on blogs and social media—I am so immensely grateful for your passion and support. Thank you!

Listing them all would take up many pages and repeat some already mentioned names, so I won't do that, but a big thank-you to the other writers—especially in the romance genre—whose work (published or not) has inspired me and improved my own storytelling.

I am extremely fortunate to have wonderful, ultra-supportive parents, and I truly wouldn't have been able to manage the last few years without their help. Thank you so much to my mom in particular for always showing interest in my life and in my work, and for spending countless hours keeping my daughter occupied so I could write. Many thanks also to Chuck and Joyce, Nan, Ariel (who told me back in 2019 to "just start writing and see what happens," although she now says she doesn't remember this), Madeline, Meganana, and the other family and friends who have encouraged me from the very beginning.

My path to becoming an author is closely intertwined with my role as a parent, and watching my daughter grow and learn about the world has made me both a better person and a better writer. Hazel, more than anything else, I'm so grateful I get to be your mom.

Houston, I could not have asked for a better partner in life, and none of this would be possible without you. You've been my trusted first reader and sounding board from day one, and helped shape this book from its earliest stages (including coming up with the title!). Thank you for supporting me, protecting my writing time, telling me when my ideas are bad, talking through plot problems in the car, and for always believing in me every step of the way. You've given me my own happily ever after, and I'm so immensely thankful for everything we've built together.

If you're a person I should have thanked but forgot to because my brain is nothing but a quarter pound of raw, tail-on shrimp jumbling around inside my skull these days, please accept my apology and know that you absolutely have my gratitude as well.

And to my readers: Without you, this all would mean nothing. I cannot express my appreciation and absolute bemusement that you chose to spend some of your valuable time and mental energy reading my words. Thank you, thank you, thank you. ♥

MRS. NASH'S ASHES

SARAH ADLER

READERS GUIDE

Behind the Book

I WROTE PART OF THIS BOOK IN A TACO BELL PARKING LOT.

Why? Because it wasn't my house, it was relatively quiet, and the Wi-Fi signal was strong enough to connect to while sitting inside my car. It was winter, and almost a year into the pandemic, and anywhere that checked those three boxes was fair game whenever I became desperate for a change of scenery. I spent many evenings driving around local shopping centers in search of a reliable internet connection. I awkwardly balanced my Chromebook between my stomach and the steering wheel and typed away while parked outside of fast-food joints and closed coffee shops until the shelter of my car became no match for the bitter cold, my toes going numb inside my boots the usual indication that it was time to head back home.

Knowing this, it's probably not all that surprising that I chose to write about an early-summer road trip that ends at a beach in Key West. Millie and Hollis's sunny and open world full of travel, eating at weird restaurants, and meeting new people became both a playground for my brain and a source of hope when I needed it most. Writing this book allowed me to practice basic social skills that were beginning to atrophy (early drafts of the scenes at José Napoleoni's had some truly bizarre customer-waitstaff interactions).

But, more important, it helped me remain optimistic that we might eventually return to a world more like Millie and Hollis's. And for a little while, it provided an escape to somewhere that wasn't a suburban Maryland parking lot.

Appropriately, the first spark of the idea for *Mrs. Nash's Ashes* also came to me while I was in my car. I was driving home after heading into DC on an errand, taking full advantage of the periodic free SiriusXM trial that my husband absolutely hates when we get because I change the channel every thirty seconds or so in a FOMO-fueled attempt to find the very best song playing at that exact moment. (Also, I know it annoys him, so sometimes I do it on purpose.) But that day he wasn't with me, so I was listening to just one channel, The Bridge, which SiriusXM describes as "mellow classic rock" (i.e., all of Millie's favorites). Sometimes they also play brief excerpts of musician interviews. So there I was, driving north on Georgia Avenue, when Rock and Roll Hall of Famer Graham Nash—no relation to any characters in this book, just for the record!—started talking about how, when his mother died, he took her ashes on tour with him and sprinkled them on every stage he played. And, I mean, how do you hear something like that and not have a hundred follow-up questions? How do you not think about it *constantly*?

That's why I had ashes on my mind when I started brainstorming a modern take on the 1934 classic romantic comedy film *It Happened One Night*. If you're unfamiliar, this is the basic story: A beautiful socialite whose father has forbidden her to marry this guy named King Westley (his name isn't important, I just can't resist including it because *King Westley*) tries to get from Florida to New York to reach her betrothed, but instead falls for the charming reporter with whom she winds up traveling. It's extremely good; Clark Gable takes his shirt off in it. Anyway, as I thought about what my version might look like, I knew I wanted Hollis to be the one who starts out intending to reach someone else. So what would Millie's deal be then? What would be her motivation to get to where she was going, and fast?

Suddenly, it all came together, and Millie was on a train, clutching a box filled with human remains.

I scrapped the train setting pretty quickly; it didn't take long to realize that this book isn't about getting from one place to another on a set track, which is the thing that trains are best at doing. It's about the ways that our journeys are often disrupted. By canceled flights, olive oil spills, and deer with death wishes, yes; but also by the other things that tend to spring up out of nowhere and force us to recalculate our routes: love, death, lust, fear, grief. And it's about how, sometimes, the results of our detours can lead somewhere even better than we originally intended.

Basically, this book needed to be centered around the freedom and unpredictability of a road trip. It needed a car.

So perhaps it's fitting that so much of *Mrs. Nash's Ashes* was written in mine.

Discussion Questions

1. Millie tends to be eager to trust others, while Hollis is extremely hesitant. Where do you fall on the Millie–Hollis Trust Spectrum?

2. Despite their seventyish-year age difference, Millie and Mrs. Nash become fast friends. What do you think each got out of their friendship? If you have any intergenerational friendships, what have you gotten out of them?

3. Why do you think Hollis pretends he doesn't remember Millie when they encounter each other at the airport?

4. Millie and Hollis wind up in town for Gadsley's Broccoli Festival. Have you ever been to a festival, fair, or other community celebration centered around an unusual theme?

5. The decor of the Mustard Seed Room at Gadsley Manor tells us a lot about its proprietress, Connie. How would you decorate a room at a bed-and-breakfast, and what might it tell visitors about you?

6. Have you ever had travel plans go awry? What happened, and how did it turn out?

7. How do you think Millie and Hollis's relationship will be different after their trip is over and they return to their "normal" lives?

8. Rose's postwar plans primarily centered around raising a family, while Elsie's were focused on her career in medicine. Do you think their lives and values would have ultimately been compatible had they remained together?

9. Millie and Hollis are pleasantly surprised by the Mexican-Italian dishes they order at José Napoleoni's Rio Grande Trattoria. What is the most interesting fusion cuisine combo you can think of, and what would a restaurant specializing in it serve?

10. What would be on your road-trip playlist?

Books You'll Find Sarah
Reading in the Passenger Seat
(Even Though She'll Definitely Get Carsick)

Welcome to Temptation by Jennifer Crusie

A Week to Be Wicked by Tessa Dare

Cold Comfort Farm by Stella Gibbons

Boyfriend Material by Alexis Hall

Act Your Age, Eve Brown by Talia Hibbert

You Deserve Each Other by Sarah Hogle

Temporary by Hilary Leichter

How the Marquess Was Won by Julie Anne Long

The Duke Who Didn't by Courtney Milan

A Gentleman in Moscow by Amor Towles

H. D. Kinney

Sarah Adler writes romantic comedies about lovable weirdos finding their happily ever afters. She lives in Maryland with her husband and daughter and spends an inordinate amount of time yelling at their mischievous cat to stop opening the kitchen cabinets. *Mrs. Nash's Ashes* is her debut novel.

CONNECT ONLINE

SarahAdlerWrites.com
SarahAdlerWrites
SarahAAdler